THE ARROWS OF HERCULES

THE

ARROWS

OF

HERCULES

by

L. Sprague de Camp

an imprint of

ARC
MANOR

Rockville, Maryland

ISBN: 978-1-61242-190-2

www.PhoenixPick.com
Great Science Fiction & Fantasy
Free Ebook Every Month

Published by Phoenix Pick
an imprint of Arc Manor
P. O. Box 10339
Rockville, MD 20849-0339
www.ArcManor.com

ACKNOWLEDGMENT:

Lines from Sappho's first ode, Richard Lattimore, translator, from *Greek Lyrics* (Chicago: The University of Chicago Press, 1960), p. 38. © 1949, 1955, and 1960 by Richard Lattimore. Reprinted by permission.

The material from Diodorus of Sicily VI reprinted by permission of the publishers and the Loeb Classical Library. Translated by G. H. Oldfather, Harvard University Press, 1954.

DEDICATION:

To Isaac Asimov and Bob Heinlein
in memory of our own Ortygian days

CONTENTS

INTRODUCTION   11

CUMAE   15

VELIA   40

TARAS   71

SYRACUSE   96

CARTHAGE   127

UTICA   159

ORTYGIA   187

MESSANA   210

MOTYA   236

PANORMOS   272

AUTHOR'S NOTE   299

INTRODUCTION

by Harry Turtledove

At the beginning of the fourth century BC, Dionysios I, tyrant of the Greek city of Syracuse on the island of Sicily, created the world's first research and development center to make more weapons and to invent new ones. That center, and particularly the quest for a practical catapult, forms the heart of L. Sprague de Camp's fine historical novel *The Arrows of Hercules*.

De Camp was an expert on the history of science, engineering, and technology. His nonfiction book *The Ancient Engineers* is a classic in the field. A copy of *The Ancient Engineers* has sat in a bookshelf near my writing chair for close to forty years, ready to grab whenever I need some arcane fact about how the Greeks made statues or the Romans built roads.

And de Camp was an expert on military research and development in another way. As he was fond of saying, he fought World War II with flashing slide rule: he was an officer in the Navy Reserve (he eventually reached lieutenant commander), and served in an R&D center in Philadelphia. Among those with whom he served at the center were fellow writers and friends Robert A. Heinlein and Isaac Asimov. Now, when Dionysios created his research center, he put it on the island of Ortygia, just off the coast from the Sicilian mainland, no doubt partly for security reasons. And de Camp's dedication for *The Arrows of Hercules* is "To Isaac Asimov and Bob Heinlein in memory of our own Ortygian days."

Among the assignments he talks about in his autobiography, *Time and Chance*, he discovered why the trim tabs on the new Grumman Hellcat fighter were freezing up at high altitude, which some-

11

times caused crashes. He found that the lubricants used with them got sticky in extreme cold, and the handwheel pilots used to adjust the tabs was too small to compensate. A bigger one would give the fliers greater mechanical advantage and let them overcome the cold, sticky oil. De Camp said as much in a report … but, right up till the end of the war two years later, no change was made, and Hellcat trim tabs kept freezing up.

He also worked on an improved de-icer for aircraft windshields. He came up with a radical new system. The only thing wrong with it was that he couldn't make it work. Then someone from Washington told him they wanted something much simpler, something he could have designed very quickly if his original instructions had been more precise. Once he found out what was required, he created the gadget the Navy had wanted in the first place, and several hundred of them were installed aboard torpedo-bombers. He does not think this made the least bit of difference in the way the war turned out. He wished he'd got better instructions, but also blamed himself for not asking his superiors to make things clearer.

When he left the Navy, he took with him lasting memories of what it was like to work in a large, complex, government-funded research establishment. Those memories give the bureaucratic wrangling and bureaucratic bungling in *The Arrows of Hercules* a realistic feel they could not get any other way. De Camp is plainly writing from experience.

He writes from experience in another way, too. The Second World War, of course, was among other things a war of unleashed ethnic and racial hatreds. The Nazis did their best to exterminate Jews and Bolsheviks. The war in the Pacific was a race war, with neither side giving or asking for much quarter. In the United States, we mocked Hitler and his followers and were actively encouraged to hate the dirty Japs. We sent Japanese-Americans to concentration camps, and whites grabbed their property in almost the same way Germans seized Jews' belongings after National Socialism came to power.

De Camp projects these ethnic struggles back almost 2,400 years in *The Arrows of Hercules*, to the conflict between Dionysios' Greeks and the Phoenicians who uneasily shared Sicily. The Greek word barbaros, from which we get *barbarian*, originally meant someone who didn't speak Greek, but made unintelligible *bar-bar-bar* noises (in the same way, the Russian word for Germans, *Nemtsi,* literally means tongue-tied ones or stutterers). By the turn of the fourth century BC, *barbaros* was coming to have the pejorative flavor it does to this day. De Camp plays on the rivalry between Greeks and Phoenicians, and on the Greeks' distrust for anyone not of their own kind no matter how talented an engineer the man might be.

His protagonist, the engineer Zopyros of Taras (now Taranto, down at the bottom of the Italian boot) and Zopyros' friend and colleague, Arkhytas, suddenly lose their desk jobs and have to go to war with Dionysios' army—and the horrors of the war Dionysios fights are shown vividly indeed. Both Zopyros and Arkhytas are actual historical figures about whom little is known: the ideal sort of people on whom to center a historical novel. Arkhytas, interestingly, also has a bit part in Mary Renault's excellent *The Mask of Apollo.* Her characterization of him is different from de Camp's, but both, I think, are plausible—and what more can a reader hope for in historical fiction?

Sprague was always a meticulous researcher. He traveled through the Middle East and Central Africa to see as much of the ground for his earlier historical, *The Dragon of the Ishtar Gate,* as he could. While he was in that part of the world, he also toured Sicily, so his descriptions of the terrain in *The Arrows of Hercules* also have that well-earned feel of authenticity.

And, finally and most important, he tells a ripping good story. Zopyros' problems in inventing one of the earliest catapults—and his problems in dealing with the people around him—always keep the reader turning pages. Like so many of de Camp's leading characters, Zopyros is a long way from perfect, and his own flaws make life harder for him than it might be without them. But they also make him a recognizable, individual human, not a Hero with a capital H. If living, breathing humans are what you're after in your stories, you couldn't possibly come to a better book than *The Arrows of Hercules.*

CUMAE

It was spring. A blustering boreal wind whistled down from the flanks of the snow-crested Apennines, making the umbrella pines nod and the slender cypresses sway. It roared across the dark green Campanian plain, drying the brown mud of the fields around the villages and ruffling the sky-blue puddles left by the recent rain. The wind rushed on over the Phlegraean Fields, a weird, legend-haunted region of sharp-ridged volcanic craters, of hot springs and sulfur-breathing lakes, of mysterious caverns which, men said, led to the underworld. It stirred the dense, dark thickets of ilex that crowded round the base of the citadel of Cumae. It flapped the woolens of those who clustered about the door to the Sibyl's chambers, on the seaward side of the hill. It billowed the Campanian magnate's scarlet cloak, the Roman knight's chalk-whitened toga, the white cloaks of the bourgeois, and the brown cloaks of the soldiers and workers. It fluttered the threadbare shirts of the shivering slaves. It stirred the Tyrrhenian Sea at the foot of the hill until the water sparkled in the reborn sun like the swords of a distant battle. Overhead, the leaden pall of the last ten-day rolled away to southward, leaving a deep bright sky streaked with snowy plumes of cirrus.

On this morn of the tenth of Elaphebolion,[1] in the first year of the ninety-fifth Olympiad, when Laches was Archon of Athens, a runner pounded south on the coastal road, panting as he ran. As he sighted the acropolis of Cumae, he slowed and glanced back along the road by which he had come. No pursuers were in sight.

---

1   Approximately March.

Above him, unaware, the crowd of seekers milled about, clutching their cloaks against the blast. The priests ushered out of the grotto a pair of swarthy, hooknosed, long-robed Phoenicians, with rings in their ears and conical caps on their curly heads. As the Phoenicians went their way, murmuring in their own guttural tongue, men in the crowd began waving their arms, snapping their fingers, and calling out:

"Next!" "It's my turn!" "Take me next, O priest! I pay the god well!"

The clamor swelled until a priest beckoned the trio of Tarentines. One of these was a stooped, elderly man with a wreath on his scanty white hair. The other two were young, wearing hooded cloaks and high Thracian boots. One of the two was short and stout, with soft, rounded features. The other was tall, bony, knobby, and angular. Deep-set eyes looked out between his craggy, overhanging brows and wide cheekbones. A prominent nose, like a curved knife, divided his face, and the curly brown beard beginning to sprout from cheek and chin did not yet fully mask the sharp angles of his big jaw.

At the priest's gesture, the three started forward. The oldster moved slowly and painfully, with the short one bouncing on one side and the tall one shambling on the other. The Campanian magnate said loudly in Oscan:

"By the gods and spirits, I have waited long enough! After all, I am Gavius Trebatius!"

The priest smiled blandly. "All in good time, my lord."

"Surely a man in my position should precede these polluted foreigners!"

"My dear sir, you will hardly dispute precedence with the Archon of Taras!"

"Most reverend sir ..." The voices of the two dropped to an undertone as they continued their argument face to face, with gestures of angry impatience. The Tarentines paused uncertainly. At the elbow of the tall young Tarentine stood a big Celt in tunic and trews, checkered with a gaudy pattern of yellow, red, and green. Grinning through his luxuriant bronze mustache, he murmured in accented Greek:

"'Tis a good point that the holy father has, my lad. Did I not hear you say the old fellow was a king, now?"

"Not exactly. That's what the title means, but in our city the Archon has only priestly duties. Nothing political."

"You mean the poor man cannot have the head off anybody he thinks would look prettier without it?" The Celt clucked. "If that's your civilization—"

The red-cloaked Trebatius turned back into the crowd, scowling. The priest said in his oily voice: "You may come now, my friends."

"Wake up, Zopyros!" said the elderly Tarentine. "Are you doing figures in your head again?"

The tall youth grinned sheepishly. "I was working out how many oboloi a word the Sibyl's prophecy will cost our treasury."

"Abandoned scoffer! Come along."

The three paced sedately behind the priest, who led them to the tunnel hewn out of the rock of the hill. At the entrance, the other priest stood with his hand out. The Archon fumbled in his scrip and brought out a small, thin-leather sack, which he dropped with a clink into the upturned palm.

The first priest fed them into the tunnel. At the threshold, Zopyros stumbled. The priest and the others frowned at the omen, but Zopyros quickly recovered and walked on as if nothing had happened.

This tunnel was sixteen feet high, several plethra[2] in length, and of peculiar form. The lower third was roughly square in cross section, while for the upper two thirds the walls leaned inward, forming a trapezoid with a narrow strip of ceiling along the top. Light came through, from a series of lateral galleries of the same six-sided form, cut through to the surface of the hill on the right. The stretches of light and dark tunnel made a series of concentric hexagonal patterns, which drew Zopyros' entranced gaze down toward the audience chamber at the far end.

Zopyros walked in a daze. It seemed that there must be some cosmic meaning to this piece of mountain-hewn geometry. Could he but grasp the pattern in its entirety ... The volume of a trapezoidal prism, he thought, would be—let's see—the length, times the height, times one half the sum of the width at the base and the top ...

Still pacing slowly, they reached the audience chamber. This was a large rectangular room, dark except where a shaft of sunlight slanted down through an overhead skylight and lit a patch of the

---

2   A plethron = 100 feet

rocky wall. Off to the left were more rock-hewn chambers, where the prophetess lived.

In the center of the chamber, an elderly woman—large, strongly built, and swathed in many cubits of black woolens—sat on a fantastically carved oaken throne. Stray strands of the woman's gray hair picked up the splash of sunlight on the wall. The air was heavy with incense.

Beside the throne stood yet another priest. The two priests murmured together in the dimness. Then the priest who had been standing beside the throne said:

"O Sibyl, the Archon of Taras seeks counsel for his city."

For a hundred heartbeats the woman sat silently, staring at the Tarentines. Then her keen gaze filmed over. Her eyelids drooped; her breath came heavily. She gasped, faster and faster, and burst into speech. She spoke in a loud, harsh voice. It sounded to Zopyros like some peculiar Oscan dialect, but the Sibyl spoke so fast that he could not be sure whether it was such a dialect or mere gibberish.

The woman ceased. The priest beside the throne said: "This is the word of the Sibyl:

O fair Taras, grim Sparta's lighthearted mule,
The Wolf of the South like a watchdog, shall guard
   thee well,
But the Wolf of the North—beware! he shall swallow
   thee down.

The Sibyl also has a personal message for you," the priest concluded. "Wait."

They waited, while the wind whistled in the skylight and the galleries. The woman gasped, trembled, and again burst into speech. This time the priest said:

"For the Archon, she sees an Etruscan candle, burnt nearly to its end. For the short youth, she sees seven golden crowns. For the tall youth, she sees an immense bow. It is the bow of Hercules himself. Many men try to bend the bow but fail. Then this youth steps forward.

"With a mighty effort he strings the bow and fits one of Hercules' arrows to the string. He draws the bow to his breast—he lets fly—

18

and the arrow strikes the world and shatters it to bits, like a dish of pottery struck by a stone!"

Zopyros gasped; the Tarentines exchanged appalled glances. "*Oi!*" exclaimed Zopyros. "I, a peaceful engineer, smash the world to fragments?" He turned to the priest. "Woe is me! Can the Sibyl explain?"

"The Sibyl never explains," said the priest. "It is not she who speaks, but the Far-Shooting One who speaks through her. The God of the Silver Bow allows us a glance through the misty veils of time and distance, but we ourselves must make what we can of these glimpses."

"This way, my sons," said the priest who had guided them in. As they walked down the corridor, the Archon said:

"I suppose the verse means that we must ally ourselves with Dionysios of Syracuse. The 'mule' refers to the story of the Partheniai, our bastard ancestors begotten by serfs on Spartan women while the Spartan men were away fighting. But this Wolf of the North—who could that be? The Campanians? The Celtic tribes, which yearly swarm over the Alps in greater numbers?"

"It could be one of many northern powers" said the short youth. "Anyway, it's up to the Council to make sense of the verse. But how about those personal messages for us?"

"By our lady, it takes no seer to interpret the burnt-out candle!" said the Archon dryly. "She means I had better not make plans twenty years in advance. My creaky old bones tell me that, anyway. As for your seven golden crowns, Archytas my lad, she does but confirm what I have said, that anybody with a tongue loose at both ends, like yours, is wasted if he doesn't try politics. And Zopyros—well, world-smasher, what do you think?"

"I don't know what to think," said Zopyros. "The gods know I'm no—ah—'Hercules.'" (Zopyros winced, for it vexed him to hear these Italians mangle the name of the mighty Herakles.) "A Pythagorean should harm his fellow beings as little as possible. ..."

They came to the end of the passage. As they stepped out the portal, the scarlet-cloaked Trebatius bustled past them. After the cave, the brightness was dazzling. Zopyros, squinting northward from the shelf of rock on which the inquirers were gathered, took in the curving shore line, the reedy swamps of Lake Licola, the dark green belt of pines along the sandspit that sundered lake from sea, and the blue dish of Lake Literna beyond. Ahead, to the west, lay the sparkling sea; to the left he could see the swampy Lake Acherusia with the mottled hills of Cape Misenum beyond. The Phlegraean Fields, the Campanian plain, and the distant Apennines were out of sight, behind the hill on which the acropolis stood.

The Celt flashed a friendly grin at Zopyros. "Did the wise woman tell you how you could turn the sea into gold, or marry the Great King's daughter, now?"

"Not quite, but she gave us much to think about."

"She gave good luck, I hope. I cannot wait to hear my own fortune. But himself in the red cloak has gone in, and by the time they get down to us common folk, I don't think I will be hearing her the day. *Ara!* What's this?"

The rasp of sandals on the path from below and the sound of panting caused heads to turn. The runner stumbled up the last step to the place of assemblage and gasped:

"P-pirates! Etruscan pirates!"

There was an instant of blank silence, then a rising chorus of exclamations: "*Ototoi*, pirates!" "*Oimoi!* The gods protect us!" "Run for your lives!"

The crowd began to stir and break up, like a swarm of ants whose nest has been kicked apart. A few near the top of the path bolted down it, toward the clearing where stood the beasts of burden. The Tarentine Archon said:

"Pest! We can't have this. They'll all run back to Cumae, every man for himself, and we shall be caught at the tail of the procession and have our throats cut by the sea thieves. Stop them, lads!"

"I'll try," said Archytas. He pushed through the jabbering, gesticulating crowd to the head of the path, spread his arms to block those behind him, and shouted:

"Why are you running away? Are you men or mud-hearted cowards?"

"I'm a coward," said a Neapolitan in a blue embroidered cloak. "Out of my way, dog-face!"

The man laid a hand on his knife hilt. Zopyros, ranging himself beside Archytas, drew his own knife. Archytas shouted:

"If you're brave enough to threaten me, you're brave enough to fight the robbers!"

"But I'm not armed!" cried the Neapolitan, his voice going shrill.

"You have your dagger and cloak, haven't you? Perhaps they are only a few. Here, you!" Archytas spoke to the youth who had brought the warning and who was now beginning to slide down the cliffside, past where Archytas stood. "How many are there?"

"I don't know. Perhaps thirty."

"Which way are they coming from?"

"Down the coast road from Lake Licola. Let go of my arm, curse you!"

"We can do it!" shouted Archytas. "With these temple guards, we are as many as they! With danger, even danger's overcome!"

But the crowd still cried: "You're mad!" "Let us by!" "They are hardened fighters and we but peaceful folk!"

More men slid down the hillside to the right and left of the path. From below, Zopyros could hear the drum of hooves as the first of the mounted fugitives got his mule headed south along the coastal road.

Now help came to the Tarentines from unexpected sources. The Roman knight, shouldering up to the head of the pathway, cried: "These young men are right, and the more shame to the rest of you! I have a sword in my gear below; who will stand with me?" He was an erect, tight-lipped man of early middle age, who bore himself with self-conscious dignity. Zopyros could barely understand his dialect, quite different from the local Oscan.

"Does your honor mean," said the Celt, "that this is not a private fight? Anybody can get in?"

"Quite so, quite so, man. Have you a weapon?"

"That I have, and I will show you how we make heads fly from their shoulders in the north country. To arms!" With a bloodcurdling shriek, the Celt bounded down the path. Others followed.

The crowd spread out on the hitching space and began rummaging in their gear for shields and weapons. They wrenched open bags, fumbled through their spare clothing, and shouted to their servants. Zopyros and Archytas threw off their cloaks, under which they wore chitons or Greek tunics—short-sleeved, knee-length, belted woolen shirts. They buckled on each other's bronze-studded leathern corselets, strapped on the smallswords, and took up the spears and shields they had brought from Taras. Somebody called:

"Who shall be our general?"

"I am a tribune of horse, who has commanded against the Veientes," said the Roman. "Does any man outrank me? Not so? Good. Now, where is the best place for an ambush?"

"The road passes under a steep bank, a few plethra to the north," said the trembling youth who had brought the message.

The Celt had doffed his tunic and strapped across his hairy chest a baldric, from which hung a long sword. A bronzen helmet with a little wheel on top now covered his long hair, and his left arm bore a big wooden shield with a bronzen boss. "Your honor," he said to the Roman, pointing at a chariot, "is that pretty thing yours?"

"Not so; it belongs to Trebatius, I believe."

"The fellow in the red cloak? I'm thinking, sir, that if I was to drive it full speed around a bend into the pirates, it would stir them up a bit."

"Trebatius would not like it."

"Ah, but he is in the cave with the wise woman, learning whether his next-born will be a boy, a girl, or a purple pig." The Celt pushed aside the slave guarding the chariot and began to unhitch the two white stallions, who shied and rolled their eyes at him. "Just give me the signal, Roman dear, and I will show you a charge like all the Persian king's chariots rolled into one."

"To the afterworld with Trebatius, then. Stand by," said the Roman, who had given his toga to his slave. He now stood in his tunic, which displayed the narrow purple stripe of the equestrian order. A heavy Samnite broadsword hung from his right side, and his arm bore a shield. "Are not the rest of you ready yet? In the name of the gods, hurry! ...

The coastal road wound along the rocky shore, a few cubits above the waves. South along the road came thirty-four armed men at a fast walk, now and then breaking into a lope. They were a scarred, sun-tanned, fierce-looking lot, with here and there a missing eye or ear. They were dressed every which way, some in tar-stained stolen finery of brilliant hues, some in the short Etruscan shirts that left the genitalia exposed. Gold and silver flashed in the morning sun; jewels in rings, bracelets, and necklaces gleamed and winked against their dirty hides. All bore spears—some heavy thrusting pikes, some light casting javelins—and shields. Swords dangled from belts and baldrics. Half a dozen had helmets on their tangled hair; the rest were bareheaded or wore round seamen's caps. Only three wore cuirasses.

Crouching above the bank, Zopyros almost held his breath in the effort to keep from either talking or raising his head to peer at the foe. His heart pounded with excitement. The Roman knight had just threatened to break a spear shaft over the back of the next man who spoke.

The clangor of the pirates now came clearly, above the sigh of the wind and the splash of the waves. Swords clanked in scabbards; spears knocked against shields. There was the sound of many sandaled feet, of hard breathing, and of muttered curses and complaints in a harsh, grating, unknown tongue. Zopyros tried to estimate the number of the enemy by the volume of the sound.

Out of the corner of his eye, Zopyros saw the Roman wave his arm. At once there came the crack of a whip and the rattle of a chariot. Someone among the unseen pirates cried out. The hoofbeats grew louder. The Roman shouted:

"Stones!"

Zopyros sprang up, grasping a ten-pound stone in both hands. He raised the stone and hurled it down on the straggling mass of men below, while others to his right and left did the same. As Zopyros stooped for his second stone, Trebatius' gilded chariot, drawn by the whites at full gallop, hurtled around the bend on one wheel. The Celt screamed horribly, rolling his eyes and showing his teeth, as the chariot thundered toward the pirates.

"At them!" yelled the Roman. The four temple guards, moving heavily in their full panoply of polished bronze, began stumbling down the slope.

Zopyros threw his second stone, picked up his spear and shield, and bounded down the bank. Others, some with rolled-up cloaks in lieu of shields, charged on either side of him. All, as the Roman had commanded, shouted at the tops of their voices. Although a few of those who had gathered at the Sibyl's cave had now slunk away, the attackers numbered over a score.

In the milling mass below him, Zopyros made out one man lying in the road. Just before he reached level ground, the chariot flashed by. The vehicle bounced into the air as the wheels struck another body.

Then Zopyros was in the mellay, jabbing wherever he saw an opening, catching a spear thrust and then a sword cut on his shield. He felt his point strike home. Then he saw a spearhead coming at his face and knew he could not bring his shield around in time. He stepped back, turned his foot on a loose stone, and fell sprawling. He rolled over to get his shield above him, groped for his spear, and scrambled to his feet.

The pirates were no longer around him. The Roman cried: "After them! Do not let them get away! You!" he shouted at Zopyros. Catching the young man by the shoulders, he spun him around and with a mighty push sent him staggering northward along the road.

Zopyros tripped over a body, recovered, and panted after a straggle of fighters, running north in pursuit of a little knot of pirates. Zopyros saw those in the lead overtake one man; saw the man go down under spear thrusts. The rest of the fugitives broke and scattered into the scrub like quail. The pursuers spread out after them but soon gave up the chase.

Zopyros, leaning on his spear and breathing in great sobbing gasps, caught an occasional flash of human hide among the ilexes. But the pirates, having thrown away their loose gear, ran faster for life than their pursuers ran for law and were soon out of sight.

Back at the battlefield, Zopyros found men bandaging wounds, while others snatched the jewelry from the corpses, hacking off fingers to get the rings. The Roman was coldly driving his sword into the body of a wounded pirate who still writhed and moaned. The Celt held his long sword and, by its hair, a severed head. Blood dripped slowly from blade and head.

"Is he not the fine trophy, now?" said the barbarian. "'Tis sorry I am not to be going home to hang him in the hall. But you Greeks are funny about battle trophies. You will hang up an omadhaun's helmet but not the head that went inside it."

Zopyros was counting: "... seven, eight. Are those all we got?"

The Roman said: "Some fell or leaped into the sea when we charged them; I do not know whether they drowned or got ashore again."

24

"Is that man one of ours?" Zopyros indicated a well-dressed body among the corpses.

"It is. That is the man from Messana, the one with the young woman."

A Samnite spoke: "His name was Nestor, and I heard the girl call him 'uncle.'"

Zopyros stepped closer for a better view of the corpse. The gray-beard had several gashes, some of them deep body wounds. His tunic, once white, was now mostly crimson.

"Still," said Zopyros, "we did well, considering that we had fewer on the battle line than they."

The Roman said: "I have seen it before. When one side breaks and runs, even the lightly wounded are struck down from behind as they run or speared as they lie on the ground. Therefore the losses of the losing side are many times those of the winners, even though the battle was close and hard-fought. When I fought at—"

The sound of horses cut off the Roman's sentence. A squadron of horsemen cantered around the bend, their horsehair plumes whipping in the breeze.

"Hercules! What's this?" said their officer. "I mean, are you the pirates or the people who fought against them?"

The Roman bared his teeth in a grimace of exasperation. "What do *you* think, my Campanian friend? Jupiter blast you, must I put on my toga to prove that I am Quintus Cornelius Arvina, of the Equestrian Order of Rome? Do I look like a pirate?"

"I'm sorry, sir," said the officer.

"Well, ride hard to the outlet of Lake Licola, and you may catch the remnant of the pirates before they board their ship."

The horsemen threaded their way through the fighters and corpses and took up their pursuit. As they galloped off, Zopyros turned to help Archytas bandage a scratch on his leg. All were in high spirits, chattering and laughing. Even the Roman cracked a thin smile. Landlord, peasant, and mechanic freely exchanged names and congratulations, differences of rank for the moment forgotten.

The Celt, pulling on his tunic, said to Zopyros: "It is Segovax son of Cotus that I am, young man, and the bonniest fighter that ever came out of Gaul. And who might you be?" He was almost as tall as Zopyros and much heavier, with merry blue eyes in a ruddy, weather-seamed face and hair, once bronzen, now streaked with gray. His cheeks and chin were shaven, but the hair on his long upper lip, uncut, hung down on either side of his mouth, then swept out and up like a buffalo's horns. Zopyros guessed his age at forty.

The Tarentine replied: "I'm Zopyros son of Megabyzos, and my friend here is Archytas son of Mnesagoras. Taras sent the Archon to consult the Sibyl, and we were chosen by lot to go with him, to run errands and protect him from evildoers. What brings you to our sunny southland?"

"I'm after having a bit of trouble at home, and I thought the wise woman could tell me where to find a good job as a hired soldier. I did it before in these lands, years ago, so I will not be finding it strange."

"Is that how you learned Greek?"

"It is that; and Oscan and Punic, too. The fairy that watched over my birth gave me the gift of tongues. Maybe you could—Valetudo preserve us, but look at all the people!"

A crowd had appeared on the road from Cumae. Among them were the servants who had watched the beasts of burden at the foot of the path to the Sibyl's cave, the priests of the Sibyl, the women and old men among the pilgrims, and a swarm of peasants and townsmen who, hearing of the victory, had come out to celebrate. Among them was the red-cloaked landowner, Trebatius, crying:

"This is an outrage! My beautiful chariot, all hacked and spattered with mud and blood! Who told you you might make free with my property, you stinking barbarian?"

The Celt looked up. "Is your honor addressing me, now?" he said softly, his hand stealing to his hilt. "Because if it is a fight you want to make of it—"

"Shut up and let me handle this," barked the Roman. "You, my good Trebatius, cower in the Sibyl's cave while the rest of us fight, and then you have the insolence to complain because somebody put your car to good use in your absence?"

"How was I to know what was going on?" said Trebatius. "When I came out from my hearing, everybody had gone. But this temple-robbing lout—"

"He is a better man than you." Others in the crowd took up the cry: "To the crows with Trebatius!" "Trebatius is a coward!" "Trebatius hides in a cave while the heroes are fighting!" "Let's give Trebatius a ducking!"

"You wouldn't dare!" screamed Trebatius, leaping into his chariot and turning the horses. "Out of my way, scum!" He lashed his horses furiously and rode at reckless speed through the scattering crowd.

The young woman from Messana was sobbing over the bloody body of her uncle. An elderly man with a wreath on his head stepped forward.

"Hail!" he said. "I am Aulus Gellius Mutilus, president of Cumae. This splendid victory has saved the shrine from the most unholy and tragic pollution. By the Heavenly Twins, how did you ever do it? You are not a trained army, but a mixed crowd of men of many nations, speaking different tongues, brought together by chance at the shrine. Yet you defeated a gang of well-armed, hard-fighting robbers, more numerous than yourselves."

Cornelius Arvina shrugged. "The Tarentines here dissuaded them from running away, and I told them what to do. After all, I am a Roman knight."

"You make it sound miraculously simple, best one. As chief magistrate of Cumae, I invite all our saviors—all those who took part in the battle—to a banquet this evening at the town hall. It is a small return, but the best we can do."

"I thank you," said the Roman gravely. "Meanwhile, did anyone think to bring us some wine? Fighting is a thirsty trade. … Ah, that is better!"

Zopyros noted with surprise that the sun was halfway down the western sky. At least two or three hours had passed since their audience with the Sibyl. The young woman still wept. Three men stood around her: two slaves, and a burly bodyguard who had fought against the pirates. Bashfully, Zopyros said:

"Young lady, can I do anything for you? I understand this man was your uncle."

She raised a tear-stained face. "I thank you, stranger. I don't know what to do. How shall I ever get Uncle Nestor's body home?"

"You don't want it buried here?"

"By the two goddesses, no! That would be terrible. His spirit would never be happy anywhere but in the family plot at Messana, and he would haunt us forever. But now ..."

"Well, the first step is to take it back to Cumae. How did you get here?"

"I rode an ass; the others walked."

"I'll lend you my mule, because it's a long walk for a little girl."

The girl looked doubtful "I don't know ..."

"You have nothing to fear. I am Zopyros of Taras, a humble follower of the divine Pythagoras, and this is Archon Bryson of our city. Assure the young lady she can trust us, O Archon."

"My dear young lady," began the Archon. "I don't know your name ..."

"Korinna daughter of Xanthos. If these young men are with you, Archon, I'm sure they are honorable."

The Cumaeans stripped the bodies of the pirates and piled the naked corpses in a heap. Others cut brush to burn the bodies. As the three Tarentines, together with Korinna and her servitors, started south along the coastal road, a crackling orange fire, a pillar of dark smoke, and a smell of burnt meat arose from the pyre.

Plodding back to Cumae, Zopyros walked beside Korinna's ass. Ahead, the bodyguard led Zopyros' mule, on whose back the corpse joggled and swayed.

"I don't know how I shall ever get back to Messana," said Korinna in worried tones. "It is hard, very hard, for a woman to travel alone. Uncle Nestor arranged everything."

"What about the three with you?"

"Sophron"—she nodded toward the bodyguard—"seems a good fellow. I don't think he'd try to dishonor me; but the big Cyprian ox is too stupid to manage anything. As for the slaves, you know what they're like. You saw how all three stood helplessly by until you told them what to do."

"How did you come from Messana?"

"In Captain Strabon's ship. He plans to sail for home tomorrow."

"We came overland, by way of Venusia and Aquilonia."

"How was the journey?"

"Smooth enough, save for a close escape from robbers near Malienta, and a snowstorm on Mount Tifata. Of course these Italian roads, so called, are mere goat tracks. I wonder how you, a young girl, came to make this voyage with your uncle?"

"I, not my uncle, was the inquirer."

"Oh?" Zopyros raised his bushy eyebrows.

"I … I wanted to find out how to get my child back. You needn't look startled. I am a respectable twice-widowed woman, once by death and once, by divorce."

"By Mother Earth, you don't look old enough to have been married even once!"

"Nonsense! That's your sly Tarentine gallantry. I'm nearly twenty—practically an old woman."

"Then my eyesight must be failing. Where is the child?"

"After my first husband died, I returned to my father's house and asked Father to find me a more interesting husband. Poor Aristeas had been sweet but terribly dull, you know."

"Many men are, I fear," said Zopyros. He added with a malicious little smile: "You found his successor quickly enough, didn't you? Did he prove more fascinating?"

"I once thought so. But love is like looking in a mirror; when you turn around, everything is on the opposite side."

Korinna fell silent. Zopyros, striding beside her, felt awkward and ineffectual. Thinking that, if he could get her to talk, it might lift some of the sadness from her small pale face, he groped for words:

"Who—what was he like, your second husband?"

"Elazar was a Phoenician building contractor and a childless widower. Father dealt with him while building a market in town. I saw them together once, standing in our courtyard, studying the plans. Elazar fascinated me—a big, strong man with a touch of gray in his beard, widely traveled and worldly wise—so different from Aristeas. Of course, Father didn't want me to marry a foreigner; but to please me he agreed."

"I take it that Elazar proved less fascinating when you came to know him better?"

"Oh, Elazar is quite a man in his way; and being a Phoenician's wife has its advantages. Did you know they give their women much more freedom and responsibility than we Hellenes do?"

"I know them well; I lived three years in Tyre. What happened then?"

"Elazar took me back to Motya, his home town, where he had a contract to rebuild part of the city wall."

"That's at the western tip of Sicily, isn't it?"

"Yes, on an island in a bay."

"Do they expect an attack by the Hellenes, then?" asked Zopyros.

"Not right now. But the warehouses of any Phoenician city bulge with goods gathered by their traders from all over the world, from the plains of Scythia to the Pillars of Herakles. Any warlord would love to loot such a place, and the Phoenicians know it. The Motyans are rich. We lived well. I could have learnt to put up with Elazar's gruff ways if we had not had a son."

"A son? Most families look upon a son as a blessing."

She lowered her voice, as if oppressed by the memory. "Elazar is a pious man in his way, and little by little I learnt what he had in mind. In times of peril to their city, leading Punic families give up their first-born to be burnt alive in the statue of Baal Hammon. If danger ever came to Motya, that's what Elazar meant to do with my beautiful baby."

"By Zeus the Savior! I saw that custom practiced once in Tyre. It's even crueler than the Italian custom of arming slaves or prisoners and making them fight to the death. What did you do?"

"At first I was so terrified that I couldn't think. Then I planned to run away with the child. Needing a confederate, I bribed the nurse. That was a mistake. Then I bribed a ship's captain to take us on his next run to Messana. I planned to visit another Hellenic woman when Elazar was out and, from her home, slip down to the pier. The nurse was to meet me there with the baby.

"I went to my friend's house and put on a white wig. Carrying a small bundle of my things, I went to the piers and boarded the ship. But the nurse never appeared. Instead, Elazar came storming down, looking for me. Luckily, nobody thought he was describing the white-haired old lady who had just gone aboard. I hid among the cargo, and Captain Philon—Artemis bless him—never gave me away. My friend later wrote that the nurse, having taken my bribe, went to Elazar and disclosed the plot to get an extra reward from him."

"Death take her! What happened next?"

"I suppose I could have gone back to Elazar and taken my punishment. But that wouldn't have saved little Ahiram; for Elazar would have seen to it that I never got another chance to touch the child. In the end I sailed away without the boy. Perhaps I was a coward ..."

"I think you're a heroine," said Zopyros. "And then?"

"Father was dreadfully upset, of course; but he got the Archon's Court to grant me a divorce. When he wrote Elazar, demanding his grandson, he got no answer. He sent my brother Glaukos to Motya to offer a ransom—besides giving up his claim to my dowry—but Elazar practically threw Glaukos out of the house. That's why I came here to ask the Sibyl's advice. Since Father isn't well enough to travel, Uncle Nestor brought me. Now Uncle Nestor's dead, and it's all my f-fault. ..." She began to cry again.

"Now, now," said Zopyros, feeling inadequate. "The Fates snip out threads as they please, and your uncle died a hero's death."

She wiped her eye with her veil. "Full is the earth of ills, and full no less are the waters.'"

"Are you still going to interview the Sibyl?" he asked.

"I've already done so."

"How is that possible?"

"By the time Trebatius came out from his hearing, nearly everybody else had left the acropolis. So I asked the priest if I might have my turn, thinking the pirates would be too fearful of the gods to invade the sacred grotto."

"Clever girl! What advice did you get?"

"She said:

"To recover thy child from the isle of the setting sun,
Thou shalt seek the aid of a man from the lands of morn."

"That describes Motya, all right; but it sounds as if you needed the help of some Easterner—an Ionian, or perhaps even a Tyrian."

"Don't ask me to get mixed up with Phoenicians again! To me they're hateful as the gates of Hell."

"I have good friends in Tyre; but I can understand your feeling."

They moved quietly for a time. The sun sank lower toward the Tyrrhenian Sea, which blazed with golden coruscations like the flames in the belly of Baal Hammon. At length she said:

"I've done all the talking. Tell me about yourself."

"There's little to tell. I'm just a hard-working engineer, in business with my father in Taras."

"An engineer? You mean a machine maker?"

"Machine making is one of our tasks. We do much else, besides. We design fortifications, build aqueducts, and survey roads. When a man like Master Elazar finds a task too complicated for him, he sends for us to calculate him out of trouble."

"I don't believe we have any engineers in Messana."

"There aren't many in the West; it's a new trade in Great Hellas. It calls for a lot of travel, and it's a chancy business. Somebody—perhaps a private contractor; perhaps the president of a city—puzzles over a technical problem until he's nearly mad. Then he calls us in. We solve the problem, and the man who has hired us says: 'Why, that was easy! I could have done as much! And do you scoundrels really think I'll pay you a hundred drachmai for that?'"

"The last time one of them talked like this, my father said: 'All right, I'll say no more about the fee, if you will make a little bet with me.'"

"'What's that?' said the builder, who was a notorious gambler."

"'I'll wager I can tell a hard-boiled egg from a raw egg without opening it. Will you bet a hundred drachmai that I can't?'"

"The builder took him on. We got a dozen eggs, boiled half of them, cooled them, and mixed them with the six raw eggs. My father easily picked out the hard-boiled ones."

"How?"

"You stand the egg on end and spin it. If it spins like a top, it's hard-boiled. If it flops over, it's not. One of my Tyrian friends taught me that trick."

"How funny! What were you doing in Tyre?"

"My father sent me there for my technical education. He apprenticed me to Abdadon, a colleague who specializes in shipyards and docks. The Phoenicians are far ahead of us Hellenes in engineering."

"Really? I thought Hellenes led the world in everything."

"So they like to think; but some foreigners know a thing or two. The Phoenicians encourage invention by deifying their great inventors."

"What did you say your father's name was?"

"Megabyzos son of Zopyros."

"Those sound like Persian names."

"They are." Defensively, Zopyros said: "I'm only one quarter Persian. My grandfather Zopyros was a Persian nobleman who fell out with the Great King and fled to Athens, where he married a Hellene. When my father grew up, he moved to Taras, because he heard it would be easier to become a citizen there. You know how exclusive the Athenians are. If you're not of pure Athenian descent, it's easier to steal a gryphon's egg than to gain Athenian franchise."

"Did the Tarentines grant him citizenship?"

"Oh, yes; we are now solid citizens despite our mixed blood. Without family or city, a man is nobody—Mistress Korinna, why are you staring at me like that?"

"Why ... you must be the man from the lands of morn, of whom the Sibyl spoke! You're part Persian, and you have lived in Tyre."

"Dear Herakles! Don't expect *me* to rescue your boy from his father!"

"You have been chosen by the gods for this task!"

"My dear Korinna, I have my duties to my city and my family, and Pythagoras placed duty and responsibility before all. Besides, the Archon would never let me go galloping off on such a chase."

"You won't help me, then?" Her lip trembled.

"I should be delighted to, but ... You have friends and kinsmen in Messana far better placed than I to cope with Elazar. I've never even been to Sicily."

"But they don't fit the Sibyl's pronouncement; you do!"

Zopyros squirmed in an agony of indecision. He liked this small, dark, pretty girl immensely. He had seldom had an opportunity to talk at length to a girl of his own class outside his immediate family. As Zopyros plodded on, frowning at the road before him, Korinna said:

"You might at least escort me back to Messana. Otherwise I don't know how I shall ever get home safely. Then, you could catch an eastbound ship and be back in Taras before your comrades."

"I'll ask the Archon. ..."

When Zopyros and his fellow Tarentines, bathed and oiled, appeared in front of the town hall of Cumae, a low red sun was staining the white stucco of this edifice rosy pink. The town hall was a boxlike building of stuccoed mud brick. A pair of Doric columns, of stucco-covered local limestone, relieved the plainness of the building and testified to the precarious lodgment of Greek culture on the barbarous Italian coast.

"O Zopyros!" It was Korinna, who stepped out of the shadows where she had stood with Sophron the bodyguard and her two slaves.

"Rejoice!" said Zopyros. "Dear old Bryson says I may take you to Messana. But not a step further; he made me swear by the holy tetractys to return thence at once to Taras."

"We may never get to Messana!" she said. "A terrible thing has happened."

"Zeus! Don't tell me Captain What's-his-name has sailed off without you!"

"No, but it's just as bad. He absolutely won't take a corpse on board; he babbles about ghosts and sea daemons and bad luck."

"Furies take him! We can't delay. If we get a warm spell, your uncle won't ... Well, I'll try to find another ship."

"Where?"

"I don't know." Zopyros waved an arm. "I'll inquire at the banquet. If there is none here, perhaps there's one at Neapolis. I'll manage something. Now get a good night's sleep."

Inside the town hall, oil lamps shed a soft yellow glow on the banquet tables. The president and a few men of the highest rank were already reclining on dining couches at the far end of the room. The other diners sat on benches at long tables. Zopyros tried to count the assemblage but gave up; too many people were moving about.

"Welcome!" said Gellius Mutilus. "I am sorry we cannot accommodate you all in proper style, but our little basilica is not large enough for so many couches. I hope you will drink enough of our best Falernian so that you shall not notice the difference."

Zopyros found himself between Segovax the Celt and the Neapolitan with whom he had had words before the battle.

"Rejoice, Master Zopyros!" said the latter. "You and your friends did what I thought impossible; namely: made me a hero in spite of myself. It proves that the gods do indeed intervene in human affairs; for, without divine help, you, I, and our fellow heroes should all be weltering in our gore. By Herakles' balls, I wouldn't have bet a moldy olive against a golden Persian stater that a raggle-taggle crew like ours had a chance against a gang of professional murderers!"

Zopyros said: "My friend Archytas, here, has a mysterious knack of talking people into doing what he wants them to do. Some god takes possession of his tongue."

"Anyway I, like a sensible man, prepared to go elsewhere. Only, as things turned out, common sense was not sensible after all. Your health, sir!"

"Thank you, Master Ingomedon," said Zopyros. "Tell me: how can I catch a ship from here—or from Baiae or Neapolis, for that matter—bound for Messana? A ship, moreover, whose captain is not superstitious."

"Taking the old Messanian home, eh? Let me see. Strabon is leaving tomorrow, I believe."

"He won't carry the cargo in question."

"Well then—hmm—do you see that fellow over there, with the earrings and the necklace of glass gimcracks?"

"The lean one who twiddles his fingers and drums on the table?"

"Yes. He's a Phoenician captain who put in a few days ago. He was at the Sibyl's grotto ahead of us this morning. I don't know his name or his home port, but you could ask him. What he's doing here, I can't imagine, since he is neither a hero of the battle nor a Cumaean citizen. Maybe the president owes him money, or maybe they have some shady deal. Some say all Phoenicians are thieves, although I have no prejudice against foreigners. Why, some of my best friends—"

"I'm part Persian myself," said Zopyros with emphasis.

"Think nothing of it." Ingomedon hastily swallowed a mouthful of diced octopus and resumed in a lowered voice. "Actually, purity of blood is a sore subject in Cumae. You see, the Cumaeans are of bastard origin, just like you Tar—excuse me, but you know what I mean.

Not two generations ago, when Cumae was still Greek Kymê an army of Samnites seized the town, slaughtered the men, and grabbed the women. Some of those old brigands are still alive. The Samnites settled down with their new women and begat as fine a crop of little half-breeds as you ever saw. Since most of the women were Hellenes, however, the children grew up to speak more Greek than Oscan. They still do, albeit with that weird Italianate accent you hear. But they carry Oscan names, since the man has the final say in that."

Zopyros asked: "Is there a Pythagorean Society around here?"

"You mean a gang of philosophical fanatics, plotting to seize power and make everybody stop eating beans?"

"No, nothing like that! The Pythagoreans haven't touched politics for years, save in Rhegion. Nowadays they are simply men interested in mathematics and the other sciences—seekers after the hidden truths of the universe."

Ingomedon laughed. "Not around here! We Neapolitans think of three things only: our purses, our bellies, and our pricks. Excuse me; my food is getting cold."

Zopyros asked his other neighbor: "How goes it with you, O Segovax? Have you seen the Sibyl?"

"That I did, young sir. The wise woman told me: 'Seek thou the place where the island rules the shore.' Now where would that be?"

Zopyros frowned. "I hear the Dionysios makes his headquarters on the island of Ortygia. Thence he rules the Syracusans on the mainland of Sicily and a lot of other peoples besides."

The Celt nodded sagely. "I am after thinking about him. I once soldiered for the fellow they had before him, Hermokrates, and a grand man he was. What did the lady druid tell you?"

"She told me I should someday smash the world."

Segovax's blue eyes widened. "You don't say, now! I hope I'll be somewhere else when that happens. You look like a nice lad, not one who goes around breaking up worlds, and them so pretty and all."

"She also," said Archytas from the other side of Segovax, "told us to beware of the Wolf of the North, whoever that might be."

"Hold your tongue, you polluted rattlepate!" said Archon Bryson from further down the table. "Such sacred matters should not be blabbed from Karia to Carthage."

"Ah, well," said the Celt, "wine makes the tongue wag easier, like grease in the hub of a chariot wheel. But you will not be talking of Sibyls and prophecies now, I'm thinking."

The buzz of conversation died as a dancing girl sprang into the cleared space in the midst of the tables. Clad in a thin shift of purple Koan silk, she went into gyrations to the tune of a double flute with a nose piece, blown by another girl in the corner.

When the girl had finished her dance, the men whooped and applauded. The girl curtseyed and ran off. Soon she was back, juggling knives and balls. The applause was louder.

The third time, the girl placed on the floor several candlesticks bearing lighted Etruscan candles. Then she cast off her shift and, naked, turned cartwheels and did handstands amid the candles, which cast golden highlights on her well-oiled skin.

"Isn't he the sour-face, though!" said the Celt in a loud whisper.

"Who?" said Zopyros.

"The Roman, that Cornelius Arvina."

Segovax nodded toward the couches on the dais at the end of the hall. The Roman knight, wearing a look of chill disapproval, was sitting up on the side of his couch, with his feet dangling, pretending to adjust his toga so that the stripe on his tunic showed. The Celt continued:

"The lassie is after having the hair of her crotch shaved off. Is that the way they do in your city, now?"

"Some Italians do it," said Zopyros. "It's an Etruscan custom. Some of the rich young Tarentines do it, too—you know, those beautiful youths who spend their days striking statuesque poses in the gymnasium. But not us working folk; before I'd let anybody near *my* family jewels with a razor—"

"We have the hairs pulled out in Neapolis," said Ingomedon.

"Ouch!" said Segovax. "The things folks will do to be in style—"

"Zeus, Apollon, and Demeter!" cried Ingomedon. "Look at that!" The Neapolitan burst into a loud guffaw, in which the entire company joined until the town hall shook with a thunder of mirth.

For the dancing girl, with a final flip, turned a somersault and came down on the lap of the Roman knight, with her arm around his neck and her face buried in his beard. Expressions of stark horror, dismay, and rage chased each other over the Roman's stern visage. For an instant it looked as if he would rise and stalk out. But, with the naked girl clinging to him like a limpet, this would have involved a scuffle, even more unseemly and undignified than his present position. Seeing that all the rest thought it a good joke, the Roman tried to smile but managed only a ghastly grimace.

The girl leaped down from her perch and made her bows to thunderous applause. When she had snatched up her shift and run out, Gellius Mutilus, the president, rose and said:

"To finish the evening, we shall auction off that little spinning top, for the night, to the highest bidder. Her kindly owner asks me to tell you two things: First, he promises that she may keep half the money the auction brings, for her very own self; and second, she need not take any man who displeases her. What am I bid, gentlemen? Do you care to open the bidding, good Cornelius Arvina?"

"I do not!" snapped the Roman, adjusting his toga.

Pointing, Ingomedon said to Zopyros: "There's your Wolf of the North."

"You mean Rome?"

The Neapolitan wagged his head affirmatively.

"I can't believe that!" exclaimed Zopyros. "Rome is a small, distant, backward, unimportant state, without sea power. How could Rome ever threaten Taras? Other peoples are far more menacing—the Lucanians, the Etruscans, or the Celts. Why, your fair Neapolis might be a greater threat than little old Rome!"

Ingomedon said: "I have been to Rome, man, and know whereof I speak. The Romans are a conservative people—exceedingly dull, in fact. They wouldn't even laugh at a comedy of Aristophanes. With them, custom is king. But they have discipline. We don't."

"Do you mean 'we Neapolitans' or 'we Hellenes'?"

"I know the Neapolitans best, naturally; but the remark applies to others as well. The Spartans have discipline, but cursed few other Hellenes. I have no discipline whatever. Hellas is full of pillow knights—lions in the bedroom, rabbits on the battlefield."

"They tell me the Spartans have been corrupted by success since they overcame the Athenians."

"That may be, but the Romans have a more complex organization than the Spartans ever thought of. Moreover, when the Romans conquer a neighboring people, they admit them—after a waiting period—to full citizenship. Thus their power grows."

"Hellenic cities are much more exclusive," said Zopyros. "Our local gods are jealous gods, who hate having strangers attend their rites."

"Exactly. So, when a Hellenic city gains an empire, as the Athenians did, it looks upon the other peoples of the empire as subjects to be exploited. Naturally, the subjects hate their masters and seize the first opportunity to break away. I don't know by what trick of theology the Romans get around the obstacle of common worship; but they do." The Neapolitan yawned. "By the Dog of Egypt, here I am, trying to play the oracle when I can't even foresee my own affairs a day in advance! The bidding for the girl has already risen beyond the reach of my purse, so I'm going. But remember what I have told you. If you live long enough, you'll see what Rome can do."

A stout, bald landowner won the dancing girl. As the party broke up, Zopyros marked the lean, intense-looking Phoenician sea captain and pushed his way toward him through the crush.

As the sun rose the next morning, Zopyros called at the inn where Korinna occupied one of the two private rooms.

"It's all arranged," he told her. "We sail this morning on the *Muttumalein*, of Captain Ethbaal."

"Another Phoenician!"

"I can't help that. He's the only one besides Strabon who is leaving within a ten-day. Let's gather our gear and be off!"

VELIA

The strong north wind of the previous day had fled away, but a brisk breeze lingered. The *Muttumalein* lay in the shelter of a small stone jetty, which curved from Cumae's harborless beach out into the turquoise Tyrrhenian Sea. A precarious plank extended from the sand of the jetty to the high gunwale of the ship. She was a tubby, flush-decked craft with a black hull, about sixty feet long by twenty feet wide. She had a single mast with a yellow square sail and, near the stern, a cabin not much bigger than a doghouse. Oars were piled at the base of the mast; a pair of boarding ladders, one long and one short, were stowed at the stern.

Workmen, shouting in Oscan, were passing casks of wine and olive oil, bolts of linen, and bags of salt down into the hold. Eight swarthy Punic sailors, stripped to loincloths, hauled on ropes and stowed ship's gear. The passengers waited on the jetty for the loading to be completed.

Captain Ethbaal stood on his deck where the plank reached the gunwale, scratching marks on a waxed wooden tablet as each item was brought aboard. Instead of the embroidered robe he had worn to the Sibyl's cave the previous day, he was now clad in ordinary Phoenician seaman's garb: a short-sleeved shirt and a pleated kilt, over them a short cape against the morning chill, and a round cap on his head. About his neck still hung the necklace of little glass and copper images of the Pataecian gods. He was a man of average height, slightly stooped, and lean to gauntness, with a nose like a vulture's beak.

Two local merchants stood, also marking tablets, on the deck near Ethbaal. Now and again the loading was held up while Ethbaal and one or the other of the merchants engaged in a last-minute haggle.

The captain's mate, a commonplace-looking little man, stood at the hatch, directing the stowage of cargo into the hold. When the last bag of salt had been stowed, Ethbaal beckoned Korinna's attendants, Sophron the bodyguard and the one remaining slave. (The other slave had run away.) At the signal, these two picked up the ends of the poles that formed the litter for the shrouded body of Nestor, carried the body aboard, and lowered it gingerly into the hold.

Now Ethbaal turned to the other passengers on the jetty. "Come aboard!" he called in heavily accented Greek. "But do not enter the cabin!"

They filed up the plank: a middle-aged couple with a twelve-year-old boy; an old Etruscan with a shaven upper lip, who wore a wide-brimmed hat and walked with a crutch; a younger man who was his servant; Segovax the Celt; a traveling singer with his lyre in a linen case; and finally Korinna of Messana. The *Muttumalein* had no amenities for the passengers, who crowded up forward to be out of the sailors' way. They camped on the bare boards along the bulwarks, making themselves as comfortable as they could with their cloaks and bedding rolls.

Zopyros bid farewell to the Archon and to his friend Archytas, while the two slaves who belonged to the city of Taras, and who had been sent along to serve the three pilgrims, held the mules near the base of the jetty. Zopyros said to Archytas:

"Don't talk the city into electing you president before I get back! You're too young for the office."

"And don't you get so absorbed in counting the waves that you fall overboard," retorted Archytas. "You might ask in Messana if there is a Pythagorean Society there. It would be nice if our little club had another with whom we could correspond now and then, besides that gang of oligarchs in Rhegion."

"I'll do that. Farewell, Archon; Hermes attend you both on the homecoming!"

A shout of "Hurry up, you!" came from the ship, Zopyros slung the bag containing his shield and spare clothing over his back and, using his spear as a stick, strode up the plank. As he hopped down to the deck, Captain Ethbaal said:

"Zopyros the Tarentine, eh?"

"That's my name." Zopyros laid down his burdens to get out his fare.

"Handsome young fellow, eh?" said Ethbaal.

"I'm glad somebody thinks so."

"Well, keep away from my cabin!"

Zopyros did not like the man's tone, nor yet the gleam in his eye. Somehow Ethbaal gave the impression, even when standing perfectly still, of being as tense as a bow drawn to the release point. Hoping to get on a friendlier basis with the captain, Zopyros said in Punic:

"Why, Captain, what holds the cabin that were too deadly to approach? A gorgon's head, that would turn us to stone?"

"The cabin holds my wife, that is all," snapped Ethbaal in the same language. "The most beautiful woman of Egypt, and I will have no lecherous Hellene sniffing on her trail!"

Zopyros managed a smile. "Fear nought, gallant Captain. Pythagoreans keep their hands off other men's wives." He turned away to claim a section of deck near where Korinna and her two attendants had spread their gear.

"Asto!" yelled Ethbaal. "Cast off the plank; hoist the anchors. Put four on the oars and tell the others to stand by to hoist sail!"

The mate jumped to the task, shooting nervous glances at his captain. The captain himself grasped the tiller bars, forward of the cabin, which controlled the two side rudders. A murmur arose as the passengers and their friends ashore prayed to their various gods. A lapping of waves mingled with a groaning of oars in their locks and ropes in their blocks, as the *Muttumalein* swung slowly away from the jetty. The yellow sail rose by jerks, fluttering and filling. The ship heeled and headed out from shore at an angle, blue and white water boiling away from her blunt black stem. The sailors shipped and stacked their oars. Gulls wheeled and squealed overhead; while, farther out in the sapphire sea, a school of slate-gray porpoises rolled and leaped.

Once clear of the coast, the *Muttumalein* fell into a steady pitch as the south-marching swells thrown up by Boreas overtook her. Wave after green wave raced up astern, slapped at the ship's rounded counter, boosted the hull upward, and rolled by underneath, foaming away on both sides. The sailors donned their shirts and kilts.

Segovax gripped the rail, staring toward the porpoises. His ruddy coloring had turned a greenish gray. He said:

"Master Zopyros, was there not one of you Greek fellows who invented a pair of wings that a man could fly with? A gigantic idea! Only the poor loon flew too near the sun, and the heat melted the glue, and the man fell into the sea and drowned, and him so clever and all. I do remember hearing somebody tell of it when I was soldiering for the General Hermokrates."

"That's Ikaros," said Zopyros. "At least, Ikaros was killed using the wings, while his father Daidalos is said to have made them."

"Whatever the man's name, it would be a more comfortable way to cross the sea than these ships, I'm thinking."

"It's just a legend," said Zopyros. "Remember to use the lee rail if your stomach gets out of hand."

"But this is *good* weather!" said Asto, the timid-looking mate. "With the wind like this, we shall make Messana in less than a tenday. Walk about the deck a bit and you will feel better. You should see how we suffer when the wind blows foul for a month at a time, or we are caught by a sudden storm at sea! Or when sea monsters rise out of the deep to seize us. ..."

"You'd better not say too much about monsters if you want to build up a good passenger trade," said Zopyros. "How is trade along this coast?"

"The Sibyl helps," said the Phoenician. "People come from near and far to consult her, thus rendering profitable some voyages that would otherwise not pay. The Campanians love imported luxuries, but their own products are mostly bulk staples for which there's not much market in Great Hellas. So, without the pilgrims, we should often have to return in ballast—"

"*Asto!*" came the yell of Captain Ethbaal. "Take the helm, Milkarth smite you! I go below to inspect."

"Coming!" shouted Asto, then to Zopyros: "Ethbaal is counted the most daring skipper of the Inner Sea, putting out the first in spring and laying up the last in autumn. Not even ill omens stop him.

But he's also the most vigilant; nothing is ever shipshape enough to suit him. Coming!"

The little mate bowed low to Zopyros and ran off, his bare feet slapping the damp deck planks. The old Etruscan was sitting on the deck with his lame leg stretched out in the sun before him, shading his eyes with his hands as he watched the wheeling flight of the gulls. He said in bad Greek:

"What was all this talk in Punic?"

Zopyros answered: "He was telling me our captain is a veritable Odysseus for craft and courage, who lets nothing—not even a bad omen—delay him."

"The more fool he and more unlucky we," said the Etruscan. "Everything that happens is presaged by omens. That is why I watch the birds. I am *zilath* of Tarquinii, wise man and important official. I know what I talk about."

"What do the birds tell you about this voyage?"

"Nothing good. Somebody will have disaster."

"Who?"

"Do not yet know. Tell you later." The Etruscan resumed his bird watching.

Segovax held his head and moaned. Korinna leaned against the rail and gazed shoreward. Zopyros came to stand beside her. As the ship passed through the channel between Cape Misenum and the island of Prochyta, the vast Bay of Neapolis opened out eastward. It formed an irregular semicircle from the island of Aenaria on the left, behind them, to that of Capreae on the right, before them. Towns and villages lined the shore of the bay like white beads on a green string. Amidst them, the pendant on the necklace, rose the walls and temples of great Neapolis itself, while to the right loomed the dark, towering cone of Vesuvius.

"It looks like mighty Aetna, in my own land," said Korinna. "But Aetna smokes and sputters, while this mountain seems still."

"There's a tradition that Vesuvius, too, was once a fiery mountain," said Zopyros. "But its fire seems to have gone out for good."

She glanced at the wretched Segovax and made a grimace. "Somehow I don't feel well, either. My head aches. I think I'll lie down."

The singer also looked unhappy. The middle-aged couple, sitting side by side on the deck beneath a little tentlike awning they had rigged, stared off across the waters with expressions of such blank stolidity that one could not tell whether they were suffering or not. That left the twelve-year-old boy, the servants, and the sailors.

However, Zopyros' shyness kept him from striking up a conversation with any of them. Unlike his friend Archytas, he tended to become tongue-tied in the presence of strangers. He had little small talk. Faced by a stranger, he was inclined either to monopolize the conversation by a lecture on his professional experiences and beliefs, or to subside into glum silence and leave the whole burden of the talk to the other.

Now, having nobody with whom he could easily converse, Zopyros contented himself with trying to count the waves, trying to estimate the speed of the ship from the time it took bubbles and flotsam to slide the length of the hull, and trying to calculate the volume of the little cabin aft. Thinking of the cabin brought his mind around to the strange behavior of Captain Ethbaal.

From time to time he had stolen glances at the structure, expecting to see some gorgeous woman in the glittering raiment of timeless Egypt come forth. But nothing happened; the cabin gave no sign of life. When Zopyros saw that his curious glances brought a suspicious scowl from Captain Ethbaal, he resolutely turned his gaze in other directions.

As the day wore on, they sailed through the channel in the southeast horn of the Bay of Neapolis, between the Promontory of Athena and the isle of Capreae. The passengers unwrapped the simple lunches they had brought aboard—mostly bread, cheese, grapes, and olives—and fell to eating. Zopyros, about to toss aside an olive pit, looked up to see Ethbaal glowering down at his passengers.

"Throw your garbage overboard, please!" growled the captain. "My ship is not a pigsty."

As they passed a cluster of rocky islets south of the promontory, Korinna came to the rail. She said to Zopyros, also leaning on the rail and staring at the water:

"On the ship from Messana, they told me those were the Siren Isles, past which Odysseus sailed with plugs in his ears."

"Perhaps. Others locate the Sirens on the Brettian coast, near your own city."

"Oh." She sounded a little put out.

"Don't be vexed, Mistress Korinna. I don't doubt that Odysseus did indeed explore these waters. But half the towns of the Inner Sea have decided that it would fetch travelers and trade if they could point out a place as the site of one of his adventures. So they've gone over the epic poets like a boy picking fleas from his dog, looking for some place that could, by a stretch of the imagination, be identified with their own city." He turned to Asto, who had just come up. "Where shall we stop the night?"

"With this good wind, the skipper is headed for Poseidonia. Usually we stop the first day at Salernum, or at best the Sanctuary of the Argive Hera. But this time the gods have been good to us."

Korinna went back to her place on deck and talked of feminine matters with the mother of the twelve-year-old boy. Zopyros asked Asto: "Why didn't we stop at Neapolis? It's a much bigger port than Cumae."

"We did, on the way north, and loaded cargo. To have stopped again would have cost us a day to small profit. Usually Neapolis is the end of our run. But Ethbaal," Asto chuckled, "can smell a cargo as a hound scents a beefsteak half a league upwind. He heard that some goods had piled up at Cumae, awaiting the first voyages of the season; and *zzip!*" Asto made a darting motion with his hand. "Off we went for Cumae, like a flying fish with a tuna on its tail!"

Poseidonia lay on a stretch of pine-forested plain beneath a purple sky. Beyond the forest, black in the fading light, rose the snow-flecked ridges of the Alburnus. As the *Muttumalein* anchored in the reedy mouth of the little Salsos River, the sunset reddened the snowy stucco of the temples, whose tops were visible over the trees. The sailors thrust the long boarding ladder over the side and into the mud as far from the ship as they could reach with it. Passengers and crew climbed down the ladder and splashed ashore. Zopyros said to the captain:

"Aren't you coming ashore, Master Ethbaal?"

"And leave my ship and my wife unguarded, in a land infested with lecherous, light-fingered Greeks? Do you think me mad?"

Zopyros turned away from this crosspatch with a shrug, to climb down the ladder. Korinna followed him, and he carried her ashore. The contact made his heart race.

There were a few Poseidonians at the landing place: some fishermen, and a couple of boys with an ass to rent. Zopyros hired the ass for Korinna. It was a good twelve furlongs to the city.

Poseidonia, Zopyros learned, had but one small inn. This was even dirtier than most and, furthermore, had no private room in which he could lodge Korinna. For her to sleep in the common dormitory with the men would be unthinkable. Fortunately, the city had a Messanian *proxenos*. The consul found lodging in a decent home for both Korinna and the mother of the twelve-year-old.

In the inn that evening, Zopyros listened to tavern talk. The natives were restless, it was said. The Lucanian tribes were stirring. They had long looked enviously at the gleaming Greek city in their midst, and now …

"We should arm to the teeth," said one, "and drill daily, as the Spartans did in their great days."

"Then how should we earn our livings?" said another. "The Lucanians can always put ten men in the battle line to one of ours. If our so-called government were really clever, they'd stir up dissension among the barbarians, so they'd fight each other instead of us."

Another: 'They've been doing that; but the foreigners seem to have caught on. Now our best hope is to be quiet and polite, avoid provocation, and hope they won't notice us."

"They've already noticed us," said another. "It's too late for that. Besides, that's cowardly advice. We ought to hire some good stout mercenaries, like our Gaulish friend there. Oh, Celt! Would you fight for us for pay?"

"I might that," said Segovax, to whom wine had given back his ruddy color, "if the wage was right. But not this year; I'm after seeing the wise woman at Cumae, and she told me to carry a spear for Dionysios. Next year, maybe."

"You see!" said another speaker. "It's hopeless. The omens are against us. We should hire some ships and quietly sail away, as the Phokaians did when menaced by Cyrus' armies."

"But whither? All the other shores of the Inner Sea swarm with bloodthirsty, envious barbarians. No! By the God, this is our land, won by the spear, and we should defend it with our good right arms. Union gives strength. What we need is a firm alliance with the Neapolitans, the Velians, and the other Hellenes of the coast—"

"Death take those dirty foreigners! Those haughty, cowardly, treacherous, temple-robbing braggarts would want supreme command. They'd put our men in the most exposed position and, if they saw things going badly, run away and leave us to be slaughtered. What we really need …"

And so it went, until Zopyros sought the bug-ridden dormitory for a night of troubled slumber. In his dreams, Korinna and the Sibyl and Etruscan omens and Herakles' mighty bow were all jumbled up.

Next morning, Zopyros paused on his way back to the ship to examine an old temple. "Not," he told Korinna, "that the religious aspects concern me overmuch. But look at those obsolete methods of construction! Mud brick instead of marble or even the rough limestone they use in the West; wooden columns instead of stone. … It's a wonder to me the old thing hasn't fallen down long since. And see all those little terra cottas around the entablature! That's Etruscan influence. …"

Sophron stood silently nearby, scratching a fleabite and leaning on his spear with an air of patient resignation. The bodyguard seemed devoted to his task of guarding Korinna but had about as blank a mind as Zopyros had met. When they boarded the ship, they found themselves the last arrivals and the captain in a fouler mood than usual.

"By Tanith's teats!" roared Ethbaal. "We've waited an Egyptian hour for you! Next time we'll sail off and leave you in the lurch!"

Velia lay another day's sail down the coast, around the Poseidion Promontory. When they left Poseidonia, a brisk offshore breeze carried them far out to sea, until the coast faded to a mottled olive-brown streak along the horizon. The crew swung the *Muttumalein* so that she headed shoreward at an acute angle, her yellow sail clewed around as near as it would go to the fore-and-aft position. Still the northeast wind drove her farther and farther from land. With the wind abeam, the deck heeled over at a constant slope; but the ship was otherwise steadier than before. Zopyros found Asto alone and asked in Punic:

"Go we not a great way from shore?"

"Fear not," said Asto. "Belike the wind will turn shoreward by even. At worst, you might have to pass the night on deck. What we truly fear is a mighty onshore gale against a rocky coast. Then, if your sail be new, perchance you can claw off; but, if it be old and baggy like ours, the crabs will pick your bones."

Most of the passengers were feeling better than the day before. Hippomedon the singer marked off a section of deck into small squares with a piece of charcoal and played robbers with Sophron the bodyguard, using black and white beans for pieces. The weather warmed so much that Zopyros put away his laced Thracian boots and donned a pair of sandals. In rummaging through his belongings, he came upon a little portable game set for playing Sacred Way. He undertook to teach Segovax the game. The Celt proved an apt pupil but a reckless plunger. After a few games, Segovax said:

"Zopyros darling, wouldn't it make the game livelier, now, to put up a small stake?"

This, thought Zopyros, will be easy. "All right; I'll bet you a penny on the next game." And he rolled the die.

However, sudden reversals of fortune were characteristic of Sacred Way. Zopyros had gotten one of his men home and had taken three of Segovax's men prisoner when, with his remaining man, the Celt took one of Zopyros' men, then another, and soon had swept the rest of Zopyros' men from the board.

The next two games followed the same pattern. Out of pocket threepence, Zopyros began to worry. Half an obolos might make the difference between eating a decent dinner and going hungry someday. He was just as glad when the Celt, looking up, said:

"Praise the gods, 'tis headed back toward land that we are! I had begun to fear we would sail on until we fell over the edge of the world."

"According to the latest theories, the world hasn't any edge. It's round, like a ball."

"Oh, come now! If it was round; all the water would run off at the bottom."

"No, it wouldn't, because 'down' is the direction toward the center of the earth. So, if you were on the opposite side of the earth from me, your 'down' would be my 'up' and vice versa."

"You wouldn't be having a bit of a joke with a poor simple Celt, now would you? Everybody knows that up is up and down is down, and how can the one be the other?"

"Why, it's as if we were on opposite sides of the mast. Then it might be south of you, but north of me. So, if somebody asked us which way the mast was, we should each give a different answer, but we should both be right."

Segovax shook his head. "With all respect to your honor, I still don't believe you. The next thing, you clever Greeks will be telling folk that spirits don't cause sickness, or that men are descended from monkeys."

"We might at that. One philosopher has already suggested that we come from fish."

"*Ara!* A man can't ever be easy with you people around. Just when he thinks he knows something, along comes a spalpeen like you and upsets him by saying 'tis not so at all." He yawned and stretched. "I'll be taking a bit of a nap, before all them theories have addled my wits for fair."

As the mate had predicted, the wind had backed to northwest. The setting sun saw the *Muttumalein* drop anchor in one of Velia's two splendid harbors—that at the mouth of the Hales. Around the margins of the harbor, fishing vessels and coastal merchantmen rode at anchor or lay canted on the beach. Several were still being refitted after their winter lay-up. Men climbed over them, caulking and painting hulls and repairing rigging.

As the people from the *Muttumalein* plodded toward the city, they saw before them a broad plain, covered with houses and girt with frowning walls. Above the walls, temples gleamed on the acropolis. Zopyros said:

"I didn't know Velia was such a great city."

"Oh, but it is," said Korinna. "It ranks with Taras and Neapolis. The Velians call it the Athens of the West, because of its philosophers."

"We should at least find decent lodgings. By the way, has anyone seen Captain Ethbaal's fabulous wife yet?"

Hippomedon the singer said: "Not I. I begin to think the woman's dead, and he has a mania for keeping her body with him."

Segovax, rubbing the sleep from his eyes, added: "If the poor lady is a dead corp, you will be knowing it soon."

"Unless she's packed in salt," said Hippomedon, "like the lady Korinna's uncle. I once knew a man who so loved a corpse that he—"

The musician broke off as Ethbaal jogged by on a rented ass, his head bowed and his face bearing its usual preoccupied frown.

"He goes to town to find a merchant with a stock of salted fish," said one of the sailors.

This time the inn was good, with private rooms for the women. In the tavern below, Hippomedon unlimbered his lyre and sang in a clear tenor:

> *"Painter, by unmatch'd desert*
> *Master of the Rhodian art,*
> *Come, my absent mistress take,*
> *As I shall describe her: make*
> *First her hair, as black as bright,*
> *And if colours so much right*
> *Can but do her, let it too*
> *Smell of aromatic dew;*
> *Underneath this shade, must now*
> *Draw her alabaster brow;*
> *Her dark eyebrows so dispose*
> *That they neither part nor close ..."*

As the singer was passing his cap, Captain Ethbaal appeared in the doorway and said in his harsh voice: "My people may sleep late tomorrow. I shall be loading fish until market time; but then we shall sail promptly. Don't be late!"

The morning sun warmed the agora of Velia, where sellers of cakes and blood sausage were unpacking their wares, sellers of roasted nuts and hot scented water were building their little fires, other hawkers were setting up their displays, orators were tuning up their voices, and beggars had begun to whine. A fortuneteller laid out a battered skull and other magical paraphernalia; a juggler tossed a few balls to limber his muscles; and the owner of a trained bear shared a loaf with his pet.

In the center of an admiring circle, three philosophers argued vehemently about the difference between Being and Becoming, and whether the Real Existent were basically One or Many. Among the crowd stood Segovax the Celt, in his checkered coat and trousers, with his mouth open. Zopyros, Korinna, and the latter's two servants approached from the acropolis, where they had made a brief tour of the temples. Several small boys, sensing foreigners, rushed up and began shouting for money with their hands out.

"Go away," said Zopyros, then to Korinna: "My dear, why are you crying?"

"They made me think of my little Ahiram. Isn't there anything I can do to persuade you to undertake his rescue?"

"Don't torture me, please! I'd do anything for you—but you know what I promised."

"Promises are made to be broken."

"To you as well as to other people? I'm not that kind of fellow. … E, Master Segovax, hadn't we better be getting back to the ship?"

The Celt roused himself like a man coming out of a dream. "So we had, young sir, so we had. The talk of the wise men was so beautiful I could have stood all day listening, and me not understanding a word of it. Tell me, does all that grand talk really mean something, or is it after listening to a lot of madmen that I am?"

"That's what they were arguing about; whether or not their subject of discussion is real. But I'll tell you a secret. It's a put-on job, like a make-believe sword duel in which nobody gets hurt."

"And why would they be doing that?"

"To show how clever they are, so they can enroll more rich young men in their classes. It's what we call higher education."

"And the young men pay to learn all about this Being and Becoming?"

"That's right. They also learn to reason, to argue, and to make speeches."

"Ah, a grand thing it must be to be a rich young Hellene and learn all about arguing and speechmaking! We have some powerful orators among the Celts, too; but I'm thinking they could learn a thing or two here."

As they climbed the ladder to the deck of the *Muttumalein*, the last basket of fish was just going into the hold. A heavy smell of fish hung in the air. Zopyros shot a covert glance at the cabin, but no sign of life appeared. The sky had again become overcast.

The last passengers had come aboard, the ladder had been pulled up, and the crew were winching up the anchors when a shout from the shore caused heads to turn. A young man was waving from the beach. As they watched, he ran through the shallows toward the ship, splashing mightily. He leaped up, caught an anchor, and climbed aboard like a monkey. Dripping and panting, he approached Captain Ethbaal.

"Have you room for another passenger?" he asked when he got his breath. "How far are you going?"

"Yes, we have room. We're going to Laos, Tempsa, and Messana; then west to Panormos and our home port, Motya."

"I'm trying to get to Syracuse. Could I take passage with you to Messana and catch another ship from there to Syracuse?"

"I suppose so. There's plenty of coastal shippings. Your fare will be one drachma."

"By Herakles, that's outrageous! I could buy passage on a state galley for that!"

Ethbaal shrugged. "Take it or leave it. Somehow I don't think you'll climb over the side and wade back to shore."

Ethbaal was staring shoreward. On the road to the harbor, small in the distance, appeared a group of running men. One of them wore a magistrate's purple cloak, which he clutched with both hands as he ran. Some of the others carried spears.

The young man, with a frightened glance shoreward, mumbled: "*Phy!* I suppose I shall have to take it. Here!"

Coins clinked. Ethbaal said: "Up sail, Asto! Now, young man, who are you?"

"Alexis son of Krates. I—"

The running men reached the shore. Their voices came thinly across the water: "Captain Ethbaal, come back! Bring back that young man! We want him!"

"What?" shouted Ethbaal, making a trumpet of his hands.

The yells from shore continued, growing fainter as the distance widened. Ethbaal shouted again:

"I can't hear you. I shall see you again in a month; tell me about it then!"

Ethbaal allowed himself a bitter little smile. "When you appeared in your shirt, without cloak or other baggage, I knew you weren't leaving Velia of your own accord. I could have made you pay twice as much, so count yourself lucky."

"Speaking of cloaks," said Alexis, "it'll be cold on the water. Could I borrow one for the voyage?"

"You may rent one for an extra obolos."

"Why, you—" began Alexis, but glanced shoreward and choked down his words. "Here!"

"Thanks. Just remember to stay away from the cabin, where I keep my wife, the most beautiful woman of Egypt."

"Oh? If you say so. Don't think I did anything wrong at Velia; it was just that I—"

"Young man," said Ethbaal coldly, "the less I know about your private affairs, the better for all of us. Now please permit me to run my ship."

The new arrival turned to the other passengers, who sat or squatted by the rail, an interested group all staring at him. "Rejoice, everybody!" he said. "I'm Alexis son of Krates, on my way to the court of Dionysios, and I'm pleased to know you all. Do tell me your names!"

He went through the list, greeting each affably, with a special smile for Korinna. He was a few years older than Zopyros, but smaller and slighter, with light brown hair worn long and blue eyes in a face of striking if slightly effeminate beauty. Strangely enough in that company of bearded men, his face was innocent of hair. Zopyros envied his easy way with strangers. He asked the newcomer:

"Why did you leave Velia in such a hurry? We are interested, even if the captain isn't."

Alexis waved a hand airily. "Just philosophy, that's all. Some of my friends and I got together to promote the higher wisdom, and the whipworthy magistrates thought they smelled a subversive plot. Ridiculous, of course."

"What school of philosophy?" said Zopyros.

"The Eleatic or Velian, if you know what that means."

"I'm not ignorant," said Zopyros. "As a boy, I studied under the great Philolaos."

"The man who said the earth flies in circles around the moon, or something? Beastly idea! Then you're a Pythagorean?"

"People call me one because I learned from them and have followed mathematical studies. But I'm not a teacher or lecturer by profession. I'm an engineer, and a good one if I do say so."

"Why, so am I, of sorts! We're shipbuilders. That's what my friends and I were trying to convince the Velians of: that their state should be ruled by a technocracy of scientific experts. But the stupid, benighted Assembly—well, anyway, I may find more sensible folk elsewhere. Do you suppose we could persuade the Tarentines to adopt such a government?"

"I don't know. We like our government as it is. Anyway, I keep out of politics."

Alexis clucked. "A well-rounded citizen can't keep out of politics; least of all a philosopher. A citizen's polis is the center of his existence."

"Well, I prefer to be less well rounded and to follow my own bent in peace."

The old Etruscan spoke up: "All this Greek word-chopping you call philosophy is a waste of time. For all your scientific—how you say—pretensions, you cannot change universe. You can only learn to fit yourself to it. And that you do by studying omens by which gods make their plans known to men, as nymph Vegoia taught us Etruscans to do at beginning."

"Which gods?" said Segovax. "At home we worshiped our own gods: Esus and Cernunnos and Epona and the rest. When I was in the Etruscan country, they said the true gods are Tinia and Uni and Minerva and others whose names I'm forgetting. The Latins had another lot, with a fellow named Jupiter as high king; and the Greeks and the Phoenicians have still others. Now, what I'm wanting to know is: Are all these gods different, with each ruling only a little patch of the earth like a mortal king? Or are they all the same gods with different names?"

"We philosophers of the Eleatic school," said Alexis with a supercilious expression, "hold that there is really only one God—a universal divine principle, you might say—but this principle manifests itself in various guises and has been different names in different places."

"You mean," said Segovax, "like the different numbers on the different sides of a die, even though the die is still one little square piece of bone?"

"That's a good example. We certainly don't believe that any gods worthy of the name go about seducing each other's wives and clouting each other over the head. And we disagree as to how our God principle can be known. Some think it can be grasped by observation and reason; but others doubt that observation and reasoning are adequate. Zenon, who taught my father, proved by his paradoxes—like his story of Achilles and the tortoise—that the combination of observation and reason are inadequate for grasping the true nature of reality. Observation tells us that Achilles could catch the tortoise, while reason says he couldn't. It follows that the phenomenal world is not the real world. This must be sought by some other mode of perception, such as dreams or divine inspiration."

Zopyros: "I wouldn't give up observation and reason just because they failed in one case. If my tool breaks when I'm making a machine, I don't say tools are no good for machine making. No, I get another and—I hope—a better tool. All Zenon proved was that *his* reasoning was faulty. As to this divine principle, I don't doubt that, if it can ever be known at all, it will be found out by observation and reason."

"True high gods are unknown to mortals," said the Etruscan. "We only know the Elder Gods exist, not who they are or anything about them. Elder Gods have planned everything that happens on earth. Little gods we worship are—how you say—just errand boys for Elder Gods. Lesser gods must do as they are told. Everything fixed in advance, including omens that tell us what gods have in store. Everything run in cycles. Etruscan nation will run for ten cycles only; then we lose power and disappear."

"So it doesn't matter what I do," said Segovax, "because these Elder Gods have it all planned anyway?"

"That right."

"Then why shouldn't I go into battle next time without a shield? If the gods have decided I'm not to be killed, it wouldn't make any difference."

"If you do not carry shield, is because gods have planned you shall not carry shield."

"Valetudo save us! It seems I can't win. Now at home, the druids told us we have not one life but many, one after the other. And, if we try to do right in this life, we may get a better job in the next, like being promoted at the court of the Great King. According to you, it does a man no good even to try."

"That's a Pythagorean doctrine, too," said Alexis, "although I don't know about the promotions. Personally I have always known I'm a reincarnation of Daidalos."

"The fellow who made the wings?" said Segovax. "That the son of him was drowned trying to fly with?"

"That's the one—the greatest inventor and artificer the mortal race has produced, if we believe the traditions."

"How do you know you're Daidalos reborn?" asked Zopyros.

"I've dreamt of my former life as Daidalos, and the idea agrees with my mathematical and engineering skill."

Zopyros grinned. "That's odd, because when I was a boy in school, learning the Pythagorean doctrines, I was sure I was a reincarnation of Daidalos. Obviously, Daidalos might or might not be reborn in one of us, but hardly both at the same tune."

"I know what I know," said Alexis sulkily.

"Well, whatever the truth, I doubt if we can really remember our former lives, save perhaps by special divine favor. That's the trouble with metempsychosis. Not remembering your former lives, you go on making the same stupid mistakes over and over."

Alexis put in: "But I *can* remember mine!"

"Congratulations."

Segovax, trying to keep up with the spate of ideas, stood leaning against the rail, frowning and tugging his mustache. He asked Zopyros: "What did your Pythagoras say about the gods?"

"Much the same as the Eleatics. Pythagoras taught that God may be symbolized by a sphere, which is the perfect figure. When it came to more precise details, however, the Man became vague or confessed that the inner nature of divine was unknowable. Anyway, these doctrines were only for members of the sect. We must always, he said, assure the masses that there are gods, and these gods take an interest in mortals, rewarding virtue and punishing sin, because without such threats and promises the masses will not behave themselves."

Segovax chuckled. "The trouble is, who are the wise philosophers and who are the masses? Everybody will be thinking he's a wise man, and 'tis the other fellow who is one of the vulgar herd. Is it not so?"

Zopyros smiled, for he loved this kind of discussion. "You should have been a philosopher instead of a warrior, man. When I was in Tyre I heard still another doctrine. The Babylonians claim the gods were the stars—or the stars were the chariots of the gods, it wasn't clear—and they controlled events on earth by their movements around the heavens."

"Now, isn't that the massive thought though?" said Segovax. "But a star moves around the heavens in one certain way, over and over. So I don't see what good it would do to pray to one, because he'll go right on moving the same way as always and making things on earth come out the same as before. That's as bad as the Etruscan gentleman's— excuse me, sir, what's your name?"

"Vibenna."

"As Master Vibenna's idea, that the Elder Gods have laid out one master plan for the world, and everything that happens is according to that plan. What do you think of the gods, Master Zopyros?"

"I suspect they're the mathematical principles that rule the universe," said Zopyros.

Segovax said: "But prayer wouldn't help a man change your mathematical principles, any more than he could change the mind of a star, or Alexis' divine principle, or Vibenna's grand world plan."

"Perhaps not. But, if a man learns how these principles work and puts them to practical use, perhaps he can better his lot in the world of the living."

"I think you are all wrong," said Asto the mate, who had been quietly bossing the sailors. "And, if you will excuse me, very impious men. You speak of learning the truth about the gods." Asto glanced upward and touched his chest, lips, and forehead. "Can a man catch a whale with a fishhook, or climb to the moon by a ship's ladder? Then, how can the little spirits of mortal men understand the mighty thoughts of the gods? All we know is that the gods are strong, and jealous, and terrible. We are to them as insects under the feet of men. If we abase ourselves before them and give them all they ask, including our first-born, perhaps they'll let us live—for a while. To talk of measuring and weighing the gods is madness. We must obey them without thinking. Why, if one of them overheard you speaking about him in this insolent way, he might puff the world out of existence, as you blow out a taper!"

"How do *you* know what the gods wish?" asked Zopyros.

"The priests tell us. If they didn't know, how could they be priests?"

"They could be men seeking their own power and wealth," said Alexis.

"That's your wicked Greek atheism, and I will have no part in it!"

"Who's an atheist?" said Alexis. "The Libyans worship baboons, and anybody who kills a baboon is put to death for atheism."

"You know what I mean," persisted Asto. "What the priests say must be true, because the gods would never let them live if they lied in such matters."

"You mean," said Zopyros, "that there must be gods because the priests say so, and the priests must tell the truth because the gods compel them to?"

"That is right."

"Alexis, it seems to me there's a flaw in our friend's logic, even if I can't quite put my finger on it."

"He's assuming what he wishes to prove. It's arguing in a circle," said Alexis. "I'm clever enough to see that."

"So it is! One could argue just as logically, as did Kritias, that the priests invented the gods to frighten the common people into behaving themselves."

Asto shuddered at this blasphemy, rolled his eyes heavenward, and muttered a short prayer in Punic. Then he said: "Your logic is just a game with words; but I have faith, which is better. My faith tells me there are gods, as the priests say. I don't need logic; I *know* I am right. You Greeks get yourselves tangled up in big words, like those men in the agora this morning. While I am not an educated man, I think half your arguments are not about the real world at all, but about the Greek language. Because you have a word like Becoming, you think there must be something in the real world that the word answers to. If you learnt other languages, you would know that this is not always so."

"My dear fellow!" said Alexis. "Do you actually expect Hellenes to learn a barbarous dialect like your Punic speech, with all those funny sounds made down in the throat?"

"It would be good for your national self-conceit if you did. I can speak with men all over the Inner Sea, but Master Zopyros is almost the only Hellene I ever met who knew any language but his own. Well, in the Canaanitish tongue we don't have fancy expressions like—what is it you call them?—Phenomenal Universe and—ah—Essential Being. So we get along very well without them. By Milkarth's bronzen balls, I should like to see Ethbaal try to sell fifty amphorae of your Becoming in the harbor at Syracuse!"

"There are things of greater worth than vulgar trade," said Alexis.

"Such as cutting your neighbors' throats, as you Hellenes so love to do?" said Asto. "Any fool with a spear can go out and kill, but it takes skill and courage and effort to build up a flourishing trade route. Without us men of business to carry the world's goods to your harbors, where would all your clever philosophers and handsome athletes and brave warriors be? Wearing stinking sheepskins and living like the Lucanians in huts of mud and reeds, with pigs underfoot, that's where!"

A silence followed this impassioned speech. Zopyros thought, the little man has more fire in his belly than one would guess from his mousy appearance and diffident manner. At last Segovax spoke:

"I'm thinking I like Master Vibenna's gods pretty well. If they won't help us, at least they won't puff us away unless it's already in their great plan, and that's some comfort. But I like my own Celtic gods best of all. Maybe they are not so wise as Master Vibenna's, nor so powerful as Master Asto's, nor so scientific as those of Master Zopyros. But they're a comfortable, easygoing lot of gods, the which a man can get along with if he flatters them a bit, and gives them a little meat and beer, and now and then burns a thief or a slave in their honor. So, begging your pardon, I'll say a little prayer to old Esus and take me a nap."

"And I," said Vibenna, "shall watch flight of birds, to see what I can learn of next stage of divine master plan."

At dusk they anchored at the mouth of the Pyxous River and passed the night in the town of the same name. As they were going ashore, Alexis said to Zopyros:

"I'm eaten with curiosity about this so-called wife, whom Ethbaal keeps so completely out of sight. I'm going to get a look in that cabin."

"I wouldn't," said Zopyros. "A sea voyage has risks enough, without inventing new ones."

"Spoilsport! You wait and see. Now as I was telling you …"

Alexis resumed his lecture on his plan for building a lighthouse as tall as a mountain at Syracuse, and on his sanguine hopes for persuading the tyrannos of Syracuse, the mighty Dionysios, to adopt his plan. "They say he's hiring gifted men like me. Why, a mere ten-day ago, an agent from Dionysios stopped at Velia to tell the young men of the fame and fortune awaiting them at Syracuse."

Zopyros had begun to find Alexis' charm wearing thin. The fellow was such a tireless talker, always chattering about himself and his own inexhaustible virtues. He also had a habit of pushing up against his hearer. When he stood beside Zopyros at the rail, he pressed his arm gently against that of Zopyros. When they sat on deck, he slid a foot over so that it touched that of Zopyros, until the latter got up and moved away.

Zopyros surmised that the man was seeking a male lover. Although no Greek regarded such a liaison as anything extraordinary, Zopyros was not attracted by the idea, since his own preference, like that of many others, was wholly for women. He regarded male love affairs as an absurd aristocratic pose, along with the drawling voices, the languid gestures, and the shaven pubic areas affected by the rich youths of Taras.

"O Alexis," said Zopyros, "I'm afraid you'll never make a living as a philosopher."

"And why not?"

"For the same reason some women can never earn their keep as harlots: because you give away what you ought to charge for."

"*Phy!* By Hera, if I bore you, I'll find somebody else to talk to, who better appreciates the profundity of my knowledge!"

So Alexis lagged behind the rest and kept pace with lame old Vibenna, to whom he poured out his stream of random thoughts. Zopyros hurried to catch up with Korinna, whose company he craved more ardently with every passing hour.

The next day Zopyros was late for the ship again—he had gotten into a discussion with a Pyxountian about the local water supply—and had to take another scolding from Captain Ethbaal. Soon the ship was heeling to the offshore morning wind. It was drawing away from the coast, when Zopyros was startled to hear Ethbaal shout at Alexis:

"*Ai*, you! Get away from there! Don't you dare go sneaking around the cabin!"

"I was not looking into your fornicating cabin! By the God, I was merely watching the sea—"

"I saw you with my own eyes! By Tanith's teats, I'll kill any man who so much as lays a lecherous glance upon her—"

"Captain, sir!" cried the mate in Punic. "Pray excite yourself not; the youth did but—"

"Hold your tongue, Asto! As for you, young man, if I see you in the after part of the ship again, I'll leave you at the next stop!"

"Then give me back my fare!"

"Try to get it!"

"Cheat! Temple robber! Dung-eating knave!" screamed Alexis.

Both men had their hands on their knives when Asto, Zopyros, and the bodyguard Sophron thrust themselves between them, coaxing and soothing. Segovax said:

"A pity it is to stop a good fight, but I suppose we must have a live captain to run the ship. I'm after bringing a little jug of wine on board, thinking a drop now and then would make the day pass quicker. If everybody will get out his cup, I'll pour you each a wee dollop. Not too much at a time on this bouncing boat, or the fishes will get it. Now, who can sing a song or tell a tale? You first, Master Hippomedon."

The singer tuned his lyre while Segovax poured. Alexis, his rage quickly forgotten, took his share; but the captain declined with curt thanks. "I need all my wits," he said.

The singer swept his fingers over the strings and sang:

> *"Throned in splendor, deathless, O Aphrodite*
> *Child of Zeus, charm-fashioner, I entreat you*
> *Not with griefs and bitterness to break my spirit, O goddess ..."*

When Hippomedon had sung several songs, Vibenna told some of the secrets of the augur's art:

"Our ancient religion is set forth in Sacred Books. Of these, one of most important is Book of Lightning, which tells of different kinds of lightning and thunder and the meanings of each! Are eleven kinds of lightnings, and nine gods have power to send lightning. Of these Tinia, sky-father, has three lightnings, all blood-red in color. Of Tinia's three lightnings, the first is warning to men; he can send it whenever he wants. Second kind of lightning is full of peril; Tinia sends it only on advice of other lesser gods. Third kind brings destroying fire of heaven; it is so dangerous that Tinia must have permission of Elder Gods to send it. Other gods and goddesses like Uni also have lightnings.

"Book of Lightning divides sky in sixteen parts. Lightning interpreter faces south, so he has eight sections of sky to left and eight to right. He interprets lightning by direction it comes from and place where it strikes ground. Lightning coming from left is good luck; from right, bad. ..."

Next, Asto related Phoenician legends. He told of the war of the hero Milkarth against the demoness Masisabal: "... and he pursued the she-monster, whose tail writhed over the dead leaves like a silver brook, into the forest, and came to a plain where women with the hinder parts of dragons stood round a fire, erect on the points of their tails. The blood-colored moon was shining within a pale circle, and the scarlet tongues of the dragon-women, forked like fish spears, curled outward to the very edge of the flame. ..."

Alexis regaled them with riddles and paradoxes. When Zopyros' turn came, he recited passages from the Hellenic national epics:

> *"Here in a sleep of exhaustion lay long-tested, god-like Odysseus;*
> *On to the Phaiakes' city however proceeded Athena.*
> *Once they resided in spacious Hypereia near the Kyklopes*
> *Who with superior power did evermore plunder them until*
> *Godlike Nausithoös thence unto Scheria brought them*
>   *and placed them*
> *Distant from laboring men. ..."*

At Laos they stopped for a day to load more wine. Then they were becalmed for a day. The passengers and the crew killed time in various ways. They gathered on the beach to watch Alexis and Segovax shave each other's chins, with many a jest at the cost of the amateur barbers. Vibenna said:

"What this? Some new barbarian fad?"

"Whatever it is," said Sophron, "it's un-Hellenic, by Herakles!"

Asto: "They do it in Egypt; and I hear the pretty boys of Athens do it, too, in order to hold their lovers."

The father of the twelve-year-old boy said: "Beards were good enough for my father and my grandfather, and they're good enough for me. I say, leave your face as the gods intended it."

Zopyros: "Alexis can't bear to grow up."

"*Oi!*" said the twelve-year-old boy. "He's cut himself."

"What did I tell you?" said his father. "That's what comes of interfering with nature."

Later, somebody organized a game of hockey with a local team. In the first period, Zopyros took a bad crack in the knee. As he limped off the field, Korinna cried:

"Are you hurt, dear Zopyros? What can I do?"

"Curse my luck! It'll be all right. I could have been hit in worse places. Sophron, you're drafted to take my place."

The bodyguard grumbled something, but Korinna said: "Yes, go ahead and play!" Sophron obediently laid down his spear and began to strip. Zopyros hobbled down to the beach, leaning on Korinna's shoulder, to wash off the sweat and dust. She said:

"I need a bath, too, and they're all watching the game. Will you promise not to try to paw me or make lewd remarks?"

"I promise."

For all Zopyros' good intentions, the sight of Korinna bathing roused his manhood, so that he had to finish his bath with his back turned to her. As they dressed, he glanced toward the field, where a crowd of naked men raced about with hockey sticks, panting and yelling, in a cloud of dust. He said:

"I've always been a dub at sports: I'm as clumsy as an ass on a roof. But my stomach tells me it's lunchtime. Why don't we pick up some food and go off by ourselves for a picnic?"

"We should have to take Sophron out of the game."

"Why not leave him? He's happy."

"No, he must stay with me. My father gave us clear commands."

"He'd never even notice we were gone."

"Listen, friend Zopyros. Sophron may not be intelligent, but he is honest and faithful, and there are few enough people of whom you can say that. Suppose we did sneak off without him. When he gets back to Messana, the first thing my father will ask is: Did he keep a faithful watch over me? And the poor stupid fellow will say: 'Yes, all but that day in Laos, when she gave me the slip.' And then the perfume will be spilt into the soup for all of us. I love my father and don't want trouble with him.

"Moreover, as a twice-wed woman, I am not altogether ignorant of men. You all want your bit of fun; and, when it's over, off you go, not caring if you leave the woman to pay the price of your pleasure. In this godless age, no one believes any more in stories about Zeus's visiting a maiden in the form of a swan or a shower of gold."

"I swear by the divine tetractys not to lay a finger on you! After all, I am a Pythagorean of sorts."

"That's what you say now; but I know better. Though you were as chaste as Melanion, once we were out among the asphodels you'd want a kiss—just one little harmless kiss—and then anything might happen." Zopyros was silent, because just such a possibility had been running through his mind. With downcast eyes, Korinna murmured: "I'm not made of marble myself, you know."

He caught his breath and grasped her hand. "Korinna—"

"Yes?"

His shyness choked him, but at last he stammered: "I l-love you!"

She looked at him steadily. "I'm fond of you, Zopyros. More than that it wouldn't be proper for me to say. If you mean what you say, speak to my father when you meet him in Messana."

"I mean to. But there will be problems."

"Of course; there always are."

"After all, I am part Persian."

"Dear Zopyros, don't always talk of your Persian blood in that defensive way! It's not as if you were applying for Athenian citizenship. After marrying me to a Phoenician, Father could hardly deem you a foreigner. I was thinking more of property settlements and things like that. And there's my child."

Zopyros waved a hand. Those things can usually be worked out in time. I should have to get my father's permission, too."

Then let's not talk of love until we can do something practical about it. Agreed?"

"I thought I was a logical person, but you make me look as woolly-minded as Alexis."

"Do you agree? I want a straight answer."

"Oh, very well."

In the end, they had their picnic; but Sophron sat with them, gnawing a leg of fowl and listening blankly as Zopyros discoursed on aqueducts and fortifications.

They sailed on to Tempsa, where they spent a day loading copper ore. As the ship was now fully laden, they had to anchor well out from the beach and go to and from shore in a harbor boat. On the morning of the eighteenth, all were aboard except the captain, whom some commercial complication had delayed ashore. At last the harbor boat put out from the beach with Ethbaal huddled in the stern.

Zopyros, glancing about the deck, was alarmed to see Alexis crouching in front of the entrance to the little cabin and plucking at the flaps that closed it. Fearing another dispute, Zopyros wanted to shout a warning. He was, however, torn by fear of arousing Ethbaal's attention and also by distaste for meddling in others' business. For an instant he stood undecided, with his mouth half open. It took him a few heartbeats—which seemed like an age—to pull himself together. He finally called: "*Ea*, Alexis! Get away—" just as Captain Ethbaal's head appeared over the rail.

The captain took in the scene at a glance. With a snarl he vaulted over the rail, threw off his cloak, snatched out his dagger, and rushed toward Alexis. He had covered half the distance before the Velian looked up to see the gaunt Phoenician bearing down upon him, eyes glaring and foam on his lips.

Alexis leaped to his feet and started to run, dodging zigzag through the rest of the ship's people. All the latter were now on their feet, beginning to shout advice to or to cry out to each other to seize the pursuer, or the pursued, or both. But the two moved too fast. Missing Alexis in his first rush, Ethbaal spun around and raced after the young man across the deck.

At the rail, over which Ethbaal had leaped aboard, Alexis turned. He tore off his rented cloak, whirled it, and tried to throw it over Ethbaal's head. The Phoenician struck the garment aside, and it did not impede him long enough for Alexis to dive over the rail. It did, however, check him sufficiently so that, as he closed with Alexis, the latter caught the wrist of his knife hand. There was an instant of furious struggle. Ethbaal strove to drive the dagger home, while Alexis strained to keep it away from his body. Then the pair toppled over the rail and disappeared. A crash and a splash from below released the company from its momentary paralysis.

Zopyros, still limping a little from his mishap of the day before, rushed to the shoreward rail with the rest. At the ship's side, the harbor boat was rocking, partly filled with water, while the boatman, shrieking curses, sought to steady it. There was a foamy splashing of limbs in the water alongside.

The splashing stopped. Alexis' head appeared. He caught the gunwale of the harbor boat and clung, gasping and coughing water.

"Where's Ethbaal?" shouted Zopyros.

Alexis wordlessly pointed downward. The people on the deck of the *Muttumalein* shouted advice to do this, that, and the other thing.

Zopyros doffed his cloak, tunic, and sandals and dove naked over the side. He opened his eyes and swam around under the water. In the green-gold shimmer between the sandy sea bottom and the black hull, furred with green plumes of seaweed and fanged with white clusters of barnacles, Zopyros sighted Ethbaal. The captain lay on the white sand, motionless save for a slight to-and-fro movement imparted to the body by the water.

Zopyros had to surface for breath. He came up too steeply, cracked his head on the hull, and scratched a hand on a barnacle. But a kick took him out from under the ship. He trod water for a few long, gasping breaths, ignoring the shouts from above. Then he upended and dove again. This time he caught an ankle and pulled Ethbaal to the surface. Korinna's slave dove in beside him. A rope was passed down from the deck, and by this means first the captain and then the two swimmers were hauled up.

They laid the captain across the rail to force the water out of his lungs. They fanned him, massaged him, and tried to pour wine down his throat to revive him. Alexis, standing aside and wringing the water from his wet shirt, said:

"I think you're wasting your time. He hit his head on the gunwale of the harbor boat as we fell."

The body remained limp and cold. The passengers, drawing back a little, fell silent save for a mutter of prayers and incantations. At length Asto the mate cried: "He's dead," and burst into tears. "He was a hard master and more than a little mad. But he was the bravest and most skillful skipper of Motya. He brought us rich trade, and we shan't see another like him soon. It's all your fault, too." He glared at Alexis.

Alexis was busy toweling his nakedness with the rented cloak. Tossing it over one shoulder, he said: "Oh, to the crows with that stuff! He brought it on himself with all his mystery about the cabin. Somebody was sure to try to peek. What *is* in there, anyway?"

"Go and look," said Asto.

"We-ell, I don't know—it's really of no interest …"

"Go ahead! You started this; you finish it. You can't hurt Ethbaal now."

Under the stares of the whole ship's company, the Velian approached the cabin and gingerly untied the flaps, as if he expected a lion to issue forth. At last he bent over, put his head through the narrow opening, and said:

"Well, I'll be an Aethiopian!"

He turned a blank, bewildered face back toward the spectators. Zopyros, whom Korinna was helping to dry himself, called:

"What is it?"

"There's nothing; nothing in there at all!" As several spectators made gestures to ward off the evil eye, Alexis continued: "What is this? Witchcraft? Or was this wonderful woman a figment of Ethbaal's imagination?"

As he stepped forward with his cloak trailing, people parted so as not to be touched by him. Asto said:

"That is right. Ethbaal did once have an Egyptian wife, before I sailed with him. One day on the Lykian coast, she left the ship to bathe in a secluded bay, and some of the local louts came upon her. After the usual rape they cut her throat and left her for Ethbaal to find. So"—Asto spread his hands—"he went slowly mad. But he harmed no one so long as we respected his fancy, and you had no right to rouse him. As I am now master of this ship, you shall have your just desert."

As the Velian, sudden alarm on his face, moved toward the rail, Asto rapped out a command in Punic. Several sailors threw themselves upon Alexis and held him fast.

"Hold on there!" said Zopyros. "What are you going to do?"

"Hang a murderer, my lords, that's all," said Asto.

"Wait! This man may not be any hero, but nobody's convicted him of any crime."

"I convict him. I am now captain, and on shipboard what the captain says is done."

"Not in a Hellenic harbor." A sidelong glance showed Zopyros that Segovax was quietly rummaging in his luggage for his sword, and that Korinna's bodyguard had grasped his spear. "Look, friend, let's not quarrel over this. We all want your first voyage to be smooth."

"Well then? What punishment do you advise?"

"Let's all sit down and discuss the case. If we decide a crime has been committed, we'll lay information before the magistrates of Tempsa and bear witness. Since they don't know the people involved, they can judge the case more justly than any one of us."

Asto seemed about to demur but, seeing the weapons, thought better of it. The sailors tied Alexis to the mast. Asto and the free men among the passengers talked the case over through the morning, while Alexis looked unhappy in his bonds. For some time Asto held out for punishing Alexis; but at last he yielded to the others' arguments.

"If he'd really tried to seduce the captain's wife " said Zopyros, "that would be different. But there was no wife to seduce."

In the end they agreed that, while it had been wrong of Alexis to look into the cabin, it had hardly been a crime. Moreover, Alexis could not be fairly blamed for trying to keep a madman from killing him. The death of Ethbaal had been due to the ire of some god, or the mysterious workings of Fate. The sailors released Alexis on the latter's promise to pay for Ethbaal's grave marker.

"Do you mean to take the body to Motya?" Zopyros asked Asto.

"No. We are not so fussy about corpses as you Greeks. Seamen often die on far shores; we can't bring them all home. We'll bury him deeply and hire a local mason to carve him a simple stela. Then tomorrow we shall sail for Messana."

Zopyros noted a new decisiveness and air of command about the hitherto gentle mate. "What will you do then, Asto?"

"Take the *Muttumalein* back to Ethbaal's partners in Motya, of course. Trade must go on. Maybe they'll give me a ship of my own. In any case, I shall want letters from you and the other gentlemen to confirm my story."

Later, Korinna said: "Zopyros, you were wonderful, the way you stopped that dispute before it got started. How did you ever have the courage?"

"Between you and me, I was frightened witless. But I saw what would happen if I didn't step in. One of these racial feuds would arise. After threats and insults, there'd be a battle, either right then or—what would be worse—after we'd put to sea. The Hellenes would be on one side and the Phoenicians on the other, with Segovax whacking at everybody with his great sword for the fun of fighting. Being part Persian and having lived among the Phoenicians, I was the logical peacemaker."

TARAS

The red sun dipped behind the Hills of Poseidon as the *Muttumalein* nosed into the shelter of the Sickle, the curved peninsula embracing Messana's harbor. The yellow sail came flapping down; grunting sailors heaved at the oars. When the ship was tied up, the passengers filed ashore and separated, with handshaking, backslapping, and waving.

Zopyros, thrusting his way through the swarm of donkey boys, beggars, pimps, guides, drunken sailors, broken-down whores, and idlers, picked out a likely-looking stripling and asked:

"Do you know where Xanthos son of Glaukos, the landlord, lives?"

"*Kai malista!*"

Zopyros gave the boy a sheet of papyrus and a bronze penny, with a promise of another when the message was delivered. The boy ran off with the letter, which Zopyros had composed to give Korinna's family time to prepare themselves before the travelers appeared with Nestor's body.

Zopyros and Sophron picked up the litter bearing the body and, followed by Korinna, the slave, and two hired porters, set out. The slave and the porters staggered under the baggage of the entire party. At Xanthos' house, Sophron rapped and shouted:

"*Pai!*"

The door was opened by a servant. A fat, elderly man appeared in the opening. Korinna threw herself into his arms, talking and weeping. At last she pulled back and introduced Zopyros to her father.

"Come in, O Zopyros," said Xanthos. "Give your cloak and shoes to the servant."

71

Others hovered behind Xanthos: a couple of servants; a slight, black-haired youth who was Korinna's brother Glaukos; and a small, middle-aged woman, her mother Eirenê. While Korinna's parents fussed and wept over their daughter, Zopyros and Sophron set down the corpse at one side of the courtyard. Then Glaukos showed Zopyros to a room.

Some time afterward, Zopyros was summoned to the courtyard. Eirenê and Korinna had disappeared into the women's quarters, and Zopyros knew he was not likely to see them again save for some very special occasion. Xanthos clasped Zopyros' hand.

"Thrice welcome, O Zopyros!" wheezed Xanthos. A big belly pushed out the front of his cloak, and bushy tufts of curly gray hair stood out from the sides of his large bald head. Several amulets hung around his neck. He moved slowly and ponderously and seemed to have trouble with his breathing.

"I'm sorry to meet you on such a sad occasion," said Zopyros.

The Messanian replied: "My brother had led an active life, and his time had come. When I got your letter, I imagined dire things about my daughter. But I have questioned her and Sophron, and I believe you acted honorably."

"I am an honorable man, sir."

"Good! Many would deem her utterly abandoned, traveling about thus with a strange man for a protector. Even though she's not a virgin, we adhere to respectable standards in this house. But man cannot fight the gods, and you did what had to be done."

When his servants had served the dinner of sow's udder stuffed with pepper and salted sea urchin, Xanthos poured a small libation and prayed. Then he said: "As we eat, tell me of your adventures."

Zopyros talked as he ate, now and then stopping long enough to gulp a bite. He told of the narrow escapes of the Tarentine mission on its way to Cumae, of the battle with the pirates, and of the doom of mad Captain Ethbaal. After the wine had been mixed, he led the talk around to the matter that had been in his mind:

"Sir, have you thought of marrying off your daughter again?"

Xanthos looked at his guest from under heavy lids and smiled faintly. "Naturally! One must do what one can for one's own. Of course there are certain—ah—difficulties."

Glaukos grinned so that his teeth showed in the dusk. "Father means, Master Zopyros, that the lousy ready-for-aught won't give back my sister's dowry. Under our law he'd be compelled to, but safe in Motya he can tell us to go futter the moon."

"That's not the only difficulty," said Xanthos, looking sternly at his son. "Why do you ask such a question, young sir?"

Zopyros' throat seemed to have grown a lump that all but strangled him. At last he stammered: "Be-because I—ah—I wondered if you might consider me as a son-in-law. Of course I realize that it's a bit irregular—my family ought to make the arrangements with you—but they're in Taras, and—ah—ah—" His voice died away in an ineffectual gasp.

Xanthos nodded sagely. "I thought you had some such idea in mind. As you say, it's irregular for persons of our class; but then so is Korinna's present status. So let's not look down our noses at each other." The stout old man smiled. "I suppose you're in love with my daughter."

"Yes, sir, I certainly am!"

"Well, any wise man will tell you that love before marriage is a mistake; the love that follows a marriage prudently arranged by your parents is the only kind you can bank on. But, in view of Korinna's lack of dowry, I'm not inclined to split hairs. What would your father say?"

"I don't know, yet."

"Who is he? What sort of family have you? What is their property? What their ancestry? I might as well tell you that my lineage is as noble as the noblest, and my wife's is nearly as exalted. I trace descent from three gods and two heroes. How about you?"

"If you must know, sir, I'm part Persian. My father ..." Zopyros told of his family and their business in Taras.

Xanthos said: "We have here a lot of irregularities to set off against each other. Your Persian blood does not disturb me, since the Persians are after all the most aristocratic of the barbarians. Your father sounds respectable enough; but his estate is in business, not land, which is, of course, proper kind of property. Mine is in land.

"I wouldn't let Korinna go to you utterly destitute, although you need not expect the sum you would get if she were a virgin bride.

Unless, perhaps, you can manage to steal her portion back from the god-detested Elazar. Tell me about yourself."

Zopyros, smiling, spread his hands. "What shall I tell you, sir? If I tell you how good I am, you'll deem me a braggart; if I tell you how bad, you might believe me."

"Go ahead and let me judge. For instance, what is your attitude toward religion?"

"I'm a Pythagorean, albeit I fear a somewhat imperfect one."

"Hm. A heretical school, but one about which I am inclined to be broad-minded, in view of their high ethical standards. I notice that you ate the meat served you."

"That's what I meant by being imperfect. The Man urged his followers to use their reason, and my reason has never been able to take his rules of eating very seriously."

"How would you describe your own character?"

"Well, sir—ah—I have, I suppose, my good and bad points like other men. I'm a competent engineer, and I think I shall always be able to make a decent living. I try to fulfill my promises and meet my obligations. I'm temperate in my vices and have never been convicted of a crime. On the other hand, I don't pretend to be a great hero, or a beauty, or an athlete, or a leader, or a demagogue. Most men of your class, sir, would not even consider me a gentleman, because I work hard and don't mind getting my hands dirty."

"What's your politics? Are you a sound conservative, with due respect for the ancient and divinely established order of things? Or are you a wild-eyed radical who wants to pull down the better sort of people to his own base level?"

"I pay little heed to politics. I had rather follow my trade and let others work themselves into a frenzy over political questions."

"People," said Xanthos, "are generally satisfied to mind their own business when it is worth minding."

"Thank you, sir; I'll remember that the next time somebody rebukes me for lack of civic spirit. But, to be honest, it's lack of aptitude. One cannot be first in everything. To me, stone and wood and bronze are quiet, trustworthy things that do what you expect of them. But people—*phy!* One never knows what they'll do next. Some men, like my friend Archytas, are born with an instinct for handling them; but not I. I'm cut out for minding my own affairs and letting the world go by, instead of leaping in and snatching the helm from the helmsman on the slightest pretext. However, I do my best."

"According to Korinna," said Xanthos, "you leaped in effectively enough in Italy. At least, by Hera, you admit to some faults, instead of merely boasting, like one of Homer's heroes, of your own ineffable virtues! Now tell me more about your lineage. Just the last few generations, please; do not bother to trace it back to the time Apollon impregnated some remote female ancestor on a hillside, back before Theognis was born. I hardly expect you to display a more exalted pedigree than Korinna's."

Zopyros tried not to smile. "As I said, I'm of mixed descent. My great-grandfather was the satrap Bagabukhsha, or Megabyzos as Hellenes say it, the head of the Daduchid clan and one of the most powerful men of the Empire. You may have heard of his fantastic career under the Xerxes and the first Artaxerxes."

"Indeed?" said Xanthos. "That is interesting. Have you kept up with the Persian branch of the family? Such a connection might be useful if one were forced to flee to the empire, as befell the great Themistokles."

"No, sir; I don't know any of those people. If I were traveling in the realm of the Great King, I suppose I could look them up. Noble Persian families almost never die out or get killed off, because of all the wives the grandees have."

"True; but let us get back to your family."

Zopyros resumed his tale: "One time when Megabyzos was in revolt against his royal master, his son Zopyros fled to Athens. There he married Thia, the daughter of an Athenian citizen. How the Athenian permitted his daughter to wed a foreigner I don't know, but you've heard how impetuous Persians are in matters of love.

"Anyway, Zopyros soon lost his life leading Athenian troops in battle, leaving my grandmother Thia with a small child. When my father grew up, he was apprenticed to Rhatoses, an Egyptian engineer living in Athens. When Father attained an age to set up in business for himself, he removed to Taras in order to obtain citizenship, bringing my grandmother with him. In Taras he married Agatha, daughter of Bessas, son of Myron of Miletos.

"This Myron had served at the court of the Great King. There the Xerxes sent him and his friend, a Persian named Bessas, to find the headwaters of the Nile. They had an extraordinary journey, fighting an ape the size of a buffalo and meeting other strange adventures. It was on this journey that Myron conceived the idea that the earth is round, an idea many philosophers now hold. When his mission was over, he migrated west and ended his days in Taras as a respected philosopher.

"Although Myron was in his fifties when he arrived in Taras, he nevertheless married a middle-aged widow and begat a son, whom he named for his old comrade-in-arms Bessas. And Bessas' daughter Agatha is my mother. My father has often told me, with much amusement, how back in Persia there was a bitter feud between this Bessas and his friend Myron on one hand, and the Daduchids on the other. To this day, when he and my mother have an argument, he'll say: 'Now, my dear, you're not reviving that old feud between our families, are you?'"

"Your lineage is more interesting than mine," said Xanthos, "even if it is not pure Hellenic. There's one thing more. I want my grandson."

"Oh?"

"Yes. At my age a man thinks about death, and I mean to have my ghost properly served by a line of legitimate descendants. Oh, yes, I know"—he waved Zopyros to silence—"you hope to beget more children on the girl. But the Fates have their own way with such intentions, and a live descendant here and now is worth several yet unborn. Besides, I want to give the poor little bastard a proper Greek name and education.

"Korinna has told me about the Sibyl's prophecy. So we'll toss that requirement into the scale pan. Get the boy, and you'll find me reasonable in matters of property. Otherwise, no hymns to Hymen."

Zopyros' heart sank. "I told you I'm no hero. Did Korinna also tell you I have promised to return to Taras?"

Xanthos flipped a hand. "Of course you must, if you promised. The other matters can always be settled in good time."

"I was hoping to wed her now and take her home with me."

"Why, you immoral young scoundrel! Without the customary discussion between your family and me, your father's permission, formal betrothal, and so on? Draw your chariot back to the starting line! But then, the young are always impatient in such matters. I understand, even if I can't approve."

Xanthos swallowed the last of his wine, set down his kylix, and yawned. "I must arrange for my poor brother's funeral. Glaukos, why don't you take our young friend to Kylon's?" To Zopyros he said: "That's our leading tavern. Since Kylon rents the lot from me, I have a vested interest in his trade. Everybody said he was crazy to build so big a place—seats for twenty, and you can squeeze in forty if nobody breathes deeply. It's the biggest tavern this side of Athens; and everybody, including myself, thought he'd be bankrupt in a month.

"But Kylon had a scheme. He offers free grog to sea captains who spend an evening answering questions, and telling the news of far places. So he packs 'em in, night after night, and is coining money. Some of his girls aren't bad, either; you might pick yourself one. After keeping your paws off my daughter for the last ten-day, your yard must be as stiff as a pikestaff."

Kylon's was crowded indeed. As Glaukos and Zopyros pushed through the mass, men spoke to Glaukos, commiserating with him on the death of his uncle. Three young men clustered around, and Zopyros learned that they were the late Nestor's sons-in-law. Soon the four young Messanians put their heads together and began talking in low, solemn tones about property and inheritances.

"Look, Zopyros," said Glaukos, "I shan't drink, because it wouldn't look well with Uncle Nestor still unburied. But that's no reason why you shouldn't enjoy yourself. If you wriggle through there, I think you can get a seat on that window sill before somebody else grabs it. I'll join you later."

Zopyros started toward the window in question, but another man got there first. While he stood in perplexity looking about, a voice with a Punic accent said:

"Come here, Master Zopyros! My friend and I can squeeze apart to make a place for you."

It was Asto, the mate of the *Muttumalein*. As Zopyros, ignoring scowls and muttered threats from the men crowded aside to make room for him, wormed into the space they made for him on the bench, the Phoenician continued: "O Zopyros, this is Evnos the Karian, a ransomer by trade. I've carried him hither and yon about the Inner Sea on his errands of mercy. Evnos, meet Zopyros son of Megabyzos, a Tarentine engineer."

"Be in good health!" said Evnos. He was a stocky, barrel-chested man with a large wide head, a hooked nose, and a close-cut, bristly black beard. Though not handsome, he seemed friendly. "Yours must be a fascinating trade."

Zopyros shrugged. "It's a living. Yours sounds far more exciting. How did you ever get into it?"

Evnos gave a gap-toothed smile. "In the worst possible way: namely, by being a slave myself."

"Oh?"

"That's right. I can't be bothered trying to hide the fact. I'm beyond such petty affectations. One winter we had a famine in Karia, and my parents, who were poor country folk, sold me to a slaver. You needn't look shocked. It saved my life, when all the rest of my family died of hunger. It was the only way they could assure me of one good meal a day. Necessity is a hard master."

"But then how did you come into your present occupation?"

"Well, I had three masters in the next few years. One was pretty good, but the other two were real temple-robbing bastards. Especially the last one—the Athenian."

"What was the matter with him?"

"He was the foulest-tempered man I have known, and every time he got a little drunk he took it out on his slaves. I was lucky—he only knocked out a couple of my teeth. One of my fellow slaves he blinded in one of his rages. Still, in the long run his vile temper got me my freedom."

"How so?"

"After he'd beaten one of us to a pulp, he'd feel sorry and treat us kindly for a while. It made him uncomfortable to see us around all marked up. Conscience, I suppose. So he let me work for other men and keep half my pay. In a few years I bought myself off.

"At about that time, a kinsman of my last master wanted me to go to Syracuse to redeem his son, who was held prisoner in the quarries after the defeat of the Athenian invasion. So I did. Then another such bit of business came my way, and one thing led to another. I had been moved around quite a bit during these experiences, and I'm pretty good with languages. So travel doesn't frighten me. Now I journey all over the Inner Sea, arranging for people to ransom relatives who have been captured in war, or seized by pirates, or kidnapped and sold by slavers. If such a calamity should befall you, I am the best man in the Inner Sea to rescue you."

"Are the ransomees grateful?"

"Sometimes, although you'd be surprised how many try to wriggle out of paying the last installment of my fee. Still, I don't complain. When I was a barefoot country boy I always wanted to travel and, by the gods, I've had my share! I've seen strange things, and moreover I get home so seldom that my family really appreciates me when I am there."

"Where do you live?"

"In Syracuse. You understand, I have certain—ah—arrangements in other cities as well, but my wife and children are in Dionysios' metropolis."

"What was your strangest adventure?"

"Let me think. I suppose it was the time I was on my way to ransom a captive from one gang of pirates, and another gang captured me."

"By Zeus on Olympos, man, tell me!"

Evnos: "A rich family in Corinth hired me to redeem their breadwinner, one Chremes, who had been taken by Cilician pirates on his way to Cyprus. This gang was headed by a Numidian named Zamar, with headquarters in Kelenderis.

"I sailed from Corinth with a good stout bag of tetradrachmai at my belt. My captain was a Phoenician, Sadid of Cyprian Soloi, on his way to his home port. The awkward thing about ransoming is that you can't buy passage to the pirates' lairs on a real merchantman, because no merchant skipper in his right mind goes within ten leagues of such a place. So you have to make the last stage of your journey in some little cockleshell of a fishing craft, sailed by a fisherman more than half mad, because otherwise he would never have undertaken such an errand. Although most pirates leave such humble craft alone, you are dealing with strange and unpredictable people."

"I find all people strange and unpredictable," said Zopyros. "But go on."

"Well, Sadid meant to cut across the Pamphylian Sea to Cyprus. But a southern duster drove us within sight of Cape Anemourion, and a sixty-oared hemiolia pounced upon us. Captain Sadid, though, didn't mean to give up without a fight. He had a big stout ship fitted with a dolphin. Do you know what that is?"

"You mean one of those leaden weights slung from a boom at the top of the mast?"

"Exactly. When the hemiolia hove to alongside, Sadid had the boom swung out above the pirate's deck, and he cut the rope that held the weight. Down went the dolphin. But alas! At that instant a wave carried the ships apart. Hence the dolphin, instead of smashing a hole in the hemiolia's bottom, fell into the sea between the ships.

"Of course then the perfume was in the soup. The pirates swarmed aboard, screeching like harpies. When Captain Sadid went down fighting, those of his sailors still on their feet gave up. I can't blame them, because they were outnumbered four to one. But surrendering did them no good. The freebooters killed every one of them, to teach them not to resist honest pirates. I shall never forget the sight of their heads rolling back and forth across the deck, bumpety-bump, as the ship wallowed.

"They bundled us passengers into their galley, raped the women, searched us, killed a couple who resisted, looted the merchantman, set fire to it, and shoved off. Naturally, they grabbed my bag of money. However, before the boarding, I had torn up my spare shirt to make a bandage and tied the bandage around my left arm, with a fistful of silver hidden in it. During the fight I managed to get some blood on the bandage. Although they searched me pretty thoroughly—hoisting my shirt to make sure I hadn't shoved anything up my arse—they never thought to unwind the bandage.

"A Phoenician, Yerubaal, headed this band. When we got to Captain Yerubaal's home port of Nagidos, he quartered us in the village. I protested against being detained and having my ransom money confiscated. I argued that ransomers ought to be inviolate, like priests and physicians, and that such highhanded actions as his would ruin the ransom business, to everybody's loss. But Yerubaal was a tough old temple robber. He only laughed, and slapped his big paunch, and quoted proverbs to the effect that a fish in the net is worth ten in the sea. He added that I had better hold my tongue if I wanted to have one to hold.

"It takes a long time for a pirate to send out ransom demands and receive replies. While the ten-days passed, I became friendly with the people in whose hut I was quartered; especially with the boy in the family, who was fired with ambition to become a real throat-cutting pirate like his father. From him I learned that Kelenderis—my original destination—was only two hundred furlongs or so from Nagidos. Moreover, there was bad feeling between Yerubaal and Captain Zamar, who was holding my client Chremes.

"I won't go into all the details, but in the end I bribed the stripling to carry a letter to Zamar, telling him of the fate of the money meant for Chremes' release. Soon Zamar's hemiolia anchored at the mouth of the river. His pirates swaggered ashore, Zamar shouting a demand to speak to Yerubaal.

"'Here I am,' said Yerubaal. 'What do you want, prick-face?'

"The two captains were very different. Yerubaal was fat and jolly, a great eater, drinker, talker, joker, and boaster. Zamar, on the other hand, was tall, lean, and dark-skinned, with a solemn manner.

"'I want my ransomer, Evnos the Karian, and the money he brought to redeem one of my captives,' said Zamar.

"'Futter you!' said Yerubaal. 'By Tanith's teats, what I have, I keep! Besides, that money has already been paid into the common fund.'

"'Your conduct is whipworthy and unethical, you branded sodomite!' said Zamar. 'If you don't give me the man and the money, by the gods I'll take them!'

"'Go ahead!' said Yerubaal with a grin. 'You've never seen me run from a fight yet.'

"Zamar looked around at his men, who were drawing swords and poising javelins, and at Yerubaal's men, who were doing likewise. All the captives and the villagers were spread out behind Yerubaal's gang to watch. In fact, some of the prisoners began laying bets. Then Zamar held up a hand to check his own men and said:

"'For a long time, sow-belly, I've wanted to cut out your stinking heart; but there's no reason why half our brave lads should die in the cutting. If you're not afraid, I'll meet you in single combat, winner take all."

"'By Milkarth's iron yard, that suits me!' said Yerubaal, and he ran at Zamar with sword and shield. Round and round they went with a great clatter—cut, thrust, duck, parry, guard, advance, and retreat. They were well matched. While the Numidian had the advantage of reach, the Phoenician was the stronger and was also quick and agile for a man of his girth. The watching pirates capered and screeched like a horde of monkeys.

"I never did find out which of the two captains was the better, because one of Yerubaal's men rushed forward and stabbed Zamar in the back. Before Zamar had time to fall, one of his men in turn hurled a javelin into Yerubaal's back. Down went the two captains, and the men of their bands rushed together in the fiercest fight I have ever seen.

"The bands, too, were evenly matched. There was a grand mellay, with everybody spearing and slashing, stabbing and kicking, biting and clawing, and blood all over the place. When neither side seemed able to win, some god sent me an idea. Whenever a man fell near the outskirts of the fight, I bravely darted forward, seized his weapon, and handed it to one of my fellow captives. Soon they were all armed.

"After a time, there were only six or seven of Yerubaal's men on their feet, and four of Zamar's. All were so winded they could barely stand and pant, and all had blood raining down their dirty hides from their wounds.

"'All right,' said I to the other prisoners, 'let's get 'em!'

"We swept forward in a line, every man of us with a sword or spear or ax and most of us with shields as well. Although we were not trained fighters, we were fresh and outnumbered the remaining pirates two to one. It was a slaughter. The pirates had hardly the strength to raise an arm. We chopped them down like saplings, except for the last couple, whom we saved for torture.

"So ended the careers of Yerubaal and Zamar and their merry men. We burned Yerubaal's ship and the smaller craft in the harbor and set out along the coast in Zamar's ship. Luckily there were seafaring men amongst us. We elected one of them captain, and between his management and god-sent winds we got to Tarsos without further trouble. Some of the gentlemen among the captives moaned at getting their hands blistered on the oars, but we had no mercy on them.

"We stopped at Kelenderis and took off Zamar's captives, including my man Chremes. And do you know, that whoreson knave tried to get back the ransom money? We debated the matter before the assembled crew. He claimed that I was entitled only to my fee, that the bulk of the ransom never had belonged to me and therefore reverted to him on Zamar's death. I argued that his family had given me the money to free him, and if he was freed it was none of his business how I disposed of the money.

"The crew voted that I should keep the money, only giving Chremes enough for ship fare back to Corinth, with a little extra for emergencies. Since this was only a few drachmai, I didn't mind. The rest paid for my house in Syracuse. And now, Master Zopyros, let me talk business with you."

"With me?"

"Yes. I'm not on a ransoming journey now, but—"

"Here's the sea captain for tonight," interrupted Asto. "He's Abdanath of Tyre. Now hush up and listen to the news, my flap-tongued friends."

Abdanath of Tyre, standing in the small cleared space and sipping wine from a beaker, said: "Excellent sirs! I have just come from Tyre, with stops at Rhodes, Athens, and Syracuse. I still have some fine purple-dyed Tyrian garments, precious Acaean glass, Athenian painted pottery, and Chian wine—"

"Yes, yes, but let's have the news!" said a man. "The commercial pitch can follow."

Abdanath bowed toward the speaker. "To hear is to obey, my lord. Know, then, that the Spartans have made peace with the Eleans and have declared war upon the satrap Tissaphernes. They have invaded the lands of the Great King in Lydia. It is said that six thousand Greek mercenaries are marching to join them. These are the remnant of the ten thousand who invaded the Empire under Prince Cyrus and had to cut their way out, across half the breadth of Asia, after Cyrus fell at Cunaxa.

"King Agis of Sparta has died and been succeeded by King Agesilaos. King Archelaos of Macedonia has been killed in a hunting accident. His young son Orestes has been slain by his guardian, Aeropos, who has usurped the throne. And the Athenians have arrested a philosopher named Sokrates on charges of spreading subversive ideas."

There was a mutter in the audience—"Isn't that what you'd expect of the fornicating fools?" Athens had been widely hated in Sicily since the great invasion fifteen years before, and the Siceliots welcomed a chance to gibe at the former mistress of the Greek world.

Captain Abdanath continued: "The Egyptian Tamôs, who was the Great King's governor in Ionia, has fled to Egypt and there been murdered by another satrap. There is much unrest in Egypt, and a famine in Thrace, and the price of olives is up in Hellas. ..."

The audience began asking questions, mostly about local politics in the cities of the East and about the prices of various goods. Evnos spoke in a low voice to Zopyros:

"As I was saying, I have a bit of business with you. Would you like a secure position, at a higher rate of pay than any other engineer in these parts? And a chance to make inventions, work out original ideas, and gain immortal glory?"

"That sounds good," said Zopyros. "But I should have to ask my father. I'm in partnership with him. Who's offering these liberal terms? Dionysios?"

"Exactly. Now that his power is secure, Dionysios has great plans for improving and beautifying Syracuse and its dependent cities, and for augmenting their military might. The trouble is to find men with enough training to do a really good job. One can always hire ordinary masons and carpenters, who will turn out adequate copies of the temples at Segesta and the walls at Akragas, or shipwrights who can whittle out a conventional trireme. But Dionysios wants something more. He wants men of genius—men with original ideas. So I've been sent to recruit such men. Whom besides yourself would you recommend in Taras?"

"My friend Archytas," said Zopyros promptly. "He's better at mathematics than I, although I have the edge over him in the actual handling of materials. Besides, he can get along with anybody."

Zopyros thought fast. He would be much closer to Korinna in Syracuse than in Taras. Once established in Syracuse, he might gain

Xanthos' consent to his wedding the girl without first rescuing the child. Or even—Zopyros winced at the thought but then faced it squarely—the Fates might offer an opportunity to do what Xanthos demanded and escape with a whole skin. In either case, logically speaking, his chances would be better in Syracuse. Of course, his parents might cavil. ...

Zopyros kept his musings to himself. To Evnos he said: "I'll talk about this offer with my father. If he approves, I may well appear in Syracuse in a month or two."

"And don't forget to pass the word to your friend Archytas. Tell him fame and fortune await him in Syracuse! I would do so myself, except that I'm on my way to Athens on Abdanath's ship, and we shan't stop at Taras."

Abdanath had finished, and Kylon brought out his dancer and his singer. As the girls performed, some heavy drinkers became noisy. Presently two men had stripped and oiled themselves and, having chased Kylon's girls off the floor, fell to wrestling in the middle of the room. Another man tried to dance the kordax on a table and fell off with a crash. As the uproar became deafening, Glaukos shouted in Zopyros' ear:

"If they're all going to scream like Illyrians, I think we had better go home."

"All right," said Zopyros, and his two bench mates agreed. As they reached the muddy street, a Messanian lounging in the doorway lurched unsteadily against little Asto. The Messanian backed off and said:

"Sorry, I—" Then his expression changed. "Another polluted Phoenician, eh? Someday we'll show you baby-burning sodomites a thing or two! Work night and day so we can't compete with you, will you? Cut prices below ours, will you? You'll get yours! Wait and see! Unless you'd like a free sample?" The man balled his fists.

"And would you be looking for a fight, now?" said a voice with a familiar lilt. Segovax the Celt had pushed out the doorway behind Zopyros and his party.

"And who in Herakles' name are *you*?" said the Messanian.

"That I will be pleased to show your honor," said Segovax, blowing on his large right fist and rubbing his left hand over it as if polishing it, "if you will be finding me a quiet place, where we can discuss the matter like gentlemen. ..."

The Messanian's friends seized him by the arms and pulled him back into Kylon's. They jabbered into the drunken man's ears: "Take it easy!" "Sober up, you god-detested fool!" "Don't start a fight with foreigners, or we shall all end up in the House!"

"Thank you, O Segovax," said Asto, taking his hand off his dagger. Zopyros could see, even in the feeble lamplight, that the small Phoenician's face had gone pale under its swarthiness. "That's the trouble with being a traveling man. Some bully decides to clean all the filthy foreigners out of his fair city, and if you're the nearest one in sight he naturally picks on you."

"He's right," said Evnos the Karian. "I run into that kind of thing now and then, too. That's but one hazard of our callings. Good night, friends."

The party broke up. The Phoenician, the Karian, and the Celt went one way; Zopyros and Glaukos the other. Glaukos said:

"Don't tell my father you're so chummy with Phoenicians. He hates them as bitterly as that man in the doorway."

"From what your sister tells me, he didn't used to."

"No; but that experience changed his mind. Not that I criticize you. I understand how you, in plying your trade, have to mix with all sorts of barbarians. But Father is of the older generation. He will never understand us progressive-minded moderns."

Zopyros found himself with a day to kill before the next ship left for Taras. If he had been able to spend the time with Korinna, he would have been happy to prolong his stay. But, with the girl shut up in the women's rooms at the back of the house, he was impatient to get away, to start negotiations between his father and Xanthos. Patient waiting was not his style. Watching him pace and fidget, Glaukos said:

"Aren't you the restless one, though? Most people are glad of a day off from work and care. Let's take the dog for a walk around the city wall."

The wall of Messana measured a mere fifteen cubits high and four cubits thick. Moreover, it was badly crumbled in places, so that strollers had to watch their step for fear of a dangerous fall. Zopyros said:

"A determined foe could overrun this wall with scaling ladders alone, without these new siege engines we hear about. Why doesn't your Council hire competent engineers—like my father's firm, for instance—to build them a proper one? If there's another big Carthaginian war ..."

Glaukos shrugged. "Long ago some oracle—I forget if it was that of Delphoi, or Cumae, or what—told us:

In this city shall men of Carthage be bearers of water.

So you see that, if the Carthaginians attack, we shall overcome and enslave them."

"Hm. People have gotten into trouble before this, by trusting in oracles instead of in strength. Croesus of Lydia, for instance."

"True." The young man looked troubled. "I'm not so keen on omens and oracles myself, though I have to be careful what I say at home."

"Your father must be a man of some influence in the city. Why don't you put him up to agitating for a new wall?"

Glaukos held up his hands. "He's the biggest omen-monger of the lot! He never does anything without consulting the priests of several temples. A saying like the one I quoted to you might have been given him by the Far-Shooter in person. I admit the oracles seem to work for him, since his business enterprises have prospered."

"If General Nikias hadn't taken omens so seriously, his Athenians would never have been trapped and destroyed at Syracuse."

Glaukos shrugged. "No doubt, but such arguments would get nowhere with Father. How about a cockfight this evening?"

Next morning Zopyros and Korinna, surrounded by the latter's family, stood on the wharf at Messana. They faced each other, not touching, with tears slowly running down their faces.

"Come, come," wheezed Xanthos. "It's not so tragic as all that. It is not as if I had said you might never marry."

"Oh, let him kiss her, Xanthos," said Eirenê. "It can't do any harm, and the lad may never get back to Messana."

"Who can foresee what the gods have in store for us?" said Xanthos. "Go ahead, Zopyros."

Zopyros embraced the girl, strained her to him for a long instant. Then he picked up his gear, slung it over his back, and climbed over the rail of the *Atalanta* of Syracuse. As the ship drew away from the wharf, he remained at the rail, waving with his palm turned inward, until the figures on shore grew too small to distinguish.

The *Atalanta* wallowed across the Tarentine Gulf under fair spring skies. Zopyros, wrapped in his cloak, dozed on the deck and dreamt. He dreamt that he stood on the forested lower slopes of Aetna. As he watched, the mountain spat fire and smoke and presently turned into a naked, hairy giant with a single red-glowing eye in the middle of his forehead. The clouds formed a wreath around his shaggy head. Then a deep voice behind Zopyros said:

"I need your help, little man."

Zopyros turned and saw the demigod Herakles, complete with lion skin. Although twice as tall as a mortal man, Herakles was still but a pygmy compared to the Kyklops. Herakles continued:

"The gods have laid another labor upon me, to slay the giant Polyphemos. For that task my regular bow, which Apollon gave me to use against the Stymphalian birds, were too small. I have made an arrow of suitable size"—he held up an arrow as long as himself, like a ship's yard with feathers—"but I have no way to shoot it. It would need a bow twenty or thirty cubits long, and that were too large even for one of my stature. But Apollon tells me that you are a clever lad, as mortals go, and can devise a means to launch this arrow. Quick, now; the Kyklops approaches!"

And indeed the giant was coming on, treading down trees with his huge horny feet and swinging a club made from a tree trunk.

"Hasten!" growled Herakles. "The world will be lost if you use not that wit wherewith the Averter of Evil credits you!"

Zopyros tried desperately to think, while the Kyklops drew closer. Then something snapped. He cried:

"Cut the branches from one of these pines, O Herakles, but leave a cubit or two on a pair near the top. Then cut off the trunk just above this pair of stubs, so that the tree shall have the form of a fork. Hook the head of your arrow into that fork, pull it back until the tree trunk is bent into a curve, and let it go!"

Herakles began lopping branches with his ax, climbing as he cut. In a few heartbeats the tree was bare save for the pair of stubs near the top.

"I cannot reach the top from the ground, even with my stature!" said Herakles, dropping back to earth with an impact that shook the ground. "How shall we bend the tree?"

The Kyklops came closer, his fiery eye shooting gleams through the forest. Trees crashed down before his tread.

"A rope!" cried Zopyros. "Use the tail of your lion's skin!"

Herakles swung the tail—which seemed to have grown to the needed length—and whipped the end around the top of the polled tree. Then his mighty muscles creaked as he hauled in the improvised rope. The tree trunk bent like a bow, quivering with stress. When it was pulled back to within easy reach from the ground, Herakles tied the loose end of the lion's tail around another tree trunk. He placed the head of his huge arrow in the fork of the polled tree.

"Now," he said, "stand you by with the ax, and when I say, 'Now,' cut the rope. Are you ready?"

"Ready," said Zopyros. He no longer dared to look at the Kyklops, so close the monster loomed.

"Now!" roared Herakles.

Zopyros brought down the ax. The rope parted; the tree whipped up with a swish. Away soared the monstrous arrow …

And Zopyros found himself sprawled on the deck in a tangle of cloak. A roll of the ship, more severe than most, had tumbled him over.

The *Atalanta* threaded her way along the channel between a pair of rocks—the Choirades—and Cape Phalanthos. The low, flat Messapian plain spread out before her. Instead of the frowning fence of the Apennines that faced the sea off most of the coasts of Italy, here but a few low ranges of hills were to be seen, far inland. Ahead lay Taras, a streak of color against the olive brown of the coast. The afternoon sun shone brilliantly on the bed of roof tiles, the white of marble and whitewashed walls, the buff of mud brick.

Straight ahead, the rocky hill of the acropolis rose from the isle where stood the old city. This island plugged the entrance to the Little Sea behind. A wall of brick ran around the island a few cubits above the water level. To the right, on a hump of land, the huge temple of Poseidon, with massive Doric columns, loomed above the wall. Smaller temples marched up the main hill to its summit.

To the right of the temple of Poseidon, the land dipped beneath the sea to form the East Passage, deep enough only for small craft and crossed by a wooden bridge. Beyond the East Passage spread the suburb, in its turn protected by a brick wall. The ship angled to port, toward the deeper North Passage.

Down came the sail. Under oars, the ship forged through the North Passage into the Little Sea, the finest harbor in southern Italy. The *Atalanta* tied up at the wharf along the inner side of the island acropolis.

When Zopyros stepped ashore, the shadows of late afternoon were lengthening. Since it was a long walk to his home, he allowed himself the luxury of hiring a porter to carry his bag of belongings. He strode ahead, using his spear as a walking stick and dodging other pedestrians. Many of these were slaves or free workers bearing heavy burdens, some so bulky that Zopyros had to flatten himself against the wall to let them pass. The city smells of sweat, produce, cookery, and decaying waste matter filled his nostrils.

The streets of the old city, too narrow and crooked for wheeled traffic, formed a chaotic tangle. They were paved with a rough surface of lime and pebbles; but in many places this had disintegrated, leaving stretches of mud into which garbage and ordure had been trodden. The brick walls of one-story houses, which crowded in from either side, were practically blank, save for massive wooden doors and an occasional high, small, barred window. The walls of the more prosperous houses had been whitewashed; the others remained in their natural mud-brick buff.

A few months before, Zopyros and his father had presented the Assembly with a proposal for rebuilding the city in accordance with a master plan, such as the great Hippodamos had made for Peiraieus, Thourioi, and Rhodes. The rebuilt streets would gradually have become wide and straight, crossing at right angles as in some ancient cities of the East. A unanimous roar of protest from the property owners of Taras, however, had instantly squelched this ambitious plan.

The streets grew a little wider and straighter after Zopyros crossed the bridge to the suburb. At last he came to the familiar door of his home. He knocked and called: "*Pai!*"

Soon he was smothered in his family's embraces. Zopyros' father who, although gray and not so tall, strongly resembled his son, shouted toward the kitchen:

"Fetch some wine!"

"Did you catch cold?" asked his mother Agatha.

"Tell us your adventures!" begged his brother Perseus, a smaller edition of Zopyros, not yet bearded.

His sister Thia, a buck-toothed, gangly girl of twelve, said: "What about this beautiful widow whom Archytas says you went off with?"

"One at a time, dear ones!" cried Zopyros. Presently they were all seated about him in the courtyard, listening to his account of his journey after he had separated from the Archon's party. When he told of his arrival in Messana and his reception by Korinna's family, his father said:

"I suppose, son, that your relations with this young lady were—and are—motivated by simple friendship?"

Zopyros blushed, choked, and stammered. "N-not exactly. As a m-matter of fact I should like to marry her."

"So my passionless logician has at last allowed himself to be swayed by sentiment? Your mother and I have thought that it was time we started looking for a wife for you, son. I'm sure we can find a more suitable match here in Taras. Besides, from what you tell me, this girl has had a somewhat—ah—colorful history " He held up a hand as Zopyros started to protest. "I know, you'll tell me it wasn't her fault. But marriage is a business proposition, and one must look at it from all angles. It has hazards enough without needlessly adding to them, as by wedding a wench from another city, with whom one's own city may someday be at war. Besides, think how hard it would be for Xanthos and me to make the financial agreements, shuttling between two cities!" Megabyzos tossed his head back in the negative. "No, I can't see this marriage as good for the family. I won't rule it out for the present, but I certainly cannot approve."

Agatha added: "You can trust us to seek your best interests, Zopyros darling."

Zopyros was silent for a moment, biting his lips. Then he spoke: "Another thing, Father. The Dionysios offers high pay to engineers and skilled craftsmen who come to Syracuse to work on his projects. I've been urged to go there—"

"Zopyros! I wouldn't think of such a thing. We have more contracts than we can handle now, and—"

"But it would be good for the firm, to have an entrée to the most powerful man in Great Hellas—"

"You've only just got home," said Agatha, "and already, you're talking about going away again!"

"I know what you have in mind!" said Megabyzos. "You want to be near that girl—"

"But, dear ones!" cried Zopyros. "It's an opportunity; and Perseus is old enough to help—"

"Nonsense!" said Megabyzos loudly. "He hasn't even begun his apprenticeship—"

They were still arguing, shouting and gesticulating, when a furious rapping cut off the dispute. The porter admitted Archytas, sweating and disheveled, with a small bag in his hand.

"Zopyros!" he said in a hushed voice. "They're after us! Get ready to flee the town. Right away!"

Zopyros frowned in puzzlement. "Are you crazy? Who is after us?"

"Kteson the demagogue and his gang! They'll get you, too, because you're vice-president."

"What in the name of the Dog are you talking about?"

"This started when I ran for the Council. The election is in a tenday. When it looked as if I should win Kteson's seat, Kteson brought a charge of treason against me."

"I never thought the people would take that silly charge seriously," said Megabyzos.

"They did, though!" said Archytas. "Kteson told the Assembly our poor little Pythagorean Society was plotting to set up oligarchic rule and stop everybody from eating beans. The next step, he said, would be to make the Tarentines live on barley porridge. So today he pushed through an indictment against both of us, as president and vice-president of the club; and his bravos are out on the streets now, looking for us."

"*Oi!*" cried Zopyros, and all his family burst into exclamations.

"What's the quickest way to get out of town?" said Archytas.

Zopyros: "Captain Phaiax's *Atalanta* sails for Syracuse tomorrow, if he can complete his loading. And, luckily, I haven't yet unpacked my gear. We'll hide in his cargo overnight. Father, it looks as though some god meant us to try our luck with Dionysios, willy-nilly."

Megabyzos sighed. "Who can fight against Fate? I shall miss you, son. And how shall I ever catch up on my work?"

Zopyros took the shield out of his duffel bag. "Mother," he said, "is there a clean shirt that I might have? Thia, can you get us something to eat on the way? A loaf, a cheese, and a sack of dried peas would do. ..."

Wearing the hoods of their cloaks pulled down over their faces, Zopyros and Archytas hurried toward the waterfront on the northern side of the suburb. They had almost reached the shore when a voice cried:

"*Ea!* You two!"

Zopyros hurried on as if he had not heard. There came a sound of running steps. A man brushed past them, turning to peer under the hoods.

"Aren't you Zopyros and Archytas, the Pythagoreans?" said the man. "Yes, I'm sure you're Archytas! I've seen you making speeches in the market place. In the name of the Assembly, I arrest—"

"And who in Milkarth's name are you?" roared Zopyros in a thick Punic accent. "I'm Elibaal of Siden, and this is my first mate. Out of the way, you greasy, boy-loving Greek!"

"You don't fool me! You don't fool me!" cried the man, capering in his excitement. "In the name—"

While Zopyros was speaking, Archytas had slipped around behind the man and dropped to hands and knees. Zopyros gave a quick glance up and down the crooked alley in which they stood. Nobody was in sight for the moment, since most Tarentines were indoors eating their dinners. Zopyros pushed the man in the chest, so that he fell backward over Archytas. Then, as the fellow started to struggle up, Zopyros whacked him over the head with the hilt of his dagger. The man collapsed like a ruptured bladder.

"Jolly good!" said Archytas. "But I do hope you haven't killed him. That would ruin my political prospects for good."

"No; just put him to sleep for a while. At least, I hope so."

"Maybe we'd better shove him into a corner where he won't be seen so quickly."

"No time for that. We're almost to the harbor, and some small-boat fishermen tie up at the foot of this street. Come on!"

They hastened on. Archytas had to trot a few steps now and then to keep up with his companion's long strides. At the end of the street, they found a fisherman tying up after his day's fishing. Since his catch had been meager, it was easy to hire him to row them westward toward the *Atalanta*'s wharf. They told him to swing wide of the shore.

While the fisherman rowed, the two young men sat in silence, casting fearful glances shoreward lest a boat put out after them or a group of armed men appear on shore to cut them off. The sun dipped behind the temple of Poseidon. Zopyros said:

"Pull in there, behind that Rhodian."

"Why don't you have him drop us at the *At*—" began Archytas.

"Shut up!" Zopyros began talking broken Oscan. "If we climb from this craft directly aboard our ship, the fisherman will know exactly where we went. Then, if anybody questions him, he'll put them on our track. We shall run less risk if we disembark a plethron or two away and walk along the shore."

At last they came to the wharf that Zopyros had designated. They climbed ashore, heaving their duffel bags over their shoulders. They were not conspicuous, because men in traveling gear were always going to and fro on the waterfront. As they strode along the street, the odors of a cookshop wafted to their nostrils. Archytas said in a plaintive voice:

"Can't we stop for at least one good cooked meal before boarding?"

"Dear Herakles! You'd think of your belly if you were writhing in the Hydra's jaws. Come along!"

As the sun set, leaving a band of green and gold along the western horizon, they boarded the *Atalanta*. Captain Phaiax, loading bales of Tarentine wool, was surprised to see them. But, when they paid their fares to Syracuse, he asked no questions. He was used to that sort of thing.

SYRACUSE

They stood at the rail of the *Atalanta*, watching Syracuse grow before their eyes. Before them lay the main city, the Achradina, occupying a semicircular mass of land thrust out into the Ionian Sea. Behind the Achradina, the suburbs rose stepwise to the plateau of the Epipolai, famed for fierce fighting during the great Athenian siege. Much building seemed to be going on in these suburbs. New houses were springing up on the plateau and the slopes leading to it, among the groves and tombs and shrines.

Inland, beyond the city, rose the long slopes of the Heraean Mountains, which filled all of southeastern Sicily. Typical Sicilian mountains, though huge in bulk, they were not craggy like the mountains of Old Hellas. Their smooth, grassy slopes culminated in rounded, breast-shaped summits. They bore few trees, save for patches of woods in the deepest clefts between the ridges.

Northward, the colossal mass of Aetna stood half hidden by clouds. A pallid, shadowy blur betrayed the snow fields of its lower slopes. Remembering his dream, Zopyros shuddered. Nevertheless, he stared at the volcano, wishing he had the vision of a god, so that he could see right through the mountain to Messana and his beloved. Then he looked back toward the shining city to southward.

"Sicilian cities have such a *new* look," he remarked.

The reason is simple," said Archytas at his elbow. "As fast as the Siceliots get a city built, some army sacks and destroys it. Then, when the survivors trickle back, they have to start anew. Think of Kamarina, Selinous, Akragas, Gela, almost any place you can name. ... They say Syracuse will soon be a greater city than Athens. I, too, could

96

build the world's largest city if I were allowed to kidnap the people of neighboring towns and force them to live in mine, as Dionysios has done with the Naxians and the Leontines."

"By the Silver Egg!" exclaimed Zopyros. "I'm a stupid ox!"

"I knew that all along," said his friend with a grin. "But what proves it now?"

"If I had only stopped to think! I'm sure my father has at least one hospitality token from somebody in Syracuse. I know he's done work for several Syracusans, but I can't think of a single name."

"Well, considering how suddenly we left Taras, I don't blame you. Yet we must have acquaintance with *somebody* in Syracuse."

"I'm thinking. If there were a Pythagorean Society in Syracuse—"

"You'd better not go around asking for one," said Archytas. "The Dionysios is said to be a very suspicious ruler. If our own democratic city can go into a frenzy over imaginary Pythagorean plots, you can imagine what Dionysios would do."

Zopyros grumbled: "The godlike Pythagoras' biggest mistake was to let his followers mix in politics."

"Somebody has to run a city, and who better than philosophers?"

"Well, you know what happened. Philosophers seem to like power for its own sake just as other men do. Perhaps we ought to rename the Pythagorean Societies after some other truth-seeker, such as Philolaos."

"Ah, but he, too, was suspected of political ambition. That's why he fled to Old Hellas. ... "What are you thinking of, old chap?"

"Zeus on Olympos! I just remembered. Do you recall, in our last year under Philolaos, there was a younger student from Syracuse, Archonides son of Philistos?"

"Only vaguely."

"Well, I saved this boy from some bullying, so he became attached to me for a time. He was a terrible snob, always boasting of his father's position and wealth and lineage. However, I remember hearing from others about this Philistos, a man with pretensions to being a philosopher. He financed Dionysios' early rise in politics, when Dionysios was just a humble clerk in the tax office. Perhaps Archonides could put in a word for us."

"How shall we find this Philistos in so vast a city?"

"I've been wondering, too. But speaking of the tax office, everybody knows where it is, doesn't he?"

"Certainly, unless he's a blind beggar."

"And the tax office is the one place where they keep a record of where everybody lives. So we'll ask at the tax office. That's logical, isn't it?"

"Yes, unless they toss us in prison as tax delinquents."

The island of Ortygia, guarding the southern flank of the Achradina, came into view. Massive battlemented walls girded the island. Behind it lay the Great Harbor with its dockyards. The masts of ships, tied up at the wharves and anchored in rows in the harbors, formed a leafless forest. Out in the sea, a squadron of triremes maneuvered. The coxswains' flutes came faintly across the water.

"Look, Archytas!" said Zopyros. "Dionysios has built his walls of stone!"

"By the Mouse God, so he has! With these new Phoenician battering rams and suchlike engines coming into use, I suppose we shall see many cities replacing their brick walls with stone. At least, there'll be plenty of work for us engineers."

The tax office lay to landward of the wooden bridge that joined Ortygia to the mainland. Here Zopyros and Archytas learnt that Philistos lived on Ortygia, along with the tyrannos' other trusted friends.

A pair of soldiers stood at attention on the far end of the bridge. As Zopyros and Archytas stepped out upon the resounding planks of the bridge, Zopyros grasped his companion's arm.

"Look at that!"

"Those chains?"

"Yes!" They start here—and go through those holes in the wall over there—" Zopyros, becoming excited, rushed about the bridge like a dog on the scent. "Dionysios must be able to haul the bridge up whenever he doesn't want visitors. Oh, plague! Why didn't I think of that?"

"I say, Zopyros!" cried Archytas, becoming excited in his turn. "Look at this gate affair that slides up and down!"

Zopyros rushed to examine. Where the island met the water, he saw massive stone fortifications. Beyond the drawbridge the walls were pierced by a lofty gateway, which tunneled through the masonry. A pair of heavy wooden doors stood open at the far end of the tunnel; while at the near end, instead of a pair of hinged wooden door valves, the passage was controlled by an openwork portcullis, which was made of iron-sheathed timbers and which slid up and down in a slot in the masonry.

Zopyros became so fascinated by these novel mechanisms that, in striding about and craning his neck to see better, he bumped into one of the soldiers of the guard.

"*Ê!*" roared the man, recovering his balance and aiming his spear at Zopyros' midriff. "What in the afterworld do you think you're doing, you collared rascal?"

"Excuse me," said Zopyros, feeling very cold inside as he gazed at the spearhead. "I was so interested I didn't see you—"

"Maybe you'd like a few ten-days in the House?" snarled the other soldier, also bringing his spear to the stabbing position.

"Now, now, it's too nice a day to quarrel," said Archytas. "You see, boys, my friend is such a genius that half the time he doesn't see what's going on around him. I'm sure the price of a drink will make up for his clumsiness. ... Now could you tell us how to get to the house of Philistos?"

"Where's your pass?" growled the first soldier.

"Must we have passes?" said Zopyros.

"By the gods, you two *are* new here, aren't you?" said the second soldier. Listening to their accents, Zopyros guessed them to be Campanians, Lucanians, or perhaps half-barbarous Sikels from the interior of Sicily. "Of course you have to have a pass, or else an escort." The speaker turned his head and bawled: "File leader Segovax!"

The Celt appeared from the guardroom, wearing the panoply of one of Dionysios' non-commissioned officers. The sweeping mustache and the long sword, however, betrayed his barbarian origin.

"By the horns of Cernunnos!" he cried, wringing their hands. "If 'tis not the brave Tarentine lads! Are you here to get a job from himself, too?"

"Perhaps," said Zopyros, smiling warmly at the sound of a friendly voice. "We thought we'd call on Philistos first, since I used to know his son."

"That's the clever Hellene for you, always thinking ahead. Master Philistos is the second man after himself." He turned his head and shouted: "Egnatius! Escort duty!" He turned back. "When you are settled, come and see me for a bit of a talk and a drop of wine."

The escort guided them through a maze of fortifications and past Dionysios' palace and the temple of Apollon and Artemis. In front of the temple stood a heroic statue of a nude Apollon bending his mighty bow. They trudged past barracks and other governmental buildings for half the length of the island. About them was a constant bustle as the dictator's soldiers and civil servants came and went. At last, near the huge Olympieion, they stopped before one of the few private houses on Ortygia and rapped.

The doorkeeper swung open the heavy door. Behind him stood Philistos, a heavy-set man in his forties, with the first streaks of gray in his beard. He leaned on a crutch-headed walking stick. To Zopyros' questions he answered:

"No, my son is not here. He is in Athens, studying under Gorgias. You claim to have known him in Taras, eh? Have you a token to prove it?"

"I'm afraid not, sir," said Zopyros.

"Well, it doesn't matter. For the next ten-day my house will be full of kinsmen, gathered for the religious rites of our clan. So I could not invite you to stay here in any case. However, the President is granting audience this afternoon. I am on my way thither and can introduce you to him."

Following the limping Philistos and the escorting soldier, Zopyros and Archytas retraced their steps around the temple of Apollon and Artemis to the palace. The palace of Dionysios resembled an ordinary square Greek courtyard house, except that it was larger and was made of stone instead of mud brick. The escort spoke briefly to the two soldiers who stood sentry go at the doorway.

"Raise your arms," said one of the sentries, stepping forward.

"Do you want our swords?" said Archytas politely. "We'll save you the trouble of finding them."

He laid his bag of belongings on the ground, reached up under the hem of his chiton, and unbuckled the scabbard strapped to his thigh. Zopyros did likewise. At the sight of the smallswords, the soldiers and Philistos scowled suspiciously.

"You see," said Archytas smoothly, handing over his sword, "we have just arrived in Syracuse and have no place, yet, to leave our gear."

The soldier who had spoken nevertheless ran his hands over the bodies of the Tarentines. There was a muttered conference among the three soldiers, which ended when one of them said:

"All right, take them in, but warn the big boss."

Inside, a fountain played in the courtyard, its drops flashing rainbow gleams in the sunshine. More soldiers stood at attention behind well-polished shields, while several audience-seekers waited silently in the shade of the portico around the courtyard. Beside the fountain, on an ordinary chair, sat Dionysios, looking up at a small man who was talking earnestly to him.

Dionysios shifted his level gaze as the new arrivals entered. He called: "Rejoice, Philistos! Come and see what you think of this tax proposal."

While the three men put their heads together, Zopyros studied Dionysios. The President of Syracuse, he called himself, although everybody knew that under his rule the form was all that remained of the democratic constitution. Dionysios was a full-fledged tyrannos, whose power rested upon the fortifications of Ortygia and upon his tough mercenary troops.

Dionysios was a strikingly handsome man, about thirty years old, with regular features and clear gray eyes. He was as tall as Zopyros, mightily muscled, and clad in a simple but spotlessly clean white tunic. His dark hair and beard were shaggy. Zopyros remembered the story that Dionysios insisted on either trimming them himself, or having them singed with a hot coal, for fear of letting even a barber close to him with any sharp implement. His movements gave the impression of vast controlled power. One minute he would be sitting as still as a rock, listening; the next, he would blur into motion as he jumped up and strode about. A secretary sat nearby, writing busily, at a table piled with waxed wooden tablets and rolls of papyrus.

The little man with the tax proposal was through at last. The next petitioner showed a toy-sized model of an armored four-horse chariot, with roof and sides covered over with iron scales. After listening, Dionysios said:

"This looks promising, O Simon. Make me a set of detailed drawings, with estimates of weight and cost. Then we shall go on from there. Rejoice! Who's next?"

The escort stepped forward and spoke in low tones to the tyrannos. At last Dionysios beckoned, and the two young engineers approached his chair.

"Are you the son of Megabyzos?" he abruptly asked Zopyros.

"Yes, sir."

"I know of him and should be glad to have him work for me. What chance of getting him to come?"

"I doubt if he would leave Taras."

"Too bad. What can you do?"

To his horror, Zopyros found that his voice refused to obey him. A gag of shyness choked him, so that he could only croak: "I—ah—I—"

"He's a good all-around engineer—" began Archytas, but Dionysios silenced him with a gesture.

"Come, come," said Dionysios. "I didn't expect an orator, but I thought you could at least answer a simple question. What can you do?"

"I—ah—" Then Zopyros burst out, hardly knowing why he said it: "I can make machines to cast missiles farther than any bow or sling can shoot. I needn't tell you, sir, the advantages of range in missile warfare."

"That is interesting," said Dionysios. "You shall have your chance. Are you sure you are not trying to learn pot making on a wine jar?"

"No, sir, I am not. What I say I can do, I can do."

"Well then, after so bold a claim, you had better produce something useful. By the bye, are you not a Pythagorean?"

"I have had the training," said Zopyros, wondering how the tyrannos knew. "But I'm not a very good one, I fear. I eat meat and, sometimes, even beans. I work on contracts for military engineering, not all of which, I think, the godlike Pythagoras would approve of."

"I do not care what you eat," said Dionysios. "But I do care about organized cults and clubs with political programs."

"Oh, sir, my Pythagoreanism is strictly non-political."

"Strictly?"

"Yes, sir. Rhegion is the only place I know of where the Pythagoreans have any political influence or interests."

"Your interests had better remain strictly non-political; for I, Dionysios, do not tolerate subversive conspiracy of any kind. Now you, young man!" He wheeled suddenly on Archytas, so that the latter started.

"Oh, ah, I'm an all-around engineer, too," said Archytas. "I can handle waterworks, fortifications, shipyards and docks—"

"Fortifications? My architect Pyres is designing a new fortress for the Epipolai, and he needs an assistant. You shall work for him. You, Master Zopyros, shall report to Drakon, my master of the Arsenal. Pyres and Drakon report to Philistos here, who commands this citadel; and Philistos reports to me. Prepare preliminary designs and estimates of the materials and workmen you will need."

Zopyros said: "Sir—ah—how much—ah—"

Dionysios flashed a brief smile. "Naturally, where there is no fee there is no art. How would two drachmai a day suit you?"

This was excellent pay for young men without established reputations. Both murmured their pleasure.

"I also pay bonuses to men who achieve outstanding results," added Dionysios. Then he spoke to his secretary. "Enter Zopyros son of Megabyzos and Archytas son of—what did you say your father's name was?—Mnesagoras, both of Taras, on the payroll at two drachmai a day. Prepare passes for them."

Zopyros said: "O President—ah—do you mind—we have always helped each other in our work."

"By all means continue to help each other. I shall be glad to see a little cooperation between different teams, instead of the usual jealousy and mutual interference. What count with me are *results*. I expect hard work and achievement, and I pay well for them. No la-di-da young gentlemen who want to spend their days in cultivated leisure, and who are horrified at the thought of working with their hands, need apply here. My men will tell you how I've worked with my own hands on our fortifications. Right now, our task is to strengthen the state against its foes. We never know when the enemy will strike."

"Enemy?" said Archytas innocently.

"*That* enemy," said Dionysios, pointing southwest, in the direction of Carthage. "The accursed moneygrubbers hate our superior Hellenic culture. They do but await an opportunity to destroy us. To hold our own against them, we must work harder than they. Well, that's enough oratory for today. You will find Drakon and Pyres in the Arsenal. Be in good health! Who is next?"

The secretary had meanwhile prepared the passes. These were two disks of clay, each with a hole through which a thong was passed to tie around the wearer's neck. On each disk, the secretary had scratched the name of one of the new employees, together with an identifying symbol.

The Arsenal, on the west side of Ortygia near the fabled spring of Arethousa, was a huge boxlike building of mud brick. Inside the building, along the two long walls, ran a pair of balconies. Down the center of the main floor, a row of columns paralleled the balconies to permit extra width. The balconies and the main floor beneath it were piled with military and nautical gear: spars, sails, rope, oars, anchors, and planking; jars of nails, tar, paint, and grease; spears, javelins, swords, shields, cuirasses, greaves, bows, arrows, and sling bullets. Steel and bronze glimmered in long lines where weapons and defenses hung on pegs in their racks.

The central part of the building was divided into working areas where teams of men strove at various tasks. The flames of forges lit the floor with a flickering, reddish light; the din of hammers made it necessary to shout. Here a man was pouring molten bronze from a crucible into a multiple mold for arrowheads; there another was shaving a pikestaff, looking along it endwise between strokes to test its trueness.

"Look at this!" said Archytas.

A huge blacksmith, naked but for a leathern apron, was holding a red-hot object on an anvil with tongs and hitting it with a hammer. As he came nearer, Zopyros saw that the object was a breastplate. Then he blinked. It was a breastplate of iron. A matching back plate lay, unfinished, on the earthen floor beside the anvil. Sparks flew as the smith hammered; black scale crumbled from the cooling surface.

"Excuse me," said Zopyros, "but are you making an *iron* cuirass?"

The breastplate ceased to glow. The smith dropped his hammer, picked up another pair of tongs, and with tongs in each hand pushed the breastplate back into the furnace. His apprentice, pumping a bellows, fanned the coals to a golden glow.

"That's right, son," said the smith. "Everybody says it can't be done, but I'll show 'em."

"Won't it be pretty heavy?"

"We'll try it first on the President. If he can manage it, then we'll see about the rest of you pygmies."

Zopyros turned away to hunt for Drakon. A voice called: "*Ea!* Aren't you the Tarentine who was on the *Muttumalein?*"

It was Alexis the Velian. The young man had been crouching over some large sheets of papyrus on the floor and drawing on them with a charcoal pencil. Now he rose and slapped the charcoal powder from his hands. Zopyros introduced Archytas.

"Glad to have you among us," said Alexis. "I told you the Dionysios would appreciate my talents. I'm planning the largest galleys ever built."

"Whose idea was that?" said Zopyros.

Alexis hesitated, then said: "The President made the original suggestion, but of course all the real mental work is mine."

"How can you make war galleys larger?" asked Archytas. "If you lengthen them more, they'll break their backs in a heavy sea."

"These ships will be, not longer, but wider," said Alexis smugly. "Instead of three rows of oars on each side, they shall have four or five rows!"

"Pest!" cried Archytas. "Why didn't I think of that? Just because standard warship had had three banks of oars ever since King Midas' reign, we've stupidly assumed that it would always have three banks."

Alexis said: "Don't feel bad; we can't all be the reincarnation of Daidalos. But, even without the divine spark, I don't doubt you will both turn out some good, sound engineering."

"Thanks," said Zopyros. "But, man, how will you ever get so many rowers packed into one hull and all moving in time? I can see difficulties."

"That's where the divine spark comes in. The greater the difficulty, the greater the glory. See you later." Alexis waved in a careless manner and turned back to his drawing.

Drakon, the master of the Arsenal, sat at a table on one of the balconies, whence he could see everything on the floor below. A small, knobby, wrinkled man, Drakon sat quietly while Zopyros explained his mission. At length he said:

"Let me explain how we operate. The workers in the Arsenal are divided into teams, each with an engineer—when we can find them—at its head. The teams are of two kinds. I suppose you'd call them—ah—let's see—production teams, which turn out weapons of kinds already known, and—what would be a word for inventing new things on purpose?"

"*Hê exetasis?*" said Zopyros. "Research?"

"That's it! Research teams. As far as I know, this is a completely new idea of the boss, to hire men in time of peace and set them to inventing things against the time of war. Even in the Punic cities and the lands of the Great King, where they have brilliant engineers, the rulers never do things like this. If a man can make arms and engines of the old kinds, they're satisfied, and he has to work like a helot to get his employers to try anything new.

"Now, our President stimulates competition among the various teams, by raises, bonuses, and medals. He's generous with those who really produce, believing that a good race horse deserves to be pampered. But you'd better bring out something that works, and not be too long about it. We've had too many starry-eyed, self-styled geniuses trying to build flying chariots that won't fly and diving ships that won't dive—or, if they do, won't come up again.

"The first thing you'll need is drawing materials: papyrus, charcoal, compass, straight-edge, strings, and so forth. Make out a list on this tablet, give it to me to sign, and take it to Achilleus, in stores. ..."

By the time Zopyros had obtained his materials, it was too late to start work. He found Archytas outside the Arsenal playing ball with three small boys; for Archytas had a way with children. Together the two young men watched the sunset across the Spring of Arethousa. In a rocky pool fringed by feathery papyrus reed and sundered from the nearby sea by a natural rampart of rock, the fresh waters of the spring churned and eddied.

"Do you suppose this water really comes all the way from Hellas?" said Archytas, dangling his feet.

Zopyros shrugged. "I suppose one could find out by dumping dye into the waters in Hellas and waiting to see whether it appears here. How did you make out with Pyres?"

"No difficulty, although there's not much scope for mathematics in planning this castle. I did pick up some gossip, however."

"Trust you. What did it say?"

"It seems there's bad feeling between the teams that produce old stuff and the teams that invent something new."

"Drakon and I," said Zopyros, "call them production teams and research teams respectively."

"Yes, illustrious sir. Anyway, the research men consider the production men a lot of stupid stick-in-the muds, while the production men call the research men a band of lunatics wasting the city's money on ridiculous ideas. Each tries to steal away the other's men and materials. Since I'm in production and you are in research, we're supposed to be like Athenian and Spartan. And speaking of fantastic ideas, do you think you can really make this missile thrower?"

"Yes."

"But how? How will it work?"

"I don't know. Curse it, I had to say something when the boss looked through me with those piercing gray eyes! All I could think of was my dream of Herakles and the Kyklops. Still—

> *A man must learn by practice of the art;*
> *For, though you think you know the thing full well,*
> *You have no certainty until you try.*

I suppose the first thing to try would be a simple flexible pole, like the one in my dream."

"What would you make it of?"

"I don't know, yet. Most woods are too stiff and brittle."

"They make bows of elm, ash, and yew," said Archytas. "They're not so good as a first-class horn bow, but horn is impractical for anything of the size you have in mind."

"Now all we have to do is find a supply of elm, ash, or yew within fifty leagues of here. I don't even know if these trees grow in Sicily."

"Hadn't you better start with a small model and go on from there to a full-sized one, as the man with the armored chariot was doing?"

"I suppose I had." Zopyros sighed deeply, wondering what he had let himself in for. "The shadow stands at ten feet, so we'd better start looking for dinner and a room to rent."

"Especially dinner," said Archytas. "I starve."

A ten-day later, Archytas found his friend on the archery range, with a carpenter and an apprentice, trying out a model missile thrower. This test had been held up for several days by a southerly duster, which had swirled the sands of the African deserts across the archery range with such violence as to make any sort of missile work impractical. The model consisted of a slender wooden rod, about three feet long, standing erect on a three-foot-square wooden platform and held upright by bracing at its base. The rod had a small fork at its upper end.

Into this fork, Zopyros was fitting the shaft of an arrow, just back of the head. Then he pulled the arrow back, bending the upright rod and trying to sight along the arrow. He released the arrow, and the rod snapped upright, tossing the arrow twenty feet or so.

"How goes it?" said Archytas. "Well begun is half done, as Pythagoras used to say."

"I don't know," said Zopyros. "It works well enough in the model, after you learn not to pull back too hard and break the mast. But in a full-sized engine ... The trouble is with the auxiliary devices, to make it possible to load, aim, cock, and discharge the device. Every plan I try to draw breaks down on those details."

"I should think you could simply bend a rope around the mast, pull it back with a windlass, and cut the rope."

"All very well for the first shot, but the boss will want something you can shoot over and over. You'd have to tie a new rope to the mast with every shot. After a while, you'd have a mass of short ends of rope flapping from the top of the mast like the hairs on a Celt's head. But wait—you've given me an idea. If there were a kind of trough, with a groove in its upper surface, along which the missile could slide, you could tie the rope to the missile—"

"And how would you get it to untie itself just as the mast snapped upright?"

"Out upon you! You spoil all my divine inspirations, Archytas. How would you do it?"

"I've been thinking along different lines. I'd make a kind of giant sling, attached to the rim of a chariot wheel, whirling round and round ..."

He went into an excited description, which Zopyros soon demolished by showing that the device would have to be mounted on top of a tall tower, to clear the ground in its swings, and would therefore be of little use. Back and forth they argued, throwing up one idea after another and knocking them all down again.

Suddenly Archytas clapped a hand to his forehead. "Herakles, I almost forgot! The President is giving a banquet for his engineers in the town hall tonight. We're invited."

"Then we had better leave a little early, to visit the bathhouse."

In the town hall, Zopyros found the tyrannos moving affably among his guests. However, he still kept a soldier on each side and another at his back, so that he could not circulate so easily as an ordinary host. Dionysios knew the name of every engineer and had some idea of how each project was going: "How is that design for a fourer coming, Alexis? ... Have you finished the first story yet, Pyres? ... I like that new shield design very well, Hippias ... How about the missile engine, Zopyros?"

"I—I've run into unexpected technical difficulties, sir ..."

"Yes, yes; that is to be expected. Keep at it. I think you have a sound idea, if only you can overcome the difficulties. What you do not know, find out!"

After a round of spiced wine, the guests reclined on their couches. Zopyros was trying to count the total number when Archytas beside him said:

"I see our young genius of a shipwright is bending every effort to charm the Arsenal master."

Zopyros looked across the room at Alexis, who shared a couch with Drakon and who was talking and laughing with all the animation of a paid entertainer. Zopyros said:

"Plague! We should have thought to grab the place next to the old boy."

"I did," said Archytas, "but the polluted Velian got there first. I can see where that young man will go far in the organization."

Dionysios poured a libation and led a prayer to Hephaistos, patron god of artificers. Archytas whispered: "He doesn't give a moldy olive for the gods, but he'll stick at nothing to keep up the spirits of his servants."

Dinner included fried squid, hare stuffed with chopped liver and brains, and kid stewed in milk and honey, all generously laced with fish sauces and condiments. After the meal came the diluted wine along with the dancing and singing girls.

The engineers were in a mellow mood when Dionysios stood up and rapped on his goblet. "Rejoice, my friends! We now have a little business to discuss. Remember that we hold the ramparts of civilization against encircling barbarism, which ever seeks to break in upon us. Eighty years ago it nearly succeeded, when the Great King conspired with the abandoned baby-burners"—he jerked his head in the direction of Carthage—"to hit us east and west at the same time. You know how we barely turned them back at Himera and Salamis and Plataia.

"Perhaps it never occurred to you that the death of Prince Cyrus at Cunaxa was a stroke of luck for Hellas, despite the fact that ten thousand Hellenes—the more shame to them!—fought for this Persian prince. For, they tell me, Prince Cyrus had in him the makings of a great king—as great, perhaps, as his namesake, who founded the Empire. And, had he overthrown his brother and become king, that had been a black day for Hellas.

"But the god-detested barbarians never give up. We must always be on our guard. And you engineers are the very boss on the shield of Hellas. For the time is coming when wars will be won, not by him who puts the most spearmen in the line, but by him who commands the newest and deadliest weapons. And you are the men who invent these things. I need you and the others like you.

"Enough of that. The old-timers among you have heard my harangues on this subject often enough. Now, let us talk of other things. First, the meeting is open for beneficial suggestions to increase production. Speak up!"

There was a moment of silence, while the tyrannos' eagle gaze roved the room. Then a man held up a hand.

"Yes, Menedemos?"

"Please, sir, that pile of trash against the east wall of the Arsenal is a fire hazard. Shouldn't it be removed?"

"Indeed it should." Dionysios nodded to his secretary, who scribbled. "Next?"

Another man wanted more slaves assigned to moving materials about the shipyards. Another urged a patrol of soldiers around the Arsenal to rout out slaves and apprentices who sneaked off to loaf or sleep in corners.

When the engineers ran out of suggestions, Dionysios said: "Now I have the pleasure of announcing an award. Master Pausanias, come forward with your masterpiece!"

The burly smith approached the dais, holding the new iron cuirass, polished to mirror brightness, Archytas whispered behind his hand:

"I hope for Pausanias' sake that it fits."

It did. The guards helped the smith to put it on the tyrannos, over his head, and to buckle the straps at the sides. Dionysios drew a breath and slapped the breastplate with a resounding *bong*. He looked magnificent in it.

"I had been told," he said, "that no smith in the world could forge a complete cuirass of iron, because of the difficulty of working that metal in such large pieces. But, as you see, Master Pausanias has done it. As far as I know, he is the first. Here, sir, is a small token of my regard!"

Around the smith's neck, Dionysios hung a golden disk on the end of a golden chain. The smith, ducking his head and twisting one toe back and forth like an embarrassed schoolboy, said:

"O President, I—ah—anyway, thanks a lot, sir. Now do you want me to start production of these cuirasses?"

Dionysios cocked his head. "That is something I shall have to think about. "I may like this so well that I shall wish to keep its use exclusively to myself. In any case, you have done a noble piece of work."

As the smith retired, Dionysios said: "Three more matters before we break up. First: There is entirely too much loose talk in the city about our plans and projects. Too many of you, when you go home at night, hunt up the nearest drink shop, sit with cronies, and tell everything you know in a voice that would carry from Karia to Carthage. By Zeus the King, no wonder foreigners call us garrulous Greeks! I have never believed the tale that Pythagoras compelled his disciples to keep silent for five years, for I doubt that the God himself could render Hellenes mute for so long.

"After this, there shall be no more discussion, off the island, of what goes on at the citadel. What boots it to devise new weapons against implacable foes, if we describe them to these foes so they can equip themselves likewise? I should not like to make you live on the island in barracks; but, unless this loose talk stops, I shall be compelled to do so.

"The second matter is this: Our production of standard military items, like shields and spears, should be increased and, I am sure, can be increased even without buying more slaves or hiring more free workers. I have been considering why the Athenian potters can undersell all the others in the Inner Sea, although their pottery is finer and shipping is costly. The reason is that they use a new method of production—mass production, we might call it.

"Have you ever seen an Athenian pottery? I have not been to Athens, but my agents have described one to me. Instead of having each workman make a complete pot, the Athenians split up the task among a number of specialists. One man mixes the clay, another turns the wheel, another throws and molds the clay, another gives the pot its finished form, another paints it, and so on. Each worker, by constant repetition, becomes more expert in his particular task than he could be if he scattered his talents among several operations. Working thus, a given number of potters can turn out twice as many pots as they could if they worked each on his own. Now I, Dionysios, want you to think about applying this lesson to the making of warlike gear.

"Lastly: I have tried several means of signaling the start of work in the morning, and none works very well. The trouble is that all signals depend upon some human being to blow a trumpet or strike a gong; and human beings are fallible. As things stand, people straggle in over a period of an Egyptian hour, and those who come early cannot work efficiently because those who should fetch them materials or otherwise help them have not yet arrived.

"Now, I want some device that can be started in the evening, when I can see to its setting, and that shall give its signal the following daybreak without further attention. Think hard, my friends!

"And speaking of getting to work promptly in the morning, tomorrow is a working day, so we must all seek out our beds. Good night!"

Crossing the drawbridge on the way to their rented room, Archytas asked Zopyros: "What do you really think of the big boss?"

"I have mixed feelings, Archytas. Sometimes I think him the most brilliant man I have ever known. And he certainly can manage men. But, when he starts ranting against the Phoenicians, I don't know. I've known enough of them to realize they're not monsters, despite their horrible religion. If our aims were peaceful, I could happily spend my life in such a place, inventing and designing new things. What's your opinion?"

"Dionysios is one of those who, like the Athenians a few years ago, justify themselves on the ground that it's a law of nature to rule wherever one can. Calling his tyranny a 'directed democracy' doesn't change its nature.

"*To the wise, a throne has no allure; to joy*
In power is to be depraved thereby."

"Look who's quoting! How about your own political ambitions?"

"I have never aspired to be king of the Tarentines, as Dionysios is king of the Syracusans in all but name. Politics is something else."

Zopyros shrugged. "Play politics if you like. It doesn't interest me."

"It should! Politics is how any large group of people manage their affairs."

"Which they do badly, under any form of government."

"No doubt, but that's no excuse for being worse villains than we need be. Therefore I wonder if we are doing the right thing."

"How do you mean?"

Archytas: "Helping this tyrannos to develop machines for killing our fellow men. You know how the Man felt about aggressive warfare."

"Dionysios talks only of defense against Carthaginian aggression," said Zopyros.

"Do you really believe him?"

"I suppose not. It's a logical flaw in the divine Pythagoras' argument: every belligerent claims to be acting in self-defense; therefore it's always the other party who is the aggressor."

"Except among barbarians like our friend Segovax," said Archytas. "They're at least honest. They come right out and say: 'You've got something I want, so I will kill you for it. But I'm still uneasy about working for this eagle-eyed tyrannos, despite our handsome salaries."

Zopyros shrugged. "Men have always killed each other, for reasons good or bad, and I suppose they always will. If we didn't help him, he'd get other engineers. As for his tyranny, I think that if a people are ruled by a tyrannos, it's only what they deserve. It means there are so many knaves and fools among them that they're not competent to govern themselves. The Man said—"

"You always oversimplify political questions," said Archytas. "That's because you have no experience at politics. I know something about it at first hand. The usual reason for a tyrannos is not so much the depravity of men, but the fact that the rich have borne down too heavily on the poor and stopped them from bettering themselves. Then some demagogue says: 'Follow me, fellow citizens! Kill the rotten-rich, divide up their possessions, and live in ease and luxury forever!' And the poor boobies believe him."

"That's what I said; the masses are so stupid that they're just as well off under a strong master—"

"No, it isn't the same. You forget that, once in power, the tyrannos concerns himself much more with enlarging and securing his power than with the welfare of the masses. To protect his power, he goes to any extremes of treachery and cruelty, like Phalaris of Akragas roasting people alive in his bronzen bull."

"I should like to see that interesting piece of bronze work," said Zopyros, "but I hear the Carthaginians took it away when they sacked Akragas. However, Dionysios has done a lot for the Syracusans, and they certainly seem to admire him."

"Some do, no doubt. But many proclaim their love because they're afraid to complain. Whoever knows black from white knows what happens to Dionysios' critics."

"I thought it was years since he had any opponents killed?"

Archytas glanced over his shoulder and lowered his voice. "Yes, but they remember the last time. He bribed a Spartan named Aristos to make the rounds of the drink shops, treating people and damning Dionysios. Naturally, Aristos got many to agree. He kept a list of names, and one fine day Dionysios arrested the lot. He drowned Nikoteles, the noisiest of his foes, and put such fear into the rest that they've kept quiet ever since. You must admit it takes more than ordinary terror to make a Hellene stop talking."

"Why does he favor drowning as a method of execution?"

"Dionysios drowns people because he loves neatness and order. Hanging turns them an ugly blue, while stoning and beheading are messy and attract flies. A drowned man, on the other hand, looks almost as good as new. ... But enough of this Stygian talk. Have you heard from your girl yet?"

"No, although I've written twice. You know how it is, sending letters by sailors, who get drunk and lose ... Archytas!" He suddenly grabbed the arm of his companion, who uttered a yelp. "I just had an idea! Why am I trying to make my missile engine the hard way?"

"I'll ask; why are you? But please don't grab me like that on a dark street! I thought we were going to be murdered."

"Remember that statue of Apollon in front of the temple, with his drawn bow?"

"Yes."

"If I used a solid post—corresponding to that statue—instead of those limber rods I've been working with, and I mounted the bow on some sort of pivot ..." Zopyros rattled off details and suggestions at such speed that Archytas cried:

115

"Help! Help! Wait until you reach some writing materials, to take notes of all these ideas! I can't possibly remember—"

"Then let's hurry! Dear Herakles, I've wasted a ten-day on a false scent. Never mind bed; I want to get this stuff down. For the experimental models, I can draw a couple of standard bows from stock. Then I'll try two alternative plans: pivoting the bow about the vertical axis and about the horizontal axis ..."

"It's all very well for you to say: 'Never mind bed,'" grumbled Zopyros' friend. "You're only half human anyway, like the bronze giant Talos who guarded Crete. But I can't live on bright ideas alone."

The spring days lengthened into summer, the shepherds and goatherds drove their flocks to higher pastures, and the long green slopes of the Heraean Mountains began to turn a golden buff as the grass died. With the coming of summer, the second year of the ninety-fifth Olympiad began, when Aristokrates was Archon of Athens.

Three model engines stood on the archery range. Each consisted of a platform, a four-foot post standing upright on the platform, and a bow fastened in various ways to the top of the post. At the rear edge of each platform was tackle of cords, hooks, and pulleys.

A puffy wind whipped across the archery range, stirring swirls of dust. A young dog, barking, chased a scrap of papyrus whirled round about by an eddy. At the far end, a squad of soldiers did spear drill to shouted commands. From the Arsenal and the shipyards came the clatter of tools. Zopyros sat alone on a stool with his chin on his fists, glowering at the models.

Archytas, plump and glowing with good spirits, approached. "O Zopyros!"

"Rejoice!" said Zopyros in a lugubrious tone. "What brings you here?"

"We ran out of stone—the polluted quarrymen let us down—so Pyres gave me the afternoon off. Do you know what I've done?"

"No; what?"

"I think I've solved the problem of doubling the cube!"

"You mean an abstract, mathematical cube; not a real one?"

"Of course I mean a geometrical cube!"

"Well, I hope the boss hangs a medal round your neck, although I don't suppose he will."

"Nonsense! I did it not for medals, but for the advancement of knowledge and my own curiosity. Man was made to investigate the universe."

A movement caught Archytas' eye and he turned; so did Zopyros. At the far end of the range, where the soldiers were drilling, Drakon, the master of the Arsenal, was strolling with Alexis. They had their arms about each other's necks, and the older man was giggling like an adolescent.

"Guess who'll be promoted next," said Archytas. "If that's the price of advancement, I'll stay on the bottom rowing bench. What's the matter with you, old boy? You look as if you'd been bitten by a Tartessian eel."

"My troubles are as many as the sands of the shore," replied Zopyros.

"Well, the good are not immune to sorrow. What grieves you?"

"I can't make these cursed things work! It's easy to rig a tackle to draw the bowstring back. The problem is to make the arrow stay in place while the mechanism releases the string. Or rather, that's one problem; the other is the release mechanism itself. Either the thing lets go too soon, while you're still cranking the windlass to pull back the bowstring; or it won't let go at all when you want it to; or you have to yank the release lever so hard that the bow wobbles and spoils your aim. What's worse, there's no solid support for the arrow, which falls to the ground at the slightest jar."

Archytas stood in thought for a while, then said: "That night when you first suggested using a bow instead of a single casting arm, you also said something about a fixed beam or trough, with a groove in which the projectile could slide back and forth."

Zopyros jumped up, clapping a hand to his forehead. "How could I have forgotten! I must be losing what little mind I have. Of course that's the answer! That trough would serve both functions: to hold the missile steady, and to mount the mechanism. It'll also brace the upright structure; these single posts tend to work loose. I'll find my men and put them to work at once."

"Where are they now?"

"Alexis wanted them to help make models of his super-galleys, and I had no immediate use for them. So I lent them to him." Zopyros started down the range with long strides. When he came within shouting distance of the strollers, he called: "*Ea*, Alexis!"

"What is it?" said the shipwright with a frown.

Zopyros hurried closer. "If you don't mind, I should like Skylax and Hermon back. I have urgent work for them."

Alexis looked down his nose, as well as he could at a taller man. "So, my dear Zopyros, have I. You shall have them back when I am good and ready to send them back, and not before."

"Well, grind me to sausage! When I sent them to you, it was with a clear understanding—"

"That I should keep them as long as I needed—"

"It was not!"

"It was! The God rot you, go away and stop bothering busy people!"

"Lying knave!"

"Bungling incompetent!"

As the two young men began thrusting their faces forward and clenching their fists, Drakon pushed between them, shouting:

"That's enough! Hold your tongues, you two! You're quarreling over the shadow of an ass."

The disputants began to drench their superior in arguments, until he stamped and screamed: "*Shut up*, Zeus blast you! I'm the manager here. Now hear my judgment. Alexis is right in one way: that it wastes a workman's time to keep jerking him from job to job, like a fish on a line. So he'll keep the two men for the time being. Now, don't you hoist the red flag at me, Master Zopyros! I'll find you another carpenter and helper as soon as I can; there's always somebody who hasn't enough to do. Get along about your business, both of you, and not another word."

Alexis strolled toward the Arsenal, smirking. Zopyros returned to Archytas.

"Lover boy buggered me good and proper," he growled as he came up.

"You mean he kept your workers?"

"Exactly. Drakon promised me others, but that means breaking them in to my way of doing things. What's more, they'll probably be the men nobody else wants, for various good reasons."

Archytas clucked. "Alexis already has more men under him than any other research engineer. He can always find pretexts for adding more to his team, although half of them stand around doing nothing. I suppose he reckons that, if he can only collect enough, he can go to Philistos and say: 'My dear sir, a man of my vast responsibilities should obviously be paid more than mere tinkerers like those Tarentines.' I'm sorry I'm not with you in the Arsenal, because I can foresee these political angles."

"A murrain on this intrigue! If we could only prove that he's incompetent—"

"Don't count on that. He's a bright lad who knows his shipbuilding. But then, prosperity is harder to endure becomingly than adversity. ... Here's somebody for you."

A soldier approached with a small roll of papyrus. "You Zopyros son of Meg-somebody?"

"Yes."

"I've got a letter for you. ... Thanks."

As the soldier put his tip in his purse and walked off, Zopyros opened the letter with trembling hands. Then he gave Archytas a joyful slap on the back that almost knocked the smaller man down. "Archytas! It's Korinna! Listen to this!

All is well here, and I hope all is well with you, too. Father's health is no worse. He has received a courteous letter from your father and has opened negotiations for our marriage. On one point, however, Father is adamant. He insists that my son be recovered; and, to tell the truth, I shall never be happy without the boy. With my parents' knowledge and consent, I send you my love. Farewell.

"She loves me! She loves me! Alexis and his ships can go to the crows; she loves me!"

Zopyros bounded about the field like a satyr in spring, shouting and waving his arms. He sang in rasping, out-of-tune voice:

"Yes—loving is a painful thrill,
And not to love more painful still;
But oh, it is the worst of pain,
To love and not be lov'd again!"

"Calm down, old boy!" said Archytas. "You're not the first man in the world to be in love. I've been in love with three different girls already since coming to Syracuse."

Zopyros knew that Archytas had already made a score of friends in Syracuse. Zopyros had few indeed. Luckily for him, he had obtained access to Philistos' library, the best in Sicily. He spent his feast days in the home of his superior, pulling books out of their pigeon-holes and poring over them by the hour, unrolling them with one hand while he rolled them up with the other. He was already well into the third book of Herodotos' *History*. With a sigh he asked:

"Do you suppose I could get leave for a quick trip to Messana?"

"Perhaps; but you'd return to find that Alexis had taken over your project in addition to his own."

"I haven't seen Korinna for months! By Zeus on Olympos, I can't go on like this!"

"You can always go to the whorehouse with me when the strain becomes too great."

"And you call yourself a Pythagorean? Anyway, I don't seem to care for whoring any more."

"Genetyllides stiffen your yard! But, if you want to hold your job, you'd better stick."

"Bugger the job! Why don't I throw it up and go back to Taras? My family would be glad to have me back."

"Not so fast! Think of your future, which is hers, too. First thrive, then wive."

"Oh, corruption! I can't think; I'm too upset."

"Look, best one, you know that even a god's judgment is impaired by love. Don't do anything until you've calmed down and thought it over."

"I suppose you're right. But the first slack time that comes along ..."

* * *

Somehow, Zopyros rounded up enough help so that, by doing much of the carpentry himself, he built another model. This had the same thick post as the previous models. The bow was clamped horizontally atop this post. Another timber sloped aft from the top of the post to the rear edge of the platform. A deep groove on its upper surface ran the length of this timber, on the rear of which was mounted a winch to draw the bow. A hinged bronze trigger formed a separate part, which could be engaged with the bowstring in its cocked position and then disengaged by a handle to release the string.

Zopyros demonstrated the model to Dionysios. He placed an arrow in the groove, winched back the bowstring until the bow was taut, engaged the trigger, slackened off the windlass and unhooked the cocking gear, and pulled the release handle. The bow twanged; the arrow soared down the range.

"Ha!" said one of Dionysios' bodyguards. "By the gods, I can shoot an arrow farther than that, without all this fornicating machinery!"

Zopyros smiled. "You realize, O President, that this is only a pilot model."

"How big will your final engine be?"

"Since I plan to use a standard javelin for my missile, the finished missile launcher will be about thrice the size of this."

"Will it shoot thrice as far, though?"

"I don't know, sir. It will certainly shoot farther than a man can throw a javelin in the ordinary manner."

"Go ahead. We shall see what happens."

"That's fine, sir. But—ah—"

"What is it?"

"If I can have a few good workmen, it'll go faster."

"How many have you now?"

"Only occasional help, such as I can borrow from the other engineers. Most of the work I do myself."

"Zeus almighty! That is not efficient. It's fine to be willing to work with your hands in an emergency; but I hired you as a thinker. Have you asked for more men?"

"Yes, sir; but I'm told there is none to spare."

The tyrannos frowned. "Indeed? I'll have a word with Master Drakon about this. I want to see how this thing turns out."

"In that case, O President, I shall also need the help of your chief bowyer, to design the bow."

"You shall have him, too. What do you call this device?"

"So far I've called it simply a *katapeltḗs*, a hurler."

"A catapult it shall be, then. Push this project as fast as you can. Be in good health!"

The chief bowyer threw up his hands. "What god ever dropped me into a nest of madmen? I've been making bows for thirty years, young man, and I've never heard the like. Zeus and Apollon, a bow ten cubits long! Whom would you get to shoot it? Herakles?"

"No, he'd be too small," answered Zopyros with a smile. "Hadn't you heard? The boss has enlisted the services of the giant Polyphemos for his next campaign."

"But I thought Odysseus blinded Polyphemos, hundreds of years ago!"

"Oh, his eye grew back again; you know these demigods—"

"Young man, are you making fun of me?"

"Look, Master Prothymion, if you don't like my little joke, I withdraw it. Consider it unsaid. Now, you've seen those model catapults I've been tinkering with on the archery range?"

"Those fool things? Yes."

"Well, I'm ready to build a full-sized one, and for that I need a ten-cubit bow. Can you make me one?"

"Umm—well—I don't know. ... These engines of yours will never take the place of well-trained archers. Not that any Hellenes are what you'd call well-trained archers." The bowyer spat on the dirt floor of the Arsenal. "They're all afraid somebody will mistake them for Paris of Troy, so they sneer at archery. The Persians, now, appreciate a scientific weapon—"

"Exactly!" interrupted Zopyros. "I'm the only man around here, besides yourself, who really understands what you can do with the bow principle. So, naturally, I come to you."

"We-ell, now that you put it that way, I'll give your idea some thought. ..."

Afterward, Archytas asked Zopyros: "Did he really agree to build your superbow?"

"He said he'd try. I told him I was the only toxophilite besides himself in Syracuse, and after that we got along fine."

"Congratulations; you're learning," said Archytas. "I'd have bet a stater against an obolos that he'd find some way to shear your oars. Prothymion is a hardshelled conservative who hates new inventions and finds an infinity of reasons for not doing what he doesn't wish to do."

As the month of Metageitnion[3] wore on and the heat of summer declined, it became rare to see men strolling naked about the streets of Syracuse. When the Rhegines and Messanians invaded Syracusan territory, Dionysios mustered his army and marched north to meet them. However, the allied army, in characteristic Greek fashion, broke up through dissension. In the end, both sides marched home without bloodshed.

In the meantime Zopyros finished his drawings, while his carpenters got to work with saws and adzes on the main timbers of the large catapult. One day, when he and Archytas were studying the work in its corner of the Arsenal, Zopyros said:

"Archytas, are you very busy these days?"

"Not really. Fort Buryalos is so nearly finished that Pyres could do without me. But you know officials. No one wants to let a subordinate out of his grasp if he can help it."

"Well, there's going to be a slack time here, too. It'll be another month at least before these boys get the catapult ready to test. Meanwhile, there's nothing for me to do but look in on them once a day to make sure they haven't committed some colossal blunder, like installing Prothymion's bow backward."

"So?"

"I thought I'd ask the Drakon for a ten-day's leave to go to Messana. During that time, I should dearly love it if you'd make a daily inspection of the work. You've sweated with me so long over this thing that you know the plans as well as I. Can I leave you to watch the nets?"

"Why, I should be glad—"

"Master Zopyros!" said the voice of a barbarian mercenary. "Big boss says he want you in palace, right away."

---

3   Approximately August.

Zopyros exchanged a puzzled glance with Archytas. "I wonder what I've done wrong?" he said. "Oh, well, here's the way to find out." He set out after the soldier.

In the courtyard of the palace he found the tyrannos sitting with Philistos and two other men whose faces were familiar: Segovax the Celt and Evnos the Karian ransomer. The latter jumped up and seized Zopyros' hands.

"Rejoice, Master Zopyros!" he cried. "It's a pleasure to see you again. So you took my advice, after all!"

Zopyros greeted the others and, at Dionysios' invitation, sat down, too. A slave passed wine.

"O Zopyros," said Dionysios, "Evnos has just returned from his tour of Old Hellas. He has brought back four or five engineers and an equal number of skilled artificers. After scouring the land, he says, these are all he could persuade to come."

Zopyros said: "Surely there are many such in the great cities of Hellas!"

"There are. But some are satisfied with their present earnings. Some are anchored by familial obligations. Some are terrified of sea voyages. Lastly, some dislike my advanced form of government, my—ah—directed democracy. They prefer their old, inefficient ways of running their affairs, wobbling unstably between oligarchic oppression and mob rule." Dionysios took a sip—Zopyros had noted that he was a sparing drinker—and continued: "My other recruiter, Matris, has already scoured the Greek cities of Italy. To glean the same ground twice were inefficient, yielding but small returns. And we cannot wait for a new generation of engineers to grow up."

"What then, sir?" asked Zopyros.

"The barbarian tribes would know no more of engineering than the jackdaw knows of the lyre. There remains but one rich, untapped source of technical talent within our reach. You can guess what I mean."

"You mean Carthaginian territory?"

"Exactly." Dionysios gave one of his rare smiles. "That were a joke for the gods, to snatch the help I need from under the noses of the enemy!"

"But, sir, if you so dislike and distrust Phoenicians, how could you bear to have them working on your secret projects?"

"For one thing, I should keep close watch on them. I'd make them live on the island. For another, I do not fear that they will desert merely because I may be forced to make war upon some of their own cities. These degenerate moneygrubbers are men without honor or patriotism. They would slit their own mothers' throats if you paid them enough. But many of the branded knaves are nonetheless excellent technicians.

"This is beside the point; I did not call you here to lecture you on foreign policy. I am sending a recruiting expedition deep into Punic territory—to the Punic cities of western Sicily and to Carthage itself. This expedition shall comprise these two men and yourself. In soliciting such people, you will of course say nothing of our preparations for defense. Stress the peaceful aspects of your work—the architecture, the waterworks, and the like.

Zopyros' jaw dropped. He had been rehearsing his request for leave to visit Messana, and now he was to travel a hundred leagues in quite a different direction! He started to utter a hot protest but softened it in the telling. "Why me, sir? I thought my present work was urgent."

"I have my eye on your present work, Zopyros. For one thing, your carpenters will need only minor supervision until they complete the full-scale model. For another, amongst all my people, you three are the only men who speak Punic fluently. Although you could not pass for authentic Phoenicians, your knowledge of that tongue will make you more effective in explaining the rewards of working for Dionysios."

"O President! May I not wait—let's say a ten-day—to take care of some personal business?"

"No, you may not," said Dionysios in a voice like a well-honed blade. "Autumn is upon us. Even a day's delay might strand you in Africa when the shipping lines close down for winter."

"Why must three go, sir?"

"Because of the hazards of recruiting in a hostile land, I would not send one man alone. Evnos has the most experience in travel and in delicate negotiations. Therefore he shall decide on your routes, sailings, quarters—everything to do with travel—and he shall make the first contacts with the local people wherever you go. Since you know the most about engineering and can thus judge the worth of the men you solicit, you shall have the final choice of men. And Segovax is a seasoned warrior who, if it comes to swords' points, can best lead you in cutting your way out. Hence he shall be your leader in battle or flight. Besides"—he smiled faintly again—"with three men, if an accident does befall, at least one of you might get away to tell me the outcome."

As Dionysios spoke, while Zopyros was still boiling with suppressed rage over losing the leave he had promised himself, an idea struck him with blinding brilliance. If he were sent to recruit in the Punic lands, he might—Fate willing—snatch young Ahiram from his father after all! He covered his exuberance by a slow, deep draft of wine. When his mind stopped its dizzy spin, Zopyros raised his goblet, saying:

"To a rich harvest of Punic engineers! When do we start, sir?"

CARTHAGE

They sat around a table in the courtyard of Evnos' house in Syracuse. On the table stood three small piles of coins, and Evnos held a bag of coins in his lap. He was placing a coin from the bag on each of the three piles in turn, round and round. At last he said:

"There you are! Your pile must last you the journey. The total ship's fares shouldn't come to more than five drachmai, and three oboloi a day will feed you if you don't demand peacocks' tongues."

Zopyros, counting his pile, asked: "What does one do if there is money left over at the end of the voyage?"

Evnos grinned at Segovax. "Isn't it nice to meet a man so young and unspoilt? To answer your question, my boy, somehow there never is any left."

Zopyros asked: "When do we leave, and where do we go?"

Evnos: "We leave as soon as I can buy passage; we sail for Carthage itself."

"Why don't we try the Phoenician cities of Sicily first? They're closer, and if we had good luck in them we might not need to go to Africa at all."

"There are, true, a few engineers in the smaller Phoenician colonies, like Panormos and Utica and Tunis. But why waste time in these little places when we can strike for the big prize? Engineers are not like landowners and priests and politicians, tied to one place by their interests. Able engineers go where the big money is, and in the Phoenician world that means Carthage. There we shall find more engineers than in all the other cities of New Phoenicia put together."

"But"—Zopyros in desperation became insistent—"the Phoenician cities of Sicily are on the way to Carthage. Why don't we take a ship to Messana, then one west to Panormos and Motya? Thus we should make a clean sweep of them. That's logical."

"No. I have made up my mind. If we don't find enough good men in Carthage, it will be time enough to try the other cities."

Zopyros frowned in thought. He did not want to quarrel at the outset with Evnos, who had been given authority over travel plans. Yet he had to find some argument to persuade the Karian to stop at Motya so that he could see how things stood in Elazar's home.

"Evnos!"

"Yes?"

"I know of a man in Motya who might be able to shorten our search."

"Who? How?"

"He's a big building contractor, named Elazar. He would know all the leading engineers of New Phoenicia."

"A house builder? I doubt it. Such men work from a few standard plans by rule of thumb. They never bother with engineers or architects."

"From what I hear, Elazar is more than that. He's had experience with things like harbor works and city walls."

Evnos stared at the pile of silver before him. He scratched a fleabite, flipped a tetradrachma, caught it, and flipped it again. At last he said;

"All right, you win. Most ships plying between here and Carthage put in at one city or another of western Sicily anyway. We'll see if your contractor knows a technician from a tadpole."

At the western tip of Sicily, a long, irregular peninsula, the Aigithallos, curved down from the north to inclose the wide, shallow Bay of Motya, ten furlongs from east to west and forty from north to south. In the midst of this bay stood Motya, an island as round as a Boiotian loaf and four furlongs across. A long causeway ran north from the island and joined it to the mainland near the base of the Aigithallos.

To the east and south, the green Sicilian coastal plain spread far and flat, checkered with fields and groves. To the northeast, five leagues away, the towering crag of Eryx broke the level horizon. To the west, the three isles called Aegates lay low in the sea.

A wall of massive limestone blocks, twenty cubits high, surrounded Motya. Twenty tall square towers rose from the wall at intervals. As their ship approached, Zopyros saw that the type of masonry varied in different parts of the wall. Some stretches were made of smoothly dressed stones, while in others the stones had been left rough on their outer surface. The size of the stones and the evenness of the courses also varied, showing that the wall had been built and rebuilt over the centuries. Greek mercenary soldiers walked the wall and guarded the gates.

The skyward-thrusting houses of the city loomed over the wall. Surrounded by water, Motya could not expand outward as its population grew. Hence it grew upward, into apartment houses of four and even five stories. Zopyros thought of Tyre. There was the same ponderous stonework, the same air of plain, graceless, severe, inartistic efficiency.

The ship docked at the south side of the island city, where a ledge of rock had been trimmed away and built up to make a wharf, between the wall and the waters of the bay. Nearby, a gap in the wall gave access to the cothon or inner harbor. Through the gap, Zopyros glimpsed a number of triremes crowded together. A raised portcullis, like that of Dionysios' stronghold, guarded the cothon and its massed ships of war and commerce.

They hired a porter to carry most of their gear and, after a few inquiries, set out for Elazar's house. As they walked down the street, Segovax craned his neck to gaze uneasily upward at the towering apartment houses on either side.

"*Ara!*" he exclaimed. "It makes my balls creep just to be walking along here, and me a big strong warrior. Are you sure, Evnos darling, that these monstrous houses will not topple over on us?"

"They haven't yet," said Evnos. "I thought you'd been in Punic cities before?"

"Indeed and I have, in Panormos and Solous; but in them places they don't stack houses one atop the other. One house at a time is enough for me."

It was midafternoon. The narrow streets swarmed with Motyans, some in long loose robes, some in plain tunics, and some in singlets and kilts. Nearly all wore dome-shaped, conical, or cylindrical caps. There were also far more women abroad than in a Greek city, strolling unattended, shopping and gossiping. Many wore fine fabrics and glittering jewels. A couple of men on a street corner were haggling over a bit of business, with expressive shrugs and movements of hands, noses, and eyebrows. Their guttural speech sounded like the purring of two large cats.

The porter stopped in front of an apartment house and set down his burdens. "Elazar's house," he said, jerking his head toward the front door and extending his palm.

Zopyros knocked. The door was opened by a stocky, long-robed man with a bushy, black, scented beard sweeping his chest and a small golden ring in his nose. On one thumb he wore the ornate ring of a steward. The man said in Punic:

"Wherein can I favor you, my masters?"

Zopyros said: "Is this the house of Elazar ben-Ahiram?"

"In sooth it is, good my lords, but the master is not here. He has taken his small son back to Carthage, to dwell with him in his house there. I am his steward, Abarish ben-Hanno. What business would you have with him?"

"We are agents of the President of Syracuse, seeking to hire men of certain skills; and we deemed that Elazar could help us in this quest."

Abarish bowed low, until his beard almost touched the ground. "This house is honored! Natheless, I fear you must needs seek my master in his present domicile."

Zopyros and Evnos exchanged a long look. The latter said: "You see now, young fellow, we might better have gone to Carthage in the first place. All we have accomplished here is a delay while we hunt for other passage." To Abarish he said: "Pray, where shall we find a good inn?"

The Phoenician beetled his brows in thought. "Abdagon's is not bad—but hold!" He spoke to Zopyros. "Are you not, good my sir, a Hellene?"

"Yes," said Zopyros, "I am called Zopyros the Tarentine." He introduced his companions.

Abarish laid a finger beside his beringed nose and squinted with an expression of self-conscious craftiness. "I knew it from your speech, albeit you speak Punic well indeed. Know you aught of what the Greeks call philosophy?"

"My father gave me a good education. I studied under the great Philolaos." Zopyros frowned a little, since it did not seem to him that such matters were any of the steward's business.

Abarish's manner underwent a change. Hitherto he had been polite and helpful, but in a wary, impersonal way. Now he smiled all over, bowed, opened the front door wide, and made sweeping motions with his hands to indicate that the three should enter.

"Mot take all inns!" he said. "Here shall you stay until you depart hence for Carthage. The hospitality of the house of Elazar, poor though it be, is yours to command!"

Zopyros exchanged another glance with Evnos, who shrugged and said: "Why not?" They filed in, murmuring polite protests. Taking off his wide-brimmed hat, Zopyros stared about him. A slight shudder took him as he thought of Korinna as mistress of this house.

When he lived in Motya, Elazar occupied the entire ground floor of the house and rented out the upper three stories. The rooms of the ground-floor apartment were spacious, but there was no courtyard, such as one found in all single-family Mediterranean houses of the better class. The rooms were singularly bare; no doubt the master had taken the handsomer pieces to Carthage with him. Abarish introduced his wife and discoursed about his son, a naval cadet of whom he was very proud.

Said Evnos: "If you will kindly let me get settled, Master Abarish, ere dinnertime I'll hie me to the waterfront to seek passage to Carthage."

"And I," said Segovax, "will be looking in on the drink shops, to see if there is any news of the comrades I soldiered with when I was in Sicily aforetime."

"To hear is to obey! This way, esteemed sirs. ..."

Thus Zopyros presently found himself seated in the main room of the apartment, drinking Byblian with the steward and answering Abarish's questions on philosophy.

"Not too loudly, I pray," said the Phoenician. "Else my wife may overhear and, perchance, repeat our discourse to the master. He is a devoted follower of the old gods and contemns philosophy as base pernicious atheism. Although my dear wife wishes me no ill—I hope—women have but little skill in curbing their tongues.

"Long have I yearned to learn more of this science of the mind, but never have the gods vouchsafed me the opportunity. Although Hellenes abound in Motya, all are of the trading class, and to them shines the glimmer of a drachma brighter than the sun of knowledge. Now proceed, I entreat you."

Zopyros talked. He told of Myron's theory that the earth was round, and the theory of Philolaos, that it traveled in a circle around the Central Fire of the universe. He told of the Four Elements of Empedokles, of the atoms of Demokritos, and of the evolutionary theories of Anaximandros, who asserted that all land animals had evolved from fishes. He told of the search for the basic principle of all things, which Thales had found in fluidity, Anaximenes in infinity, and Herakleitos in fire. It was a struggle to express philosophical thoughts in the Punic tongue, which contained but few abstract terms.

The catechism continued the next day. Zopyros explained the Pythagorean ethical doctrines: rigorous self-control, imperturbability, temperance, moderation, and justice. A good man should rise early, train his memory, and keep his passions under the control of his reason. He should do his duty and faithfully discharge his responsibilities. He should perform scientific experiments to extend the bounds of mankind's knowledge. He should be kind to animals. He should have nothing to do with blood sacrifices or with aggressive warfare. He should observe certain rules of eating, "... which," said Zopyros, "I fear I seldom do." He should altogether shun drunkenness, adultery, and pederasty. He should not even fornicate before he was nineteen, and thereafter only while he remained single, and no more often than he had to.

On the third day the travelers were supposed to embark, but an adverse wind kept their ship in harbor. And still there seemed no limit to the philosophical appetite of Abarish. The man was a real devotee. He said:

"It is as if I had lived in a dark room all my life, Master Zopyros, and you have suddenly opened a window to the outer world. I know that soon shall this window close again; but, ere it do, I would drink in all I can of this world beyond the bourn of our senses."

By now Zopyros had grown hoarse as well as restless. When he got tired of pacing the room, he suggested that he be given time to tour the city, of which he had so far seen but little.

"To hear is to obey," said Abarish. "But, good my lord, think me not forward if I do accompany you. For a strange Hellene to wander abroad were not always prudent."

"Why were it not?"

"Because rumors aver that your master Dionysios plots to attack us. Certes, these rumors are but chaff; for, with a true philosopher like Philistos as his chief adviser, how could Dionysios contemplate any such base act? Howsomever, the many are not men of intellect like us and so are easily fired to witless acts."

They walked about the town together, picking up Segovax at one of his drink shops. Zopyros saw no signs of hostility from the Moty-ans, who, busy with their business, ignored the foreigners. Zopyros could not decide whether Abarish's warning had been merely an excuse to keep him talking on philosophy, or whether Segovax's fierce appearance quenched any hostile thoughts in the breasts of the citizens. In any case, the walk was peaceful.

Besides the tall apartment houses and a town hall, Motya contained a number of temples. Some were purely Greek; others Punic. At each of the latter, a high brick wall surrounded the temenos, but the gates were open so that the foreign visitors could see in, even though they might not enter without special permission. The temenos was cluttered with shrines, stelae, and obelisks placed at random, while in the midst of this confusion of masonry stood the temple.

The Punic temples themselves were small, plain, boxlike buildings of whitewashed brick. Their few decorations—sometimes a pair of bronzen pillars in front of the doors, sometimes a huge lustral bowl—were wrought in a hybrid Graeco-Egyptian style. One new temple had a whole row of Ionic columns across its front, but without the peaked roof and pediment that such a row of pillars would support in Hellas. Zopyros asked:

"In which temple burn they the babes?"

"In this one: the temple of Baal Hammon. See you the touch of Greek artistry about the fane?"

These words started a train of thought in Zopyros' mind. He asked: "Why did the lord Elazar move to Carthage?"

"He has long owned a house and possessed business interests there ..."

"Aye; but I understand he had long dwelt in Motya."

Abarish lowered his voice and glanced about nervously. "Know you not the tale of his wife and son? He wedded a Hellene of Messana, and she did try to flee back to her parents with the infant. The boy she failed to carry off, but fled herself to avoid chastisement. Now her kinsmen hound my poor master, demanding dowry—to which they have no right—and the child as well. Fearing some desperate attempt to abduct the lad, Elazar removed to Carthage where, methinks, such desperate deeds have no likelihood of success. Remind me ere we part to give you a token to present to Elazar. He's a suspicious man, and rightly so. Otherwise he might turn you out of doors without ceremony."

The next day, Abarish saw them to the wharf. He bent himself double with repeated bows and wrung their hands. Zopyros could have sworn that, as the man bade them farewell, a pair of tears ran down his cheeks into his vast black beard. Abarish said:

"Your visit has honored me, my lords! Would you could stay for months, further to enlighten me about the secrets of the universe! Never, I fear me, shall I see you again, for last night I dreamt a dream and it boded ill. Forget not, sirs: You must say nought to my master of these excursions into philosophy. For, an he knew, he'd dismiss me eftsoons as a wicked atheist."

"Have no fear of us, friend Abarish," said Zopyros, who felt he had talked enough philosophy to last him the rest of his life. "Was I not to ask you in parting for a hospitality token?"

"Aye, aye; I had forgot. Here!" Abarish dug into his wallet and handed over a half of a broken Carthaginian half shekel. "The gods—whatever gods there be—prosper you!"

On the left the sun, rising over the rocky mountains of Cape Hermes, shot ruddy beams through the scattered clouds and sprinkled the waves of the Bay of Carthage with rubies. To starboard, the long sandy beaches of the Carthaginian coast broke into rising sand dunes and then into steep red cliffs, along which ran the huge outer wall of Carthage.

The city—one of the world's greatest—crowned the end of a peninsula that jutted out into the Bay of Carthage. This peninsula broadened out at its tip on either side, so that it had the shape of a hammer or a pick. The two horns almost inclosed two bodies of water, Lake Ariana to the north and the Lake of Tunis to the south; while shallow channels, suitable for small craft, joined each lake to the sea. The city proper occupied the head of the peninsula, between the two horns.

As the ship sailed southward past Cape Carthage, the hills of the Megara—the suburb—rose behind the outer wall, which here ran close to the sea. Villas, surrounded by fields and orchards, were scattered over these hills. Here and there a temple crowned a hilltop. The glass roof ornaments of these temples caught the rays of the rising sun and shot them back to the ship in rainbow hues.

The hills of the Megara flattened out as the ship sailed on, until it came abreast the Byrsa. The Byrsa—the inner city—was surrounded by its own wall, which joined the outer wall along the waterfront to form a single enormous rampart, strengthened at intervals by towers. Behind the double wall could be seen the tops of houses five or even six stories high. Beyond these, and separated by a short distance from the hills of the Megara, stood the single fortified hill of the citadel.

Between the great wall and the sea ran a paved causeway, with a parapet along its outer edge. Ships tied up along this quay by ropes looped around the crenelations of the parapet. As Zopyros' ship proceeded, the causeway narrowed into a long point, directed south, and ended in a huge built-up stone pier. The captain tied up near the end of this pier.

As Zopyros and his companions disembarked, a donkey boy came running up, leading his animal. Knowing from the steward's directions that Elazar's house was over a league from the port, they hired the ass to carry their gear. When the three duffel bags had been roped into place, the travelers set out northward toward the base of the pier and the great wall.

To the left of the pier was a gap in the wall, through which Zopyros glimpsed the inner harbor. This harbor, rectangular and ten by sixteen plethra, was crowded with merchant ships, some in the water and some hauled out on skids around the margins. Beyond this inner harbor but connected with it lay the cothon or naval harbor, surrounded by a massive circular wall. A trireme, issuing from the cothon, nosed its way through the merchantmen, like a shark in a pool of turtles, with shouted threats and warnings to clear the way.

As the three reached the base of the pier, they approached one of the gates in the main wall. Flanking this gate were a pair of towers with a portcullis, like that of Ortygia, working between them. Behind the portcullis was the main portal, comprising a pair of wooden doors whose timbers were whole tree trunks squared, held together with massive bronzen brackets. The portcullis was raised and the gates stood open. Several soldiers in corselets of gilded metal scales mounted guard at the gate. One soldier questioned Zopyros and his companions closely before letting them into the city.

Once within the gate, the travelers followed the animal past the merchant harbor, across which they could see the tophet or temenos of the temple of Tanith and Baal Hammon, with its groves and shrines and stelae surrounding the home of the divine pair. They trailed the ass around the curve of the wall of the naval harbor into the tangle of stone-paved streets beyond.

"Valetudo preserve us, but the houses are even taller here than in Motya!" said Segovax, looking apprehensively at the towering white-washed façades on either side. The height of the buildings made dark canyons of the bustling streets, into which an occasional scorching sunbeam struck slantwise. The dust made Zopyros cough; the rank city smells were overpowering.

The travelers jostled loose-robed Phoenicians, tattooed Libyans wearing ostrich-plume headdresses, and lean, swarthy Numidians capped with turbans of wildcat skins. There were Negroes from beyond the deserts: some of them huge, muscular men; others mere Pygmies, less than five feet tall.

They brushed past snake charmers, sorcerers, and beggars holding out fly-crusted sores and the stumps of withered limbs. They dodged around the litters, borne by gigantic blacks, of bejeweled oligarchs. They pushed past the flocks of goats and sheep that flowed like freshets along the narrow streets, with a skin-clad herdsman and his dog walking briskly behind each flock.

The streets were lined with shops, identified by wooden signs inscribed right to left with lines of Punic writing. Costly goods from near and far spilled out into the street. The shopkeepers stood in their doorways, importuning passers-by with seductive cries, low bows, and sweeping gestures. One man sold Etruscan candles; another, Persian umbrellas. An Egyptian tradesman featured two of his country's products: a salve for curing dandruff, made from genuine hippopotamus fat; and some large tame snakes, which Egyptian ladies of quality placed in their laps or around their necks to keep themselves cool in summer.

Everywhere—on street corners, in the entrances to shops, and in the midst of traffic—men pursued their eternal bargaining in the purring Punic tongue. If quieter than Greek hagglers, the Carthaginians were more energetic and businesslike in their manner. Everybody seemed in a hurry. Nobody strolled about discussing philosophy or politics and illustrating his points with graceful gestures. Every Carthaginian seemed to have urgent business, to which he was hastening with an anxious, preoccupied air.

Elazar's house stood on a hilltop in the Megara, near the temple of Eshmun, amid vineyards and groves of olive, almond, and pomegranate trees. When the porter called the master, Evnos introduced himself and his companions and handed over the hospitality token they had received from Abarish.

Elazar ben-Ahiram was a tall, heavily built man, with a broad head, blunt features, and a close-cut black beard. Rings gleamed on his fingers and in his ears. On his head was a hat like a small inverted pail. His body garments were of thin, light material, but he wore a number of them. There was a loose linen gown, which hung to his ankles. Over this he wore a kind of linen apron, and over this in turn a long-sleeved thin woolen coat, cut so that it was open in front and fell to his calves behind.

He looked at his visitors from small, wary, black eyes, studied the broken coin, and grunted. "Wait here," he said, and disappeared.

Soon he returned, holding up the two halves of the coin to show that they made one. "'Tis true you come from Abarish," he growled. "Doubtless you are fain to stop at my house?"

Zopyros glanced at the Karian, to see how he would cope with this ungracious greeting. Evnos beamed and said: "Your hospitality overwhelms us, Master Elazar. I trust we impose not upon it."

Elazar frowned. He shot a sharp glance at the speaker from under heavy black brows, as if wondering whether there had been sarcasm in the words. Then he said:

"Know that you will find no abandoned luxuries here. No dancing girls or all-night revels. In this house we are sober, hardworking folk, and we keep regular hours and obey the gods."

Evnos' smile remained fixed. "After inns and ships, sir, your plainest fare will seem like unto the paradise whereto the Egyptians thought their kings ascended."

Elazar muttered under his breath, jingled the halves of the half shekel, and finally said: "Come on in."

The house was of the courtyard type, resembling that of a prosperous Hellene. Instead of the statue that a Greek might place in the middle of his courtyard, Elazar kept a sundial in the center of his. A loom stood at one side. A boy of four played with a toy chariot in the care of a Negro nurse, who sat sewing with her big black breasts drooping over the top of her single garment.

Elazar said: "I am about to depart to oversee a house I am erecting in the Byrsa. The master's eye feeds the horse, you know. My servants will see that you are settled and victualed. Take your ease until I return in the afternoon."

He was gone; Zopyros heard him giving orders. The front door slammed, and chariot wheels rumbled away.

Zopyros found that the plaster of the walls of his room was painted, but with plain panels of pastel colors instead of mythological or bucolic scenes. Little borders of egg-and-dart patterns ran around the panels. Otherwise the room was rather bare.

He made himself at home and went into the courtyard. His first task would be to make friends with the boy, and he nervously wished he had Archytas along. Archytas had such a way with children, while Zopyros found their company awkward.

However, when he entered the courtyard, he found Segovax already deep in converse with the child, whom he was entertaining with fantastic Celtic legends. Two of Elazar's watchmen lounged in the vestibule that led to the outer door, leaning on javelins and watching the visitors. Bludgeons hung from their belts. Elazar was taking no chances.

"Hello!" said Zopyros to the boy. "Are you Ahiram ben-Elazar?"

"That am I. Are you a Greek? I know Greek. *Nai. Ouk. Chaire. Parakalô. Eucharistô.* My mother is Greek."

Zopyros said: "I—"

"Pray talk not; I would hear the story Segovax tells."

The Celt threw Zopyros a wink and resumed his tale. Zopyros strolled over to the lounging watchmen. Looking as innocent as the small boy, he spoke to one of them in Greek:

"Could you tell me when the master will be back?"

Both men bowed and smirked but looked blank. One spread his hands and shrugged. When Zopyros repeated his question in Punic, their eyes lighted with intelligence. Both began to speak at once. Elazar might be home at any time from midafternoon to dinnertime. His business hours were irregular.

Zopyros turned back to where Segovax spun out his tale. "When you've finished," he said in Greek, "I should like a word with you. You, too, Evnos," he added as the Karian appeared in the courtyard.

Segovax quickly rounded off his story: "... so Prince Divico married the elf king's daughter, and the wicked stepmother was chopped into little bits and fed to the pigs. What is it, Zopyros my lad?"

The nurse took Ahiram away, and servants began setting up lunch in the courtyard. Speaking low and in Greek, Zopyros told his comrades the story of Korinna.

"You mean," said Evnos, "that this is the same woman of whom the steward told us? And you knew it all along and never said a word?"

"Ah, but he's a sly one," said Segovax.

139

Zopyros said earnestly: "I'm not telling you this now just to pass the time. I have a life-and-death task to do, and I need your help."

"Meaning," said Evnos, swiveling his eyes to the door through which Ahiram had disappeared, "you're thinking of absconding with the child?"

Zopyros wagged his head in the affirmative.

Evnos clapped a hand to his forehead. "By the womb of the Mother Goddess, what an idea! Are you out of your mind? Do you want to get us all burned in the belly of some big bronze idol?"

Segovax added: "Zopyros darling, 'tis a fine high-spirited lad that you are. But we have serious business, and we can't be letting you spoil it all with your romantical notions."

"I'm going to try it, with or without your help!"

"Absolutely not!" said Evnos. "I have the final say in such matters."

"Would you leave the poor infant to be broiled in the statue of Baal Hammon?"

"It's none of our affair. People are always killing one another; one Punic brat more or less makes no difference."

"You forget, this brat is my stepson-to-be. That is, if I can save him."

"That's your lookout, not ours. Your present duty is to see that we perform our mission. Afterward, if you want to come back to Carthage to make a snatch, that's up to you. ..."

They argued back and forth through lunch, in tense voices, which they kept from rising by conscious effort. The watchmen looked on, mildly interested in the foreigners' quarrel but giving no sign that it concerned them.

At last the disputants came to a grudging agreement. Zopyros should make no move before the engineers were all recruited. After that, if he wished to leave the group and try a coup on his own, they would not put obstacles in his way—provided he gave them a chance to get clear of Carthage first.

Shortly before sunset, the rumble of Elazar's chariot sounded outside. Servants rushed to and fro to get dinner ready. The contractor stalked into the courtyard, a scowl on his face. Zopyros braced himself for an unpleasant dinner. Then little Ahiram trotted in. Elazar hoisted his son up, hugged him, and kissed him, while the boy pulled his father's beard and chattered about the events of the afternoon.

Elazar served no wine before the meal and drank but little himself during the repast. They ate sitting in chairs instead of reclining on couches. The entrée was a tasty stew. Segovax asked:

"What's this we are eating, your honor?"

"Puppy dog," said Elazar.

Segovax clapped a hand over his mouth. Zopyros gulped. Even Evnos' gap-toothed smile became strained. Elazar shot keen glances around the table, and his lips twitched. He said:

"'Tis not your custom, and I know it. But, when I dine among Greeks, I must ofttimes eat pork or go hungry, notwithstanding that to us Canaanites the pig is an unclean beast."

Zopyros compelled himself to go on eating. Dog meat, he found, was really not bad if one fought down one's inherited prejudices. He said:

"How goes the business, sir?"

"Baal Hammon roast all house buyers!" roared Elazar, smiting the table with his fist so that the tapers wobbled in their holders. "The polluted bastards can never make up their minds. No matter how carefully one goes over the plans with them, there's ever some last-minute change. Every such change costs good shekels. The wretches try to wriggle out of paying for it and curse the poor builder as a thief because he cannot afford to absorb these costs himself. Why chose I not some safe, easy trade, like lion hunting or piracy?"

Through most of the meal, Elazar harangued the other three on the iniquity of the people who bought houses from him. Becoming bored, Zopyros sought to change the subject. He said:

"Your son seems a bright lad."

"Oh, he is; forsooth he is!" Elazar's eyes gleamed with proud eagerness. "Know you that, albeit not yet five, he knows the Punic alphabet? If the gods receive him not into their bosoms first, he'll verily be a credit to me."

Zopyros: "You mean—ah—sir—that custom of yours?"

"Certes, I mean that custom, as you call it. Unlike certain other folk, we really do revere our gods—at least the righteous amongst us do. How better to show our reverence than to give them that which we love best?"

"Is it not all equally righteous that you are?" ventured Segovax.

Elazar sighed. "That is never the way with mortal men. Our wise kohanim still debate the question: How can good gods permit evil in their world? Time was, long ago when the city was young, when the folk of Carthage gave in to luxury and license. But of late we've mended our ways. The rich care for the poor, thus averting civil conflict; and all alike strive for sober and godly conduct. Did things but continue thus, I doubt not the gods"—Elazar rolled his eyes heavenward and touched his breast, lips, and forehead—"would favor the Republic for aye, and no draft of the first-born to pass through the fire were needed.

"But, alas! I fear for the future. Skeptics and so-called philosophers from the Greek lands have begun to infect our folk with their blasphemous thoughts, saying there are no gods; or if gods there be, they care not for the petty affairs of men. Sacrilege!" Elazar shook a fist. "Other Greeks seduce our folk away from honest toil; they set an evil example of wasting time in idle argument or childish sports."

He subsided, staring morosely into his wine cup. "Forgive my vehemence, my lords," he grumbled. "I confess I'm not the most courteous man in Carthage. But these things touch me closely. To give my son to the fire would tear the heart from my breast; yet, an the gods demand it, I'll do it without cavil. Look not scornful, for other peoples have hard customs also. The Celts burn victims in wicker cages; the Italians make them fight to the death; and the Greeks abandon their weans on rubbish heaps for dogs to devour."

"The boy has no mother?" said Zopyros innocently.

"Oh, aye, he has one. My wife is—on a long visit to her kinsmen in Messana."

"Only one wife?"

"Certes; what think you? We're no Persians. Why, if men were allowed as many wives as they could afford, the rich would garner more than their share. Then would the poor be forced to remain continent or have recourse to those vile, unnatural acts that so delight you Greeks." Elazar glowered at Zopyros. "But enough of these things. You spoke when erst we met of a mission to Carthage. What is this mission?"

Evnos explained that they were recruiting engineers for Dionysios and hoped that Elazar could help them in their quest.

142

Elazar frowned. "Peaceful purposes, eh? I trust not that pop-injay in his Ortygian fortress, nor any other Greek. Methinks he's greedier than a purple-shell and will devour whatever his jaws can span. I know you Greeks. 'Tis not to your taste by tedious toil and patient, peaceful penetration to weave a web of mutual trust and obligation with those you trade with. Nay, rather, you seek by swift and ruthless onset to assert yourselves at the cost of other men. You boast of your culture; yet in many of your cities 'tis the regular yearly thing, as soon as the harvest be gathered, to sally forth with shield on arm to discover which of your neighbors you can most readily rob, enslave, or slay. What's that song?" He sang in good Greek, in a powerful bass voice:

My wealth is a sword and my riches a spear
And a buckler of rawhide I carry before me.
I plow and I sow and I reap with this gear;
I press the sweet vintage and make serfs adore me!

"Now, is that not the perfect pirate's view of life? But to return to our subject: I know but few engineers. In building houses for the citizens, experience serves the turn of plans and reckonings."

Zopyros said: "But"—he almost said "Korinna" but caught himself in time—"Abarish told me you've worked on fortifications. So you must know something about engineering and engineers."

"What if I do?" growled the Carthaginian. "You ask me to put myself out; to do your work for you, in fact, by hunting down these men. What's in it for me?"

Aha, thought Zopyros, now comes the truth. He threw a smile at Evnos, who smoothly took up the dialogue: "Oh, we plan to make it worth your while, Master Elazar. Say—a reasonable commission on the salaries of the men you can find?"

Elazar thoughtfully scratched a fleabite. "The slippery word, of course, is 'reasonable,'" he said with a grim smile. "I'm still not utterly happy about this project; but, if I help you not, you'll doubtless go to another. So let's talk terms. Say—the first three months' pay?"

"Ye gods, no!" cried Evnos. "At two drachmai a day—which Dionysios offers—he'd never agree to such terms. He has many sources of expense."

"Well can I ween. Such as a stable of pretty boys?" said Elazar, deliberately offensive.

"I think you are misinformed on that score," said Evnos evenly. "His home life, from what I've seen, is as sober and temperate as your own. But the governance of a city is a monstrous consumer of treasure."

"Well, how much had you in mind, then?"

"Let's say, ten drachmai a man—five days' pay. If you find ten men, that will come to—"

"An insult, by Tanith's teats!" cried Elazar. "A pittance! A penny thrown to a beggar! Am I a dog? Am I a slave, so vilely to be used? Why, the cost of sending letters alone were more than that. ..."

Zopyros signaled for more wine and settled back in his chair, watching the haggle. The dusk deepened, bats whirred overhead, and the stars came out. Zopyros counted stars and wondered which of the philosophers' theories about them was right. Having seen Phoenician traders at this kind of game before, he knew that hours, perhaps days, would pass before agreement was reached. Since these people had practically no sports, drama, poetry, art, science, or philosophy to amuse them, bargaining was (except for their atrocious religion) their main entertainment.

He looked across at Elazar, absorbed in wringing the last penny out of Evnos whether he needed the money or not. He much disliked the man, not least because the Carthaginian's brutal censures of everything Greek had in them too much truth for comfort. Zopyros sympathized—natural prejudices aside—with Korinna's desertion of her husband. The Phoenician was a grouchy, gloomy, grasping boor and, in religious matters, a priggish fanatic. On the other hand, Elazar was not to be underestimated. He was intelligent, energetic, and enterprising. He seemed sincerely to love his son. His blunt discourtesies were no worse than the oily overpoliteness of many Phoenicians.

* * *

144

The bargaining continued the next morning and through lunch. At last Elazar wiped his mouth on the tablecloth and held out his hands for a servant to pour water over.

"Much though I enjoy matching wits with you, Master Evnos," he said, "business calls, and I must forth to my constructions. Let's cleave the difference and make it the first twenty days' pay: half to be paid when the man is hired by you; the other half to be sent by your master to Abarish in Motya when the man goes to work in Syracuse. Agreed?"

"Agreed." The two clasped hands.

Elazar rose. "Stay you here, all of you; for your men will soon appear. I go!"

Less than an hour later, a Carthaginian knocked at Elazar's front door. He identified himself as Azruel of Thugga, an engineer specializing in siege engines.

Zopyros interviewed the candidates. It was new work for him. At first he hated to make a final decision, fearing that, if he turned down very many, the supply might suddenly fail, and he would be left without enough technicians to please Dionysios. The first few, therefore, he told to go home and wait. He took down names and addresses.

As he got more experience, however, he found that he could detect the ones who were bluffing. In the end he hired fourteen engineers and turned down three. Over breakfast the next day, Elazar said:

"That's the tally of the able engineers of Carthage. Belike I could flush one or two by writing my colleagues in Utica and Tunis."

"This were enough, meseems," said Evnos. "When I shall have paid you the promised half of the commission, the money entrusted me by Dionysios will be well-nigh gone. If my master wish further recruitment, I must needs go back to Syracuse for more."

Elazar nodded. He had become almost agreeable. "Then, I ween, you're for town and will seek passage homeward. Take my advice and ask of Bomilkarth's Sons. Their ships are roomy and well found; and, what is more, remarkably clean. Old Bomilkarth had a mortal hatred of mice, wherefore every ship of that line now carries one or more Egyptian cats, this nuisance to abate."

145

One of Bomilkarth's Sons' ships was to sail three days later. Evnos reserved passage and reported back to his comrades. The master of the house had chosen to stay home that day, checking accounts with his steward. He looked up from his work to say:

"Tomorrow comes the harvest festival. Since you have nought else to do, I thought I would show you the religious procession."

"Thank you, sir," said Zopyros. He glanced across the courtyard, to where Evnos and Segovax had their heads together. Presently they went out, saying:

"We would shop a bit in town, my masters, for pretty things to take home to our womenfolk."

Zopyros spent the afternoon playing in the courtyard with Ahiram. The boy—a sturdy, swarthy, black-haired child—had gotten used to the visitors. Aside from the fact that he tended to talk too much, Zopyros liked the boy—as well as he liked most children.

Ahiram was well developed for his age. When Zopyros played ball with him, he was appalled to find that the child was almost as good at throwing and catching as was he himself. Zopyros was awkward, whereas the child was precociously agile, slinking and pouncing like a cat.

Once, when he thought nobody was listening, he asked Ahiram: "Would you like to see your mother?"

"Father says Mother is bad. She went away."

"But would you like to go to see her?"

Ahiram considered the question soberly. "Yes, I should. When can we go?"

"I know not. If you say no word to anybody about it, peradventure something can be done."

When Segovax and Evnos came back that afternoon, the former said: "We have a bit to talk about with you, Zopyros; and I'm thinking we'll disturb himself less if we do it outside."

Elazar glanced up from his papyrus rolls and back again without a word. The three travelers went out and strolled among the olive trees. Farm workers were striking the boughs with poles and gathering into baskets the olives that fell. Evnos said:

"During this parade tomorrow, do you think you could slip away with the boy?"

Zopyros' jaw dropped. "Wh-why, I hadn't thought. What is it? What are you planning?"

"If you can, Segovax will be waiting at the corner of Shadapra and Bes—that's a couple of blocks from the route of the procession—with a mule. You can be out of the city with the lad before anybody misses him."

"*Oi!*" But—I thought you wouldn't have anything to do with this?"

Segovax grinned through his mustache. "To be sure, now, you didn't think we'd let our friend down, and him so romantical and all?"

"I—I don't know how to thank you. But what will happen to you?"

"It's all fixed," said Evnos. "Segovax and I are leaving, not on Bomilkarth's ship, but on a Greek ship that sails a day earlier. Of course Elazar won't know that."

"Where do I go when I get out of Carthage?"

"Now, that called for fast work on my part! Luckily I know unsavory characters in all the big cities. You'll follow the coastal road to Cape Utica. There's a ford across the Bagrada near its mouth."

"Do I go up to Utica?"

"No, no. You're going to visit a witch who lives in a cave on Cape Utica."

"A *what?*"

"A witch. Saphanbaal the witch. She'll hide you for a few days until you're picked up."

"Zeus on Olympos! Will she turn me into a spider, or what?"

"Good gods, no! This is a simple matter of hiding a wanted man. Don't let her profession bother you. Here is the hospitality token by which you shall identify yourself to her."

Evnos held out a length of bone—a piece of human thighbone, Zopyros guessed. It was about half a foot long. One end was a smoothly rounded joint, while the other was jaggedly broken. Zopyros took the object and eyed it doubtfully, asking:

"What about my rescue?"

"Three nights hence, a Captain Bostar will sail past on his way to Sicily and Tyre."

"What sort of man is he?"

"Not the best, I fear. He's a smuggler—one who secretly loads off open roadsteads and shaves his prices by evading harbor fees. But, if you will do desperate deeds, you can't be fastidious."

Two of Elazar's watchmen cleared a way with elbows, boots, and bludgeons through the pushing, gabbling throngs for Elazar and his guests. With much shoving, quarreling, and threats, they jammed themselves into a space along Baal Hammon Avenue. Elazar hoisted Ahiram upon his shoulder.

Zopyros, being taller than most Carthaginians, could easily see over the heads of those before them; but Evnos was not so lucky. Zopyros thrust the Karian in front of him, so that he could at least glimpse the proceedings. A line of soldiers on either side of the avenue kept back the throng with spears held level to form a railing.

They stood for an hour, not daring to move lest they lose their places. Hawkers strolled up and down the avenue on the other side of the fence of spears, crying their wares: "Hot biscuits!" "Pure water!" "Good blood sausage!" "Who's fain for dried chick-peas?" "That's tuppence ... pass it back to the gentleman, pray." "Father, when will the parade begin?" "Palm fronds to greet the gods!" "Fresh sardines!" "Amulets for good luck! Your favorite god!" "Delicious little cooked birds!" "Fine grapes to cool your throats!" "Pomegranates!" "Artichokes!" "Good felt caps, latest style!" "Hot biscuits!" "Father, when will the parade begin?"

They stood for another hour in heat and dust. Zopyros' knees began to ache. Little Ahiram fussed a little, cried a little, and went to sleep in the arms of his father, who growled:

"The accursed priests never begin these things on time. An the gods ever desert the Republic, the cause will be that they've wearied of waiting for their tardy worshipers."

At last a gong boomed, followed by a blast of trumpets. The hawkers scampered away. Men with brooms and dustpans passed along the avenue after them, stirring denser clouds of dust.

Then came the boom of drums, the clash of cymbals, the twang of harps, the clang of sistra, and the wail of flutes and pipes. The odor of incense filled the air. The first group of paraders appeared, from the temple of Bes.

In front marched a musical band. Then came groups of singers and dancers, the latter bounding and cavorting. Little girls threw flower petals at the crowd. The god himself, a painted and gilded statue on a litter borne by a dozen priests, followed. The priests wore thin, transparent robes over white loincloths. Bucket-shaped gauze caps covered their shaven heads.

The statue was that of a long-bearded, snub-nosed, dancing dwarf, naked but for a lion's skin thrown over one shoulder. Ostrich plumes waved from the corners of the litter. Other temple folk followed: priests swinging censers, which filled the avenue with blue clouds of sweet-smelling smoke; sacrificers, lamplighters, sacred barbers, lay brothers, temple slaves and serfs.

The crowd cheered the god of mirth and merriment. Another group of musicians followed, and after them came the float of Eshmun, the healer. This was a statue of a long-bearded, long-robed god seated in a gilded wagon drawn by four mules. The god held out his arms to bless the people. Priests, walking beside the wagon, wore bandages, or had their arms in slings, or pretended to limp on crutches to show the ilk of which their god cured his worshipers. After them came more ranks of minor temple personnel; for today even the meanest temple slave had his moment of glory.

More incense, more music. The next float was that of Hiyôn, the divine artificer, beating a piece of metal on his anvil. A real fire glowed in his forge. The priests who walked beside his wagon bore tools for working wood, stone, leather, and metal.

Next came Dagon, with his fish's tail. His priests carried his litter. Other priests, dressed in iridescent scales, went through the motions of fish, while yet others in blue-green cloaks swayed back and forth like waves. Pretty priestesses in green gauze sprinkled scented water on the crowd from golden aspergilla.

Then came Kusôr, the mariner and inventor. Priests pulled his wagon, which was a fishing boat on wheels. In the boat, the statue of Kusôr sat at a table and tinkered with a device of wheels and levers.

So far these were minor gods. Zopyros nudged Evnos and glanced toward Ahiram, astride his father's neck. The two watchmen closely flanked their master. Zopyros could not see the remotest chance of getting the boy away without a struggle, in which he would be outnumbered by Elazar's party and surrounded by the excited crowd. Elazar had only to shout: "Seize that rascally Greek!" and Zopyros would be torn to pieces.

Evnos followed Zopyros' gaze, shrugged, and spread his hands, muttering: "The gods of Carthage are guarding their own today. I'm sorry Segovax will miss the procession for nothing."

Now the cheers became louder, mingled with prayers and snatches of hymns. The wagon of Milkarth, drawn by white horses, came into view. The hero stood, wrapped in a lion's skin—a real skin, Zopyros noted, not a sculptured one—with his sword in one hand and the head of the demoness Masisabal in the other. Blood dripped realistically from the head. A squad of kohanim, with embroidered stoles over their shoulders, marched barefoot in front of the wagon, chanting the legends of the labors of Milkarth from scrolls they held before them.

Next came the wagon of Resheph. A pair of black bulls drew it; a white ass, to be sacrificed at the end of the day, was led behind. The statue showed the god as standing on a bull and wearing a horned helmet. In one hand he held a battle-ax and in the other a three-pronged thunderbolt. The priests carried his emblems on poles: black thunderclouds of cloth, zigzag silver spears representing lightning, and silver vultures with outspread wings.

The float of Mether bore an image of the god, in the form of a beardless youth in Persian coat and trousers, stabbing a bull. Although it was full daylight, the attendant priests carried guttering torches. Two of them walked naked with masks in the form of lions' heads over their faces and a live python draped over their shoulders.

Now the wagon bearing the statue of Anath, the warrior goddess, swayed into view. The goddess rode a lion, with a shield on her right arm, a spear in her right hand, and an ax in her left hand. A necklace of severed human heads hung round her neck. A live lion, aged and blinking, was led beside her carriage. Her priests carried shields and spears, which they clashed together in unison.

The maddening rhythm of *clang*—step—*clang*—step—made Zopyros want to shout or punch somebody. A man ducked under the line of spears and ran, shrieking and foaming, toward the divine wain.

An officer, rushing up, brained him with an ax. The body was pushed back against the feet of the foremost spectators and lay in a widening pool of blood while the procession marched on.

Next came El, seated in a chariot drawn by two red bulls. The symbols carried on poles included bulls' horns, rayed sun disks, and long blue streamers representing rivers.

Then came Ashtarth. The cheers became deafening. She had the largest band and the most exotic corps of priests. Some, their eyelids painted green, pranced in a sacred dance with their skirts hiked up to their waists, flapping their genitals at the crowds. Others manipulated phalli of painted leather, two to three cubits long, attached to the fronts of their costumes. Temple harlots danced in embroidered robes cut away to leave the fronts of their bodies bare, with multitudes of little flowers affixed in their pubic hair. Painted boys wiggled their hips.

The crowd screamed its pleasure and roared ribald jests. Zopyros nudged Elazar, caught his eye, and glanced at the painted boys. Elazar said something of which Zopyros caught only the last words: "...but that is *religion!*"

In turning, a peculiar motion had caught Zopyros' eye. Directly behind him, a man and a woman were copulating, standing against the wall. Their neighbors cheered them on, while the ecstatic pair quivered and gasped with slack mouths and drooping eyelids, oblivious to all about them.

A living woman played the part of the goddess Ashtarth. She lounged on her wagon wearing a robe of many colors, draped to expose her body, while she threw kisses to the crowd. Her priests carried spiked silver balls, representing the planet Venus, and sexual symbols made of precious metals and adorned with jewels.

The clouds of dust and incense made Zopyros cough. He shot another look at Ahiram. The boy's legs were firmly locked around his father's neck, while his hands gripped Elazar's beard. Zopyros could not see any possible way to pry him loose without open violence.

The crowd quieted down, because the greatest gods of Carthage were now approaching. The priests of Tanith marched solemnly by, wearing fillets of gold and silver about their foreheads. The chariot of the moon goddess was drawn by a pair of strange animals. They looked like mules but were covered all over with narrow black and white stripes. They shied, skitted, and pulled nervously at their bridles, gripped by a pair of stalwart Negroes who walked at their heads. The statue of the goddess wore a robe of gray doves' feathers. Priests in hideous masks danced around the chariot to scare off demons. Others bore poles with the symbols of the goddess: stuffed doves, palm fronds, silver lunar crescents, and golden pomegranates. A chorus sang a solemn hymn.

Then came the greatest god of all, Baal Hammon. The god sat on a throne on his wagon, his hands on the rams' heads that formed the arms of the throne. His beard hung to his waist, and horns curled up from his head. Some of his priests wore golden fillets, some feathered headdresses, and some tall pointed hats.

The crowd roared. Everywhere men tried to cast themselves down to the ground, although being so tightly packed they found this almost impossible.

After Baal Hammon came several minor gods. Some were served by eunuchs; some by whole priests who walked naked, lashing each other with whips or wounding themselves with knives. Some small groups seemed to be little more than gangs of sorcerers, waving human skulls and animal heads on poles. A group of Negroes beat deep drums with complicated rhythms, while a witch doctor smeared with ashes capered in their midst.

Last of all came Adon, god of the harvest, who on this occasion had the place of honor. Wild boars were led on chains before his litter, which took the form of a bier. The body of the dead god, painted white, lay supine with hundreds of stalks of wheat standing in holes in the upper surface of the effigy. A chorus dressed in sackcloth and ashes preceded the litter, singing a dirge for the dead god. Following the litter, a second chorus—bejeweled, wreathed, and garlanded—sang a hymn that rejoiced in his resurrection.

After Adon's scores of temple attendants and workers had passed, the soldiers raised their spears, allowing the thousands of ordinary Carthaginians to follow the procession. They filled the avenue like a river. Elazar said:

"We ought to do likewise and worship at one of the temples; but the boy is tired. Let us return to my house."

"I have private business, my masters," said Evnos. "I shall join you later."

Soon after Zopyros had returned to Elazar's house, Segovax walked in, whistling a wild Celtic air and carrying a chous of wine.

"By the horns of Cernunnos!" he said. "It's entirely destroyed that I am with carrying this great jug up all them hills, and the day so hot and all. I only hope it tastes good enough at dinner to pay for the labor. Master Elazar, I'm to tell you that our friend Evnos won't be coming home to dinner. The sight of all the colleens jiggling their pretty little pink teats in the air has given him ideas, I'm thinking. Zopyros my lad, could I have a word with you?"

Outside, the Celt said: "A shame it is that you couldn't get the boy away while the procession was going on, but belike it will be better this way."

"What way?"

"That jug of wine has enough drug in it to put the whole villa to sleep; so don't you be drinking any when it is passed tonight. Just pretend. I had to carry it home because I can drive Elazar's chariot, and Evnos can't. He'll be meeting us at the foot of the city wall with the mule."

"You meant to steal Elazar's—"

"Just borrow it, lad, borrow it. Now listen to what I'm saying …"

The nearly full moon was high in the eastern sky, and the only sound in the moonlit courtyard was the chirp of a cricket, when Zopyros eased open the door to the boy's room and stole in. Inside there was only a glimmer of light from the courtyard and the soft breathing of two persons. One breath was slow and heavy, with a touch of snore; the other was quick and light.

In the dimness, Zopyros could see nothing but two dark blotches against the paler tones of the stuccoed walls and the cement floor. One blotch, Zopyros knew, was the Negro nurse, sleeping on a pallet. The other was Ahiram on his bed. Zopyros, starting toward the blotch he thought was Ahiram's bed, stumbled against an unseen lamp stand. The stand teetered with a horrible noise. The lamp started to slide off. By a wild clutch in the darkness, Zopyros caught it by the spout. Carefully replacing it, he paused, sweating despite the chill of the North African night, waiting for his wildly beating heart to slow down, and cursing his own clumsiness.

A grumbling sound came from one of the blotches. One of the sleepers stirred and turned over. Zopyros' heart almost jumped out of his mouth. The sleeper was evidently the nurse; it was toward her that Zopyros had been stealing when he bumped into the lamp stand. Even though Segovax had managed to slip her a cup of the drugged wine, Zopyros hated to think what would have happened if he had tried by mistake to pick her up and carry her out.

He moved to the other dark patch, which turned out to be Ahiram asleep with his thumb in his mouth. Taking a deep breath, Zopyros gathered up the boy, blanket and all, without awakening him. Zopyros walked out, avoiding the lamp stand, and softly shut the door.

Silence reigned in the courtyard, save for small noises where Segovax fondled the head of Elazar's watchdog.

"He's after eating all that sausage I brought him," whispered the Celt. "If he sets up a barking when we go out, we're in it for fair. Come on."

They opened the front door. The dog stood slowly waving its tail and watching them with its head cocked in puzzlement. Segovax closed the door behind them, picked up their baggage, and set out with swift strides for the stable.

Ahiram stirred again and muttered: "What—whither go we, Master Zopyros?"

"We go to see your mother," whispered Zopyros. "But you must be a good boy and keep quiet."

Ahiram fell asleep again in Zopyros' arms while Segovax hitched Elazar's pair of blacks to the chariot, muttering; "A murrain on this Punic harness! All the straps go different from the way they should. It would not do at all to have the beasts gallop off without us."

At last the chariot was ready, although the horses pawed uneasily, rolling their eyes and twitching their ears. Zopyros got in with the boy, the baggage, and a coil of rope.

"Now, my beauties," said Segovax, "don't be upsetting us on the road. That's all I'm asking!"

He shook the reins. The team moved out at a walk. Zopyros fought down an urge to tell Segovax to gallop.

When they had put a few plethra behind them, Segovax clucked and brought the team up to a trot. "They're a fine pair, the darlings," he said in a hoarse whisper. "If only I could smuggle them aboard our little ship—but that wouldn't do at all, at all."

"We needn't whisper now," said Zopyros. "Where are we going?"

"Evnos says there's a stretch of wall along Lake Ariana that is not much patrolled, because nobody could climb up there from the rocks unless he had wings like that fellow you were telling me about. And, if he had them, he wouldn't be needing to climb anyway, now would he? 'Tis at the end of this stretch, where the wall leaves the lake and turns south across the big neck of land, that he'll be waiting for us."

"Do you know the way?"

"I do not. But I can steer by the stars and, the gods helping, we'll get there."

This proved easier said than done. The roads of the Megara wound around the hills. Segovax was trying to head a little south of west. Every road that started off in that direction seemed either to curve back eastward or came to a dead end at a villa. Segovax cursed in Gaulish, turned, backtracked, and tried again. Zopyros craned his neck to look back at the eastern horizon. Although they had started around midnight, at this rate he feared that the rising sun would find them groping for their direction.

Ahiram woke up and began asking questions. "Where is my mother? ... Well, when shall we see her? Why know you not? ... Are you going to bring Father along? ... Why not? ... Why mustn't I talk? ..."

At last the crenelations of the city wall manifested themselves as a saw-edged band of deeper black against the blue-black of the starry sky. The moon was low. Segovax slowed his team to a walk. Presently he stopped the horses, got out, and led them on foot, patting them and talking softly to them.

He stopped where the wall reared up before them to a height of thirty cubits. He tied the horses' bridles to the fronds of a palm that grew beside the road. To Zopyros he whispered:

"Pick up your gear, but leave Evnos' and mine. I'll be taking the rope. Now you see why I didn't bring the white horses. They'd stand out like a tulip in a basket of charcoal."

155

He led Zopyros and the boy toward the wall. Once there, they had to walk along it for several plethra before they reached a staircase. Again came the whisper:

"I'll go up and scout; wait here in the shadow. The gods willing, a sentry will be just going by. Then we count to five hundred, and over the wall we go. If we go up there when there's no sentry in sight, we never know when one will be coming."

Segovax removed his shoes and stole up the stone stairs. For a big, bulky man, he could move with remarkable quiet.

They waited. Ahiram became restless and increasingly hard to keep quiet. Zopyros did not dare to slap the child or even to threaten to do so, lest Ahiram set up a howl or run away.

Segovax came back down the stairs, as quietly as a drifting cloud. "There's no sentries at all, at all," he whispered. "Or, if there are, we can't wait till sunrise to greet them. So come on up, Zopyros dear."

They stole up the stairs, panting a little by the time they reached the top. As far as the eye could carry, no sentry could be seen along the broad upper roadway of the wall. Away to the right, the setting moon threw a broad band of silver dust across the surface of Lake Ariana. Far away a jackal yelped.

Segovax put his head out through one of the embrasures of the parapet and whistled. An answering whistle came from below. Segovax tied a loop in the end of the rope.

"You first, my lad," he said, putting the loop around Zopyros' body.

"But what about you? And whom do I pay for all this? And what shall I do with the mule?"

"Don't be worrying about silly things like money. Dionysios is paying for your escape, though he doesn't know it yet, poor man. Give the mule to the witch if you like. Now, over you go! Hold on to the parapet. ... Now put your weight on the rope, a little at a time. ... That's right. Keep the feet of you firm against the stones."

Segovax had taken a couple of turns of the rope around one of the merlons of the parapet, so that he could let the rope out a foot at a time without undue strain. It seemed to Zopyros that the descent took hours. He was glad he could see nothing below except the irregular black masses of trees and shrubs. As the rope above him lengthened, it quivered and thrummed in disconcerting fashion, and he found it harder to keep his feet braced against the masonry.

At last he felt the ground beneath his feet. Evnos helped him out of the bight of the rope and fastened it around his body.

"We shall see you in Syracuse," he whispered. "There's the mule; name's Yaphê." He looked upward and called softly: "Ready!"

Up he went, a few inches at a time. This was much slower than lowering Zopyros, even though Evnos was the smaller man. After a few pulls, Segovax had to stop, snub the rope around his merlon, and rest.

Zopyros sought out the mule in the darkness. The animal, tethered to a small tree, was munching at everything it could reach. It bore a saddle pad with a strap in back, to which Zopyros fastened his traveling bag.

When he had finished, Evnos was almost to the top. The Karian pulled himself up hand over hand for the remaining distance. There was quiet for a moment, then the sound of the rope's being paid out rapidly through one of the embrasures.

"Master Zopyros!" came a small voice. "Are you there? I am afraid! I'm being banged against the rocks!"

As Ahiram came down with a rush, Zopyros caught him. The boy had been tied in an elaborate harness, made out of the end of the rope.

Zopyros was still untying the lad when there was a whistle from above. Then came a scurry of feet going down the stair on the other side. The sound of horses' hooves and chariot wheels started up sharply and then diminished. At the same time, the sound of running steps on top of the wall approached. There was a jingle of warlike gear and a sentry's cry:

"Stand! Who goes there?"

Zopyros strained his fingers at the knots in the rope, but his comrades had done their work all too well. At last he took out the small-sword strapped to his thigh and sawed the rope apart. At that moment, the rope was snatched away from above. Another pair of running feet approached from the other direction. Zopyros heard snatches of phrases in Punic:

"Who's there?" "Somebody sneaking over the wall" "Going in or out?" "That sounded like a chariot." "Behold this rope!" "See you aught below?"

Zopyros boosted Ahiram on the back of the mule, unhitched the animal, and vaulted on behind the boy. "Go!" he said, kicking the mule's ribs with his heels and slapping its flank with the slack of the reins.

The mule stood still, continuing its repast. Zopyros kicked and slapped, to no avail. He did not dare to shout. He thought of drawing his sword and giving the balky brute a prick. He hesitated, for his Pythagorean training had taught him to be kind to animals.

"Somebody's down there!" came one of the voices from above. "What is it?" "I cannot tell." "Give them a shot whilst I rouse the guard!"

Footsteps receded. There were small indeterminate sounds, a faint whir as of a large night insect, a whistle of cloven air, and a smacking impact just behind Zopyros. A sling bullet had struck Yaphê in the rump. With a bray of pain and anger, the mule started off. Zopyros desperately clutched Ahiram with one hand and the saddle pad with the other. Then they were out on the coastal road, rocking along at a brisk canter toward Utica.

UTICA

Cape Utica ended in a wedge of sea cliffs—buff, umber, and tan-bark in the slanting rays of the afternoon sun. Above the cliffs, the land, sparsely covered with thorny bush, rolled away to southward. Scarcely any green was to be seen. The dun-colored scrub forest looked as dead as Darius the Great.

Actually, as Zopyros knew, the land was only sleeping. It was lying low, like a leopard snoozing away the noonday heat in the shade of a gum tree. With the first rains of autumn it would spring again into vigorous life.

Overhead, piles of clouds, winging in from the west, now and then obscured the sun. At the base of the cliffs, a choppy surf hammered at shiny black, sea-washed rocks. The sea, too, was awakening from its summer sleep. Soon would come overcasts, gales, downpours, whitecapped swells, and the end of sea travel.

Hoping that he had remembered his directions aright, Zopyros jogged out to the end of the point. Then he turned the mule and ambled a bowshot back along the eastern side of the point. He slid off Yaphê and tied the reins to a branch of a gnarled cork oak.

"Stay on the mule," he told Ahiram. "I shall be back."

"Waits Mother down yonder?" asked Ahiram.

"Nay. I've told you: We must needs take ship."

"I have been on a ship. But I thirst! When eat we?"

Zopyros turned away to scout along the top of the cliff. At first he failed to find a path. He had a horrid feeling that he had been hoaxed or had made some basic mistake. What in Hades should he do if there were no Saphanbaal, or if she could not be found?

Then he saw the path, snaking steeply down the cliffside. It was partly natural but had been improved by the hand of man. Zopyros walked down the slope, cautiously feeling the cliff with his shoreward hand. More than halfway down to the water, the path leveled out. Then it widened to form a ledge, on which yawned the mouths of several caves.

"O Saphanbaal!" he called.

"Who calls?" came a woman's voice, reverberating hollowly out of one of the caves.

"Zopyros the Tarentine, with a token."

"Oh?" The woman appeared at the entrance of the middle cave. She was a large woman, fat and saggy, wearing a simple dress of coarse brown stuff. Little piggy eyes looked out from a fat, round face. Most of her straggly hair had turned from brown to gray. Zopyros guessed her age at about fifty.

"I know about you, darling boy," she said, "but show me the token natheless. Show it me."

A little taken aback, Zopyros wordlessly pulled the broken shin-bone from his belt and handed it to her. As he came close, sight and smell told him that Saphanbaal had not bathed in a long, long time.

She took the bone and waddled back into the cave. Presently she reappeared, holding a second piece of bone in her left hand. She fitted their broken ends together.

"See?" she said. "A perfect fit. A perfect fit. The spirits told me, when erst I saw you, that you were a man of honor and virtue. But is there not a little lad with you?"

"Aye; I'll fetch him. I was fain to be sure. But how knew you all this? We left Carthage but last night, around twelve Egyptian hours ago."

She gave a simpering giggle that would have better become a girl of fourteen. "Now, darling Zopyros, were I not a sorry sort of witch, an I could not divine such matters? I have ways, and ways, and ways. But go fetch the boy. The poor little wight must be half dead of hunger and thirst. Go fetch him."

Zopyros went back up the path, unsaddled the mule, and moved it to a spot where it could graze on plenty of dried grass. Then, carrying his bag and holding Ahiram's hand, he returned down the path.

On the ledge he found Saphanbaal crouched over a little pile of tinder. In one hand she held a glass disk, two digits in diameter. The rays of the sun, striking through the glass, were concentrated in one glowing, rainbow-colored spot on the tinder. With the other hand she made passes over the tinder, intoning:

> *"Ye spirits of fire, come to my aid!*
> *Gulgoleth! Shehabarim! Lamia white!*
> *Come hither from gulfs of eternal night,*
> *And kindle this flame, by Elissa's shade!*

"Death take this wind!" she exclaimed. "There it goes!"

A plume of smoke whipped up from the tinder, and a small flame burst into being. The witch put twigs on the fire and soon had a blaze.

"Is that a magical fire?" said Ahiram.

"It certainly is, boy," said Saphanbaal. "It certainly is. Would you be a witch when you grow up? I could use an apprentice."

"Nay. I would be a builder like my father. But magic must be fun. Show me some more!"

"You shall see more soon enough, Master Ahiram; for tonight is the night of a big sitting. With the help of you two, I can give my truth-seekers an evening they shall long remember. Long shall they remember it. Know that I was once a beauty. I'm still a good figure of a woman, am I not?"

"It is not open to question, madam," said Zopyros, a little puzzled by the change of subject. "Live you here all alone?"

"Certes. I had a girl apprentice, but she ran away with a goatherd. 'Tis lonesome after the bustle of Utica."

"Why moved you?"

"You know how people talk and gossip about a woman who lives alone, be she never so virtuous! I had a colleague, a man witch named Shaddiel, with whom I undertook all-night conjurations. Such lengthy invocations are needed to command the mightiest spirits. The talk of the neighbors was bad enough; but what really burnt the roast was that my favorite daemon, little old Gulgoleth, became jealous of Shaddiel! Imagine, a daemon becoming jealous of a mortal! So much so that, one night, when Shaddiel by some mischance had left off his most powerful amulet, Gulgoleth sprang upon him and devoured him. Actually ate him! If you have never seen a man consumed alive by an invisible spirit, you know not what a gruesome sight is.

"Of course, the tongues wagged even more freely, and there was even talk of the magistrate's charging me with murder. And how could I have warded myself? The evidence of daemons is not accepted in court, even if I could summon the monster and compel him to confess. So, what with one thing and another, I removed to this lorn spot and have dwelt here ever since. My clients bring me the things I need from Utica. From Utica they bring them.

"But 'tis sad, sometimes, to sit by oneself and listen to the play of the waves and the cries of the wild beasts. And of course, there's the hazard"—she rolled her eyes at Zopyros and tittered—"that some strong man like you will take advantage of me. An you did, I could do nought, nought whatever, to stay you." With downcast eyes and a shy smirk, she quivered all over, like a vast mass of jelly.

Zopyros nervously cleared his throat. "Madam, no true Pythagorean would so abuse the hospitality of a virtuous woman. What's for dinner?"

Dinner was a simple repast of fish, bread, cheese, and olives. Nevertheless, after his long ride, Zopyros found it delicious. He felt he could have eaten the witch's pet daemon Gulgoleth, assuming that daemons were edible. He looked up to see the witch, who had eaten more than Zopyros and Ahiram put together, staring intently at him.

"What is it?" he said.

"I was looking at your soul, he-he!" said Saphanbaal.

"Well, it is some comfort to know I have one. What saw you?"

"Your fate."

Zopyros shifted uneasily. "What is my fate?"

"Yours will be a long life, with much joy and much grief." The witch's voice boomed, as if she were speaking from one of her caves. "Some of your ardently sought goals you shall achieve—and then either have them slip from your grasp, or find that they were not worth the striving. You will be hindered by one grave fault and upheld by one great virtue."

"And those are?"

"The fault is that you are not as other men. You feel not as they do. Matters that overjoy them delight you not, whereas you rejoice in things that are of little worth to them. Therefore, they find you cold and lacking in oneness with themselves. You will have but few true friends.

"The virtue is that yours is a hard, tough soul. You can not only endure solitude, but even take pleasure in it, for your own thoughts are company enow. When things seem at their worst, you console yourself with the thought that better men have suffered worse, that the things that grieve you will seem of little moment ten years hence, and that you may do better in that other life, whereof your philosophy teaches." She shook herself as if coming out of a trance. "Why give I such a priceless reading gratis? Some god must have put the words into my mouth. Hate you not the latter part of summer's drouth? My daemons tell me that 'twill soon be broken. Come on, both of you, and help me prepare for my clients. Now, have a care lest you tread on the toes of a spirit!"

She led them into the largest cave. Ledges had been chiseled out of the walls. On these ledges, heaped in disorder, were boxes, bags, jars, phials, rolls of parchment and papyrus, herbs, skulls and other bones, a small stuffed crocodile, tortoise shells, ostrich eggs, feathers, odd-shaped stones, and other magical accessories. Other objects hung from the ceiling: lamps, bird cages, masks, and in the center of the cave a jar. The jar hung by two strings, forming a V. Directly over it a polished circular plate of yellow metal, a foot in diameter, was set in the ceiling. The roof of the cavern seemed to sparkle with little points of light scattered over its rocky surface. Saphanbaal, following Zopyros' gaze, explained: That is the metal they call mountain copper."

"Oh." Zopyros had heard of *oreichalkos* but had never seen any. He had long wanted to get his hands on a piece to test its feel under tools, its melting point, and its other qualities. "Would you sell it?"

"And lose my moon? My very Tanith? Nay!"

"Moon, madam?"

"Let me explain the needs of my profession. Let me explain. I am a true witch, an authentic sorceress. I command spirits of fell power, utter mighty spells to work weal or woe, and see into hidden things far away or in the misty future. But"—she gave that repulsive giggle—"even the mightiest wizard knows times when his spells are countermanded by the influence of the stars, or his rebellious daemons shirk their duties to him, or his second sight wavers and blurs. Therefore must we of the magical craft impress our clients by base material means, lest they desert us for practitioners of lesser power and probity.

"This apparatus on the ceiling—the plate of mountain copper and the fish scales glued to the rock—are the moon and the stars. Ere the sitting begin, I light an Etruscan candle in this jar and cover the jar with a cloth. A string leads from the cloth back to yonder curtained niche. You, Master Ahiram, shall hold the other end of the thread. When I cry: 'Aroint you, rocks! Let the heavens be revealed!' you shall pull the cloth from off the jar and draw it back into your hiding place. The light of the candle, reflected from the plate and scales, will convince the boobies that they verily behold the moon and stars above them.

"You, Master Zopyros …" Thrusting a hand into her bosom to scratch, she gave further directions for producing thaumaturgical effects.

"You trust us far," said Zopyros. "How know you we shall not give away your secrets?"

"Ah, well, as to that, you have a secret or two yourselves, have you not? Have you not, in sooth? So we must needs trust each other, willy-nilly." She giggled. "And sure am I that no such big, beautiful man as yourself would wrong a poor lone woman! Know you that I was once beautiful, too?"

A small charcoal fire glowed on the floor of the cave. Saphanbaal, wrapped in a vast black cloak, which hid all but her face, sat cross-legged facing the entrance. Around the tiny fire six other persons, four men and two women, sat on mats on the earthen floor. All had ridden for hours, on asses, mules, and traveling carts, from Utica four leagues away. All sat silently, their faces dim in the faint, ruddy glow. The smell of incense filled the cave. Beside the witch stood a pail full of lumps of charcoal, with a small scoop resting on top of it.

Zopyros and Ahiram crouched at the back of the cave, where a sharp bend in the cavity and a jutting wall of rock provided a lair for the witch's confederates. A greasy, dirt-colored curtain divided this recess from the principal part of the cavern, and Zopyros and Ahiram now peered through the crack in this curtain. Within the recess, the only illumination was a faint blue glow from a rushlight, thrust into a cleft in the rock. The man and the boy each wore a dark cloth tied over the lower part of his face, lest his visage reflect the firelight and draw the attention of the sitters. In addition, the mask helped to remind the talkative child to keep silence.

Fidgeting, Zopyros wondered if they were going to sit there all night. Then a stir at the mouth of the cave announced the last arrival, a man of mature years and dignified bearing, albeit Zopyros could see little of him beside his long white beard and the black cloak that covered him from head to foot. This, he understood, was a visitor of no common degree. The man was one of the two suphetes or chief magistrates of Utica.

The suphete murmured a brief greeting; Saphanbaal handed a cushion to the sitter next to her, who passed it on around to the magistrate. As the suphete sat down with the rest, Zopyros thought that Saphanbaal must be no ordinary adventuress, to draw to her sittings a man from the haughty Punic merchant aristocracy, and moreover compel him to sit with rag, tag, and bobtail of her regular circle of clients.

Still the witch sat silently. At last, when Zopyros was ready to jump out of his skin with impatience, her deep voice boomed through the cavern. She intoned:

"Friends, we are gathered together here to pierce the veil that hides matters of moment from mortal sight. To this end I have spent the day in prayer and fasting." (Zopyros, smiling in the dark, recalled that she had eaten a dinner big enough for a hungry lion.) "I have cast a mighty conjuration to summon a host of fell spirits across the black gulfs of space and time. My spell went forth through all the corners of the universe, rousing the winged daemons of the lofty aether and the scaly monsters of the bottomless pits, as the twitch of a trapped fly in a spider's web arouses the spider. In mystic caverns in the cragged mountains beyond the desert, bats flew squeaking in circles to warn the black wizards who dwell therein. On ancient battlefields, the ghosts of the unburied dead stirred restlessly. The night wind whispered the spell as it flew, and were-leopard and were-hyena slunk to their lairs, whimpering with fear. The serpent under the rock knew; and the owl on its bough knew. They knew. The very gods in their jeweled heavenly palaces"—she touched breast, lips, and forehead—"looked at one another and said: 'Saphanbaal conjures again. Well, let her conjure, for she is beloved of the gods!'"

Saphanbaal picked up the scoop, dug a small quantity of charcoal out of the pail, and sprinkled this fuel on the fire. She did this a second time. After another wait, she spoke again:

"Now my attendant spirits draw nigh. I feel the magical wind of their coming. From the blue-green depths of the sea, from the jungle-lost ruins of ancient temples, from the icy caves of the Mountains of the Moon they come. If any have arrived, let them signify their presence!"

There was a long pause. Then the charcoal fire hissed. The coals moved and seethed as if something alive were under them. The sitters gasped with awe. Zopyros, watching from his side chamber, would have gasped, too, had he not helped to prepare the fuel. Mixed with the first scoopful of coals were a number of lumps of alum coated with wax. When the wax melted, the alum bubbled, stirring the coals.

"They are here!" cried Saphanbaal. They have come! Now for the sacrifice!"

Her hands came out from under her cloak. In her left hand she held one of the little birds from the cages, securely trussed. The bird uttered one cheep of protest. Then the witch cut its throat and let its blood trickle into the coals, making them hiss more loudly.

"Let us all sing the invocation to the moon!" she said. In an unmusical mixture of voices and keys, they sang:

"Infernal, and earthy, and supernal Bombo, come!
Saint of the streets, and brilliant one, that strays by night;
Foe of radiance, but friend and mate of gloom;
In howl of dogs rejoicing, and in crimson gore,
Wading 'mid corpses through tombs of lifeless dust,
Panting for blood; with fear convulsing men.
Gorgo, and Mormo, and Luna, and of many shapes,
Come, propitious, to our sacrificial rites!"

166

"Aroint you, rocks, and let the moon appear!" shouted Saphanbaal.

Zopyros nudged Ahiram, who crouched beside him in the dark. The boy, suppressing a giggle, pulled a cord and drew the cloth off the jar. Saphanbaal, glancing up, screamed:

"Behold! The heavens are above you!"

Although both man and boy had moved back into the recess for better concealment, Zopyros could well imagine what the sitters saw. The light in the jar, reflected dimly on the metal disk and the fish scales glued to the black rock above, looked to the bewildered sitters for all the world like the moon and stars as seen through a murky glass. Saphanbaal's awe-struck clients gazed up at this artificial heaven with cries of wonder. The witch boomed:

"Resheph, lord of thunder, cast thy mantle of dark cloud about us! Extend unto us thy good will! Lend us thy might!"

This was Zopyros' cue to take out a packet of powder, shake a handful into his palm, and put the packet back on the shelf. While Ahiram, flattened against the rocks lest he be seen, opened the curtain wider, Zopyros tossed the powder into the flame of the rushlight. The powder ignited with a faint *floomp*; the bright flash was followed by a cloud of smoke, which billowed out into the main cave. Zopyros instantly picked up a basket of stones weighing several pounds apiece and poured the stones out upon a sheet of hammered bronze, which lay on the floor of the recess. The stones struck the metal with a magnificent crash.

When the reverberations of this clangor had died away, Zopyros ventured another peek through the curtain. Half the sitters lay prone with their faces covered in an ecstasy of terror. Even the suphete, whose dignity forbade him to sink to the floor of the cave like the others, had his hands pressed to his face.

"The gods and spirits are present!" said Saphanbaal. They are all around us! One flits about yonder! See! See! Another peers over the shoulder of my lord the suphete!"

The suphete shifted nervously on his cushion and glanced over his shoulder.

"Ask your questions!" said the witch. "Ask, and it shall be answered unto you!"

"Who—who will win the next election of suphetes?" said the suphete in an unsteady voice.

"My gracious lord, the gods have ordained that one of the twain shall be a man of most rigorous probity, a man of pure motives and actions; whereas the other shall be a rogue of a demagogue who, while charming the citizens with flattery and promises, meaneth to enrich himself and his friends from the public till. Next."

"How can I make my wife conceive?" said a man.

"I can furnish thee with a phial of genuine water of the mighty Nile, which as all wise men know is most efficacious in causing conception. 'Tis cheap at a shekel. Next."

"Who stole the brooch from my dressing table?" said one of the women in belligerent tones.

Saphanbaal held her hands before her eyes. "I see night and darkness. I see a house, whose owners lie wrapped in tranquil slumber. I see a shadowy form flitting through the door and peering about for any loose thing to steal."

"What looks he like?" asked the woman.

"'Tis too dark to see clearly, but from his height and swarthiness I take him for some vagabond of a Numidian. Now he snatcheth up the brooch, where it lieth on the woman's dressing table, and silently goeth out. I see him, mounted upon his ass, jogging down the road toward Carthage. I doubt not thou wilt find thy brooch at the thieves' market in the great city."

The other woman said: "Can I speak with the spirit of my dead child once more?"

Saphanbaal gasped, trembled, mumbled, and then burst into childish tones: "Hail, Mama ..."

The sitting went on and on. Saphanbaal spoke in the voices of several people. The sitters swore they recognized these voices as those of persons dear to them in life. She answered more questions with artful ambiguity. More hymns were sung. The witch uttered a small sermon on the power of spirits and the wonders of magical science. At last she said:

"The spirits wax restless. I must needs dismiss them, lest they wreak harm upon the living; especially Gulgoleth, whom I employ only for the most baleful tasks." She went into a stream of gibberish, waving her arms and crying at the last: "In the name of the god who must not be named, begone! Begone! Begone!"

Meanwhile Zopyros, acting upon his instructions, had tied a bunch of tow by a string to the leg of another bird. Holding the bird firmly in one hand, with the other he touched the tow to the rush-light. When the tow blazed up, he opened the curtain and tossed the bird and its flaming burden out into the cave. The bird took wing at once, trailing the blazing tow behind it. In the darkness, only a fiery streak could be seen. As the sitters cowered shrieking, the bird circled thrice around their heads and raced out into the night.

"That was Gulgoleth," said the witch in ordinary conversational tones. "The vain creature would fain make a show of his departure. Good night, my friends; the gods be with you on your long road homeward."

When the seekers had gone, Zopyros and Ahiram came out of hiding. Zopyros felt a belated pity for the bird whose throat had been cut, since the divine Pythagoras had forbidden blood sacrifice and unnecessary harm to animals. But the Tarentine salved his conscience with the thought that the other bird, now freed, would probably survive its fiery flight.

"Splendid, splendid!" said Saphanbaal, shaking the bowl in which the sitters had placed their offerings, until the coins clinked. "I would you could go into partnership with me. We could make a fine thing of this, my dear apprentice witches!"

"Nay; I have other plans, alas," said Zopyros. "Now, with your permission, madam, we'll withdraw to our quarters. It is far too late for such small fry as my charge, here, to be up and about."

"If it wax cold in that little side cave—" began Saphanbaal with a giggle. Zopyros picked up the sleepy child and hurried out, pretending not to hear.

At breakfast next morning, Saphanbaal swatted a fly on her dirty arm and said: "'Twas cool in the night, was it not? Say not that I failed to warn you. Master Zopyros, I dreamt a dreadful dream last night, concerning you. Concerning you."

"Indeed?" said Zopyros. A slight chill made him shudder, even though he knew the woman for a charlatan. "What was it?"

"I dreamt of a great shining city, and war raged about that city." Then you came, tall as a cork oak tree, bearing a mighty bow. You set to this bow a fiery arrow, as long as a ship's mast. To the point of this arrow a bunch of tow had been tied. Another man—him I saw not clearly, but meseems he was as short and stout as you are tall and bony—kindled this bunch of tow with a torch. You let fly your arrow. It soared up into the heavens and swooped down upon the city. The flaming tow set fire to the nearby houses. Soon the entire metropolis was blazing fiercely. When the fire had burnt out, nought was left for the besiegers to loot—nought but one vast field of gray ash, stirred by the passing breezes."

"And then?" said Zopyros intently.

"That is all. Then I awoke."

Zopyros frowned. "I had a like message from the Sibyl of Cumae. Could you interpret such an oracle?"

She shook her head, as Phoenicians did to indicate the negative. "You've seen how a poor lone woman must sometimes cozen her clients when her spirits fail to furnish the wonders they demand. Mark you: I could easily concoct an interpretation to salve your soul. But it were not the true one. The true one, I do confess, I know not. But this dream frights me. It frights me, so vivid it was."

They finished their breakfast in uneasy silence. The morning was passed in chopping wood for Saphanbaal, watering the mule, and playing hide-and-seek with Ahiram. As he finished a meager lunch, Zopyros asked:

"Will there be another sitting tonight?"

"Nay, not for seven more. For we Canaanites hold the number seven sacred. Hence sittings are held at intervals of seven nights: on the nights of the full, half, and new moons."

"We Pythagoreans hold ten in equal honor," said Zopyros.

"Be that as it may, Captain Bostar comes tonight, if all go well and he see my signal, to snatch away you and the lad."

"How shall we get out to his ship, without any landing place?"

"I have a little skiff, hidden in yonder small cave. You shall row to the ship in it."

"How, then, will you get your boat back?"

170

"A cord is coiled within the skiff. I shall hold the end of this cord and, when you are safely aboard the *Sudech*, shall pull the boat back to me. You are not the first to be thus whisked away, he-he! The old boat leaks a mite, wherefore you must needs ply the dipper you'll find with the oars."

Zopyros entered the cave she had indicated and confirmed her statements about the boat. When he returned to the ledge, she said:

"It grieves me that you'll not be here long enough to learn more of the secrets of magic; for my occult powers detect a rare sympathy betwixt you and myself." She fluttered her eyelids at Zopyros and giggled, so that her double chin and mountainous breasts quivered. "I could teach you other arts, too, my fair young lord! For I have seen much in my life. Said I that I was once a dancing girl?"

"Nay."

"I have danced before many great ones—the suphetes of Carthage and the Persian governor of Egypt. Was I lithe and graceful then! Although hateful age has brushed me with its bony fingers, once I was fair indeed. Really beautiful!"

"I'm sure—" began Zopyros, but she rushed on:

"Why, the governor offered half a talent for me! In those days half a talent went farther than it does today. That Persian was a lordly, manly man. Why, seven tricks a night might scarce abate his ardor! You resemble him in feature, dear Zopyros, but whether you'd surpass his prowess in lectual matters remains to be seen.

"Would you were here in spring, when the flowers bloom! Then is this dusty corner of New Canaan a fair land to see. Where was I? Oh, yes, a dancing girl was I ere I sought the higher wisdom and perforce forswore the pleasures of the flesh. When I danced before the king of Tyre, he said: "By all the baals, her breasts are fairer than the moon at its full. …""

Saphanbaal went on and on. Zopyros, embarrassed, did not know how much to believe. At least half, he thought, was surely fiction. He started a quiet game of tic-tac-toe with Ahiram to keep the boy occupied and, he hoped, to keep the child's attention off Saphanbaal's vulgarities.

Saphanbaal kept right on, tirelessly boasting of her former beauty and of the havoc she had wrought among the men who saw her. Her garrulity, her lies, her sudden changes of subject, her irritating giggle, her coy flirtatious winks, her elephantine attempts at seduction, her trick of repeating sentences, and her self-absorption combined with her personal uncleanliness to make her one of the most repellent human beings Zopyros had ever known. On the other hand, he dared not treat her brusquely lest she betray him.

There were people, he reflected, who, deciding they did not like Saphanbaal, would simply cut her throat, board the ship, and leave her body to the vultures. But, as a Pythagorean, he could not consider such a ruthless course. Moreover, he did not know the signal that would fetch Bostar in to shore.

At last, to stop the inane flow of chatter, he suggested a game of Sacred Way with her. Saphanbaal had never played the game but seemed to learn it readily enough, Soon she suggested a small stake. Nevertheless, she made foolish moves, no matter how often Zopyros pointed them out and tried to teach her better. Finding herself losing, she loudly insisted upon larger stakes and called upon her stable of daemons to aid her.

The daemons, however, seemed to have taken the day off. The pile of shekels, drachmai, and smaller coins in front of Zopyros grew. At last she cried:

"Recreant knave! By Bes's beard, at this rate, you'll not leave me enough to eat on for the next month!" She angrily knocked the board aside, so that the die and the men flew hither and thither about the ledge. "Even though I eat no more than a bird!"

"*Ea!*" said Zopyros. "You need not destroy my set, just because you've been losing! As for the bird, no doubt you are right if you mean the ostrich of the African desert." He picked up the pieces and counted them. "Harken, madam; I have no wish to impoverish you. I'll return my winnings if you will give me my pick of your magical gear."

"Oh, forgive a foolish old woman! Forgive me, dear, sweet boy!" she cooed. Those terms were just enow, specially since you've promised me the mule. Ask what you will."

"I want that metal plate you use for a moon."

"*Ai!* I am shent! Anything but that! The man-made heaven is one of my best stocks in trade! In the name of your Greek gods, I beg you!

Deprive not a poor old witch, who holds you in warmest esteem, of her means of livelihood!"

"Well," said Zopyros, disappointed, "what else could you offer?"

She clawed in her billowy bosom and brought out the burning glass. "How about this? For a traveling man, it is ofttimes quicker than flint and steel; and certes 'tis better far than rubbing sticks together."

"Will that not leave you as badly off as the loss of the plate?"

"Nay; I have another. Here, take it!"

Zopyros, who had heard of such lenses but had never seen one, happily slipped over his head the cord from which the object hung. Then he said:

"My dear Saphanbaal, to leave Yaphê in good condition, I must needs exercise him. Come, Ahiram; we go for a muleback ride."

When a blocky black shape showed clear against the moonlit waters, Saphanbaal kindled a torch and, standing on the edge of the ledge, waved it thrice up and down. A spark appeared against the blackness of the ship, moving likewise. The ship grew larger as Captain Bostar crept in toward shore. Zopyros inched the little dugout down the rough rocks from the ledge to the water's edge.

"'Twill be some moments ere he comes within rowing distance," said Saphanbaal. "Darling Zopyros, could you not—ah—leave me with a fond memory of your stay? ..."

"I am honored, madam," grunted Zopyros, looking up from his struggle with the boat, "but I am much too nervous now." He slid the hull into the water, hoping that he had not aggravated the leaks. Then he carried his bag down to the water, climbed to the ledge again, and said:

"Come here, Ahiram."

Zopyros picked up the child, hugged him, and swung him astride one hip, saying: "Hold tight, now!" As Ahiram grasped Zopyros around the neck, Saphanbaal muttered something about boy-loving Greeks. Ignoring her, Zopyros groped his way down to the water, clutching Ahiram with one arm and steadying himself with the other. At the boat, he lowered Ahiram into the stern, saying;

"Now sit there and, whatever you do, do not stand up!" He placed his traveling bag in the bow, so that it would serve as a back to the thwart. Then he gingerly lowered his own weight into the craft, sat down facing aft on the thwart, put out the oars, and pushed off. Somewhere in the distance a hyena laughed.

"Ahiram!" said Zopyros. "Take that dipper." He indicated the dipper of wood and leather in front of Ahiram's feet. "Now scoop up the water in the bottom and throw it over the side—*phy!*—I did not say to throw it at me!"

Zopyros wiped his arm across his face, from which a dipperful of water ran down. On his second try, Ahiram got most of the water in the dipper overboard.

"That's right; keep on bailing!" said Zopyros, bending his back to the oars.

A light but strong cord, fastened to the stern of the boat, curved up to the ledge where Saphanbaal stood. As Zopyros rowed out from shore, Saphanbaal paid out the cord. The boat bounced perilously in the slight swell, and water began to come aboard—some over the gunwales, some through the leaks in the bottom.

"Bail, Ahiram, bail!" said Zopyros. Then he called across the water: "Farewell, O Saphanbaal! Many thanks for your kindness! The gods of Canaan prosper you!"

He could afford to be cordial, now, because he was out of her reach. (Unless, the horrid thought struck him, she decided to haul the boat shoreward by its cord!) He rowed faster, glancing over his shoulder at the dark shape of the merchantman. Ahiram, bailing, asked:

"Is Mother on the ship?"

"Nay, lad. We have a way to go yet."

"I liked Saphanbaal. Are all witches like her?"

"I hope not. Keep bailing, or we shall find ourselves in the sea!"

For some minutes Zopyros rowed and Ahiram bailed. But, every time the talkative infant spoke, he forgot to bail, and Zopyros had to bark at him. At last, feeling the water rise around his ankles, Zopyros snatched the dipper from the boy and, with a score of rapid scoops, got the water back down to a less ominous level. While he bailed, the boat drifted, bobbing and rocking.

Zopyros handed the dipper back to Ahiram, saying earnestly: "Keep bailing, son, no matter what!"

"I tire of bailing."

"There's no help for it, unless you would swim the rest of the way."

"But I wax sleepy!"

"We cannot have you going to sleep, because I can't bail and row at the same time. Wake up!"

The water was rising again. As it rose, the boat moved more sluggishly. Casting about for some means of keeping Ahiram awake, Zopyros said: "Let's play a game. Let's pretend we have forgotten Punic and speak nothing but Greek. How would you say: 'I'm sleepy' in that tongue?"

"*Eimai—eimai hypnôdês.*"

"Good! Keep bailing! Faster!"

Despite Zopyros' efforts to hold Ahiram to his task, the water gained again. Again Zopyros had to stop rowing and take the dipper himself. By the time he had beaten the water level back to within a digit of the bottom, Ahiram had fallen quietly asleep. From then on, it was a nightmare struggle to row the waterlogged craft a few strokes, bail frantically, then row some more. Each time the water seemed to gain more between bailings, and the ship appeared to come no closer. ...

At last they reached the ship. Zopyros had to risk capsizing by standing up in the wretched skiff to grasp the gunwale of the merchantman. With his free hand he boosted Ahiram up into the waiting arms of the sailors, tossed his wet bag after, and climbed over the rail himself. The half-filled boat wallowed shoreward as Saphanbaal reeled in her line.

A stout figure, standing before Zopyros on the moonlit deck, bowed and said in Punic-accented Greek: "Rejoice, my lord Zopyros! I am Captain Bostar of the *Sudech*, and your humble servant. How can I serve you?"

"Be in good health," said Zopyros in the same language. "We must find a place for the boy to sleep—"

"Harkening and obedience! But he seems to have found a place for himself," said the captain, pointing.

175

Ahiram had curled up on the deck and fallen asleep again, with his head on his arm. In obedience to the mate's orders, the sailors hurried about, letting out the sail and swinging the ship's bow eastward. Zopyros wrapped Ahiram in a blanket and moved him to a safer place. Then he followed Captain Bostar into the cabin aft. Although this cabin was larger than that on the *Muttumalein*, Zopyros still had to stoop to enter the tiny room. A chair, a stool, a small three-legged table, and the captain's bunk took up most of the space.

They sat across from each other at the little table. Over the table a small bronze lamp, suspended from the ceiling, swung back and forth with the motion of the ship. In the dim yellow lamplight, Captain Bostar was seen to be a man of medium height, powerfully built, with a large curly black beard. Besides the usual rings in his ears and on his fingers, he wore a costly-looking necklace of amulets alternating with semiprecious stones. On his head sat a cylindrical cap with a scarf wound turban-wise around it. Below the turban, pouchy black eyes peered out on either side of a large, fleshy nose.

"Will my lord deign to sip a drop of wretched Byblian?" said Bostar, pouring from a small jar into a beaker.

"Thank you," said Zopyros. "You seem to run an efficient ship."

"Your lordship is much too kind! May the gods of Hellas requite your courtesy! By the way"—he suddenly changed his language to Punic—"speak you the Canaanitish tongue?"

"No, alas," said Zopyros. He had remembered Evnos' warning that Bostar was not the most trustworthy of sea captains. Besides, the man's excessive politeness made him wary. "Have you a regular arrangement with the witch?"

Bostar shrugged, spreading his hands. "In my trade one must have contacts with people of many kinds, in many lands. Else, how should I learn of profitable deals before my competitors do? How long was your excellent self in New Phoenicia?"

"Not so long as I should have liked." Two could play at the game of evasion. "I found Carthage a most impressive city. Will this be your last voyage of the season?"

"That is as the gods of the weather decide. ..."

The conversation became a dull repetition of polite phrases. Zopyros finished his wine, excused himself, and went out on deck. He found a sheltered place near the child, wrapped himself in his cloak, pillowed his head on his duffel bag, and fell into uneasy slumber. The gentle roll of the ship, the groan and creak of timbers, the song of the wind in the rigging, and the rhythmic splash, splash of the blunt stem smiting the waves were woven into his dreams.

The sun was up when the sound of voices awakened Zopyros. The captain, the mate, and two sailors were standing in a group, arguing in Punic. As he opened his eyes and saw that they were watching him, he caught the tail of a sentence:

"... I told you not to speak so loudly; now he wakens!"

This, thought Zopyros, was interesting. He smiled, yawned, stretched, said "Rejoice!" and pretended to go back to sleep.

"No harm is done," said Bostar's voice. "He knows not the Punic tongue."

"But the boy does!" said another voice.

"The boy's gone aft, out of earshot." Zopyros recognized the voice as that of the mate.

"'Tis not too late to seize them now—"

"Nay," came Bostar's voice again. "He wears a sword beneath his raiment. He's a big, strong youth and no man's fool. In the cabin, he turned my questions aside as neatly as you please. Did we not succeed at the first grab, by Milkarth's iron yard, he'd have a head or an arm off one of us ere we secured him! Tonight were better."

The mate said: "When he slumbers tonight, we'll bind and gag him and the lad and hide them below deck, lest they cry a rescue whilst we stop at Akragas."

A sailor said: "Feed him well and ply him with wine and he'll sleep during the day."

"Aye," said another. "The sooner he's trussed the better. What think you he'll fetch on the block at Tyre, sir?"

Bostar: "With his wit and education, he should bring at least eight or ten pounds of silver. And the boy will fetch at least the half of that when he's been to the castrator's."

The mate said: "Won't this queer future deals with Evnos, Captain?"

"Bugger Evnos! I'll not reject the gifts of the gods for any mealy-mouthed ransomer in the Inner Sea. ..."

Speech sank to murmurs as the group moved off. Zopyros cast off his pretense of sleep and got up. He was shaking with rage and fear, although he tried to hide the fact by staring stonily seaward. Seize him and his protégé to sell in the Persian Empire—the boy as a eunuch—would they? He'd see about that.

For a time he stood at the rail, so filled with fury that he could hardly think. Little by little his mind cleared. It was lucky, he thought, that he had awakened when he did and frightened them off. A few heartbeats more and they might have nerved themselves to throw themselves upon him right then. ...

Dirty, treacherous, murderous, baby-burning, money grubbing, Phoenician swine! It served him right for ever trusting one of them. ...

He checked himself. That was no way for a Pythagorean to think. Pythagoras had stressed the worth, or lack of it, of the individual man, regardless of his tribe or nation. One of his closest friends had been a barbarian from Scythia; another had been a Thracian. Zopyros had found Canaanites good, bad, or indifferent like other men. At the moment he was having a run of bad Phoenicians, just as the die of his game set might turn up a three several throws in a row.

Meanwhile, he must think of some means of escape. What would happen if he simply drew his sword and started dashing about the ship, killing every man he came to? He might get a few, but the rest would gang together with knives, oars, and boathooks. In addition, Bostar probably had a chest of weapons stowed away against pirates. In the long run, they would probably kill or capture him. Even if he did slay all the scoundrels, the ship was much too large for one man to sail, even if that man were a sailor, which Zopyros was not. ...

"Master Zopyros!" said Ahiram. "That thing the witch gave you—"

Zopyros spoke slowly and softly in Greek: "You forget, Ahiram, that I don't speak Punic."

"Oh." The boy frowned, then tried in stumbling Greek: "That—that thing—make fire—you know—"

"Oh, you want to see it make fire? Then fetch me some scraps of oakum and stuff for tinder."

Presently the boy had gathered a handful of litter. Zopyros placed it on the deck at the stern, next to the bulwark, where the rising sun shone upon it. To make the performance more impressive, he waved his free hand and murmured the chant that Saphanbaal had used:

"Ye spirits of fire, come to my aid! ..."

A curl of smoke arose from the litter, to be whisked away by the wind. When a shadow fell athwart his fire, he looked up to see the mate and a couple of sailors staring at him. The captain shouldered past them, crying:

"What do you, Master Zopyros? Try to set my ship afire? Stop it at once!"

Bostar pushed Zopyros brusquely aside, stamped on the smoldering tinder, then kicked the litter so that the wind snatched away the fragments.

"I was only showing off this magical crystal to the boy," said Zopyros with a weak smile. "I'm terribly sorry, but I never thought of the risk of fire."

"Well, well, no harm is done," said the captain. "Pray forgive my rudeness, most excellent lord; but the safety of his ship is the foremost thought of every good captain." Bostar bowed, rubbing his hands together and smiling unctuously. "You have pardoned me, I hope? I'm only a poor rough mariner, unused to intercourse with such fine gentlemen as yourself. I beg you, do me the honor of stepping into my wretched little cabin and sharing the morning repast with me!"

Two plates were set on the little table. Zopyros' plate was heaped with enough food for two, and the captain pressed wine upon him. Zopyros nibbled and sipped sparingly, rolling each mouthful carefully over his tongue before swallowing it lest it be charged with some drug.

Afterward he went out on deck. He watched the sea and played with Ahiram, conscious of the sidelong glances of the sailors. They hoped he would go to sleep; he would disappoint them. Once during the long, disagreeable day he asked the mate:

"When shall we reach Akragas?"

"If the wind holds, before dawn tomorrow. The big risk in this passage is that an overcast will come up so you cannot tell direction.

Then the wind backs or veers, and you hit Libya or Sardinia when you were aiming for Sicily."

"Like that Samian who started for Egypt and ended up at the Pillars of Herakles," said Zopyros.

"I can understand a Hellene captain's making such a mistake," said the mate, "but no Canaanitish mariner ever went so far astray!"

"I'm sure your navigation is expert," said Zopyros.

Late in the afternoon, the captain invited Zopyros to dine with him. This meal repeated the earlier one, with the captain hospitably urging him to overeat and overdrink. As the dinner ended, Zopyros said:

"Captain, do you play Sacred Way?"

"A little, my lord. Have you a set with you?"

"Yes. How about a game after it gets dark?"

"Whatever pleases you will delight me, sir."

When the stars came out, Zopyros went back to the cabin, carrying his game set in one hand and leading Ahiram with the other. He said:

"If you don't mind, Captain, I should like to put the little fellow to sleep on the floor here, where I can keep an eye on him while we play."

"Harkening and obedience!" The captain bowed and smirked. "Place him on my bunk yonder."

The evening wore on. Game followed game, while the yellow-plumed lamp swayed back and forth over the little table. From time to time the mate or a sailor appeared at the door of the cabin. Sometimes they exchanged looks with the captain.

At last, Zopyros thought, the time for action had come. He threw the die, made his move, and rose abruptly, cracking his skull against the overhead.

"*Oimoi!*" he groaned, clutching at his head.

"Are you hurt, generous sir?" said Bostar.

"No; just a little bump. I deserve it for being stupid. Go on with your play while I look at the boy."

Stooping, with pounding heart, he stepped behind Captain Bostar, who was throwing the die. Zopyros quietly reached under his tunic and got his hand on the hilt of his sword. Then with one quick blur of motion he whirled, drew, reached around with his left hand, and caught a fistful of Bostar's beard. Jerking it up, he touched the edge of his sword to Bostar's throat.

"Be still!" he whispered in Punic. "One move and off goes your head!"

"What—what means this outrage?" gasped Bostar, tensely gripping the sides of his chair.

"You know well enough. Call the mate. Call him at once, I say!" Zopyros increased the pressure on the Phoenician's throat.

"Softly, pray! You're cutting me! I bleed!"

Zopyros, leaning over, saw that he had indeed made a slight cut in Bostar's flesh. "Well then, call the mate!"

"Milko!" cried the captain hoarsely.

"Aye?" said the mate, putting his head in the door. When he saw what was going on, he took a step forward. Zopyros shouted:

"Stand back, if you would not see your captain's throat cut!"

"He means it, too!" said Bostar in a quavery, tearful voice. "Stand back, Milko!"

The faces of sailors appeared over the mate's shoulders. Zopyros said: "I have just made it clear to your captain that I am fain not to be sold in Tyre. So we shall disembark at Akragas as planned."

Milko said to the captain in an accusing voice: "You said he knew no Canaanitish!"

"How was I to know?" said the captain. "The lying Greek deceived me!" To Zopyros he added: "You cozened us, you unprincipled scoundrel!"

Zopyros grinned. "Oh, I'm a terrible fellow, so to befool a gang of honest kidnappers! But we have business. Milko, fetch me a length—say, fifteen feet—of light rope. Hurry up!" He pushed the sword edge into the captain's flesh.

"Do as he says!" wailed Bostar as Zopyros increased the pressure of the blade.

When he had his rope, Zopyros said to the sailors: "Now get out on deck and stay away from the cabin. If there be any attempt at rushing us, be sure your gallant captain shall be the first to die. Go!"

Zopyros made Bostar extend his arms behind him with the wrists together. Taking one end of the rope in his teeth and manipulating it with his free hand, he took several turns around Bostar's wrists. Then he risked driving the point of his sword into the planking long enough to tie a hard knot with both hands. He passed the rope under the seat of the chair to the front and tied Bostar's ankles to the chair legs. He prowled around the chair, testing the firmness of the knots. Then he set the sword again against Bostar's throat and called:

"Milko!"

"Aye, sir?" said the mate in a hushed voice, as he appeared again in the doorway.

"Forget not to set your course for Akragas. We should reach it ere dawn, remember? So, if broad day burst upon us with no Sicily in sight …" He pointed at Bostar and drew a finger across his throat. "See you to it."

Before the mate had time to depart on his errand, there came a disturbance. Ahiram, awakened by the loud voices, sat up, rubbed his eyes, stood up, and started for the door of the cabin.

"Come back, Ahiram!" yelled Zopyros, too late. Quick as the strike of a snake, Milko caught the boy's arm, swept him against his body, and touched the point of his dagger to the boy's throat.

The mate's narrow face split in a grin. "Now, good my lord, an you slay our captain, we'll do likewise with your brat!"

Zopyros silently cursed himself for his stupidity. For several heartbeats he and the mate confronted each other over the bodies of their respective hostages. Ahiram wailed:

"But, Zopyros, I had to *go!*"

Zopyros gathered his thoughts. He wondered if he could regain the upper hand by beginning slowly to saw off Bostar's head. Then another idea struck him. With his left hand, he felt inside his tunic and brought out the burning glass, which hung from a string around his neck. "Know you this?"

The mate gave back a trifle. "Aye—it—'tis that magical crystal wherewith you started the fire this morn."

"Now," said Zopyros with a sinister grin, "belike you think that, even if I slay your captain and you kill the lad, you and the sailors can still overpower me, so you'll come out with whole skins. But I have tidings for you: namely, that by this little device I can make certain that all of us shall perish."

"How so?" said the mate, an anxious note in his voice. Behind him the sailors exchanged uneasy glances. Ahiram noisily wept.

"By burning a hole in the bottom of the ship. Can you swim ashore across half the Inner Sea?"

"I cannot swim at all," muttered a sailor.

"But you would die also!" said Milko. "I believe it not! You are shamming!"

"Oh, think you so? I fear not death, because the Pythagorean philosophy teaches that I shall live again in another body. I shall now begin the spell." Holding the lens with its axis vertical, he slowly chanted:

> "*Ye spirits of fire, come to my aid!*
> *Gulgoleth! Shehabarim!* ..."

"Smell you not something burning?" said a sailor in a loud whisper.

"Stop him!" cried Captain Bostar. "Let the boy go! Death I fear no more than most men, but I will not see my beautiful ship destroyed! 'Tis not worth the paltry price they'd bring!"

> "... *Lamia white!*
> *Come hither from gulfs of eternal night* ..."

"Stop!" screamed Bostar. "Release the child! I command it!"

Milko reluctantly loosened his grasp on the weeping Ahiram, who scuttled around the cabin to clutch one of Zopyros' legs.

"Now," said Zopyros, "be so good as to set the course for Akragas. Let us have no more nonsense. And you, Ahiram, stay behind me. Go piddle in the corner if you must."

The mate and the sailors went away. Zopyros remained standing behind Bostar. He took his sword from the captain's throat but held it ready in case of surprise.

Bostar cocked his head to look back over his shoulder.

"Ha, ha!" said he with false heartiness. "You are the world's wonder, my lord Zopyros! By the gods, a more daring rascal than I, myself! 'Tis a pity we should quarrel, when together we might achieve great deeds. Why not throw in with me? No matter that you're not a sailor.

I'll make you supercargo, to be my man of business ashore to arrange kidnappings, ransoms, illicit cargoes, and other delicate matters. In time, when you have learned enough lore of the sea, belike you may have a ship of your own."

"Nay," said Zopyros. That is not my trade."

"But think of the adventure and the profit! I know where a sunken treasure ship lies hid …"

For hours Bostar talked. He wheedled, blustered, and made promises ever more fantastic, if only Zopyros would put away his sword and unbind him. Zopyros encouraged the captain to ramble on, if only because it helped him to stave off sleepiness.

At last a faint light appeared in the doorway. Yawning, Zopyros stepped to where Ahiram lay curled in a small heap and shook the boy awake.

"Go to the door," he said, "and put your head out. Beware lest someone grab you. See if land be in sight."

Ahiram reported land on the port side. An hour later, Milko appeared.

"We near Akragas," he said.

"Good," said Zopyros. He yawned and stretched. "Tell me when the wharf is nigh."

Some time later the mate reappeared, saying: "The wharf is crowded, my lord Zopyros. We shall have to anchor in the harbor."

"Run the ship up against one of those already tied up to the wharf!"

"But my paint!" cried Captain Bostar. "You'll mar the side, if you crack not the timbers with the impact!"

Zopyros put the sword edge to Bostar's throat. At the touch of the steel, the captain moaned: "Do as he says, Milko. But if you, sir, harm my ship, I'll—I'll …"

You'll write me a letter of complaint, care of President Dionysios, Syracuse, Sicily."

The motion of the ship eased as it slid into the harbor at the mouth of the Akragas River. Sounds of harbor work, human voices, the braying of asses and mules took the place of wind and wave. Zopyros stooped and cut the rope where it bound Bostar's ankles.

"Stand up!" he said.

With his hands still bound behind him and the blade of Zopyros' sword against his neck, Captain Bostar walked—hobbling stiffly from being tied up—out of the cabin, followed closely by Zopyros and Ahiram. Far-above and fifteen furlongs away, the ruins of Akragas' magnificent temples, sacked by the Carthaginians seven years before, gleamed like a pale golden crown at the top of the long slope. The mate and the sailors, watching like a ring of wolves, moved forward a little.

"Keep back!" barked Zopyros, with a suggestive motion of his sword. He pointed. "Bring the ship in there!"

Milko took the tiller bars from a sailor and, snapping commands, guided the ship slowly toward the line of merchantmen moored along the wharf. The sailors took in sail until there was barely enough to keep the ship under way. Two sailors grunted at the sweeps.

The captain of one of the moored vessels, seeing the *Sudech* drifting toward him, rushed to the rail of his ship and began shouting in Greek: "Keep off, you dung-eating temple robber! Touch my ship, and by Herakles I'll have the law on you!" A couple of his sailors stepped to the rail of the Greek ship with boathooks.

"Keep on!" commanded Zopyros.

When the ships were less than two cubits apart and the Greek captain was dancing and waving his fists over his head, Zopyros called to a Punic sailor: "You there! You with the squint! Throw my duffel bag across to the other ship, and Baal Hammon help you if you drop it in the water!"

The sailor addressed picked up the bag and tossed it to the deck of the farther ship. The Greek sailors with the boathooks strained at their poles to keep the ships from touching. Two Punic sailors picked up oars from the deck to help in holding the ships apart.

"Ahiram!" said Zopyros. "Go to the rail!"

"I fear that angry man on the other ship—"

"Never mind him! Go, or Zopyros will spank!"

The boy went. Zopyros spun Bostar around and, with a mighty shove, sent him staggering into the midst of his own men. Then he tossed his sword across the gap, swept up Ahiram in both hands and, with a muscle-cracking effort, hurled the child across the rails of the two ships.

Seeing Zopyros unarmed, Bostar's sailors sprang at him. Just ahead of their clutching hands, Zopyros vaulted to the rail of the *Sudech* and with one long stride reached the rail of the Greek ship. His foot slipped on the second rail, so that he fell heavily and sprawled on the Hellene's deck.

When Zopyros scrambled up, the Greek captain had already planted a foot on the sword. On the *Sudech*, a rattle of commands sent the Phoenician sailors to their posts. They pushed off with their oars, and their ship began to draw away from the Greek merchantman.

"What in the name of the Dog goes on?" shouted the Greek captain. "What kind of vagabonds are you, to come leaping aboard my ship like sea daemons?"

"Merely a couple of good Hellenes escaping from a Punic slaver," said Zopyros. "I'm Zopyros the Tarentine, presently of Syracuse."

"Oh, so you're Hellenes," said the captain. "That's different." Cupping his hands, he shouted across to the other ship: "You there! Drop anchor so a port officer can board you!"

But the crew of the *Sudech*, pulling hard on their oars, ignored the command. The Greek captain turned back to Zopyros. "Shall we take those rascals into custody?"

The *Sudech* was swinging about toward the mouth of the harbor. Moving briskly, the sailors hauled her yard around and shook out her sail. She heeled to the morning breeze and started for the open sea.

"Let them go," said Zopyros. "Those rogues would be hard to catch and harder to convict, and I have my own business to attend to. I got off at the cost of a game set and a night's sleep, which is not bad considering."

ORTYGIA

The first autumnal gale, with gusts of rain, swept in from the west. Skippers beached their vessels for the winter; hence Zopyros found no ship to take him and Ahiram to Syracuse. He managed, however, to hire a traveling cart in Akragas. He had to hire a driver, too, to return the vehicle to its stable.

The journey took four days—longer than it would have by ship—and was costlier and less comfortable than a sea passage. The road was a pair of ruts of the standard Sicilian vehicle gage, lined with stone and chiseled into rock where the road crossed a ledge. Where the ruts were in disrepair—that is to say, for most of the journey—the vehicle jounced over rocks and roots and splashed through mudholes. For long stretches of wild country there was little sign of human life, save an occasional peasant's one-room hut of sticks, stones, and mud.

Zopyros braced himself as best he could on the narrow board seat behind the driver. Since Ahiram could not reach the floor with his feet, Zopyros spent most of the journey with the sometimes fretful child in his lap. Both were covered with dust and soaked by intermittent rains. At night, Zopyros slept with the boy in his arms in the rude, bug-ridden huts that served as inns.

Considering all he had been through since he had been snatched from his placid, prosperous home, Ahiram proved a good traveler. While Zopyros entertained him with stories of gods and heroes, he took the hardships of the road in his stride, showed a keen interest in every new sight, and asked endless questions about his mother.

At the Hyblaios River they cut across the southeast corner of Sicily, by way of Akrai. When Zopyros remarked upon the beauty of the

Heraean Mountains, now turning from brown to winter green, the driver looked at him queerly.

"Beautiful to you, maybe," he said. "A toff like you looks at mountains and forests and thinks of nymphs and satyrs playing orgy-tag in the brush. So you say: 'How pretty!' When I look at mountains and forests, I think of all them bloody brigands waiting to pounce on me and slit my gullet. No, sir, I don't think they're the least bit pretty!"

They arrived in Syracuse in midafternoon. Zopyros paid off the driver and left Ahiram with his landlady, who gathered the boy to her bulky bosom and cried:

"Just look at the poor little mouse, filthy from head to foot! You men!"

"Then clean him up and buy him a new shirt, my dear Rhoda," said Zopyros. "Here's some money."

Having seen to Ahiram's needs, Zopyros walked to the Arsenal. At the entrance to the building he passed Alexis the Velian, to whom he gave a casual wave. Next, Archytas rushed up to embrace him, saying:

"When you failed to return with Evnos and Segovax, I was sure you had joined the majority. They wouldn't tell me what had happened to you. What did happen?"

"Just a little job of abduction."

"Korinna's boy?"

"Yes."

"Divinity! You're a fox who can slip through any hole!"

"You might say so; we were almost kidnapped ourselves by slavers on the way here."

"By the Dog of Egypt, tell me!"

"It's too long a story. I'll tell you the whole tale this evening."

"You won't have a chance; the boss is giving another party, for off-islanders. We're invited because we are educated gentlemen, forsooth, and he wants to show the people that his friends aren't all spies and ruffians."

"At least we shall eat well; after the road—"

"How is it that you gave Alexis such a casual greeting just now? Oh, I know! You haven't yet been told that he's your new boss."

"What?"

"Yes," said Archytas. "Dionysios decided that the Arsenal gang had grown too large for Drakon alone to oversee. So he gave Drakon two subordinates: one, Alexis, in charge of all research teams; and the other, Pyres, in command of all production."

"Zeus, Apollo, and Demeter! That's a fine surprise to come home to. I shan't need three guesses to figure out how Alexis got the job."

Archytas laughed shortly. "Thrice evil to evildoers! Everybody knows he's Drakon's boy friend, and no doubt Drakon urged him on Dionysios for that reason. Now Alexis thinks he has God by the balls. Still, Dionysios is pretty shrewd. If Alexis can do the job, he'll stay no matter how much you and I hate his shadow. If he can't, he'll be out regardless of Drakon or anyone else."

"Have you had to do with him personally?"

"I've had a few brushes with him. He gives me a pain. I can laugh it off more convincingly than you can, but that doesn't make me like it."

An ominous thought struck Zopyros. "How is my project coming?" He looked around the vast floor of the Arsenal, seeking the space that had been assigned to him for the pilot model of the catapult.

"You won't like it," said Archytas. "Come this way."

At one side of the Arsenal, among the piles of oars and ship timbers, Zopyros found the parts of his pilot model, unassembled and neatly stacked. Archytas explained:

"No work was done on your catapult after you left for Carthage. Alexis claimed he had more urgent need for your carpenters and shifted them to other jobs. I complained clear up to Philistos but— Zopyros! Keep your temper! A Pythagorean never acts in anger!"

Zopyros stood still, his lips drawn back from his teeth, his eyes glaring, and his hands clenching into fist. He said in a low voice:

"By the twelve postures of Kyrenê, I'll have it out with that baby-faced catamite—"

"Wait! Calm down! Dear Zopyros, remember; if you lay a finger on Alexis, you'll be out on your arse! And then what of all your fine marriage plans?"

"I'll get that whipworthy rascal, though Dionysios has me drowned afterward!" Head thrust forward, Zopyros stalked toward the doorway, where he had last seen Alexis.

Alexis was nowhere to be found. Zopyros learned that the new assistant master of the Arsenal had gone home to prepare for the evening's feast.

"It's time we went home to wash up, too," said Archytas with evident relief.

They returned to the island at dusk. The town hall was thronged with prosperous-looking Syracusans, who stood about with a deferential air, staring curiously around them. Among them a few of Dionysios' engineers were to be seen.

The tyrannos' cronies were present in full force. These were a score of trusted friends, like Philistos, who lived on the island and shared Dionysios' table. Mainlanders called them his flatterers or parasites. In truth, however, Dionysios kept them so busy running errands, occupying executive jobs in his government, traveling about on embassies, and snooping into the affairs of the Syracusans that they had little time for flattery. Among these courtiers were a willowy poet, a scar-faced character from the underworld of some big Greek city, and a stocky man of peasant type, named Lithodomos, who seemed to be kept around mainly as a butt for the others' jokes. Dionysios' brother Leptines, the admiral of the Syracusan navy, was at his brother's side.

While the cronies spoke in loud, self-confident tones, the mainland Syracusans seemed by contrast subdued and apprehensive, glancing over their shoulders before speaking. The towering figure of the tyrannos moved freely among them with only two bodyguards at his back. Exuding charm, he pressed cups of spiced wine upon them and asked about their families and affairs.

Zopyros, studying Dionysios as he passed by, thought there was something oddly stiff and bulky about him. He wondered if the tyrannos could have put on weight during his short absence from Syracuse. The mystery was cleared up when one of the guests, having been vigorously slapped on the back, gave Dionysios' chest a playful pat in return. A small metallic sound startled the guest and told Zopyros that the tyrannos was wearing the new iron cuirass beneath his robes.

At last Zopyros caught sight of Alexis, standing in a knot of men. He wore a fine new blue tunic with golden dolphins embroidered on the breast and a matching blue ribbon on his long light hair. The shipwright was talking with elegant, languid gestures and an expression of extreme hauteur.

Zopyros, ignoring his cup of wine, started in Alexis' direction. Following him, Archytas tugged at his shirt and hissed: "Zopyros! Keep your passions under the rule of reason!"

"Don't worry, old boy. I have my tactics planned."

He strolled up to Alexis with an expression as haughty—he hoped—as that of the Velian. "Rejoice, Alexis!" he said. He raised his cup. "Congratulations on your promotion!"

"Thank you, my good Zopyros; our great leader knows ability when he sees it. And how was Africa?"

"Dusty," replied Zopyros. "How are your ships coming along?"

Alexis became animated. "The keels are being laid. You must come over to the shipyard to see them. They're the shipbuilding triumph of the age; none but I could have conceived them. By Our Lady, I shall be as famous as Ameinokles of Corinth, who invented the trireme!"

"What are you calling them?"

"The fourer will be the *Arethousa*, while I shall name the fiver the *Syrakosia*."

That's fine, Alexis. I feel the same way about my catapults. Yet, when I visited the Arsenal this afternoon, I found that my catapult project had not advanced a digit since I left."

"Oh?"

"Yes. As the new supervisor of all the research teams, you must know something about that."

"Of course I do. Our research projects call for a great deal of labor and materials. Therefore I have set up a system of priorities. Devices of questionable value, like yours, necessarily receive a low priority. It's unfortunate, but you see how it is."

"No, I don't see. Only two months ago, when I demonstrated the small model to the President, he expressed keen interest and urged me to push the project. Has he changed his mind?"

"My dear man, since then he has entrusted me with the management of all these speculative enterprises; so I must use my own best judgment. Any time he doesn't like the way I run the department, he can replace me."

"Beware the anger of the jealous gods, Alexis. I shall see you later."

Zopyros turned away. Archytas, with a sigh of relief, followed him. Zopyros stood watching Dionysios across the crowded room, then set out on a course that would bring him face to face with the tyrannos. The latter, seeing him, took a quick step forward and grasped Zopyros' arm in a muscular grip.

"Welcome home, O Zopyros!" he said, smiling broadly. "When Evnos told me you had gone off on private business, I feared I had seen the last of you. What was it? Something with soft curves and golden hair, no doubt?" Dionysios winked and dug Zopyros in the ribs.

"You might put it that way, sir," said Zopyros. "Have any of our recruits arrived yet?"

"Two came in today. They are so welcome that I can almost forget the accursed race from which they sprang."

"I'm glad you are not displeased at my taking a couple of days to promote my own affairs."

Dionysios waved a hand. "Think nothing of it. An executive must be given a degree of trust and freedom beyond that of an ordinary workman. Provided, of course, he doesn't abuse his privileges. You have the full confidence of Dionysios."

"Well then, O President, let me say I'm sorry you have changed your mind about my catapult."

Dionysios looked puzzled. "Changed my mind? How?"

"When I departed, I left orders with my carpenters to finish the first full-scale catapult. Now I find that no work has been done on it at all. My new superior, Master Alexis, has moved my men to other projects, on the grounds that my device is of questionable value." He paused. When Dionysios stood silent, looking at him inscrutably, he continued. "Understand, sir, I strive to please. If you don't approve of catapults, then put me to work on something you do value. It's hardly efficient to assign me a job and then withhold the means for doing it."

"Hm," said Dionysios. His piercing gaze roved the room until it lighted upon Alexis. His voice rose to a leonine roar: "O Alexis!"

"Coming, sir," said Alexis, hurrying over.

"What's this about your halting work on the catapult?"

"I have not halted the work, sir."

"Nothing has been done on it for nearly a month!" said Zopyros.

"Be quiet, Zopyros," said Dionysios. "Has any work been done on the catapult since Zopyros left?"

"I couldn't say," said Alexis.

"You cannot say? Why not? Are you not in charge of all the research projects?"

"What I mean, sir," said Alexis, "is that I have not given orders to halt it. Some other projects, with higher priority, have needed extra craftsmen. Therefore I've borrowed men from the catapult for these more promising projects. Any time they had left, of course, these men were supposed to devote to their original assignment."

"Any ox can see there's been no time left over!" said Zopyros.

Alexis shrugged. "That's unfortunate but hardly my fault. I have to distribute our resources of men and materials where I think they will do the most good. If I have erred, O President, I shall be glad to be corrected."

Dionysios looked hard at both young men, then said: "Give the catapult the highest—what's that word you used?"

"*To proterêma*—priority, sir."

"Well, give it the highest priority." He frowned both at Zopyros and at Alexis. "Know, you two, that I, Dionysios, want no more squabbling! I demand cooperation at all levels. I have many gifted men at work here, and gifted men are not always easy to work with. Sometimes two of them together are like quicklime and water. You must overcome these petty distractions and annoyances. You must act as if you were dear friends and comrades, whether you feel that way or not. If you do not, I shall be displeased, and I will make my displeasure felt. Do you understand?"

Zopyros and Alexis each murmured a surly assent, and the group broke up to take their places on the banquet couches.

On the way home, Zopyros said to his friend: "I've been so wrapped up in my own problems that I haven't asked you what you've been doing since I left."

Archytas said: "They made me a special assistant to Drakon, to do the calculations for the whole Arsenal. I have a desk up on the gallery near his. It means I have to be polite to Alexis, but there's plenty of work. Some of the problems are fascinating. I also have a little time for an invention of my own."

"What is it like"?

"I'll show you tomorrow."

"I'm eager to see it. ... By the way, I notice Ahiram took to you the minute he met you."

"I admit I have a way with children," said Archytas. "What are you going to do with him? We can't ask Rhoda to care for him indefinitely."

"I thought I'd ask for a few days' leave, to take the boy home to Messana."

"Gods on Olympos, don't do that!"

"Why not?"

"First: you just took a few days off without asking leave. The boss took it in good part, but if you demand another leave now it won't sit well with him. Second: Alexis has been ordered to give you back your workmen; but, unless you stick around, he'll sneak them away again on some pretext or other. Next time you might have more difficulty getting them back. Since you faced Alexis down in public, one needn't be able to see through walls to realize that he'll ruin your project if you give him the smallest opening."

"What shall I do, then? The little fellow is anxious to see his mother."

"Write Korinna at once. Xanthos is rich; he can send a traveling cart to fetch the lad."

"By that way I shan't see my darling again until the gods know when!"

"I thought that's what you had in mind." Archytas patted his friend's shoulder. "Even a god must yield to necessity."

Next morning, Zopyros was pleased to find his carpenters and their apprentices back at their jobs. He had hardly set them to work assembling the catapult, however, when Drakon's errand boy came to tell him that the master of the Arsenal wanted to see him. The impudent look on the boy's face warned him that the interview was likely to be unpleasant.

He followed the boy up the stairs to the gallery. When he reached Drakon's desk, however, the master of the Arsenal was not there. He walked a few paces to Archytas' desk, littered with sheets of calculations. Nearby stood a complicated arrangement of jars and tubes.

"What's that?" said Zopyros. "Your invention?"

"If I can ever make it work," said Archytas. "The big boss said he wanted something to signal starting time in the morning. Well, you know the clepsydra they use in law courts—a jar with a hole in the bottom? They limit speeches to the time it takes the water in the jar to run out the hole. I'm trying to make a clepsydra that shall blow a whistle."

Just then Drakon returned to his desk. Zopyros hurried over. Across this desk, Drakon's gnarled features glowered up. "Who's Arsenal master here?" he snarled in a voice like a rusty hinge.

"Why, you are, sir."

"Then what in Hades did you mean by taking complaints to the President without speaking to me first? Don't you know nothing about organization? Are you trying to kiss the President's arse in hopes of promotion? If—if—" He pounded his desk, incoherent with rage.

"I'm sorry, sir," said Zopyros. "When I saw what Alexis had done to my project, I was too angry to think about—"

"Don't you dare say a word against Alexis! He's a good, bright, hard-working boy. You're jealous of him, because he was promoted ahead of you. Now get out—*ea*, wait! Where are you going?"

"You said to go, sir."

"Furies take you! You think you can mock me, because you've had a fancy education! I'll show you! I'll—I'll ..."

Drakon subsided into silence. For some time he sat, breathing heavily. At last he spoke in more moderate tones: "Understand, *Master* Zopyros, that we have certain orderly procedures. People are expected to follow them. One rule is that you shan't carry complaints, proposals, or suggestions to a higher executive until you have at least talked the matter over with the one directly above you, and then with the one over him, and so on. Do I make myself clear in my stupid, uneducated way?"

"Perfectly clear, sir."

"Then you may go."

"Do you really mean it this time, sir?"

"Why—you—*get out!*" Screaming, Drakon snatched up his bronze inkwell, spilling ink on his papers, his desk, and the floor. Zopyros ran for the stairs.

Lunchtime came. Sitting on the edge of the Spring of Arethousa and munching bread and cheese, Archytas told Zopyros: "The gossip is all about the great Zopyros-Alexis feud. The betting was even as long as it was just between you and Alexis. But, now that you've got Drakon against you, too, they're making up a pool on how long you will last."

"Bugger all feuds and jealousies and intrigues! I'm only trying to get my work done."

"Ah, but in any big organization, there's a scorpion beneath every stone. It's a law of nature. They're gossiping about your feud merely because it's the noisiest one."

"How is it, Archytas, that people always come to you with gossip and never come to me?"

"Why, as to that, I look like the kind of person it would be fun to swap rumors with. I'm overweight and jolly-looking, and I know everybody. You, on the other hand, are tall and gaunt and serious. You prowl around with a preoccupied scowl on your face, like a leopard on the hunt. You walk past people you know without seeing them. They come to me afterward, saying: 'By Herakles, what's wrong with that Tarantine friend of yours? Is he angry with me, or what?' I have to explain: 'No, it's just the way of these creative geniuses. They are so wrapped up in their own mighty thoughts that the material world doesn't exist.' Then I assure them that you're the finest fellow on earth, when I can get you down off your philosophical cloud."

The great feud, however, was resolved in an unexpected way. A few days after his outburst, old Drakon took to his bed with a wasting disease. Arsenal gossip said that he had been suffering for some time, and that this fact explained his foul temper in recent months. Although he lingered on for a year before dying, he came no more to the Arsenal.

In his place as Arsenal master, Dionysios appointed Lithodomos, his stocky, peasantlike crony. Lithodomos called a meeting of the Arsenal workers and made a speech:

"Now, boys, I don't want nobody to think I'm putting on airs, just because I'm your new boss. I admit I don't know so much about some of these here technical details as you men who work on them. But I've been around longer than plenty of you young ones, and I've watched the President at his work, and I know a thing or two. In fact, I'm a lot smarter than you might think. And I can tell you we're going to put out bigger and better production here than ever before, see? I've got some new ideas of my own about this. In fact, I'll be disappointed if we don't double our production in the first six months. Now, boys, get in there and *produce!*"

For the next few days, the work of assembling the catapult went smoothly. Everybody knocked off for an hour to witness the trials of the armored chariot designed by Simon of Kroton, the little man who had been expounding his idea to Dionysios when Zopyros first laid eyes on the tyrannos. The vehicle, looking deadly in its coat of iron scales, towered up from the archery range. Four horses were backed up to it and harnessed.

"*Ithi!*" cried Simon.

The driver cracked his whip. The horses lunged against their neck straps. The chariot did not move.

"Go on! By the God, stir them up!" shrieked Simon, dancing about. "It *must* go!"

The driver lashed the horses, which redoubled their efforts. At last the wheels heaved up out of the holes into which they had sunk. The chariot, creaking and groaning, lurched slowly forward a few feet. Then the wheels found another soft spot and settled in again. Shouting and lashing the horses failed to move it. The animals stood exhausted with hanging heads.

Dionysios walked over to the vehicle. He prowled around it, examined the places where the wheels had sunk into the ground, put his shoulder against the rear of the structure, and shoved. He told Simon:

"You seem to have underestimated your weights, man. That thing would require a dozen horses to move it at a decent pace."

"Please, godlike sir!" wailed Simon, catching Dionysios' hand and kissing it. "I can redesign—I can modify—"

Dionysios turned his back. As he strode off the archery range, he said to Lithodomos:

"Scrap it."

Then he was gone. Zopyros went back to work with the rest. Next day they heard that Simon had hanged himself in his room during the night.

A few days later Glaukos, Korinna's brother, arrived with a traveling cart from Messana to take his nephew home. Zopyros gave a party at a wineshop for Glaukos, with Archytas, Segovax, and Evnos as company. Tongues loosened by the best Falernian, they told the tales of their adventures in Africa. Evnos said:

"I can offer a bit of gossip about the President, which the rest of you may not have heard."

"Oh?" said Archytas. "I'm all ears." The others likewise urged Evnos until, after teasing them a little, he said:

"Dionysios has begun to look for another wife."

"Whatever happened to the first one?" asked Glaukos.

"The daughter of Hermokrates? You remember about six or seven years ago, in his first big campaign, when he tried in vain to raise the siege of Gela by the Carthaginians? Our aristocratic cavalry figured he was done for. They thought it would be a fine time to get even with him for ousting the oligarchs from power and killing off their leaders. So they galloped home from Gela, sacked his house, and raped his wife."

"All of them?" said Glaukos.

"Probably no more than a troop; nobody kept count. Anyway, the poor girl killed herself before Dionysios got home with the rest of the army."

Segovax clucked. "A distressful thing. Why does any man have to be doing rape, and so many women willing?"

"Well," continued Evnos, "since then he's made do with occasional dancing girls, although I must say he's as moderate in his venery as a Pythagorean. Now, however, he's getting dynastic ideas."

"They always do," said Archytas.

"So, wanting legitimate children to leave his city to, he's been shopping for a wife. He sent one of his cronies to Rhegion, but the

Rhegines sent the man back with word that Dionysios might have the daughter of their municipal hangman if he liked."

"*Oi!*" said Zopyros.

"*Oi* indeed! He rarely shows anger; but they say that he was angrier at this than at anything that's happened since he came to power. He swore by all the gods he'd pay the Rhegines back for this insult, if it took the rest of his life, I do believe he hates them worse, now, than he does the Carthaginians."

"Speaking of cronies," said Zopyros, "does anybody know why he's made Lithodomos master of the Arsenal? The man doesn't impress me as qualified."

"I'm after hearing the story on that," said Segovax. "Himself has literary ambitions. He wants to write great plays and poetry, although your Greek poetry can't compare with that of our Celtic bards. You should hear them around the chief's hearth fire in Gaul. ... But anyhow, Dionysios thought if he could get some of the writing tools of the best writers of Athens—those who are dead and gone—the gods would somehow send him an inspiration. So he sent Lithodomos to Athens. And Lithodomos had a bit of luck, because he found a man who had the pen and writing tablets and harp of Master Euripides, and the desk of that other omadhaun—what's his name? Ai-something."

"Aischylos?" suggested Zopyros.

"That's it, Aischylos. So this man had these things that belonged to the great writers—or at least he said they did—and Master Lithodomos bought up the lot."

Archytas asked: "Did these writing tools furnish the desired inspiration?"

Segovax shrugged. "I wouldn't be knowing. I don't hear that his honor has yet won any of them literary prizes they give in Old Hellas. 'Tis a pity I never learnt to write, because I'm thinking I could write poetry that would make your Homers and Anakreons sound like so many crows calling to each other to come and eat a dead corp they've found lying. Only they'd never give me a prize, first because I'm a foreigner, and second because it would be in the Celtic language I'd be doing it, the which they couldn't understand at all."

"It's never too late to start," said Zopyros. "Come around for a free writing lesson sometime."

Thanks; maybe I will. Anyway, Dionysios was monstrously grateful to Master Lithodomos and swore to give him a good steady job the next time one opened up. And that is that."

Later, Zopyros said to Glaukos: "How are things at home?"

"She sends you her love, of course, and thanks you with all her heart for rescuing her boy."

"Yes, but how are the negotiations coming?"

"Slowly. Your father and mine are both trying to skin a flayed dog. They haggle over every detail like a pair of Phoenician jewelers."

"Plague! I wish I could speed them up."

Glaukos smiled. "One can't live with women, and one can't live without them! My sister is impatient, too. Father smiles and says, that's why the parents have the say in such matters. If left to themselves, young people, urged on by their lusts, would rush into all sorts of foolish bargains."

By the beginning of Maimakterion,[4] the catapult was assembled in the Arsenal. Not wishing to have a crowd around to jeer if the device failed, Zopyros persuaded some of his workmen to try it out early on the morning of a holy day. They hauled the engine out of doors on rollers and set it up at the end of the archery range. With the windlass at the after end of the trough, they cranked back the bowstring, digit by digit. The mechanism creaked with the strain, and Prothymion the bowyer peered anxiously at his huge bow.

At last the string was behind the trigger. Zopyros pulled back the lever that raised the trigger from its slot, holding the bowstring in place. The workers eased off the windlass, until the windlass cord went slack. Zopyros unhooked the end of the windlass cord from the bowstring and laid one of his missiles in the groove. This was a standard Javelin, to the after part of which three small bronze vanes had been added, like the feathering of an arrow. A notch had been cut in its butt to take the bowstring. He teased the dart back until its butt rested against the string. To one of the apprentices he said:

---

4   Approximately November.

"I don't know how far this thing will carry. Hagnon, go to the far end of the archery range to warn away anybody who might be strolling there."

"What if the dart comes right at me?" asked the boy.

"Be ready to duck behind a target."

The apprentice ran off. Archytas said: "Won't you feel silly, old boy, if after all your precautions the dart carries only spitting distance?"

"That's what we're here to learn. Is everybody ready? Here goes!"

Zopyros thrust the handle of the lever forward. The trigger sank down in its dot. The bowstring, released, whipped forward. There was a sharp crash of creaking wood and cloven air. The frame of the catapult quivered like a harp string, while the missile soared away with a shriek.

"Valetudo preserve us!" cried Segovax. "The thing will be flying clear to Carthage!"

The dart curved down and buried itself in the ground beyond the row of butts at the far end of the range. Archytas said:

"By the holy tetractys, I'll bet that's gone three plethra! Half again as far as an archer can shoot! Have you another dart?"

"The big boss ought to see the next one, if he's up and about. Segovax, why don't you carry the message? The soldiers at the palace will treat you with less insolence than they would one of us civilians."

The apprentice, looking pale, approached. "Master Zopyros! Was that nice, to send that thing whizzing over my head and scare me out of my wits?"

Segovax returned, escorting Dionysios and his bodyguards. The tyrannos affably greeted all present. The crew wound up the catapult again. Again the engine crashed and the dart soared away.

"Thessalian witchcraft!" muttered a bodyguard, making a sign against the evil eye.

"Zeus almighty!" said Dionysios. "I see you have one more dart. Try that, to prove this was not a fluke."

The third dart was discharged. Dionysios prowled around the engine, prodding and poking and asking questions. At last he said:

"Can you vary the range?"

"No, sir," said Zopyros. "You would have to set it up at a known distance from your target."

Dionysios stood in thought, fondling his beard. At last he said: "That too narrowly limits its use. Understand, my dear Zopyros, I think you have here the greatest advance in the military art since iron weapons took the place of bronze. Nevertheless I shall not be satisfied, to the point of ordering production, until you can vary the range. With your genius, I am sure you can overcome this obstacle." Seeing disappointment on Zopyros' face, he added: "Meanwhile, your salary is raised to two and a half drachmai a day. And I will make it known that you are to have all the men and materials you wish. You shall have the very highest—what's that word again?—priority."

Dionysios patted Zopyros' shoulder and squeezed his arm. He added: "This success makes it necessary to tighten security precautions. As soon as the new apartment building is finished, you and your team shall move to Ortygia, along with the rest of the engineers. I shouldn't care to have you kidnapped by Carthaginian spies! I heard what befell you on your return from Carthage."

"You're right, sir. One such attempt is enough; next time I might not be so lucky."

The next ten-day Zopyros spent in thought. Although he sketched mechanism after mechanism, none satisfied him. There were two obvious ways to vary the range. One was to vary the angle at which the dart was discharged. The other was to vary the distance the bowstring was pulled back before it was released.

The first solution was mechanically simple. It meant pivoting the bow and its attached trough about the lateral axis. But it entailed making the whole engine much larger, taller, and heavier. The second solution—varying the length of pull—avoided this difficulty, but it involved a tricky mechanical problem.

At last Zopyros drew up plans for several small models, embodying alternative plans. One had a pivoted bow. Another had three triggers, spaced along the trough, instead of one. Another had a heavy bronze trigger mechanism sliding loosely in the missile groove and pulled back by the windlass.

Meanwhile, things did not go well at the Arsenal. Lithodomos developed curious ideas of running the organization. For one thing, he shared—or had acquired—Dionysios' hatred of Phoenicians. However, Dionysios was careful to conceal his feelings in the presence of the fourteen Punic engineers whom Zopyros had recruited in Carthage. In fact, the tyrannos went out of his way to be cordial to them. Lithodomos, on the other hand, used them rudely. He made remarks in their hearing about "treacherous, cowardly, sneaking moneygrubbers." He taunted them when he greeted them in the morning:

"Ê, Azruel, burnt any babies lately?" Or: "Swindled any widows and orphans lately?" Or: "Tortured any prisoners lately?"

The Phoenicians bowed low with forced, sour smiles. In time, two of them disappeared. Dionysios was furious when he heard about it, as he was sure that they would go to Carthage and reveal all they had learnt of the new weapons. Apparently he had words with Lithodomos, for the latter moderated his language toward the remaining Phoenicians.

Lithodomos also interfered in the details of the research projects. Although he obviously knew no more of engineering than Zopyros did of Etruscan divination, he was always bustling about, full of ideas and insisting that they be put into practice at once. The next day he would be back, countermanding his previous orders and issuing new ones. One project after another ground to a halt as its engineer despaired of carrying out impractical and mutually contradictory instructions.

Alexis and Pyres trailed their superior around the Arsenal with unhappy expressions. They tried to moderate Lithodomos' enthusiasms and to defend the project engineers against the sweeping changes the Arsenal master demanded. There were furious quarrels between Lithodomos and the engineers, among the engineers themselves, and between Lithodomos on one hand and Alexis and Pyres on the other. Scarcely a day passed without Zopyros' hearing shouts and pounding of desks from the gallery. Much as Zopyros detested Alexis, he found himself sympathizing with the shipwright. Alexis at least knew good engineering from bad.

One day Lithodomos appeared with a dark-skinned man of medium height and slender build, with a narrow, hatchetlike face. He wore a woolen robe, belted and fringed, to his ankles, and on his head a knitted cap with a long dangling tail. His glossy black hair, carefully curled and tended, hung to his shoulders, and his beard was likewise curled and oiled. In his hand he carried a walking stick with an ivory head carved in the form of a little dragon.

Lithodomos, coming upon Zopyros, said: "O Zopyros, meet Durea of Babylon."

The Babylonian touched the end of his walking stick to his nose and said, in Greek with a strong accent: "May the divine stars bring you peace, my son!"

"He's our new scientist," said Lithodomos. "They've got a universal science out there in the East, based upon the stars. Boy, nothing's too scientific for us now!" He smirked, clucked, and poked Zopyros in the ribs.

"What is Master Durea going to do?" said Zopyros.

"He's going to revolutionize our production, that's what. Every time we have a question about where a project should go on the floor, or what priority it should have, or which of two designs is the better, we ask Durea, see? He gets out on the roof and consults the stars. Then he casts a horoscope and tells us how to take advantage of the occult influences of the different stars."

At lunch, when Zopyros neared his usual eating place on the margins of the Spring of Arethousa, Archytas looked up and said: "What's the matter? You look sick."

"I am. Have you met our new Babylonian wizard?"

"No. What's all this?"

Zopyros told him. Archytas clutched his head, crying: "No! Father Zeus, it can't be!"

"Ha-ha, that's what you think. Archytas, tell me: Why are most higher executives such a gang of knaves, fools, and incompetents?"

Archytas thought a while. "They're not, really."

"Oh, come on! You know—"

"No, it just seems that way. Many, like Pyres, are able enough. But, when a knave or a fool gets power, he can make so much more trouble for those around him. The people you're thinking of would be fairly harmless as slaves or unskilled workers. Their virtues—if any—would be the same as they are now, and they would curb their vices for fear of punishment. But give such a man power, and see what happens. His virtues are no greater, and he now thinks he can indulge his vices with impunity. After all, vices are more fun than virtues if you can choose between them."

Zopyros growled: "I'm fed up with these particular vices. I was hoping to get far enough ahead of my work so that I could strike the big boss for leave, to go to Messana. But with the chaos which that thickskin is creating, I don't see how I ever shall."

Three days later, Lithodomos called a meeting of the engineers in a corner of the Arsenal. When they were lined up, he gestured to Durea beside him and said:

"We're going to reorganize the layout according to the latest scientific principles, as applied by my special consultant here. All the projects are to be moved to new locations on the floor, the way they're laid out on this chart, see?" He held up a large sheet of papyrus. "In this way, every project will be where the occult emanations of the stars will best help it along."

Somebody groaned. Lithodomos looked around, reddening angrily. "Who said that? Who said that? Anybody don't like the scientific way we do things around here, by Herakles, he can go jump in the Spring of Arethousa! I'm boss, and what I say goes. Now, call your workers together and start 'em moving your gear to the new locations shown on the chart."

"Right now?" said a voice.

"Yes, right now. What is it, Pausanias?"

"Master Lithodomos," said the blacksmith, "how am I supposed to move my forge, which weighs ten or twenty talents and is planted in the floor?"

Lithodomos frowned at his chart. "It says here that you're to move it only a few cubits, to this new location. I guess that little change won't make much difference. So leave it where it is, at least until the others have moved."

The other smiths clamored that they, too, should be allowed to remain where they were. When Lithodomos gave in to these, the other engineers began likewise to beg to be allowed to stay. At that, Lithodomos put his foot down.

"By Zeus!" he shouted. "Everybody but the smiths got to move to the places shown on the chart, and no back talk! If you want your jobs, you'd better hop to it!"

The engineers dispersed, muttering and buzzing. A great clamor arose in the Arsenal as workmen began picking up gear and moving it to new locations. A difficulty at once transpired. All the smiths, who had been allowed to stay where they were, occupied areas shown on the chart as assigned to other teams. The other teams could not move their equipment to these places until the smiths vacated, and likewise could not vacate their own locations to make room for still other teams.

A frightful confusion resulted. Men sweated, argued, threatened, shouted, screamed, and called upon their various gods. Fights broke out among the workmen of different teams, who punched and kicked and pulled hair until their engineers stepped in to separate them. When the sun went down, the great move was not yet half completed.

Next dawn, as the men of the Arsenal assembled for work, a whisper passed among them: "Don't do a fornicating thing today, except what Thickskin directly orders!"

Some time later, Lithodomos appeared with Durea. Fists on hips, he glowered at the throng, who sat silent and immobile on their piles of gear. They stared into space or blankly returned the Arsenal masters' glare. At last Lithodomos strode up to one engineer, barking:

"Euphron! Why aren't you moving to your new location?"

"I can't, sir, because Pollis' group still occupies it."

Lithodomos walked over to Pollis and repeated his question. Pollis answered: "I can't, sir. Hylas' group is still there."

"Gods on Olympos!" shouted Lithodomos. "You watch yourselves, you people! The President don't stand for any nonsense! If this is mutiny, I'll see you all drowned!" He swept out, followed by the Babylonian.

The workmen and engineers relaxed, gossiping and throwing dice. An hour later, Dionysios and Archytas appeared at the door of the Arsenal. The Arsenal people rose to their feet.

"Easy all," said Dionysios. "I have a few announcements to make. First, Arsenal Master Lithodomos has been sent on a short vacation. He has been overworking lately, with harm to his health." The beginnings of a cheer were quickly stifled. "Second, Assistant Arsenal Master Alexis has been transferred, at his own request, to the ship-yards, since his ships are far enough along so that he will be more useful there than in the research division. Third, Archytas the Tarentine has been appointed in his place. Lastly, Special Consultant Durea, that *great* Babylonian scientist, has been recalled to Athens on urgent business and so will no longer be with us."

The men broke into broad grins, and even Dionysios' lips twitched. He continued: "For the next few days, until Lithodomos returns to duty, Pyres and Archytas will run the Arsenal. If any disagreement arises between them, they shall refer it to Philistos. Your first task will be to put all your gear back as it was before this unfortunate move."

At lunch, Archytas told Zopyros: "The big boss's one false step was not firing Thickskin altogether. I urged him to do so, but he shut me up pretty sharply."

Work went smoothly for the next few days. Zopyros decided that two of his small models, the one with multiple triggers and the one with a movable bronze trigger mechanism, showed enough promise to warrant making full-scale engines. One day in early Gamelion,[5] as he was drawing plans, a shadow made him look up. There stood Lithodomos, looking fit and rested. Archytas stood behind him.

"Ê there, Zopyros old boy!" said the Arsenal master. "How's your little old catapults coming?"

"Well enough, sir."

"Look, I never did rightly understand these things. Give me an outline of what you're doing, see?"

Zopyros explained the workings of the models. Lithodomos pursed his lips and said:

"I like this one, the one with the pivoted bow and trough. Why aren't you making a full-scale one of that?"

"Because it means a greater size and weight for the same results."

"I still like it better, because you get a full draw on your bow at all ranges and therefore a full penetrating effect. When you shoot an ordinary bow at close range, you don't aim it up at the sky but only pull it halfway, do you?"

---

5   Approximately January.

"But, sir, I—"

"Never mind. You build your first full-sized catapult to that model. Forget about the others for the time being."

Zopyros, feeling his temper slipping swiftly away, filled his lungs for a scorching retort. Then he caught a wink from Archytas and mumbled his acquiescence. Later he cornered Archytas and demanded:

"What in the name of the Dog are you doing, letting him interfere again? He'll ruin the project, as sure as death."

Archytas grinned mischievously. "Oh, I don't know. He might even be right, you know."

"That stupid—"

"He's not always so stupid as he looks."

"Of course not; he's much stupider! But stop joking. I want to know what's up. If it's another deal like that stargazer, I'll go back to Taras."

"Don't worry," said Archytas. "I'll handle him. Tell your people to go ahead and build the bed frame for one of your two favorite models, and to convert the existing one-range catapult to the design for the other. As soon as they have gotten far enough along for Thickskin to tell the difference, I'll show them to him and bring him around to your view."

"A neat trick, if you can do it. He were a clever teacher who could drive sense into a fool."

Gamelion passed in overcasts, wind, and rain. The new catapults began to take shape. Then, one day, Lithodomos again appeared with Archytas. He frowned at the catapult frames, saying:

"I thought I told you to work on the one with the pivoted trough and let the others go? Here I see two fixed troughs. What are you up to?"

"Let me explain, sir," said Archytas. "Zopyros has been in constant consultation with me. We started the pivoted catapult as you said but ran into technical difficulties. We—"

"What technical difficulties?"

"I'm telling you." Archytas spoke seriously but with animated gestures. "The trouble with the pivoted model is that in the hootnanny position, the gadget interferes with the thingamajig, and that throws the doohickey out of line. The only way to prevent this is to par-allax the gimmick, and *that* keeps the thingumbob from equalizing. So, whichever way we approach the problem, the result is always the same: it doesn't work. You follow me, don't you, sir?"

Lithodomos judiciously stroked his beard. "Ye-es, I see what you mean. Funny I never thought of that. It would seem, though, like a couple of such brilliant fellows ought to be able to figure a way around it."

"We're trying to; by the holy tetractys, we're trying to! But meanwhile we thought, rather than waste the workmen's time, we'd better convert the pivoted model to one with a fixed trough, so that if worst comes to worst we shall have something to show the President. We can always go back to the pivoted catapult if we solve this silly problem."

"Fine! I wish all my engineers was as clear-minded as you two. Keep up the good work!"

MESSANA

O n a rain-threatening day in early Elaphebolion, Zopyros' men
rolled the two catapults out to the archery range. Although Archytas came along to see the trials, few others even noticed them. The
Ortygians were used to Zopyros' experiments.

First, Zopyros commanded his men to cock the old catapult, in
which he had installed three triggers in tandem. The crew winched
the bowstring back to the rearmost trigger, engaged the trigger, and
disconnected the windlass. Zopyros pushed the release lever. With a
crash, the catapult sent its dart shrieking down the range, about as
fast as it had shot when it had only one trigger.

Then he ordered the men to cock this catapult to the interme-
diate trigger. This shot went off without incident. When the crew
cocked the engine for short range, however, Zopyros found the release lever at an awkward distance. He had to lean over the catapult
frame to reach the lever. When he pushed the lever to release the
bowstring, he lost his balance and fell forward into the mechanism.
As the catapult whanged, Zopyros' chin came down where the bowstring had just been.

He climbed out of the machine, rubbing his bruises. Archytas
said: "If you'd fallen a heartbeat sooner, old boy, your head would have
gone flying down the range like that dart."

"As good a use for it as any," growled Zopyros. He directed his
crew to the windlass of the other catapult. He engaged the hooks on
the front of the heavy bronze trigger assembly, a mechanism about
the size and shape of a brick. It had a pair of hooks like a crab's claw

in front, an eye in back to which the windlass rope was tied, and a release lever protruding from the top.

As the crew turned the spokes of the windlass, the trigger assembly crept back down the missile groove, drawing the bowstring with it. The bowstring thrummed and the bow creaked as they took the stress.

This catapult had a ratchet wheel mounted on the windlass shaft, and a dog or pawl to lock this wheel. When Zopyros judged that the trigger assembly had been drawn back far enough, he engaged the pawl. The windlass rope remained taut, still taking the pull of the bowstring. Zopyros placed the dart in the groove, seated it, and grasped the lever.

"This one, you pull back to release," he said. "Like this!"

He pulled, but nothing happened. The lever stuck. The hooks refused to open.

He pulled again, without effect.

"The polluted thing's jammed," said Archytas. "Be careful—"

"To the afterworld with it!" shouted Zopyros, giving the lever a tremendous jerk.

The hooks parted, the bow snapped forward, and the dart sped on its way. At the same time the trigger assembly, still attached to the windlass rope but suddenly released from the pull of the bowstring, flew into the air. It struck Zopyros on the head with a clank. There was a flash …

He came to his senses lying on his back near the catapult. Archytas was wiping his forehead with a wet sponge. When his eyesight cleared, Zopyros saw the rest of his team standing around him in a circle, bending over him with anxious looks.

"Wh-what happened?" he asked.

"The engine kicked back at you, as I feared," said Archytas, wiping his forehead. "Your thick skull seems to be intact, but you've got a lump the size of a gryphon's egg growing out of your scalp. It's just the gods' own luck that we haven't yet killed anybody with these things."

Zopyros sat up and groaned. "I feel as if Herakles had swatted me!"

"You'd better take the day off. Wheel the engines back into the Armory, boys."

By evening Zopyros was up and about, although any sudden movement made him wince. He and Archytas argued long and intensely in their rented room. Whereas Zopyros wanted further to develop the catapult with three triggers, each for a different range, Archytas held out for the catapult with a movable trigger mechanism, like that which had smitten his friend on the head. Their voices became so loud and so filled with passion that their landlady knocked on the door.

"Boys!" she cried. "Are you two quarreling? I won't have it!"

Archytas opened the door with a broad grin. "Now, now, Rhoda dear, fear not! We're still the best of friends."

"Then why all this shouting?"

"You don't understand the engineering mind. It's just a little technical point. I can't convince my thickskinned comrade that the President won't accept a—well—ah—never mind. Good night!" He closed the door and turned back to Zopyros, waving a clenched fist. "You idiot, don't you see? All you have to do is use a thicker dart, or put flanges on it—"

Zopyros held his head. "Old boy, my head is splitting, and I can't think straight. Look, for a year I've worked like a helot for Dionysios, without a single real vacation. Why don't you ask him to let me go for a ten-day?"

Archytas pursed his lips. "Now that's a sensible idea. What's the use of having a friend among the higher-ups if you don't use him?"

"Sure. Tell him I need to get off by myself and think."

Archytas laughed. "He'll assume you mean to think about *his* problems, but I know what you'll be thinking about. You'd better write those people in Messana you're coming."

On the fifteenth of Elaphebolion, Zopyros arrived at Xanthos' house in Messana. As soon as he entered the house, Korinna flew into his arms. Glaukos slapped his back, and little Ahiram—now renamed Hieron—danced around him, waiting for his hug.

After dinner, when the women had retired, Zopyros asked Xanthos: "Sir, how goes my suit?"

Xanthos stroked his beard. "Very well, I am happy to say. Your father and I have come to terms."

"Then shall I look forward to marrying Korinna soon?"

"Were it not for the time of year, you could."

"What do you mean, the time of year?"

"Everybody knows that the most propitious date for marriage is the full moon of Gamelion. But that is two months past."

"Zeus on Olympos! Do you mean you expect me to wait till next winter?"

"That is right, Zopyros. As a conscientious father, I want the very best for my children. I want the best luck, which can only be obtained by heeding the rules."

"Why—why—you mean, to put off my marriage for nearly a year, all because of some silly superstition—"

Glaukos tried to signal Zopyros to silence, but in his excitement the latter ignored the warning. Xanthos roared:

"Superstition! You call the holy traditions handed down by our ancestors superstition? Why, you dog-faced young infidel! I won't have such an abandoned atheist in my family!"

"But!—but if—"

"Good night, sir!" Xanthos heaved himself to his feet and wheezed and puffed his way out of the court.

"Now see what you've done!" said Glaukos.

"I did rather let myself go," said Zopyros.

"Let yourself go! By the Heavenly Twins, you spilt the perfume! I'm sorry, because I think you'd make a fine brother-in-law."

"Thanks. What shall I do, Glaukos?"

"Wait until morning, I suppose, and apologize. Abjectly."

"You mean to crawl around like something from under a flat stone and tell your old man I really believe in his days of good and ill omen?"

"That's right. I don't say it will be pleasant for you, or even that it will work. But I don't see how else you can get Korinna."

Zopyros fell into a thoughtful silence, and Glaukos excused himself. Zopyros sat in the light of the rising moon, drawing his cloak around him against the chill. Then there was a stir. Korinna, likewise cloaked, pattered out. Zopyros told his tale.

"Oh, my dear!" she said. "Why couldn't you have passed it off with some noncommittal remark? Or invented a superstition of your own to balance his?"

Zopyros groaned. "Because, darling, that's just what I am a stupid ox at. I'm a pretty good engineer, if I do say so. But, when it comes to handling people, I'm as incompetent as that man Lithodomos is at engineering."

"But, Zopyros, one has to learn these things!"

"I know, but sometimes I think I never shall. When somebody talks nonsense, I come right out and tell him it's nonsense, giving him logical proofs. And, of course, any man of the world will tell you that's not how to persuade and beguile people. Do you still want to marry such a thickskin?"

"Oh, I knew all about you when I said I'd marry you."

He reached for her, but she glided away. "No, dearest! If you once held me close, the gods alone know what might happen."

"Oh, don't be—"

"Keep your voice down! If the family found us talking unchaperoned, you'd be out the door before you could say alpha-beta. Promise you will try to handle Father in the morning, though!"

"I'll—I'll—oh, to the afterworld with all these marriage contracts and parental negotiations and dowries and ceremonies! Why don't we just elope?"

"What! You mean to have a common-law marriage, like poor working folk?"

"Well—ah—yes, I suppose I do mean that. I hope I haven't offended you?"

"No, not really. It takes a lot to shock a double widow like me. In fact, it's something of a compliment to be wanted for oneself and not for the property one brings. But I love my father and wouldn't do anything to hurt him. Besides, darling, you're not thinking far enough ahead."

"How so?"

"Your father would be as furious at you as mine would be with me."

"Let 'em. They'll get over it."

"Now—let me think—I don't know just how to say it—" She sat for a while with chin in hand, while Zopyros devoured her with his eyes. Then she spoke again:

"You're thinking: I can make a good living, family or none, so why not take what I want, and to the crows with them? Isn't that so?"

"Well, yes."

"But you don't know what nasty surprises the gods may have in store. We live in a world of frightful danger and mischance. Every year we hear that some great city has been smitten by a plague, or has been destroyed by an earthquake, or has been sacked and its people massacred and enslaved. Not a year goes by but that we learn some friend or kinsman has been murdered by robbers, or been kidnapped by slavers, or fallen in battle, or perished of disease. You think, because of your fine position with Dionysios, that you are riding in Zeus's wallet. But how do we know the future? This Dionysios is a bloody adventurer—"

"Not really. He's a brilliant statesman—"

"Brilliant, perhaps; but watch what he does, not what he says. Nature will out. So next year, you may be slain in one of his broils; and then what would become of me if I had turned my back on my family? Or suppose Dionysios were overthrown or murdered? Even if you escaped from Syracuse, where would you go then, if you were at outs with your family? We need all the anchors we can set out. A woman has to think of these things. A woman can't flit about the Inner Sea, living on odd jobs picked up here and there. So, will you please try to handle Father?"

"I'll do my poor best. Whoever said women were less practical than men doesn't know a mountain from a mushroom."

"You needn't actually crawl. Tell him that crack on the head has addled your wits—just a little, you know."

Next morning, Zopyros breakfasted with Xanthos and his family, all self-consciously taciturn and evasively polite. At last he said to his host: "May I speak to you in private, sir?"

"I suppose so," growled Xanthos. "Go on, the rest of you."

"Well, sir," said Zopyros, "first I must apologize for my rude, rash words of last night. Of course I don't really contemn the traditions of our ancestors ..."

Zopyros went on, saying little in many words, walking a tightrope between groveling and defiance, and despising himself all the while. Xanthos' jowly face never changed until little Hieron came into the court, crying:

"Won't somebody play ball with me? Dear Zopyros, please throw me the ball!"

At that, Xanthos' stern visage softened. He sighed. "For the sake of my grandson, I'll overlook a good deal. But I still won't allow the wedding until the propitious day, ten months hence."

"Necessity is a hard master, sir. But couldn't we at least have the formal betrothal now?"

"Yes, we could. How much longer can you stay?"

"Five or six days."

"Then I'll give a feast the night before you depart."

Messana's city wall was as dilapidated as ever; Kylon's tavern, as crowded. When Zopyros visited it with Glaukos, a Greek sea captain was giving the news of the world:

"… Derkylidas, the Spartan general in Asia, has made a truce with the Persians and invaded Thrace, where the barbarians were attacking the Greek cities of the Thracian peninsula. The Spartan has driven out the Thracians and built a wall across the peninsula to protect it. The Spartans have restored peace in Trachinian Herakleia by killing all the men of one faction in the recent civil strife. At home, they have crushed a plot to overthrow the rule of the Peers. The Athenians have put to death the philosopher Sokrates, whom they tried and convicted on charges of corrupting the youth of Athens and introducing strange gods into the city. The Persians have made the Athenian Konon their admiral …"

A small, nondescript man pushed through the crowd toward Zopyros, who recognized him as he came closer. "Asto! How's the bold mariner?"

Asto bowed. "By the grace of the gods of Canaan, my lord Zopyros, I do well. I have my own ship now. And you?"

"I've been working for Dionysios. Engineering."

"Indeed? Then I may see you anon; for my masters have put me on the run between Motya and Syracuse."

"How come you to be in Messana? I thought all merchantmen were laid up for the winter."

"They are; I came on muleback."

"You? A sailor?"

216

"Yes, and the sorest-arsed sailor you ever saw. My masters sent me to buy ship timbers. What are these rumors I hear of Dionysios?"

"What rumors?"

"Oh, that he will conquer the world, like a Greek Cyrus; that he will make Syracuse a greater city than Athens and Babylon put together; that he spends his time cowering in fear of assassins. Where lies the truth amongst all these fables?"

Zopyros shrugged. "The big boss doesn't confide his political plans to me."

"What in particular do you do for him?"

"Why, I'm working on a wonderful new inv—" Zopyros began with enthusiasm, but remembered and cut himself off. "I—ah—suggest—ah—improvements in the city's defenses."

Asto smiled. "I see it is true what they say, that Dionysios swears his workers to secrecy about their tasks. Well, here's hoping that his plans—whatever they be—won't bring destruction upon us all."

"I'm sure they won't. In many ways he's an enlightened ruler."

"I hope so. But you know how it is with these mighty men. To them, we are no more than insects are to the boys who pull off their legs and wings. When I was in Carthage last autumn, a man appeared before the Senate, claiming to be a Punic engineer who had worked for Dionysios but had run away because of mistreatment. He brought news of fantastic weapons, which, he said, Dionysios was preparing against the Canaanites. He told of a device to shoot arrows from Syracuse to Carthage, and a war galley the size of a city, and other marvels. I wondered if these tales had any basis."

"Oh, nonsense! We try to see that the city is well stocked with up-to-date weapons, that's all. What happened to the fugitive engineer?"

"The Senate in its wisdom decided that, since these tales were obviously untrue, the man must be a Greek spy, sent by Dionysios to spread terror in Carthage and weaken the Republic. So they had him crucified."

Zopyros concealed his feelings by a long, slow draught of wine.

During his remaining days in Messana, Zopyros had several long walks and talks with Korinna, but always with another member of the family present. On Zopyros' last night, Xanthos gave the promised feast. After the guests—a fairly dull, stuffy lot, Zopyros thought—

217

had been fed, Korinna and her mother, heavily veiled, came out from the women's apartment. Xanthos got up and, holding a fistful of papyrus rolls in one hand and his daughter's hand in the other, said:

"I, Xanthos son of Glaukos, of Messana, do hereby state before these witnesses that an agreement has been reached between myself and this young man, Zopyros son of Megabyzos, of Taras, presently living in Syracuse, and his family, concerning his marriage to my daughter Korinna. I have here three copies of the betrothal contract, because the parties to this agreement all live in different cities. Zopyros has read the contract and compared all three copies to make sure they are identical. He has affixed his signature thereto as a token of agreement with the terms set forth therein. In this contract are stated the sum of money to be settled upon my daughter as dowry; a list of the clothes, ornaments, and other personal possessions she will bring with her; and the sum that Zopyros' father, the respectable Megabyzos, will settle upon him.

"O Zopyros, in the name of Zeus, Hera, Artemis, Apollon, Aphrodite, Demeter, and the other gods and goddesses, in token of my promise to give my daughter Korinna to you in lawful marriage, on a day of good omen to be agreed upon between us, and in accordance with the terms of this contract, I now place her hand in yours."

Zopyros took Korinna's hand and said: "O Xanthos, in the name of Zeus, Hera, Artemis, Apollon, Aphrodite, Demeter, and the other gods and goddesses, in token of my promise to enter into lawful marriage to your daughter Korinna, on a day of good omen to be agreed upon between us, and in accordance with the terms of this contract, I now take her hand from you."

The guests cheered. A tipsy guest bellowed: "Kiss her!" Xanthos frowned at the indecency. The other guests, one after another, toasted the couple before the women went back to their quarters. Drinking and speechmaking went on for hours—long after Zopyros had become bored with it—before the last guest staggered out into the street and set off for home, preceded by a servant bearing a lighted link of tarred rope.

Once again, Zopyros made his overnight stop at Catana, at the foot of the colossal mass of Aetna. Five years before, Catana had been the flourishing Greek city of Katanê. Then Dionysios had invited its people to remove to Syracuse. When they refused, he bribed their President to admit his army to the city. He then sold all the Kataneans—except the President and his kinsmen—into slavery.

The city he turned over to his mutinous Campanian mercenaries, in lieu of arrears in their pay. For the victims of this mass enslavement there would be no homecoming. No Evnos could arrange their redemption, because no men of property survived the enslavement to furnish the ransom money.

Catana still stood, but with a difference. The city wall had been allowed to crumble in places. The filthy streets were full of scarred, unwashed Campanian veterans and their slatternly women, speaking Oscan and glowering suspiciously at the stranger. Ragged children played in the filth or followed the traveler, begging.

Zopyros put up at the town's one inn, then sought the market place to buy some food so that the innkeeper could cook his dinner. A boy pimp tugged at his cloak and said something in broken Greek about a nice, clean sister.

At Xanthos' house, Zopyros had suffered an agony of thwarted lust. Now he felt desire rising again. His blood pounded in his temples. He assured himself that he loved Korinna so passionately that no other woman could interest him; but this, he found, was not quite true. None of his Pythagorean training helped him. The animal in him swept aside all barriers in its demand for plain, loveless, physical relief. When the boy tugged at his cloak again, Zopyros followed him to a small door in a one-room house in a narrow street.

The whore was a buxom, muscular, cheerful Sikelian girl who appeared to enjoy her work. When the passage was over and Zopyros was sponging himself off, she said: "You were on your way to buy food, weren't you? I can cook better than that dirty slob at the inn. If you will get enough for my brother and me, I'll cook your dinner here."

"I'll gladly do that," said Zopyros.

A few minutes later, he was back with the victuals. He sat on the single stool, watching her put copper pots on the little hearth fire. The room had few furnishings other than the stool, the bed, a chest, and a washstand. Large gaps in the plaster showed the brickwork of the house walls.

Now and then Zopyros asked his hostess a question. Since she spoke some Greek and he some Oscan—a tongue akin to Sikelian—they could understand each other with a little effort.

"My name's Ducetia," she said, scratching. "My people were farm folk at Herbessus. One day when we were working the fields for our landowner, a troop of Dionysios' soldiers came suddenly by on their way to attack our city. We had no time to run back to town. I was carrying water, apart from the others, when they caught me. Three horsemen took me into a bosk to rape me.

"Never having been with a man, I thought it would be terrible. But, although it hurt a little at first, I found that by the time the third man had finished I was beginning to enjoy it. When I asked for more, they laughed in a shamefaced way, saying they wished they could oblige. I cursed them as weaklings for bringing me almost to the verge and then disappointing me. At last, one rode out of the bosk and came back with a comrade, who gave me what I demanded.

"They hauled me along with them to sell, but I gave them the slip. After Dionysios raised the siege of Herbessus, I went back to my city. But another family had seized our house and barred the door against me. They drove me out of town with sticks and stones. My own family—I have heard no word of them since.

"I took up with a traveling peddler and tramped the roads with him for a year. I had never heard of harlotry in Herbessus and was astonished to find that men would pay me for doing that which I most enjoyed. When my peddler died of a fever near here, I settled down to make the best of things. The boy whom I call 'brother,' is an orphan, too. I wouldn't say it was an easy life—we often go hungry—but it's far less work than swinging those big hoes in the vineyards all day."

"Do you ever worry about the future?" asked Zopyros.

"Sometimes. I suppose one of these days I shall get old, and then I shall have to marry one of these Campanian pigs and settle down. But I'll worry about that when the time comes. How did you like your dinner?"

"Fine," lied Zopyros.

She began to clear away. "How about another trick?"

"Dear Herakles, Ducetia, you drained me dry the first time! I'm no three-ball man."

220

"Oh, come on! A strong young gentleman like you is good for more than one a day!"

"I don't know—I was thinking of my work …"

"Well, think of my work for a change; it's more fun! Please! I'll make it half price. I need the money for charms for the witch, to keep from getting pregnant."

She planted herself in his lap, kissed him, fondled him, and slipped her dress off one shoulder. Soon they were back on the bed. As he settled in, she gave a gusty sigh of content.

"That's how I like my men! Snorting and pawing, like big black bulls!"

Zopyros walked back to the inn with mixed feelings. On one hand he felt a certain pride in his powers. On the other, although he had done nothing that any Hellene would consider wrong, he was a little disgusted with himself. He had a vague feeling that he ought to have been true to Korinna, even though they were not yet wed. Moreover, he had failed the Pythagorean ethical standards. The divine Pythagoras would have excused venery in moderation—"no more than is necessary to a single man," he had said—but Zopyros had not been moderate.

All such feelings, however, were soon swept aside by a torrent of thoughts about his project. When he had told Ducetia that he was thinking of his work, he meant just that. For, while eating his dinner and savoring the memory of his contact with her, he had been struck by the resemblance between the motions of sexual intercourse and those of the parts of a catapult. Now more and more such ideas sprang into his mind—some fantastic or impractical; some worth noting.

He quickened his pace. At the inn they had no waxed tablets, papyrus, or parchment, so he bought a fresh-cut board. Over this he crouched in the flickering lamplight till midnight, covering the yellow wood with notes and sketches, until there was room for no more.

Zopyros expected to reach Syracuse the following afternoon. It began to rain, however, while he was passing through Megara Hyblaia, a Syracusan fortress and a squalid camp-followers' village built out of the ruins of a once fine city. Fearing lest the rain wash his notes off the board, which lay exposed athwart his cart, Zopyros knocked on the door of a hut. Although he was ordinarily too shy to ask for shelter of strangers, the thought of losing his precious notes nerved him to the ordeal.

The door opened a crack. "What do you want?" said a voice.

"I should like to come in out of the rain for a while, please—"

"Get out, vagabond!" The door slammed, and he heard the sound of a bolt's being drawn into place.

The rain showed no sign of letting up. He could not stand under the eaves of this house all night. If he tried to sleep against the wall, he might well have his throat cut. So he wrapped his cloak around the board, put it back in the cart, and went on to the fortress.

His Arsenal identification disk got him in. The officer in command offered him a small, unused room, in which he spent a restless, flea-bitten night. Just outside his door, a pair of soldiers diced noisily. They argued loudly in Oscan, got drunk, quarreled, started a fight, were reconciled, diced some more, and sang discordant peasant songs.

Around noon of the next day, Zopyros appeared with the board on his shoulder at Archytas' desk on the gallery of the Arsenal. Archytas said: "You've overstayed your leave, old boy, and you look a mess. ... What in the name of the Dog is that?"

"Don't touch it; you'll smudge it. It's the solution to our catapult problem."

"Are you joking?"

"Not at all. If the big boss says anything about my being absent without leave, here's proof I was working for him all the time. Do you see this?"

"I see a lot of charcoal smears. What do they mean?"

Zopyros snatched a piece of papyrus and began drawing with quick, sure strokes. "Now, look here. Nothing says there has to be just one single trough, does it?"

"I suppose not."

"Well then, we'll have a main trough, fixed as in the present models. In this trough there shall be a big, deep groove, thus. Sliding back and forth in this groove, we have a slender movable trough. We'll call it the 'slide.' This is a complex structure. At the after end it's nailed to the trigger assembly or crosshead. On its upper surface

222

is a shallow groove for the missile. On the bottom it's keyed into the trough groove so it can't fly out.

"When we push the slide all the way forward, the trigger hook—call it the 'finger'—engages the bowstring. The windlass rope is tied to the trigger assembly. When we crank the windlass, we pull back trigger assembly, slide, and bowstring all at once. When the slide is as far back as we want it, we place the dart in the shallow groove and release the finger. The string snaps forward, sending the missile on its way. Then we unwind the windlass, push the slide forward, and start over."

"How do you hold the slide at the point from which you want to shoot the missile?"

"By a ratchet wheel on the windlass shaft and a pawl, as in the present movable-trigger model."

Archytas looked up. "By Earth and the gods, best one, I think you've thrown a triple six! This is jolly good. Wherever did you get the idea?"

"It came to me while I was—ah—um—while I was driving along the road on my way back."

"Perhaps you ought to spend all your time driving about Sicily, if this is what it does for you!" Archytas frowned. "I see trouble ahead, though."

"How so?"

"We're shorthanded. Most of the carpenters have been sent over to the shipyard to speed Alexis' supergalleys."

"Well, get 'em back! You're the executive."

"That's easier said than done. We shall have to carry our appeal clear up to Philistos, and we shall have to convince the wise Lithodomos first."

"Oh, I'd almost forgotten about him! Where is he?"

"Probably out to lunch with the other bosses. I'll find—"

A long, mournful toot struck Zopyros' ear. He started so sharply that he dropped his charcoal. "Good gods, what's that?"

Archytas grinned. "You're not the only one to invent things, you know!" He pointed to the mass of jars and tubes near his desk. The din of tools died away. The workmen swarmed out of the Arsenal, carrying the bags containing their lunches.

"So that's your alarm-clepsydra, eh?" said Zopyros.

"Yes. The big boss liked it so well that he makes me set it for noon and closing time as well as for dawn. I'm told—unofficially—that I shall get one of those medals at the next Arsenal banquet." Archytas carefully measured out a quantity of water into a graduated beaker and poured it into the uppermost jar. "But your invention is far more important, if it works. Meet me back here at the end of siesta, and I'll do my best with that god-detested idiot."

Lithodomos listened while Zopyros explained his plan. At the end he tossed his head back.

"I don't get it," he said. "You've got a sliding trough underneath, and a sliding trough above, and the dart in between them—"

"No, no!" said Zopyros. "The lower trough is fixed, while the upper trough moves back and forth along it."

"You mean the trough moves instead of the dart? You're going to shoot the trough at the enemy?"

"Let me begin again," said Zopyros, holding his temper with both hands.

After the mechanism had been explained, with drawings, three times, Lithodomos said: "I still can't understand it. I think that settles the question."

"How do you mean?"

If it's too complicated for me, it's certainly too complicated for the ordinary soldier. I know I'm not so brilliant as you educated geniuses, but the people who use these things have even less technical training than I have. If I don't get it, you can bet your last drachma they won't."

Zopyros said: "Master Lithodomos, I don't expect everybody to grasp this mechanism at first sight. It's really not complicated—just unfamiliar. The main thing is to get enough carpenters to build one."

Lithodomos: "We're short of labor. I've tried to get men from the ship side, but I get only sweepings. If I do obtain a good man, a dozen other engineers have requests in for him. You'd need a fornicating good argument to get ahead of them. All I see here is a lot of complicated junk, which wouldn't work, and which no soldier could ever be taught to use if it did. Besides, all this complication means a higher cost. The President is always short of money."

"Well, what then?"

"If you was to go back to that catapult with a pivoted trough, I could see that. I might be able to get you help."

"No!"

"Why not?"

"We've been all through that. There are various ways of solving the problem of varying the range; and by the gods, I've hit on the best one! I'll bet *my* last drachma on this! If you want me to try the pivoted catapult later, I'm game; but I won't give up the most promising design until it's been tried out."

"Then you'll have to do it without carpenters. I won't tie up my labor force in something so complicated it'll fly to pieces the first time you try to shoot it."

With tight lips and trembling hands, Zopyros rasped: "My dear Lithodomos, if you'll just enable me to build one full-scale model, all these questions will be answered. The workings of the machine will be obvious even to—to everybody."

A flush crept up Lithodomos' face, and his voice rose. "You was going to say, obvious even to a half-wit like me, wasn't you? Wasn't you? Well, look here, Master Genius, all your so-called intellect don't mean a polluted thing. It's the practical people like me who have the say. That's why I'm boss. Think you're so cursed clever, because you've been to school, eh? All that did was ruin whatever common sense you ever had. You're like that fool Simon, with his twenty-talent armored chariot."

"But—"

"*Shut up*, you dog-faced slave!" screamed Lithodomos. "You speak when I tell you—"

"By God, I will *not* shut up for a stupid ox like you—"

"Gentlemen, gentlemen!" cried Archytas, thrusting himself between the furious men.

The voices of the three blended into a single uproar. The noise brought all the work in the Armory to a halt. Smiths let pieces cool on their anvils as they gaped up at the gallery, where Archytas was dutifully trying to keep Zopyros and Lithodomos from assaulting each other.

Just then Philistos, followed by a secretary, arrived in the Armory. Seeing the spectacle on the gallery, he limped up the stairs, frowning. As soon as he came in sight, Zopyros and Lithodomos stopped shouting at each other and began haranguing Philistos. Zopyros tried to explain the workings of his engine, while Lithodomos shrieked:

"This young know-it-all is insolent and insubordinate! Fire him! Fire him! Fire him!"

Philistos, leaning on his crutch-headed stick, waited until the two ran out of breath. Then he said:

"Zopyros, were you going to build a small or a full-sized model?"

"A full-sized one, sir. Most of the problems of construction have been solved, so to save time—"

"You shall build a small model, to a scale of one third. Lithodomos, see that he gets at least one good carpenter, to build this model. And both of you are fined one day's pay for disorderly conduct, and for making spectacles of yourselves in front of the workmen. Next time it will go harder on you. Good day."

He turned and made his slow way to the stair, his stick tapping. Zopyros and Lithodomos exchanged one last scowl before Zopyros went down to the main floor to complete his plans.

The flowers bloomed and faded on the long Sicilian hillsides. As the days of spring marched toward summer, Zopyros completed his small model, powered by an ordinary bow. On trials it proved satisfactory, except that the trigger mechanism often jammed. After much weary hammering and filing, having new parts cast, and changing the design, he finally got even that balky mechanism to work.

One day when he was out on the range, shooting arrows from the model and painting small numbers on the trough, Archytas asked: "What are you doing, man?"

Zopyros explained: "This is so you can tell how far your missile will fly."

"Why not put the numbers on the ratchet wheel of the windlass shaft?"

"The windlass rope stretches with use, so a given position of the ratchet wheel doesn't necessarily mean that the slide will be in the same place next time."

"It's your baby, old chap, and I wouldn't dream of trying to bite off any of your glory. But ..."

"But what? If you have a suggestion, make it."

"Wouldn't it be better, instead of this awkward ratchet wheel, to have a straight bronze rack along one side of the trough? Then mount a pawl on that side of the trigger assembly. As the slide is pulled back, the pawl will ride over the teeth of the rack, clickety-click, until you reach the tooth representing the distance you wish to shoot. Then slack off the windlass, and—"

"I see, I see! That would eliminate any question about stretching the windlass rope. Of course, other elements vary, too. The bowstring stretches, and the bow itself tires when bent many times in succession."

"Well, you would at least get rid of one variable. Why not try it?"

"I will. And I shan't need a new model; I can install the rack and the pawl on this one."

The third year of the ninety-fifth Olympiad began, when Euthykles was Archon of Athens. The hillsides turned brown again in the blistering heat of the dry Sicilian summer. Scorching, dust-laden south winds dimmed the sun to a disk of mountain copper, like that on the roof of Saphanbaal's cave, and coated the Arsenal workers with dust until they looked as if they had been dipped in flour. Zopyros reported to Archytas:

"Your rack-and pawl system works fine. But I find I need a pair of racks, one on each side of the trough, and a pawl on each side of the crosshead to engage them. With only one rack, the unbalanced stress warped the whole engine out of line."

"Good. Now I suppose you want me to twist Lithodomos' balls until he assigns men for your big model, eh?"

There were more quarrels with Lithodomos, with shouts and threats and inconclusive endings. Zopyros said: "Dear Herakles! Why doesn't the big boss send the accursed fool on a diplomatic mission?"

Archytas shrugged. "That's human nature, old boy. There's at least one Lithodomos in every organization. If we got rid of him, we might get a worse in his place."

"That I should like to see!"

"Have a care what you say, or the gods may give you what you ask."

In the month of Boedromion,[6] Zopyros demonstrated his final full-scale model to Dionysios. Nobody else paid much heed, since Zopyros had been shooting on the archery range for over a year. The tyrannos, however, watched the demonstration with keen interest. He gave commands:

"Shot one plethron ... Fine! Now shoot a plethron and a half. ..." When it was over he said: "You have done it, Zopyros. Can you make me fifty of these things?"

"Given the men and materials, sir, I certainly could."

"You shall have them. Henceforth you shall be in the production division, under Pyres. Wear your best tunic at the next engineers' banquet, three days hence. Finally, you shall have another raise in salary as soon as the treasury can afford it."

"Thank you, sir."

"There was something else. ... How soon can you have several catapults completed?"

"'Several' is an indefinite number, O President; but I think we can have five or six within a month."

Dionysios fingered his shaggy beard. "These weapons require men especially trained to use them."

"Yes, sir! The crews will have to learn by doing, so to speak."

"How big a crew will be needed for each catapult?"

Zopyros thought. "In testing them on the range, here, I find eight or ten about right. In case of need, two men could load and shoot the engine, but that would give a very slow rate of shooting. You also need extra men to move the engine on and off its rollers, to aim it, and to relieve the cockers when they tire."

"That brings up another question. How would you move a number of catapults to a distant place?"

---

6   Approximately September.

"Zeus on Olympos, sir, I hadn't even thought! Let's see—these things weigh eight or ten talents each, I suppose. That's too much for a mere traveling cart."

"As the unfortunate Simon discovered," said Dionysios.

"Exactly. I suppose one should have a set of four-wheeled ox wains built, with low bodies. Otherwise, we might have an upset."

"See my wainwright about that; get some wains started. Now, somebody will have to command the crews. We'll start with a single crew and expand as you complete more catapults. Can you recommend anyone for the post of commander?" As Zopyros hesitated, Dionysios added: "I have brave soldiers, wise philosophers, eloquent poets, and jolly jesters in my entourage. I have nobody, however, who combines the qualities of soldier and mechanic, as these new weapons demand. I will not ruin so promising a thing by appointing some gilded incompetent." (Zopyros choked down a biting remark about Lithodomos.) "So, whom would you suggest? Would you like the job yourself?"

"No, sir."

"Haven't you had military training?"

"I've had militia drill in Taras. You might say I know enough to don my greaves before my cuirass. If my own city were attacked, I would of course fight to defend it. But I have no ambition to be a mercenary soldier."

"You're probably wise. Anyway, I need your talents here in the Arsenal. But, if not you, whom shall I get?"

"I don't know many of your soldiers, sir. There's only one I know at all well: File-leader Segovax."

"The Celt I sent to Carthage with you, eh? A good soldier, albeit too fond of the wineskin. Would a barbarian like that have the needed intelligence?"

"Segovax has always struck me as a man of ready wit, who adapts himself to circumstances and doesn't let his fondness for the grape interfere with business."

"I'll try him, then. Rejoice!"

As the tyrannos walked off, Zopyros said to Archytas: "When do you think my pay will be raised? If I'm to be married soon, I could use the money."

Archytas chuckled. "You'll get it when horses play the flute, I think. Most of us have been nursing Dionysios' promises until we've given up hope."

"You, too?"

"Certainly! I'm supposed to have become a three-drachma man long since, but I'm not. Alexis was complaining about the same thing the other day. Be glad we're not actually in arrears, as his soldiers often are."

Zopyros said: "Speaking of Alexis, it occurs to me that, when his supergalleys are finished, there ought to be some carpenters to be had. How are they coming?"

"I don't know. Let's walk over to the shipyards and see."

The shores of the Great Harbor were lined for more than a league with shipways, most of them roofed over. Zopyros estimated that there were more than two hundred of them. A few ways stood empty, their last ships having recently been launched. Other ways held triremes in various stages of completion. Some were mere keels. Some comprised keels and ribs, like the skeletons of long-dead monsters lying supine. Others had their hull planking, from the forests of Aetna, partly in place.

At the end of the row, on two larger ways, stood the *Syrakosia* and the *Arethousa*. The former—the fiver—was the farther advanced.

As Archytas and Zopyros neared the two experimental ships, they came upon Alexis arguing with a workman. When the shipwright saw his visitors, he walked over with—to Zopyros' surprise—a pleasant smile.

"Rejoice!" He spoke loudly, to be heard above the din of saw and adze and hammer. "You've never met my two sweethearts, have you? Let me show you …"

He guided them about the ships, climbing ladders and dodging among the timbers, all the while explaining his theories of ship construction. Twice, Zopyros hit his head on overhead timbers. When his ears stopped ringing, he asked Alexis:

"When do you expect to finish them?"

"The *Syrakosia* should be launched in another ten-day, and after that it will be simply a matter of cabins and deck fittings. The other may not be ready for months. Why do you ask?"

Zopyros told of his assignment to make fifty catapults.

"Oh!" said Alexis. "So, naturally, you're hoping to fall heir to the carpenters who have been working on the *Syrakosia*, eh? Well, I can't promise all of them. I shall need some for the *Arethousa*, and the other shipwrights will be watching for a chance to snatch them, too. But I think I can get you a few."

"If you'll tell me in advance whom you're letting go, and if I request those men by name, I stand a better chance than if I simply scream 'Men! Men!' to Pyres."

"Fine. I shall be glad to help—provided it doesn't interfere with my own project."

"Tell me, Alexis," said Zopyros, "why is the larger of your ships farther along than the smaller? I should expect the contrary."

"Orders from the big boss. He wants the *Syrakosia* finished and tested by the end of Maimakterion, to fetch his bride."

"What?" exclaimed Zopyros and Archytas together.

"Hadn't you heard? He's persuaded the Lokrians to give him the daughter of one of their magnates for a wife. He wants to make a spectacle of the occasion by sending his biggest ship. But what will really grind you to sausage is that, to avoid hard feelings, he will at the same time wed a local girl, Aristomachê daughter of Hipparinos."

"Two at once?" said Zopyros in amazement. "Like a Persian king?"

"Absolutely. When one of his cronies muttered something about legality, he said: 'My dear fellow, I, Dionysios, am the law in Syracuse!' He's braver than I. With all my abilities, I don't think I could manage two women at once."

Zopyros said: "He certainly doesn't let a little thing like consistency stand in his way. He harangues us every month on our duty to defend Hellenism, and you can't call bigamy Hellenic."

Archytas said: "Oh, I don't know. The Macedonian kings do it. And wasn't there a Spartan king, a fellow with a long name—you'd know, Zopyros; you've been reading history. ..."

"Anaxandrides!" said Zopyros. "Yes, but he took a second wife only because the Overseers insisted, when his first wife bore no children and he wouldn't divorce her."

"Why wouldn't he?" said Alexis.

"Because he loved her," said Zopyros. Alexis sneered. "Anyway, both wives then produced offspring, and there was the usual struggle for the throne. One of the sons was the famous Dorieus, who stirred things up in these parts a hundred years ago. Is the big boss sending his prize ship out in the middle of the winter?"

"Evidently. I wouldn't risk it myself, but he says he'll order her captain to run for harbor every time a blow appears. With reasonable luck, the trip each way shouldn't take more than two days."

Zopyros said: "Well, it's nice to have seen you, Alexis, and thanks a lot. We must get back to work."

As Zopyros and Archytas walked back toward the Arsenal, the former said: "That's funny!"

"What is?"

"Once I thought Alexis my dearest enemy; but here he's as pleasant and helpful as if we'd never had a cross word."

"Well, you've heard of friends who grow apart? I suppose enemies can grow apart, too; one gets out of the habit of thinking about them all. I'm still glad we needn't work any more with Master Alexis. He's one of those who can be charming—as long as he has his own way. But, if you gainsay him in anything, watch yourself!"

The next day, as Zopyros was eating his lunch in his usual place by the Spring of Arethousa, Segovax appeared in his polished cuirass and crested helm. Scowling, he growled:

"Bad cess to you, Zopyros my lad!"

"Why—what—"

"For ruining the best soldier that ever came out of the Celtic forests!" The scowl changed to a grin. "To be sure, 'twas kindly meant. When himself called me in and asked me to be his catapult officer, I thought: What would my noble ancestors think to see me, not charging into the thick of the fray with sword and spear, but standing ten leagues away and pulling a little handle that sends a dart flying at men who don't look no bigger than mosquitoes? 'Tis ashamed of me they would be. I was all ready to say I would not, for all the golden mountains of Persia. But he talked, and talked, and said as the catapult company got bigger, I'd be a captain and maybe even a Colonel. So I got to thinking: If I'm a file leader and get only a private's pay and the rest in promises, as a colonel he's sure to give me a captain's pay and the rest in promises. So I said I would. Still, there's one thing wrong with this colossal plan."

"What's that?"

"I can't read nor write. Dionysios says his officers have to read and write, so they can read orders from the general when he's too far away to shout at them."

"I told you to come around for lessons. Now you'll have to do it, that's all."

"Ah me, 'tis less of a brave Celtic warrior that I am every day!"

Zopyros received his golden medal from Dionysios at the next engineers' banquet. A year earlier he would have panted with eagerness for the honor. Now he enjoyed it, but his enjoyment was mixed with the irony of maturity. He would have gladly traded it for that promised raise, if there were only some way of guaranteeing the latter. But there was not. He had the medal, while the raise was as yet merely words. In case of need, the gold would fetch a hundred drachmai, which would feed a man for most of a year.

During the next three months, Zopyros struggled with his catapults. He found the problems of producing an engine in quantity quite different from those of developing an experimental model. He learned to watch like a hawk for defective materials or careless workmanship. He learned to give each catapult intensive tests; two of the engines might look alike to the eye but perform quite differently.

In Maimakterion, the *Syrakosia* was launched, fitted out, and manned. Zopyros had a glimpse of Alexis standing on the quarterdeck of the new ship, screaming curses at the rowers because they would not row in time. The rowers were hardy professionals, horny-handed, huge-muscled, and well paid. But with their mighty backs went weakly minds. To learn to row a ship of a new type was to them an almost impossible task. Being used to triremes, they found the new ship, with oars in groups of five, cramped and awkward. They bumped each other's backs and fouled each other's oars.

Back and forth across the Great Harbor they went, until their rowing was no more ragged than in the usual trireme. Alexis staged a race before Dionysios, between the *Syrakosia* and a standard trireme. The fiver won, but only by the length of her ram. Nevertheless there were cheers and a medal for Alexis.

At the next engineers' banquet, Dionysios strolled among his guests, giving each a few gracious words. When he came to Zopyros, he asked: "How is production coming?"

"Much better, sir. We're finishing at least one new catapult every ten-day."

"What took you so long to get started?"

"The problem of breaking in the workers and obtaining a steady stream of good materials. As a result of shortcomings in one thing or the other, several of our early catapults proved defective and had to be scrapped. By the way, O President, have you heard that I plan to marry?"

"Congratulations, O Zopyros."

"And double congratulations to you, sir."

Dionysios gave Zopyros a searching look and burst into one of his rare laughs. "The pains of principate, my boy! What I go through for my beloved Syracuse! If you were thinking to dun me for that promised raise, I hope to make it good within a month."

"That will be welcome, sir; but it's not what I was about to say."

"Which was?"

"I hear you plan to send the *Syrakosia* to Lokroi next month."

"Yes, to fetch my bride, Doris daughter of Xenetos."

"My betrothed lives in Messana, not far out of the way of this voyage …" He explained about Xanthos' insistence on having the wedding on a lucky day.

The tyrannos scratched his shaggy beard. "That's an interesting idea. We could drop you off on the way to Lokroi and pick you up on the return voyage. Efficiency! Besides, you could not become so mazed with love as to forget to return at the end of your leave, as happened once before. But here is a complication."

"What, sir?"

"I mean to celebrate my weddings on the full moon of Gamelion. We cannot deliver you to Messana on that day, yet fetch Doris back to Syracuse before that date. … Hold, I have it! The fourth of Gamelion is deemed as lucky for weddings as the fifteenth. If we dropped you off a day or two before the fourth and picked you up a day or two afterward, that would suit everybody, wouldn't it?" The tyrannos grinned, pleased with his own ingenuity.

"Thank you, sir! I'll write the father of my betrothed at once."

Thus it fell out that on the fourth of Gamelion, Zopyros stood beside Korinna at Xanthos' hearth in Messana. Each of them snipped off a lock of hair and burnt it on the family altar. They broke the honey cake and each ate half, while a crowd of Xanthos' friends sang wedding songs. In the early evening, after the feast, all went into the street and formed a torchlight procession. Glaukos drove the wedding chariot, with Zopyros and Korinna seated behind him. For the groom's dwelling, to which the procession led, Xanthos had persuaded one of his friends to lend a room in his house.

"It would look pretty silly," Xanthos explained, "to parade around the block and come right back here; and yet we must faithfully follow custom."

When Zopyros and Korinna had been showered with grain and olives at the entrance to the friend's house, had eaten the ritual quince, and had finally closed the door behind them, Korinna took off her veil. They gazed long at each other and then, for no particular reason, burst out laughing. In unison they said:

"Thank the gods *that's* over!"

"Shall we go to bed, darling?" said Zopyros.

"Why not? We've certainly waited long enough."

MOTYA

All through the winter and spring, Zopyros made catapults. The tempo of the Arsenal speeded up. The manufacture of arms grew to such vast dimensions that smithies and woodworking shops were set up in the market place of Syracuse. They were set up even in the temenoi of temples and in the mansions of the rich. Men tramped through the streets of the Achradina bearing bundles of arrows, javelins, and spears, and bags of sling bullets. The tyrannos was ever on the prowl, inspecting, checking, and exhorting, praising here and blaming there. Normal business in Syracuse slowed to a crawl as more and more of its people were sucked into this gigantic military effort. One goldsmith was kept busy making the medals, wreaths, and crowns for Dionysios to bestow upon his champion weaponmakers.

Zopyros had settled down with his wife and stepson in a small rented house in Syracuse. Archytas, at the tyrannos' insistence, moved to the island of Ortygia. Zopyros was spared this move because the apartment house that Dionysios had ordered for his married engineers was not yet completed. Dionysios, likewise, had settled down with his two new wives, who shared the women's quarters in Dionysios' austere palace.

"He seems to manage his women as efficiently as he does everything else," said Archytas over a cup of wine after a dinner at Zopyros' house. "They say he treats them well, and they're both devoted to him, in spite of their—ah—unusual status."

"How does he do it?" asked Zopyros. "Do they sleep three in a bed, or does he take turns?"

Archytas laughed, bouncing little Hieron on his knee. "The boss hasn't told me, and of course I almost never see the girls. What I tell you is mere backstairs gossip, with which Ortygia buzzes like a beehive. The latest is that there will be a general assembly of the Syracusans a few days hence."

"What for?"

"I don't know. I suppose the Dionysios will harangue them on their duty to pay taxes cheerfully and to gird their loins against an attack by the accursed Phoenicians."

"Or he'll announce some move of his own against them. Several times lately he has sent word to ask how my catapults were coming. I think he's growing impatient."

"That fits in with some things I've heard," said Archytas. "A lot of Syracusans—and not just members of the old oligarchy, either—long for the return of self-government. They're not taken in by Dionysios' talk of 'directed democracy.' Quite a few have been slipping away to Phoenician territory, in western Sicily. It's the one place where they needn't fear murder or kidnapping by his agents. It infuriates the big one to hear of their forming a party-in-exile with impunity. But how are your catapults coming?"

"Not so well as I should like. I used to think research was frustrating; well, production is worse! When you get some timber and bronze to work with, you find that your men have taken sick, or have been moved to another project, or have disappeared. Then when you get the men lined up and ready to work, you find that your materials have been stolen by some other engineer, or won't do the job. When at last you get both men and materials ready, it's a holy day and no work may be done."

"That's life, my boy. How many catapults are completed?"

"We tested Number Eighteen today. That's not counting the defectives that were broken up for salvage. But catapults aren't my main worry right now."

"What is?"

"The missiles, of all the silly things! You'd think if the Arsenal can turn out a complex engine like a catapult, we could make a simple thing like a catapult dart. But we've got a labor dispute."

"*Oimoi!*"

"You see, a dart isn't exactly an arrow, nor yet is it a javelin. It's a weapon with some of the characteristics of both. So the fletchers claim they should make the darts, and the spear makers that they should, and each gang threatens to stop all work unless its men get the job. I don't think they'd actually strike, being too much in fear of Dionysios, but they slow things up. I'd been hoping to get to work on the design for an improved catapult; but all my time has been taken up with this polluted management—threatening and wheedling and bullying and soothing a lot of overgrown children, plague take them!"

"So now you know what a boss does with his tune," said Archytas.

"Speaking of Phoenicians," said Zopyros, "guess whom I saw today!"

"Whom?"

"Captain Asto, my old friend from the *Muttumalein*. He's in town on the first voyage of the new season."

"I should like to meet him. He sounds like a good man."

"I wanted to invite him here tonight." Zopyros glanced toward the kitchen, where Korinna was washing dishes, and lowered his voice. "But you know Korinna's feelings toward Phoenicians. In fact, this brought about the first real dispute of our married life. I argued. I showed her how illogical it was to condemn the poor man, after he'd been so nice to us on the *Muttumalein*. But it did no good. If I were a proper Hellenic husband, I should have said: 'Woman, serve my friend, and no nonsense!' But somehow it didn't work out that way."

"My dear fellow, you ought to know better than to argue with an emotion! Trying to change somebody's feelings by logic is like trying to kill a lion with a fly whisk. I don't say it couldn't be done, but I shouldn't recommend the method."

"Well, Master Know-all, how would you change somebody's opinion?"

"First, make the person like you. Then, because he thinks you're a good fellow, he infers that your ideas must be right. It's crazy logic, but that's how the minds of mortals work."

"That's all very well for you, who drip charm as a wrestler drips oil. But Korinna won't come around to my way of thinking, just because she's my beloved wife. She has a mind of her own. It might be different if we had a bigger house, with separate women's quarters and servants to do the dirty work. Then she wouldn't even see my guests."

"You could afford a bigger place," said Archytas, glancing around. "Not that this isn't very nice, you understand. Didn't your father settle some money on you?"

"I've only received the first installment, and I don't want to throw my little capital to the winds."

"Well, you always were a man to squeeze every drachma until the owl hooted for mercy."

"Yes, I have all the unattractive virtues: thrift, accuracy, sobriety, industry. ... I suppose people are born with either charm or character, but rarely both. I fear the gods gave me character only."

Archytas grinned. "Meaning I'm a dissolute charmer?"

"No; you're one of the rare exceptions, blessed by the gods with both."

"That's good of you, old boy! Good enough for us to pour another drink. To the gods, by whose grace we were born free, not slave; men, not women; Hellenes, not barbarians!"

The market place was packed with Syracusans. As the sun rose out of the Ionian Sea, its vermilion beams crossed the Little Harbor and pierced the city, shining into narrow streets and over red-tiled roofs, painting the white walls orange. Dionysios, wearing his iron corselet over his tunic, mounted the dais in the market place. The rising sun flashed a brilliant red-gold on his armor. It glanced from the helms and cuirasses of his guards, as they stood in double rank around the dais; it glowed on the statues of polished bronze and painted marble on plinths around the market place."

"O Syracusans!" Dionysios began. "Long have I warned you of the threat from the west. I have told you of the vile moneygrubbers, sitting at their counting tables with twitching fingers and greedy eyes, who plot to destroy our precious Hellenic civilization. ..."

"Here we go again," muttered Zopyros to Archytas.

After his usual rant against the Phoenicians, Dionysios spoke of the iniquity of allowing these human vermin to rule over several Greek cities in western Sicily: "... the very gods must be grieved and ashamed to see these baby-burning barbarians insolently lording it over Hellenes—Hellenes! The only truly civilized people on earth; the gods' chosen race; the enlighteners of the world! This abomination, this monstrous perversion must not be! It shall not be!"

Dionysios paused to allow his claque to work up a cheer. He continued: "I, Dionysios, have therefore sent a just and moderate demand to the so-called Senate of Carthage, that they free these cities at once. My demand, although couched in courteous terms, was rejected with scorn and insult. What policy remains us?"

The claque set up a rhythmic cry of "*POLemos! POLemos! POLemos!*" Soon thousands were chanting "War! War! War!" until the noise became deafening.

At last Dionysios raised his arms for silence. As the noise died away, Zopyros muttered in Archytas' ear: "So now we know!"

"My people!" cried Dionysios. "You have spoken! I, your leader, can but obey!

"The struggle may be hard. The foe, if timorous, is crafty and treacherous. If the cowardly Carthaginians have no stomach for cold steel themselves, they have money—vast piles of it—wherewith to hire hardy mercenaries: Numidians, Ligurians, Iberians, and other barbarians.

"But, whatever the danger, whatever the sacrifice, we shall vanquish! Carthage has been weakened by a plague. They will not be able to defend their Sicilian satellites. The glory will be great, and the booty even greater! *Iô Hellênes! Iô Syrakosioi!*"

As the crowd broke up and streamed away, Zopyros and Archytas headed for Ortygia and the Arsenal. An hour later, Zopyros was directing the work on his catapults when Archytas came to him and said in a low voice:

"I hear that mobs have formed to attack and plunder the Phoenician metics. You'd better get home to protect your family."

"Could you come with me?"

"Of course. Wait till I get my sword."

The streets of Syracuse near the bridge to Ortygia were strangely deserted. Doors were closed, windows shuttered. From a distance came a subdued roar, which rose and fell. The two men walked swiftly, speaking in low voices and looking apprehensively at the blank walls on either side of them.

As they turned a corner, the roaring suddenly swelled. Around another corner, a Phoenician in loose robe and slippers came flying, panting and pumping his arms. After him pelted a yelling horde of Syracusans, brandishing knives and clubs and screaming threats. Archytas and Zopyros flattened themselves against the wall. The mob rushed past them unheeding. The eyes of the pursuers glared; foam spattered their beards. Then they were gone.

Zopyros and Archytas looked at one another. Zopyros said: "Let's hurry. The way these people are worked up, the gods know what they'll do."

They hastened on, until at one corner a smell of smoke and a crackle of flame drew their attention. Zopyros exclaimed:

"Zeus on Olympos, those fools will burn down the city!"

A mob of a hundred-odd men had gathered in front of a small house in the middle of the block, closed and shuttered like the rest. Some were kindling torches and throwing them to the roof of the house, already blazing briskly. Smoke curled up from the closed shutters.

The door flew open, and a young man rushed out. Zopyros caught only a glimpse of the man before the mob, with a roar, closed in on him. Knives flashed in the sunlight; clubs rose and fell. The mob fell back in a semicircle from the remains on the street. Presently the door opened again. This time a woman ran out. The mob closed in again, stabbing and flailing. Then came a small boy, who was likewise done to death. At last an old woman hobbled out, but a step from the door she, too, went down.

Members of the mob, screaming and foaming, rushed about waving severed arms and legs and spattering blood in all directions. One of them kicked a head along the street like a ball. Others dashed into the smoking entrance to try to grab house furnishings before the blazing roof fell in.

A squad of Dionysios' mercenaries appeared. They marched up to the burning house and thrust the mob back with spear shafts. Ignoring the dismembered corpses, they organized a line to bring buckets of water from the nearest fountain to quench the blaze.

Archytas and Zopyros worked free of the crowd and resumed their march toward the latter's home. Now and then they passed a mangled body lying in a pool of blood. When Archytas had trouble keeping up with Zopyros' long strides, he panted:

"Slow down, old boy, slow down! I dare not run, lest some mob of citizens think me a fugitive."

They found Zopyros' door closed on an empty street. Zopyros knocked and called until Korinna opened. They slipped inside. The closing of the door plunged the interior into gloom. Korinna embraced her husband, trembling. Hieron clung to his mother, asking endless questions, until Archytas took him aside and began to tell him a story. Zopyros got his sword out of his chest.

There came a sharp knocking. "Who is it?" said Zopyros.

"It is I, Asto! Let me in, in the name of your gods!"

Zopyros knew a moment of hideous indecision. Ordinarily he would have admitted the Phoenician without question, since he counted the man as a friend. But now he feared to endanger his family. He looking despairingly at Korinna, saying:

"It's Captain Asto. If I keep him out, he'll be killed; if I let him in, they may come for us—"

"Let him in; let him in! Quickly!"

Zopyros opened the door. Asto, sweating and panting, ducked inside. Before Zopyros could close the door, the roar of a mob rose. The horde streamed around the nearest corner. Zopyros quickly slammed the door and shot the bolt. To Asto he snapped:

"Go to the back room. Under the bed, quickly!"

There came a thunderous hammering on the door, and yells: "Open up!" "We know he's in there!" "Open, or we'll burn you down!"

Archytas, pale, thumbed the edge of his sword. "We shall have to open the door, or they'll fry us. Perhaps we can talk our way out of this."

With racing heart, Zopyros whipped his cloak around his left arm for a shield, threw open the door, and blocked it, sword in hand. Archytas, likewise armed, crowded up beside him.

"What do you want?" said Zopyros in a voice that he made especially deep and harsh.

The nearest members of the mob gave back at the sight of the swords. Somebody shouted: 'There's a polluted Phoenician in there! We saw him go in! We want him!"

"Phoenician? Nonsense! There's no such person here."

Archytas added: "We opened the door to look out when we heard the noise. You only saw us close the door. Your Phoenician ran that way." He pointed.

"Then, by Herakles, let us in to see for ourselves!"

Archytas said: "Are you mad? Don't you know who we are? We're the President's chief engineers, and this house is full of his secret devices."

An argument broke out among the crowd. Some said yes, these men were really governmental officials. Others said no, they were lying, and in any case a search should be made.

Zopyros glanced up and down the street If only Segovax were to appear at the head of a squad of soldiers! But there was no sign of help. Segovax would be out on the archery range, drilling his catapult teams.

A lean, shabby youth with eyes like a dead fish circulated among the rear ranks, shouting; "Go on! What are you afraid of? We know the moneygrubber is in there. Even if he isn't, these men may be Carthaginian spies. Anyway, they'll have some loot worth taking. Go on! Go on!"

Every time the youth got several men organized to push forward, they drove those in the front rank closer to the door. When Zopyros and Archytas flourished their swords in the loot-hungry faces of the foremost, they pushed back, so that there was a continual stir in the mob. All the while Archytas kept up a running fire of argument, firm but not ill tempered.

Zopyros had an inspiration. Still facing the mob, he called: "Korinna! You know my burning glass? Get it for me."

Presently he felt the lens thrust into his left hand. He held it up in front of his left eye and called to the youthful agitator in the rear: "*Ea*, fish-face! You in the blue shirt!"

"Who, me?"

"Yes, you! You don't believe we have secret devices here, eh? Well, here's one. It's a device for casting the evil eye. Shall I show you how it works?"

He stared through the glass at the blurred image of the youth, who gave back with a cry: "Don't you dare point that thing at me! By Zeus, I'll kill you if you do! Put it away! Turn it away from me!"

As the young man spoke, he seized another of the crowd and hid behind his body. The second man struggled and whirled the youth in front of him in turn. The youth freed himself, dodged about among the crowd, and ran down the street, shouting threats and obscenities. Several others ran witlessly after him. Another man led a group off in the opposite direction, crying:

"Follow me! I'll show you some real Punics with lots of loot!"

The rest of the crowd hastened off, singly and in groups, glancing back apprehensively at Zopyros and his glass. Soon they were all gone.

Safely back in the house, Zopyros and Archytas sat down weakly, the latter mopping his forehead. Zopyros said: "I don't usually drink in the morning, but … Ah, thank you, darling. One for Archytas, too. Hieron, fetch Daddy that lamp."

Zopyros touched a pine splinter to the hearth embers, blew until the splinter caught fire, and used the flaming splinter to light the lamp.

"That was a cursed near thing," muttered Archytas. "By the Silver Egg, I haven't been so frightened since old man Pelias caught us stealing his plums and set that great savage dog on us!"

Zopyros patted Korinna, saying: "You were brave to let Asto in, considering how you feel about his people."

"Asto? I wasn't thinking of him!"

"You weren't?"

"No, I was thinking of his family in Motya. I know what it's like to be a lone widow with a child to bring up."

A plaintive voice came from the bedroom: "Please, my lords and lady, is it safe to come out now?"

"No; stay where you are," said Zopyros. "We'll call you when things quiet down. Son! Carry this cup of wine in to Asto; he doubtless needs it."

The day wore on in anxious waiting. Now and then one or the other would crack open a shutter for a quick look outside. Sometimes all seemed quiet. Then again they might hear a mob roar, sometimes near and sometimes far, or the crackle of a burning house. Smoke drifted overhead in thin clouds and streamers.

* * *

Late in the afternoon, a commotion reverberated in the street outside. Mingled with the usual crowd noises was the clatter of soldiers' gear. Zopyros peered out the crack between the shutters and saw a squad of mercenaries driving a mob before them. When one of the tardiest mobsters turned with a snarl on the soldier nearest him, the soldier thrust at him, jerked the spear out of his body, and strode on over the corpse.

A big, bronze-colored mustache caught Zopyros' eye. "Segovax!" he shouted, flinging wide the shutters.

"Eh there, Zopyros my lad!" said Segovax, striding across the street to the open window. "In a little while the city will be as safe as a nursery. Himself has given orders to put down the shindy, if we have to kill a few spalpeens to teach them their civic duties."

"Too bad you weren't here this morning, when they nearly mobbed my house!"

"Why would they be doing that, and you as Greek as olive oil?"

"An old friend of ours lies hidden here." Zopyros added in a loud whisper: "Asto of Motya!"

Segovax grinned. "Not a word of what you're saying have I heard. And now I must be off after my men. Good luck to all!"

After Segovax had clattered off, Zopyros called: "Come out, Asto!"

A disheveled Asto appeared with lint in his beard. He threw himself to his knees, touched the floor with his forehead, and kissed Zopyros' hand, swearing eternal gratitude. When he turned toward Archytas, the latter said:

"Oh, get up, man! Don't make so much of simple thanks. We'd better start thinking how to get you home safely."

"The first thing is to make a Hellene of him," said Zopyros. "Off with the Punic cap, Asto. I'll lend you a chiton. My shirts are too long for you, but who cares? Your hair must be cut. And we must get rid of those earrings. Must we file them off?"

"No. You pry the points apart."

"Where's your ship?" asked Archytas.

Asto spread his hands. "I do not know, noble sirs. It was in the Little Harbor. But the company's orders are, in case of civic disturbance, to put to sea at once with such of the crew as can reach the ship in time."

"We'll look in the harbor to make sure. If the ship is gone, you have another long muleback ride ahead of you."

The next morning a Hellenized Asto set out on muleback for the Phoenician-ruled western tip of Sicily. Zopyros, having seen him safely out of Syracuse, arrived at the Arsenal during the lunch hour. A messenger boy told him to report without delay to Dionysios in the palace.

He found the tyrannos in his courtyard, sitting at a long table with his secretary and Philistos, examining rolls of papyrus and piles of waxed tablets. Dionysios said: "Sit down, O Zopyros. How are the catapults coming?"

"We are putting the finishing touches on Number Twenty, sir."

"That's a long way from the fifty you promised to have ready for me by now."

"We've been turning them out as fast as circumstances allowed, sir. In the past month we have completed—let me think—six."

"How many can you make in the next three months?"

"At the present rate, eighteen. As the men become more skillful, we might even turn out twenty."

"If I gave you more workmen, could you make thirty in that time?"

"Possibly. But I don't think additional workmen alone would do it."

"Why not?"

"I should need more space in the Arsenal for the men to work in, and of course more materials. Moreover, there will be some delay in breaking in new workmen. Few have ever worked on anything so complicated; it's hard to make them realize that every part must exactly fit every other."

Dionysios looked at Philistos, who said: "I don't think Dinon's project—that big shield on wheels—will amount to anything. We might as well close it out and give Zopyros the space Dinon's team now occupies."

"So be it," said Dionysios, nodding to his secretary. To Zopyros he said: "I'm also giving you Abdashtarth of Tunis as an assistant. And speaking of Phoenicians, I hear you had a little trouble yesterday."

"Nothing serious, sir," said Zopyros, impressed by the tyrannos' minute knowledge of his subjects' affairs. "There was a lot of damage in the city, though."

"No more than one would expect. The same thing is happening in the other Siceliot cities. It's a long-overdue purge."

Zopyros said: "May I ask a question about your policies, sir?"

"You may ask. I may not choose to answer."

"Why, then, did you wait until late afternoon to order the soldiers to put down the mobs? Many innocent people were killed; and besides, when the Syracusans set fire to all those Phoenician houses, it's just the gods' own luck that the air was calm. On a windy day the whole city would have burned."

Dionysios combed his beard with his fingers. "Let me tell you something about your fellow man, Zopyros. I am informed that some philosophers believe man to be descended from the lower animals. I think they are right, because of the qualities I see in the people around me. Your average man is full of impulses to do good, to be brave, to sacrifice himself for others, and so on; but he is also full of depraved and selfish urges to seek the pleasure of the moment, to abuse the weak, to steal and torture and kill. Sometimes one set of impulses rules; sometimes the other. Why does a company that has fought long and bravely, in the next battle, turn tail and run like rabbits? Because the men have drained dry their supply of bravery. So they follow their animal instinct, to save themselves at all costs.

"Now, as you know, I keep a firm hold upon the Syracusans. I expect much from them: civic virtue and orderly conduct in peace, courage and endurance and discipline in war. But all the time I know that their impulses in the opposite direction are building up, like the pressure of air in a bellows when you stop up its nozzle. These urges must have an outlet—or they will make an outlet for themselves, sooner or later, willy-nilly. I deem it better to unstopper the bellows by letting them slaughter a few worthless Punics than to have my bellows burst. People need a disturbance like this from time to time, to stir them up and let them satisfy their animal lusts, as the *marobia* stirs up the mud and seaweed along the Sicilian coasts."

Zopyros said: "And the fact that a lot of unoffending people were torn to pieces doesn't matter to you?"

"Not really. A great ruler cannot afford to be squeamish about the fate of individuals; and I, Dionysios, am a great ruler. Would you deny that?"

"No, sir!" said Zopyros emphatically, thinking the while: Dear Herakles, what does the fellow expect me to say when I'm in his power? Dionysios continued:

"So, you see, if a ruler took no action lest it cause harm or death, he would never accomplish anything. He would gain no glory. Furthermore, his very inertia would tempt others to impose upon him. In the end he would have to fight anyway, and just as many men would die. Besides, most of those slain yesterday were foreigners. It's not as if there had been a massacre of Hellenes.

"The trouble with you technicians is that you travel too much and study too much. Travel and study weaken a man's natural loyalty to his city and his race."

"If my natural loyalty, as you call it, were as strong as all that, I should have remained in my native city. So would your other engineers; and thus, sir, there would be none here to serve you."

"True. But here we are; and you and I must make the best of it. And now I have other business, Zopyros. You know my wishes in the matter of the catapults; do your best to meet them. Rejoice!"

One holy day, Zopyros crossed the bridge to Ortygia and approached the Arsenal, which was deserted save for a single sentry outside. He meant to examine his catapults and to think up ways to speed the work. At one end of the building, under the gallery, piles of ship's stores had been cleared out to make room for his completed catapults. Zopyros strolled down the rank of deadly war engines, twanging a bowstring here and working a lever there. He felt the sort of pride in these contrivances that he supposed a poet felt when he saw his completed epic reduced to papyrus and ink.

As he neared the end of the row, he noticed something odd about one of the catapults. There were several thin yellow streaks on its timbers, at right angles to their long axes, as if freshly painted with a fine brush. When he looked more closely, his heart almost stopped beating. The lines were the kerfs of saw cuts; the yellow color, that of freshly exposed wood. A small pile of fine sawdust, lying on the floor under each of the cuts, confirmed his suspicions.

The damaged catapult stood third from the end. Zopyros hastily moved to the last two. They had also been sawn; in fact, these cuts were more numerous and ran deeper into the wood than the first cuts he had observed. It was as if the saboteur had tired or been frightened away before he finished his work.

Wild with fury and excitement, Zopyros ran all the way to the Ortygian house that Archytas shared with several other single engineers and foremen. In response to Zopyros' knocks and shouts, his friend appeared, draped in a blanket, yawning and rubbing his eyes.

"By the Dog of Egypt!" he said. "Can't a man sleep late even on a holy day?"

"Come quick! Some abandoned sodomite has been at my catapults! Three have been ruined!"

"Zeus almighty! One moment till I dress."

Half an hour later, Zopyros and Archytas returned to the Arsenal, accompanied by Pyres, Lithodomos, Philistos, Dionysios, and the tyrannos' bodyguards. They examined the damaged catapults.

"Zeus blast the dung-eating rascal!" growled Dionysios. "Has anybody searched the Arsenal yet, to make sure he is not hiding behind a coil of rope?" When the others said they had not, Dionysios turned to his bodyguards. "Search every digit of this building, you two! Telesinus, take the ground floor; Vertico, do the balconies!"

"But, sir—" began one guard.

"Never mind my safety!" snapped Dionysios. "Hop to it!" He turned to Philistos. "Carthaginian spies, don't you think?"

"Could be," said Philistos.

"I know who done it!" said Lithodomos. "It's those fornicating Punic engineers you hired, boss. Why don't you drown 'em all?"

Dionysios said: "I will, if they deserve it. What is your evidence, Lithodomos?"

"Everybody knows what treacherous bastards these men are, and naturally they'd sympathize with Carthage. They've got motive and opportunity. What more do you want?"

"I should want a lot more before I condemned them; good engineers are too precious to execute on mere suspicion. Did you see one of them sawing away?"

"No, but I know they done it. It stands to reason—"

"Did you even see one leaving the Arsenal with a saw in his hand? No? And suppose one of them is guilty; how about the others? There are ten of them. If all ten had been working at the job, they would have done much more damage than this." Dionysios stood silent for a moment, then resumed: "Let us speak of things we know about at first hand; amid too much wrangling, truth is often lost. Zopyros, how has your assistant conducted himself?"

"Abdashtarth? He couldn't be better. He doesn't like Carthage any better than you do, because the Carthaginians squeeze tribute out of his native city."

"What would you say of the others, Pyres?"

Pyres shrugged. "They're like all engineers. Some are better than others, but they all turn in a good day's work. I have no grounds for suspecting any one of them."

"Bugger that stuff!" cried Lithodomos. "You're a bunch of babies! You know cursed well they're only waiting a chance to burn down the Arsenal, or the shipyards, or the whole city. If they haven't been caught at treason yet, it's because they're too clever. By holding off, they hope to make us overconfident and careless. This is just a taste of what they'll do if we let them run around loose. Drown the whoresons, I—"

"You'll drown *my* assistant over my dead body!" cried Zopyros.

"Sure! You stand up for him, because you're not a real Hellene yourself. You're part Persian, so you take the barbarians'—"

"O President!" said Zopyros. If you really want to win your war, get rid of the man who's done more to hinder the work of this Arsenal—the man who has cost us more production—than all the spies and saboteurs put together!"

"Who is that?"

"Lithodomos!" Zopyros pointed. "He's been driving all of us crazy ever since you appointed him Arsenal master. You know he got that Babylonian stargazer in here and fouled up the work for a ten-day. He tried to force me to choose one catapult for production when I knew another model was better. Everything one can do wrong, he does wrong, and spends his spare time sneering at us engineers because we're not stupid illiterates like—"

"Why, you dog-faced, temple-robbing—" yelled Lithodomos, and launched a long swing with his right fist. In an instant they were slugging toe to toe, cursing and panting. Zopyros had the advantage of reach and age; but the burly Lithodomos gave as good as he got.

"Separate them!" said Dionysios to his guards, who had just returned from their fruitless search of the Arsenal. Dropping their spears, each guard seized one of the fighters from behind, pinioned his arms, and pulled him away from his opponent.

"That'll cost each of you two days' pay," said Philistos.

As Zopyros and Lithodomos, panting, continued to mutter insults, Archytas said; "O President, may I speak?"

"Go ahead, Archytas," said Dionysios. "You seem to have a cooler head than many."

"I just wanted to say that this talk about who's the saboteur is idle chatter, because it could have been one or many people. True, it might be a Carthaginian spy, or a Phoenician engineer. But it might also have been a Greek engineer jealous of Zopyros' success. It might be a workman, trying to assure himself more employment. It might be some citizen of Syracuse who doesn't want to fight the Phoenicians or who doesn't like your rule, sir. We may never learn the truth, unless you believe in oracles."

Dionysios smiled. "I find it politically expedient to let each man think I believe in him and all to think I believe in the gods. Now, have our bold Hector and fleet Achilles cooled down enough to be turned loose?"

The soldiers released Zopyros and Lithodomos, who stood silently, rubbing their bruises.

"Since you two are so eager to fight," continued Dionysios, "you shall have your chance. I appoint both of you to my staff for the coming campaign against Motya. Lithodomos, you shall be quartermaster, responsible for seeing that the men are fed. Zopyros, you shall be my adviser on engineering questions, especially those having to do with catapults. Each shall have the rank of captain. You will draw uniforms from the armorer. Part of your pay will be withheld to pay for the armor. Now, Zopyros, how does the damage to these catapults affect your production schedule?"

"I can patch up the third one, sir. The others will have to be scrapped for salvage. Luckily the saboteur didn't damage the cross-heads, which are the hardest parts to make."

"Can you have your fifty completed by the end of Mounychion?"[7]

"I'm sure I can reach forty, sir. I'm not certain about the rest. But, at the present rate of production, the number of catapults won't be the limiting factor."

"What do you mean?"

"We shall be short of wagons to haul them in. At the rate the wainwright is going, I doubt you'll have twenty-five of those special wagons by the end of Mounychion."

Dionysios fingered his beard. "Why didn't you tell me this sooner?"

"Sir, I didn't know you wanted to haul the whole lot of catapults to the other end of Sicily, and so soon! Besides, the wainwright is not under my orders."

Dionysios sighed. "Even I cannot think of everything. Well, keep up production. Any surplus catapults can be mounted defensively on the walls of Syracuse. I shall order double guards around this building. Pyres, you are now master of the Arsenal. I'm putting the wainwright under your orders; try to speed him up. Lithodomos will start at once on his new duty, gathering food stores for the campaign. Philistos, round up all the soldiers who have stood sentry go here since yester-day. They probably know nothing, or we should have had word; but I mean to question them anyway. Rejoice, all! Stay, Zopyros; I have more to say to you."

The group broke up. Dionysios, followed by Zopyros and the bodyguards, went out of the Arsenal. Dionysios questioned the sen-try, but the man had seen nothing. The tyrannos turned away and strolled along the edge of the Spring of Arethousa. To Zopyros he said musingly:

"A ruler cannot afford to take so casual a view of treason as our friend Archytas seems to. Perhaps he is right in thinking we shall nev-er find the culprit, but I mean to try." Dionysios struck his open hand

---

7   Approximately April.

with his fist. "But how? The villain was not so obliging as to drop his wallet at the site of the crime. What I need, even more than new engines of war, is an infallible method of uncovering spies and conspirators. While I have little faith in the supernatural, I would not overlook any means ..." He turned to stare at Zopyros through narrowed eyelids. "I understand you had some experience with a witch in Africa?"

"Yes, sir; I spent a day and a night in her lair."

"Did she give you any reason to think that such a person could help us?"

"No, sir, she did not; although she mightily impressed the other Phoenicians who came to her sitting."

"How did she do that?"

Zopyros told about Saphanbaal's little tricks—the alum in the fire and the fish scales on the roof of the cave. "... and when they asked her questions, she gave the same sort of artful, ambiguous answers that our oracles give. You know, when the Pythia of Delphoi told King Croesus:

If Croesus shall o'er Halys River go,
He will a mighty kingdom overthrow,

she carefully neglected to state *which* kingdom would fall. But such was the sitters' faith that half the time they almost answered the questions themselves. When Saphanbaal hesitated, they prompted her. They didn't try to expose her chicaneries; they wanted to believe."

"Hm," said Dionysios, tugging at his beard. "So the effectiveness of your witch lies, not in the power she actually possesses, but in that which her followers impute to her, eh?"

"That's it exactly, sir."

"One might say the same of rulers like me—albeit not in public, of course."

"You mean," said Zopyros, "you may never find an infallible means of detecting conspiracies; but, if everybody in Syracuse believed you to have such a method—"

Dionysios snapped his fingers. "You've thrown three sixes!" He spoke to his bodyguards: "Lag behind us ten paces, boys. I would speak in confidence to this man." He turned back to Zopyros. "If my people thought I had such power, the guilty might either give themselves away by their actions or, at least, refrain from further treasonable acts. Is that what you mean?"

"I don't doubt it, O President. The Phoenicians have a saying: 'The guilty flee where no man pursueth.'"

Dionysios chuckled. With a cynical smile on his handsome features, he said: "Zopyros, my boy, how would you like a pound of silver for doing absolutely nothing?"

"Why—ah—sir, money is always useful. ..."

"Especially to a thrifty fellow like you. By doing nothing, I mean simply keeping your mouth shut. To most of our fellow Hellenes, that were a harder task than walking on red-hot sword blades; but you do not seem to be a typical Hellene. Can you do it?"

"Yes, sir."

"Good! Hold yourself in readiness at the next engineers' banquet, which is—let me think—six nights hence."

Zopyros and Archytas sat on the edge of the Spring of Arethousa. Archytas said: "I say, are you really going to join his army?"

"I think so. It's a chance to get a wider variety of engineering experience."

"Take care that, in grasping at the shadow, you lose not the substance."

"Don't you approve?"

"Approve? I think you're crazy!

> *War never slays a bad man in its course,*
> *But evermore the good. ...*

Why risk your gore for a city other than your own, and moreover one ruled by a tyrannos instead of by its citizens?"

"It doesn't sound very risky, being on the boss's staff. The catapults should be out of bowshot."

"Yes, until Dionysios tells you: 'Captain So-and-so has just been killed; Captain Zopyros, take his place and lead his company up the scaling ladders!' And whoever told you Dionysios stays back out of the fighting? Here in Syracuse he's cautious to timidity, wearing that iron vest, accompanied everywhere by guards, and having all visitors searched. But in the field, they say, he's quite the dashing hero."

"One's fate is in the hands of the gods."

"Moreover, the divine Pythagoras would never approve. What have you got against those poor devils in Motya?"

"Nothing, but I don't think my presence will add much to their danger. What else could I do, Archytas? The Dionysios is not a man to take no for an answer."

"You could gather up your family, slip quietly out of town, and go back home to Taras. Kteson is in disgrace, so there shouldn't be any trouble from that source."

"That's craven advice! Is this what you plan to do?"

"I can't," said Archytas.

"Why not?"

"Because I haven't yet persuaded Klea's father to give her to me in marriage."

"Ah, love!"

"Look who's talking! But seriously, aren't you letting your head be turned by the pretty officer's uniform?"

"Oh, I admit I shall look rather well in a crested helm. But the real reason I'm joining is the chance to get ahead in my profession. Any city would hire a man who had been engineering officer on the staff of the great Dionysios in one of his campaigns."

"Well, it's your fate. I still think you'll be sorry. You haven't considered the most ominous possibility of all."

"That I shall be killed? One must take some chances—"

"No. I mean that, if you survive, you may become one of the big boss's cronies."

"What's so bad about that?"

Archytas smiled. "Then you will have to listen to Dionysios' endless recitals of his mediocre poetry, and you'll have to act enthusiastic about it!"

* * *

Korinna was much perturbed by the news of Zopyros' new post. She clung to him, crying that he would be killed. When Zopyros reassured her, she said:

"But Hieron and I shall be here all alone! You can't go off, leaving us in a strange city, with hardly any acquaintances, and no man to watch out for us in time of trouble!"

"I can move you to Ortygia. Some quarters in the fortress will be vacated when the officers set out on the expedition. I'm sure I can make arrangements with the President."

"You don't understand, Zopyros dear. Ortygia may be safe against outside attack, but it's full of those ruffianly foreign soldiers. Who's to protect me against them?"

"Most of the mercenaries will be away on the campaign, darling, and you can always call upon Archytas."

"Oh, I know he's your friend; but he's too fat and sleepy to be of much use in a brawl."

"You'd be surprised, if you ever saw him in a brawl."

"Well then, why don't you take us home to Messana until the war is over? At least I should he among my own people."

Zopyros frowned in thought. "I know you'd be happy there. But—have you ever taken a good look at the city wall of Messana?"

"I've often walked along it. Why?"

"Haven't you noticed how ruinous it is?"

"I did once sprain an ankle on it."

"And it's of obsolete brick, not up-to-date stone. Even if it were of stone, it's too low and too narrow for an effective defense. Under modern conditions of war, you might as well camp in the open fields as to count upon the wall of Messana to protect you. You would flee the ashes to fall into the coals."

"But Messana isn't at war with anybody. ..."

They argued far into the night. Zopyros flatly refused to send Korinna and the child to Messana, and she likewise refused to promise not to go thither if her father sent for her. Thus, for several days, a certain acerbity entered their relationship, since, despite their ardent love, each was a person of strong will and opinions.

* * *

At the next engineers' banquet, when the time came for awards, Dionysios' voice boomed across the hall: "You all know Zopyros the Tarentine, the brightest star in our crown of inventive genius. I had thought that the invention of the catapult were triumph enough for one lifetime. But no, he has now surpassed himself. His latest godlike inspiration is an infallible method whereby a ruler can detect all spies, saboteurs, and conspiracies against the government." Smiling, Dionysios let his gaze rove slowly over the audience. "Naturally, I cannot reveal the precise method. Suffice it to say that the device is so simple that any of you would kick yourselves for not having thought of it. O Zopyros, stand forth and receive from me, Dionysios, one pound of silver—one hundred freshly minted drachmai!"

As Zopyros, his face carefully composed, made his way forward, Dionysios loosed the cord at the mouth of a bag he held. Dipping one hand into the bag, he brought out a handful of silver coins and allowed them to trickle back, jingling, into the bag. They glittered in the lamplight like a metallic waterfall.

Although the applause was adequate, Zopyros sensed a slight constraint about it. In fact, more than one engineer turned his head this way and that, staring with manifest unease at his neighbors.

The following day, an officer of the mercenaries, followed by four soldiers, came through the Arsenal. The officer stopped to question every engineer and foreman in turn. When he came to the catapult section, he asked Zopyros:

"Have you seen Alexis the Velian today?"

"No."

"Did you see him after he left the engineers' banquet last night?"

"No."

"Has he said anything to you lately, indicating that he might be leaving?"

"I haven't spoken to the man. What's this all about?"

"I can't tell you that," said the officer, moving on to the next section.

Later, Zopyros sought out Archytas, who as usual was a mine of the latest gossip. Archytas said: "Absolutely, old boy; he's gone. He must have scooped up his money and his most precious possessions as soon as he got home last night and bolted, letting himself down from the city wall by a rope. I guess that settles the question of who sawed up your catapults."

"So he kept his grudge after all, despite his pleasant words?"

"Evidently. As I reconstruct the events, they went like this: Dionysios, I hear, refused to authorize any more superwarships, because the two that Alexis built did not show enough advantage over the standard trireme to justify their extra cost. Much disappointed, Alexis brooded over the unfairness of your success. One night, getting a little drunk, he determined to do something about it. It was no trick to slip into the Arsenal, with only a single sentry to dodge. ..."

"Many good-bys to him! I wonder where he's gone?"

Archytas shrugged. "He'll probably turn up in Carthage, or Athens, or the gods know where, full of bright ideas and prepared to give a good kick in the balls to anyone who stands in the way of his rise. He's shrewd enough to avoid the places where Dionysios could lay hands upon him. Why, are you nursing a grudge, too?"

"Not I! I was furious at first, of course. But he did me no real harm, and I can't be bothered with such people. I care much more about carrying out my projects and saving up my pay. I have no time for enemies."

"What, no implacable hatreds or lifelong feuds? What kind of Hellene do you call yourself? If all Hellenes felt as you do, we should rule the world!"

Flowers still bloomed along the roads that wound among the fields and groves of western Sicily, when Captain Zopyros cantered up to the Bay of Motya. He approached the bay by the road from Akragas and Selinous. He had ridden along the southern coast, where huge limestone crags, eroded into fantastic shapes, stood up from the plain like the half-buried skulls of long-dead monsters.

Since much of Zopyros' work was done on horseback, he wore a horseman's high leather boots. His cuirass, worn over a padded tunic, was made up of several layers of linen canvas, molded on a form and glued together. If less effective in stopping spears and arrows, such a defense was much lighter than a foot soldier's bronzen corselet. His sword was longer than a foot soldier's, too. Behind him cantered two mules, one of them bearing a hired servant and the other his shield and baggage.

On Zopyros' left, the bay's calm waters opened out; beyond the bay, the dunes and scrub of the Aigithallos Peninsula lined the horizon. Along the mainland, where Zopyros rode, hundreds of tents were ranked. They stood in clumps, with gaps between the groups where Dionysios had drawn off most of his forces to ravage the Phoenician lands of western Sicily. The bay swarmed with hundreds of tubby merchant ships, some moored, others moving slowly under sail and oar as they brought in supplies to Dionysios' army or departed to fetch other loads. Drawn up on the beach were rows of triremes, each one chocked and braced lest it tip or slide.

The island of Motya rose on the left, in the midst of the bay. Nothing was visible at this distance but its frowning walls and the tops of its towering apartment houses. Northward, where a narrow spur of land reached out toward the island, Zopyros saw the coming and going of antlike specks. As he rode on, the specks grew into men bearing burdens to and fro. The Motyans had torn up most of the causeway linking them to the shore. Now, a detachment of Dionysios' troops patiently carried baskets of stone and dirt out to the broken end of the causeway, dumped them, and went back for more.

At last Zopyros reached the big headquarters tent at the northern end of the bay. Back from the shore, a horde of carpenters, with a great din of hammers and saws, were assembling ram tortoises and belfries—movable siege towers. Engineering troops dug trenches in their search for the leaden pipe that carried fresh water under the bay to the island of Motya. Zopyros found Leptines on the shore, watching the rebuilding of the causeway. He delivered the tyrannos' orders:

"… he wants the triremes launched as soon as possible, sir, to meet Himilko's fleet. He also plans to put every man available to work on the causeway, to make it several times as wide as it now is, so that he can move his siege engines upon it. He wishes you to supply each man with a basket or other container for carrying earth."

Leptines, who looked much like his brother Dionysios, smiled. Zopyros had always found him kindly and good-natured, without Dionysios' drive and cold passion for power and authority.

"Well done, Zopyros," said Leptines. "It's too late to start launching the ships tonight. We'll get at it in the morning. As for baskets, I don't know where I could get so many on short notice."

Zopyros said: "If I may suggest it, sir, a man can pile quite a load of stones or sand on a shield, and two men can carry it."

"Excellent! My brother made no mistake when he gave you the job of proposing ways and means. Good night."

Zopyros learnt that he was to share a tent near the headquarters tent with several other staff officers. He left his servant stowing his gear, turned his horse over to a groom, and set out on foot for the artillery park. Thirty-three catapults had started from Syracuse on their special wagons. Three had failed to make the journey. Two wagons had broken down; a third catapult had been damaged when its wagon upset. They were supposed to follow shortly, but Zopyros guessed that the drivers would find excuses for delaying their arrival until after the battle.

"Where's Colonel Segovax?" he asked a soldier.

"That big tent, sir," said the soldier, pointing.

Zopyros found Segovax sitting on his bunk with a goblet of wine in his hands. The Celt looked up blearily.

"By the horns of Cernunnos, 'tis my old friend Zopyros! How's the brave Tarentine lad, and him so handsome and all in his new soldier suit?"

"I'm worn down to a stump," said Zopyros. "Could you—"

"Of course, of course, have yourself a drink! Here, let me pour. In the tent we don't observe the niceties of rank with our old friends." Segovax hiccuped. "Here ye are. My lad, you are beholding the soldier's ruination, the which is sitting on his arse and doing nothing, day after day. No wonder we take to the drink."

"Here's to ruination!"

"Here's to indeed. But—I thought you were with his honor, ravaging the territories of the accursed Phoenicians. What brings you back to us?"

"I'm carrying messages to Leptines. The Dionysios arrives tomorrow."

"Did he take all them cities he was talking about?"

"No; he's raised the siege of Entella and is marching this way. He learnt that the suphete Himilko is bringing a fleet from Carthage to relieve Motya."

"Is that the fellow who attacked Syracuse? We've had all sorts of rumors, like he's captured the city and killed everybody in it."

"No; Himilko only raided the harbor of Syracuse. He sank many merchantmen but never even tried to land. He sailed back to Carthage to refit, and now he's headed here. How are the catapults?"

"The catapults are fine, but the men are not. It's the idleness. I'd like to give them a bit of target practice, but we can't shoot out into the bay for fear of using up our darts, and we can't shoot along the shore for fear of hitting our men. Did you bring any orders, like?"

"They were for Leptines, but I don't mind passing on the one that concerns you. The big boss wants the catapults set up along the shore, between the beached triremes, at the narrow entrance to the bay. He wants half of them on this side and half on the Aigithallos."

"Hm." Segovax stroked his mustache. "Did you by any chance bring me a written order?"

"No. It's all in my head."

"You mean to say I'm after spending hours and hours, when I could have been wooing fair lassies and drinking good wine, learning to make them little marks that look like fishhooks and pitchforks and bedbugs, so I could read an order—and now you're just saying it out of the mouth of you?"

"Don't give up, old boy; you'll find use for your reading and writing yet. I suggest you alert your men, but for Hera's sake don't move any catapults until you get the command from Leptines. Dionysios is fussy about who gives orders to whom. Working through official channels, he calls it."

The next morning, a southerly duster blew up, coating men and materials with African desert dust, cutting vision to less than a bowshot, and kicking up a powerful surf at the entrance to the bay. As a result, only a few triremes had been launched by late afternoon, when Dionysios' army marched up the coastal road to take its place in the vast encampment.

First came mounted scouts, lightly armed and unarmored, galloping hither and yon, yelling and making their horses curvet and caracole. Then came a thousand regular cavalry. At their head rode Dionysios astride a huge black steed, looking like a god in his polished iron armor and flowing crimson cloak. Since no ordinary horse could have borne all that weight, it was said that this stallion had been smuggled out of the Persian Empire, where such horses were bred for the mighty cavalry of the Immortals.

Following the horse came the foot. Here marched, to the tune of flutes, citizens of Syracuse and allies from many Siceliot cities. Here, too, came thousands of barbarian mercenaries: Sikelians, Lucanians, Campanians, and Samnites. There was even a battalion of trousered Celts from the valley of the Padus, in the extreme north of Italy, with sweeping mustaches, huge elliptical shields on their arms, bundles of javelins over their shoulders, and long swords at their sides.

Dionysios tried as far as possible to equip each troop of mercenaries with its national arms. He believed that the men would fight better with familiar weapons than with strange, if superior, Greek equipment. Behind the long lines of swinging kilts and gleaming crested helms of the foot, another thousand horsemen brought up the rear.

Waiting in the anteroom of the headquarters tent, Zopyros overhead Dionysios angrily demanding of his brother why more of the ships had not yet been launched. He heard Leptines' soothing replies. He ate with the other staff officers and turned in early. Although still bone-tired from the campaign, he could not sleep for a long time. Swirling round and round in his mind were ideas for improved catapults, homesickness for his family, and worry as to whether he was right in soldiering for Dionysios.

It seemed to Zopyros that he had hardly fallen asleep when the trumpets sounded the alarm. When he emerged from his tent, men were looking and pointing toward Mount Eryx, where glowed a red spark against the lightening sky. Dionysios—Zopyros remembered with the little knot in his stomach that always preceded a battle—had commanded a watch fire laid on the mountain to signal the appearance of Himilko's fleet.

During the next few hours, the staff officers rushed about in Dionysios' wake like hounds after a stag. Along with the others who attended the tyrannos, Zopyros ran errands and relayed orders down the chain of command. He gave advice about catapults when asked for it.

The catapults had been set up between the triremes along the beach. Later at Dionysios' command, hundreds of Cretan archers and Baleric slingers climbed up to the decks of these ships and readied their missiles.

Men began pointing and shouting: "Here they come! See the polluted Punics!" The masts of Himilko's fleet formed a picket fence along the horizon—a fence whose palings bobbed and swayed with the motion of the ships' hulls. Soon the hulls themselves rose over the curve of the sea.

The oncoming ships drew slowly nearer. To the watchers on the shore, it looked as if each ship, seen bow on, had only three oars on each side, rising and falling in perfect rhythm. By counting the masts, Zopyros estimated that Himilko had about a hundred galleys—half the number that Dionysios commanded. Although Dionysios' soldiers and sailors, pulling on ropes to rhythmic chants, were launching galleys as fast as they could, most of the Greek ships still lay helpless on shore.

Closer and closer came the Carthaginians. Dionysios, with his staff trailing behind him, galloped around the northern end of the bay and out on the Aigithallos. The tyrannos cursed as the Carthaginian galleys broke formation to dash after a number of Greek merchant ships in the open sea. Some were under sail; others were anchored in the shallows. Running or standing, the enemy caught them all. Some were rammed and sunk; others were boarded and towed away, while Punic marines tossed overboard the bodies of the slaughtered crews. Hundreds of naked Greek sailors, who had dived from the doomed ships and swum for shore, staggered out of the surf along the peninsula.

The sun rose higher. The Carthaginian ships, like an army of intelligent centipedes, crept back together. Signal flags fluttered; trumpets called across the water. The ships formed a huge rectangle, ten by ten, and crawled into the entrance to the bay.

"Zeus blast them!" snarled Dionysios, sitting on his huge horse. "If we had half our ships in the water, we could surround the head of their column and crush it, as the Hellenes crushed the Persian fleet at Salamis."

Since the bay curved sharply to the north, behind the sheltering peninsula of the Aigithallos, the Carthaginian fleet made a slow column-left as it entered the narrows. Inside the bay, Dionysios' remaining merchant ships struggled slowly northward under sail and oar, toward the far end of the bay behind Motya. In the meantime, the few Syracusan triremes afloat formed a line across the bay to protect the merchantmen from the oncoming enemy.

Dionysios, peering beneath his palm at the Punic fleet, said to his staff: "They think, if they stay in the midst of the channel, we cannot reach them with missiles from shore. Soon they shall learn differently. Go, Zopyros, and give the command to shoot when you think it best."

Zopyros galloped down the peninsula to the narrows at the entrance to the bay, where half the catapults were posted. Cantering down the line of ships and war engines, he raised his arm and shouted:

"Quiet, everybody! Get ready to shoot! Stop talking, all of you! Prepare to shoot!"

On came the Carthaginians. Zopyros could hear the flutes of the coxswains sounding slow time, to keep the ships in formation and ready for surprises.

"Shoot! he yelled, bringing his arm down smartly.

Trumpets sounded. There was a vast snapping of bowstrings, hissing of arrows, and whir of slings. The air was filled with missiles. Some fell short; some reached the nearer ships.

Then the catapults began to discharge: crash, crash, crash. Their darts arched high into the air and shrieked down upon the Punic fleet. Some fell among the ships in the middle of the channel. Like an echo, the sound of missile fire came from across the bay, as the troops on the mainland discharged their projectiles. The crews of the catapults strained at their windlasses to get off a second volley, and a third.

Trumpets sang across the waves. The Carthaginian galleys stopped rowing and sat in the waters of the bay with lifted oars. Commands were shouted from ship to ship; flags fluttered. The rain of Greek missiles continued as the galleys pushed forward with their oars on one side and pulled back on the other. With much roiling of the water, the ships slowly turned about, each in its own length.

Still bows twanged and catapults crashed. The Punic ships filed out of the bay, some of their oars trailing limply where the rowers had been struck at their benches. Zopyros raised his arm. The catapult men and the archers and slingers stopped shooting. Thousands of soldiers, drawn up in formation during the battle of missiles, burst into cheers.

All along the shores of the bay, gangs of men, who had been sweating to get triremes into the water, renewed their efforts. Outside the mouth of the harbor, the Carthaginian fleet formed a half circle, facing the channel into the bay. Dionysios growled:

"They hope we shall come rushing out into their jaws. We outnumber them two to one, but we cannot bring our numbers to bear. Herakles! How can we get two hundred ships into the outer sea without their being crushed one by one as they emerge?" His cold gray eyes searched each of his staff officers in turn.

Zopyros said: "You could haul the ships overland across that low neck of land at the base of this peninsula, sir—"

"And what would keep the foe from destroying them one by one as they were launched on the seaward side?"

"You could set up the catapults along the beach. The Carthaginians fear catapults out of proportion to their real danger, because they've never faced these weapons before."

"Good!" Dionysios showed his teeth in a tight-lipped smile. "Young man! Take an order to Leptines and remain with him to help with the work. ..."

All the rest of that day and through the night, the Siceliot army hauled ships across the isthmus at the base of the Aigithallos. Thousands of men dragged each ship by scores of ropes. Although the ships slid easily across the muddy, marshy ground, the soldiers sank to their knees in the muck. Not a few were killed when they slipped and fell on the churned-up ground and the ships were hauled over their prostrate bodies.

By the following dawn, more than a hundred Greek triremes rode the waves of the outer sea; but the Carthaginian fleet had vanished.

* * *

Thus, as the fiery heat of the Sicilian summer beat down upon besieged and besieger alike, began the fourth year of the ninety-fifth Olympiad, when Soundiades was Archon of Athens. The siege of Motya dragged on. The gap in the causeway was filled at last and the causeway itself enlarged.

The last stages of rebuilding the causeway were the most costly, for the Greeks had to carry the widened structure up to the very walls of Motya. Here a natural ledge extended out into the bay, west of the main gate of the city. This ledge provided Dionysios with a platform on which to mount his siege engines.

All day and all night, men trotted across the causeway with stones and sand to enlarge the ledge. In the daytime they went in pairs, one carrying his basket of stones while the other held a shield over the heads of both to ward off missiles from the walls. The corpses of Dionysios' soldiers littered the Motyan end of the causeway. Every night there was a mass cremation on the mainland, sending a smell of burnt meat through the besiegers' camp.

If Himilko's failure to relieve Motya discouraged its citizens, they did not show it. Day and night they showered missiles upon the Greeks working under the walls, while under bombardment themselves from Greek archers and from catapults on the causeway. From time to time, smoke rose above the temple of Baal Hammon as the first-born of the leading Punic families were passed through the fire. Every time he saw this smoke, Zopyros was glad that he had rescued one child, at least, from this cruel fate. At these times, especially, he worried about his family, hoping that they had had the sense to stay in Syracuse.

At last Dionysios' large siege engines—the belfries and rams—rolled out upon the causeway. It took several days, under the ceaseless downpour of missiles, to bring them one by one to the walls of Motya, to lever them around to the right, to roll them out on the ledge, and finally to turn them to the left again to face the beleaguered city.

With a flourish of trumpets, the next phase of the attack began. The two ram tortoises moved up to the wall. The rams inside these engines, swung by chains from the roofs of the wheeled sheds, began pounding the masonry. Day and night they pounded—*boom*—*boom*—as if two demented gods were beating a pair of cosmic drums, a little out of time. As the crew of each ram tired, another crew relieved it.

The Motyans dropped fire, stones, and heavy beams down upon the tortoises. Now and then one was damaged or caught fire. Dionysios' men would draw it back, put out the fire, and repair the damage. Then they pushed it forward to the attack again.

At last, the wall in front of one ram crumbled and collapsed with a frightful roar and a vast cloud of dust, burying the front end of the tortoise. Trumpets sang; infantry, brave in bronze cuirasses, greaves, and crested helms, climbed into the breach. Missiles rained upon the soldiers. Many fell, writhing in pain or limp in death. Others pressed on. The Motyans and their Greek mercenaries met them shield to shield, jabbing with spears, swinging swords and axes, and grappling body to body. Time and again the besieged thrust back the attackers.

Meanwhile Dionysios' men, with shovels and even with bare hands, hauled away the debris that had fallen from the wall. Then the wall in front of the other ram collapsed in its turn, and another bloody struggle took place in the breach.

Little by little the Siceliots gained the upper hand. They enlarged the breaches with pick and shovel and crowbar. They leveled the broken wall down to the ground, pulled back the tortoises, and pushed forward the two belfries. These were wheeled wooden towers sixty feet high—to overtop the tall houses of Motya—and very narrow to go through the winding streets of the city. They swayed alarmingly as they rolled slowly forward, pushed by hundreds of sweating soldiers. Coatings of green hides, nailed to their outsides, protected them against the torches and firepots the Motyans threw at them.

The belfries did not get far into the city, because the Motyans had thrown up barricades across the streets in front of them. From the stalled belfries, some Greeks attacked these barriers with picks and shovels. Others invaded the houses on either side, battering down the planks that had been nailed across the doors and windows. Planks were thrust out from the tops of the belfries to the roofs and upper windows of the houses. Syracusan soldiers charged clattering across these planks. Motyans rushed from their hiding places and out upon the planks from the other ends. The foes met in the middle, grappled on the narrow ways, and crashed to the streets far below. Other men fought across the housetops, through rooms and hallways of the buildings, up and down the stairs.

Little by little the invaders enlarged their hold upon the city, but at a fearful cost. The dead ran into thousands.

Dionysios made a practice, each day at sundown, of breaking off the battle. Then, when he had accustomed the Motyans to this routine, a sudden night attack through the captured apartment houses carried the defenses, and the attackers poured into the city through a dozen gaps.

Some defenders, losing hope at last, fled to the temples or tried to hide in their homes. Others, guessing the fate in store for them, cut the throats of their wives and children and rushed snarling upon the invaders, to die in a last wild fury of hacking and stabbing. Up and down the streets the slaughter raged.

Dionysios, entering with his staff on foot through one of the breaches, saw his soldiers running about and striking down old men, women, and children in a frenzy of blood lust. He roared:

"What do the abandoned fools think they are doing? How shall I ever pay for this war, if I have no prisoners to sell? Stop them at once!" He addressed his staff. "Go through the streets, crying: 'Cease all killing, by order of Dionysios!'"

Zopyros and the others scattered to try to stop the slaughter. But, although they bawled themselves hoarse shouting, "Cease all killing!" their efforts proved useless. The soldiers paid no attention but continued unchecked their raping, torturing, and slaying.

Zopyros walked the section of the city assigned to him, shouting his message. As he walked, he kept looking for Abarish, the steward of Elazar who had been so in love with Greek philosophy and who—if he still lived—must have revised his ideas on the subject. Failing either to check the slaughter or to find Abarish among the living or the dead, Zopyros reported back to Dionysios. So did the other staff officers. The tyrannos commanded:

"Go out again, men; but this time cry to all Phoenicians to take refuge in the Hellenic temples! Pass the word: all Punics to the Hellenic temples!" He spoke to the captain of his bodyguard. "Agathias! Split up your men and post a guard at each Hellenic temple. They shall protect the Punics who take refuge there. Order your men to cry the message loudly as they pass through the city. All Punics to the Greek temples!"

"But how about you, sir?" said Agathias.

"I can take care of myself. Get along with you!"

Dawn saw a few thousand surviving Motyans huddled on the grounds of the Greek temples. At each temple, a squad of Dionysios' bodyguards blocked the gate in the wall of the temenos with leveled spears while, outside, thousands of soldiers milled about, gripping armfuls of loot and growling threats. Their eyes gleamed with eagerness to resume the slaughter.

Dionysios, red-eyed from lack of sleep but still a dominant figure in his iron breastplate and scarlet cloak—the latter now stained with blood and smoke—strode through the corpse-littered streets. His staff, reeling with fatigue, staggered in his wake. Several houses were burning. A few officers tried, with little success, to organize bucket brigades of soldiers.

Most of the soldiers had completely thrown off discipline. They rushed about after loot, hurling household furnishings they did not want from the windows of the tall houses, to the peril of those in the streets below. Others swarmed about the entrances to the temenoi of the Greek temples, not yet quite mutinous enough to rush the squads of guards who protected the Motyans within.

Seeing the blood lust on the faces of the soldiers and knowing that the lives of the surviving Motyans hung by a thread, Dionysios muttered to his staff: "If I don't do something to appease the dogs, they'll butcher the prisoners in spite of me. I have it!" He raised his voice. "All Hellenic mercenaries who fought for the Motyans are to be separated from the rest of the prisoners, bound, and marched to the mainland!"

By noon the captive Greeks—bloodstained, hollow-eyed, and stripped to their shirts—stood bound in long lines on the shore of the mainland near the end of the causeway. Thousands of Dionysios' soldiers—dirty, wild-eyed men of various arms and nations all mingled together—moved restlessly around them. From his great black horse the tyrannos harangued them:

"... the Motyans, scoundrels though they be, at least fought for their own. But *these* slimy traitors, these renegades from Hellenism, these unnatural men, these parricides—no easy fate shall be theirs! We must set an example for all time, to any Hellene who would offer his sword to the implacable foes of Hellas. And so I say—crucify them!"

The soldiers cheered frantically and beat their weapons against their shields. They jeered the prisoners and gleefully taunted them with their coming agonies. All afternoon, cross after cross arose in an endless line along the beach, each with its burden. By sunset every one of the Greek prisoners hung, dying slowly and painfully, upon his cross.

As for Dionysios' soldiers, by nightfall their avidity for blood, pain, and death had been sated. They quietly rejoined their units, scrubbed the blood and dirt from their bodies in the waters of the bay, and cleaned and put away their weapons. Some got roaring drunk; some gambled away their loot; some rolled up in their cloaks and slept like exhausted animals. Some gathered around campfires to tell stories and sing, for all the world like kindly, good-natured men who had never butchered a prisoner in their lives.

Meanwhile, far into the night, in battered Motya, captive after captive was hustled to the slave block for the swarming slave dealers to bid on.

As the sentries called the end of the first watch, Zopyros stared at the line of crosses, black against the starlit sky, and once more wondered if he had done the right thing. Although no more squeamish about death than most men of his brutal age, he knew that such massacres as he had witnessed were contrary to everything Pythagoras had taught. Yet what could he have done, either to stop the carnage or to avoid becoming involved in it? If he had followed Archytas' advice and refused the commission that Dionysios had pressed upon him, even more Phoenicians would have been killed; for he alone, of the members of Dionysios' staff, was able to call out the message to flee to the Greek temples in the Punic tongue.

For that matter, what could Dionysios have done, once he had committed himself to the siege? Deprived of the pleasure of this mass crucifixion, the soldiers might have wrought an even greater slaughter among the defeated. To be sure, the victims expiring on the long row of crosses were mercenaries, and such an end was a normal hazard of the soldiering trade. Why, thought Zopyros, he, now a mercenary, might someday face such a fate himself! With a shudder he drew his cloak about him and turned back toward his tent.

PANORMOS

On the plain behind Cape Plemmyrion, west of Syracuse, Dionysios drew up his army. Despite losses in battle, the departure of his Siceliot allies to their own cities, and the detachment of besieging forces at each of the recalcitrant cities in Phoenician Sicily, he still commanded over fifty thousand men. The Syracusan citizens formed one contingent; the various mercenary nationalities, others. They stood in long, even lines, the sun glinting on their spearheads and the wind ruffling the horse-hair crests of their helmets.

Dionysios reviewed the men, praised them—briefly, for he knew they yearned to go home—and ordered the Syracusans to stack their arms. The men piled their weapons with much clatter, as others loaded the sheaves of spears and piles of shields into wagons. Zopyros, sitting his horse behind Dionysios, whispered to an older staff officer:

"We're a long way from Syracuse yet. Why must they stack their arms so soon?"

The officer snorted. "Sometimes, my boy, you don't seem bright. There are always traitors, malcontents, and agitators. What do you think a few thousand such men would do if they entered the city with arms in their hands?"

"Oh."

As soon as he was dismissed, Zopyros hastened home, fearful that Korinna had gone back to Messana after all. But she was there, welcoming him with open arms as if they had never disagreed. After he and Korinna and Hieron had hugged the breath out of one another, Zopyros said to his stepson:

"Hieron, how would you like to go out and play until dinner?"

"Will you play with me, Zopyros?"

"Not this time. I have things to discuss with your mother."

"Then I'll stay home with you. I love you so much."

"I love you too, Hieron dear. But now I want to be alone with your mother."

"Why, Daddy?"

"Never mind. Look: here's a nice, new penny. Go to the market place and buy yourself a drink of sweetened water, or a toy, or whatever you like. Just don't come back before sunset."

"No, I want to play with you."

"Either you go, or you shall spend the afternoon studying your alpha-beta!"

"I don't want to study my alpha-beta today."

"Then go! And take your penny!"

During the winter, the store of weapons in the Arsenal grew, albeit at a slackened tempo. Zopyros, back at his job in the Arsenal, called Segovax, Archytas, and his assistant Abdashtarth into conference on a new catapult design. Segovax said:

"If you put the windlass farther back, the boys can get a better hold on it, without barking the knuckles of them against the frame."

Archytas: "And these stretchers are thicker than they need be. You can save weight ..."

Abdashtarth: "May it please my lord Zopyros, Master Prothymion thinks he can get more range by reinforcing the bow with a strip of sinew, as do the Scythians. ..."

As Archytas had predicted, Zopyros found himself drawn into the circle of Dionysios' personal friends. Late one afternoon, he and Archytas were sitting with the others in the andron of Dionysios' palace, sipping Lesbian wine under the watchful eyes of the bodyguards. Damokles, the willowy poet and the most outspoken of Dionysios' flatterers, was holding forth on the greatness of his patron, when Dionysios entered with a letter in his hand. As the guests rose, the tyrannos said:

"At last, my friends, Lithodomos has written us from Neapolis— no doubt concerning his mission to buy grain for the next campaign."

Damokles cried out; "By the gods, O Dionysios, that's good!"

Dionysios looked at Damokles with a puzzled frown. "Since I have not yet opened the letter, how do you know whether he sends me good news or bad?"

Damokles, not put out of countenance, chuckled. "By the gods, Dionysios, that's good—reproof! You always know what to say! Such godlike speed of mind and tongue—no wonder you are the most accomplished, most fortunate, and happiest of mortals. If, that is, you are indeed a mortal."

"Were it not for this iron vest I wear," said Dionysios, "my mortality would, I fear, have been proven ere this. But speaking of happiness: are you then eager to change places with me?"

"Oh, no sir!" cried Damokles. "Does a mortal take the place of a god? One must not seek to climb the sky or to wed Aphrodite. My own shortcomings make such thoughts absurd—nay, blasphemous."

"Someday," said Dionysios, "you shall taste the joys of my position. Then, perchance, you'll chatter less about my ineffable happiness. How is your new catapult coming, Zopyros?"

Zopyros told him. Dionysios said: "Try to get the pilot model under way before the end of Anthesterion.[8] The Carthaginians are stirring, hot to avenge last summer's defeat; we must start our campaign early."

Zopyros discussed the forthcoming campaign that evening at dinner with Korinna and Archytas. Both urged him to flee to Taras. But the revulsion he felt after the fall of Motya had faded. He refused, saying:

"If I quit Dionysios' service at the end of my first campaign, people would suspect he's dismissed me in disgrace. Besides, these campaigns don't promise any real danger to a staff officer. This time we're just cleaning up a few little sieges."

Archytas said; "Old boy, I'm afraid your head has been turned by Dionysios."

"Not at all! I see through his rascalities. Although you must admit that, if a city can't manage its own affairs, it could do worse than be led by a man like him."

---

8   Approximately February.

Korinna said: "It's all very well to talk about your career; but your family ought to mean more to you. You leave us in danger while you pursue glory with that man."

"All right, all right, I promise to quit after this campaign. Just one more try for reputation, that's all!"

During the next few ten-days, Syracuse buzzed with rumors about the Carthaginians' vast preparations. Zopyros, along with Archytas, was asked to another dinner with Dionysios' intimates. The tyrannos walked in upon his guests clad in a long robe of royal purple and wearing a golden crown. A couple of guests whistled in amazement at this gorgeous spectacle.

"Your attire, sir," said Damokles, "confirms my suspicion of long standing, that we have befriended, not a man, but a god."

"Hm!" snorted Dionysios. "Could I but persuade the Carthaginians of that, all my problems would vanish. Understand, my friends, I don't intend to flaunt this raiment before the Syracusans just yet. To them I am still merely their President, and republican simplicity of dress is in order. But, now that I rule most of Sicily, I must experiment with the symbols of a wider sovereignty. Could the Great King retain the loyalty of all the many peoples of the Persian Empire if he strolled about the streets of Babylon in the garb of a common man, talking and joking with the vulgar as if he were one of them? I doubt it."

"How are the Carthaginians' preparations coming, sir?" asked another guest, as they took their positions on the dining couches.

"So far, I have received more rumor than fact. Still, I am told that Himilko will lead a million men to Sicily."

Some of the guests exchanged glances of alarm. Dionysios, taking off his crown and rubbing his scalp where it had chafed him, continued: "But every soldier knows what wild guesses people make about the size of a hostile army."

Zopyros said: "That's right, sir. Even Herodotos, whose history I've been reading, attributed an army of a million eight hundred thousand to Xerxes in his invasion of Hellas. From simple calculations of food and transport, and of the organization of the Persian Empire, Xerxes would have done well to assemble one tenth that number— actual combatants, that is."

"I trust that rumor as greatly exaggerates reality in this instance," said Dionysios. "Whatever the enemy's numbers, however, we must bestir ourselves. You may expect orders to march within a ten-day."

"Ah, with a Dionysios to lead us, we fear nothing!" said Damokles. "One Dionysios is worth a million ordinary men. Happy are we, to be able to bask in the sunshine of his happiness ..."

Dionysios stared fixedly at Damokles until the latter's voice died and his obsequious smile melted away. Then Dionysios slowly raised his eyes to the air over Damokles' couch.

Damokles craned his neck to follow the tyrannos' glance. What he saw made him turn pale; his goblet clattered to the floor. A sword was suspended from the ceiling by a single horsehair; it hung, point down, directly over Damokles' couch. As Damokles stared in frozen horror, Dionysios raised his resonant voice:

"I told you once, my dear Damokles, that the next time you blabbed about my happiness, I would give you a taste of what it is like to be a ruler. Now you know. Plots and intrigues hang like a sword above my head. Malcontents and traitors at home, exiles and foreign foes abroad, stand ready at all times to remove me from this earthly scene.

"Know that a nation is always filled with men who hate their ruler, be he as wise as Sokrates, as noble as Perikles, or as successful as Cyrus the Great. Nothing would satisfy them save to be the ruler themselves. Since there is room for but one ruler at a time, most of these envious men must be disappointed. I shall have had the gods' own luck if I rule this land for another decade without being murdered by someone I trust or torn to bits by a revolutionary mob. You may leave your couch now, Damokles."

Damokles squirmed off his couch to the wine-stained floor with the speed of an octopus slithering into its lair. Majestically, Dionysios rose, took a spear from a guard, and struck the hair that held the sword. The sword fell heavily, deeply burying its point in the upholstery of the couch. Dionysios pulled out the sword and handed both weapons to the guard. No one spoke or moved.

"I must have that cut mended," said Dionysios mildly, fingering the tear in the couch. He resumed his own couch.

Damokles rose to his feet with purple wine stains on his tunic. Red-faced, in a voice choked by suppressed anger, he said: "After all, godlike sir, nothing compels you to go on being—ah—President."

"Indeed? Do you know another better qualified to lead the Syracusans in these perilous times?"

"N-no, sir. I—ah—"

"Or perhaps you favor a full constitutional democracy for Syracuse?"

"I—I have never thought much about it."

"Well, I have, and I will tell you what I think about democracy. Democracy is a delightful form of government, but it succeeds only where the people are qualified to practice it. The Athenians made a success of it for nearly a century, because they disciplined themselves and placed the duties of citizenship above selfish personal interests. This, however, does not happen often. Democracy assumes that every citizen is born wise, prudent, farseeing, just, altruistic; but this, we know, is not true.

"Sometimes a great crisis, like the Persian wars, inspires men to attain these heights of virtue for a while. Sooner or later, however, they fall back into their normal swinishness. They listen to demagogues who promise them wealth without work, safety without arms, and public services without taxes. Then they stand amazed when they find themselves powerless and destitute, with the enemy battering down their gates.

"I did not steal democracy from the Syracusans. You, yourselves, let it die, because you did not love it more than your personal lusts and whims and ambitions. I have defended you from grasping politicians within and envious foes without. I have built the ships for your trade and made you rich among the cities of all the world. But I cannot give you these things and democracy, too. Yes, Damokles?"

"I beg my President to excuse me," said Damokles stiffly. "I feel unwell."

"You may withdraw; but think twice before you call me happy again. Rejoice!"

The skies were blue, and the earth lay brown beneath the scorching summer sun, when the Syracusan army marched back home once more. This time Dionysios did not disarm the citizens outside the

277

city but marched them straight in without halting. He did not fear rebellion; for everyone knew of the huge Carthaginian army and the desertion of the Syracusans' allies. They knew that a long, grinding siege, as desperate as the Athenian attack of eighteen years before, was in prospect.

Zopyros returned on foot, with his left hand bandaged. As soon as he was dismissed, he trudged wearily home. The house was completely empty, but he found a note on a sheet of papyrus, lying on the bare floor:

Korinna to her beloved husband Zopyros, greeting:
    Father has sent Glaukos with a traveling cart to fetch Hieron and me home. I go with him. As you know, it terrifies me to remain in this strange city without you. Archytas has arranged to store our furniture on Ortygia. I long to be reunited with you when this dreadful war is over. Farewell.

Zopyros stared at the letter, holding it in trembling hands. Then with a curse he slammed the door behind him and set out with long strides, his fatigue forgotten, for Ortygia. He found Archytas at his desk on the gallery of the Arsenal.

"Why did you let her go?" he snapped.

"My dear fellow, how could I stop her? By force? Her brother was there to prevent that. I repeated all your arguments about the crumbling walls of Messana, but it did no good. She's used to having a family around her, and she's been miserable alone while you were gone. What happened to your hand?"

"Just a burn. The Segestans made a sally at night and put the torch to half our camp. A lot of horses, including mine, perished. What in Hades shall I do now?"

"How should I know? I tried to warn you that you might be taking the pitcher to the well once too often—"

"Go ahead, say: 'I told you so.'"

"I did, but I won't rub it in. How's the war? Were we beaten?"

"No, aside from that setback at Segesta. But Himilko landed more than a hundred thousand at Panormos—rumors said three hundred thousand. The allies, believing the rumors, dashed back to defend their own cities. Leptines was supposed to sink the Carthaginian fleet, but their galleys engaged him while the transports gave him the slip. Although he had some small success, by the time Himilko had called up contingents from the Phoenician cities of Sicily, the Punics again outnumbered us two to one. So Dionysios went on the defensive."

"Where's Himilko's army?"

"I hear he's recaptured Motya. I hope he treats the garrison we left there better than our men treated the Motyans. Archytas! If you were Himilko and controlled the western end of Sicily, which route would you take to Syracuse?"

"The southern route, I suppose. You're worrying about Messana, aren't you?"

"Yes. But, you know, Himilko has a lot of his force at Panormos, on the northern coast. If he came by the northern route, Messana would lie in his path. ... I'd better ask the big boss."

Zopyros went to the palace. Long after dark, he was admitted. He found Dionysios, looking wan in the lamplight, standing over a table littered with scrolls and sheets and tablets. The tyrannos said:

"What is it, Zopyros? Be quick."

"Sir, I haven't asked many favors of you, have I?"

"You've asked so few that it makes me uneasy. What is it that you want."

"I want to know which route Himilko is taking toward Syracuse."

Dionysios, despite his fatigue, looked sharply at Zopyros. "You think I know that?"

"If anybody does, sir, you do."

Dionysios hesitated, then said: "He is advancing along the northern coast toward Messana. Let me see—Messana—your wife comes from there, doesn't she? And didn't I hear that she had returned thither?"

"Yes, sir. I want leave to go fetch her. That wretched wall at Messana will never keep out the Carthaginians."

"You may not go."

"Wh-why not?"

"In the first place, it would do no good. Himilko has already reached Peloris, a day's march from Messana. He'll almost certainly

get there before you. In the second place, I need you here. Let me see
…" Dionysios fumbled among the sheets of papyrus. "Here's a list of
things for you to do. You're to study the city's fortifications and decide
where to emplace our catapults. Report back by this time tomorrow,
with a list of recommended sites."

"But, sir, I've got to get my wife out of that trap!"

"We have a few days to prepare for a siege as great as the siege
by the Athenians," roared Dionysios, "and you distract me with your
private problems? Who do you think you are? Zeus? Get to work
on those catapults, and no more nonsense! You're a soldier now. If
you leave town, you will incur my severe displeasure. Now get along
with you!"

Clenching his fists, Zopyros held his temper. Although it went
against his grain to dissemble, too much stood on the razor's edge
to allow himself the luxury of saying what he thought. He muttered:

"Aye, aye, sir. I'll do my best."

As he left the palace, he considered appealing to Archytas again
for advice. Then he thought better of it. If he antagonized the tyrannos, he did not wish to involve his friend in his own disgrace.

An hour later, he left Syracuse. When he explained that he was
on his way to Megara Hyblaia, to examine the defenses there for the
President, the sentries let him through the gate. The soldiers failed to
notice how strange it was for a staff officer in full uniform to be driving a traveling cart.

The two horses, although no destriers, were good animals as hack-
neys went. Zopyros pushed them as fast and as far as he dared that
night. He found a pasture where his horses could graze and slept in
the cart. Before dawn he was on the road again, driving all day and
staying his hunger by gnawing a loaf as he drove. From Catana to the
ruins of Naxos—a Siceliot city razed by Dionysios seven years before—he had the vast mass of Aetna, smoking ominously, on his left.

About noon of the following day, he neared Messana. All morning he had passed groups of refugees, with fear on their faces and
bundles on their backs. Several times he stopped to question them
about the Carthaginians, but their answers were contradictory: "Oh,
I'm sure they have taken the town. …" "… No, there was no sign of

them when I left. ..." "We decided to leave before the foe arrived; but some, relying on the oracle, stayed behind. ..." "They're right behind us. ..."

Zopyros drove on along the coastal road, skirting the feet of the Poseidonian Hills. The groups of refugees became thicker and thicker, slowing his progress. Between halts he lashed the horses to a gallop to try to make up time. Although he shouted himself hoarse, the refugees stood in stolid clumps in the middle of the road, staring blankly until he was almost upon them.

At noon he came upon refugees running past him. Others were scrambling up the hillsides. They did not stop to answer his queries. Grimly, he drove on. He had, he thought, escaped from his would-be captors on the ship *Sudech*; why not again? He still had a chance.

Around the next bend in the road he spied a troop of horsemen galloping toward him. They were lean, dark men in kilts, with vermilion-dyed goatskin mantles and turbans of wildcat fur. Each had, slung across his back, a large quiver from which several light javelins protruded. As they sighted Zopyros and his cart, they spurred their mounts, bending low over their horses' necks.

Zopyros pulled up and tried to turn his cart around. But the road was narrow, with little room to spare between the hillside and the sea. The cart tipped wildly as the horses backed it off the road. Zopyros had nevertheless almost completed the turn when the dark horsemen came upon him.

They swarmed around, yelling and poising their javelins. One man grabbed the bridle of one horse; a second man, the other.

Zopyros leaped from the cart. A javelin whizzed through the empty space above him; another glanced from his helmet with a metallic sound. He had not brought a shield or a spear on this journey, since he had not meant to fight and planned to travel light. To engage the horsemen with sword alone would be suicidal. Instead, he rushed at the nearest horse, seized the rider's nigh leg in both hands, and pushed it upward.

The man toppled off his horse and fell into a bush. Zopyros gathered himself to vault to the horse's bare back, for the Numidians rode without even a saddle pad. But, as he placed his hands on the animal's back and sprang into the air, the horse bounded forward like a rabbit.

Zopyros fell sprawling. Before he could recover, several of the men were on top of him.

They hauled him to his feet, punching, kicking, and whacking him with the shafts of their javelins. The blows were painful but not crippling. He wondered why they had not killed him outright, when he became aware of a Carthaginian officer on a horse, waving a battle-ax and shouting something in the Numidian tongue. From the man's gestures, Zopyros inferred that the order meant "Take him alive!"

With yelps of glee, the Numidians stripped off Zopyros' crested helmet, sword, dagger, purse, canvas cuirass, and boots. They divided up the loot. Two tied his wrists together, while others turned the cart horses around until the wheels were again in the ruts. They boosted him into the cart and started him for Messana.

The Carthaginian officer and three Numidians escorted the cart. Two Numidians led the horses along the road, while the third rode abreast of Zopyros, ready to spear him if he made a false move. The other Numidians galloped off to southward.

The officer leaned toward Zopyros and said in broken Greek: "You who?"

Zopyros opened his mouth but found himself unable to speak. He was a churning mass of fear, rage, dismay, and self-blame. He was, he told himself, the most useless, clumsy, stupid, incompetent ox—

"Who you?" said the Carthaginian again.

Zopyros swallowed, stammered, and finally said in Punic: "I hight Zopyros the Tarentine, O Captain."

The officer replied in the same tongue: "One of Dionysios' mercenaries, are you not?"

"Aye, sir."

"Then what in the name of Baal Hammon were you about, driving a cart into the midst of the Carthaginian army in broad daylight? A scout on horseback I could fathom, but this madness ..."

"I had hoped to rescue my wife and son. They were in Messana."

"Ah, that I can understand."

"I needed the cart to bear them away in. I take it you saved me from being skewered by these barbarians?"

"What use is one more corpse? You will fetch a good price on the block, and I shall get a share of that price. You are lucky to get away with your life, considering how you lying, boy-loving Greeks murdered so many of our folk."

"Have you taken Messana?"

"Aye, Greek; it fell this morn. Some of its citizens fought, but with that paltry wall 'twas like mashing a gnat with a hammer."

Zopyros glanced about. The land had opened out. Soldiers swarmed the fields and groves: marching, drilling, setting up tents, loafing, and quarreling over loot. There were earringed Carthaginians in cuirasses of gilded scales. There were black-cloaked Iberians in purple shirts and tight knee breeches, with little round black bonnets on their heads and double-curved falchions at their sides. There were bronze-plated Greeks, ostrich-plumed Libyans, and veiled Garamantes. Huddled in blankets were companies of black spearmen from beyond the great desert, with shields of rhinoceros hide and wooly hair trimmed in fantastic shapes. Horsemen cantered by; a column of scythe-wheeled chariots rumbled past.

There were thousands upon thousands of tents. They filled the plain around Messana like the waves of the sea. Messana's pitiful wall stood jaggedly above this sea of tents. A few plumes of smoke ascended languidly from fires still raging inside the city. From within came rumbling crashes as Himilko's men overthrew the walls of houses.

Zopyros' captor delivered him to another Carthaginian, who was in charge of a long line of prisoners chained hand to hand. Other prisoners were brought in from time to time. The officer in charge looked them over as they arrived. As he encountered those enfeebled by age, whether male or female, the officer made a signal to a common soldier who stood by. The soldier smote the aged prisoners over the head with his battle-ax. As a pair of blacks carried the bodies off to throw on a huge stinking pyre blazing a bowshot away, others chained the living together.

The prisoners stood with hanging heads. For hours Zopyros stood with them, equally dejected. Now and then he peered up and down the line, searching for a familiar face. He kept telling himself that he was worthless, worthless, worthless. ... How could he ever save Korinna now? To be a slave and yet to live! Slavery, like death, was part of the natural order of things. Like death, it lay in wait for everyone. But a gentleman and a hero would never be enslaved; he would either die fighting or slay himself first. Yet he, Zopyros, had failed to do either. Through his head rang the lines of the Poet:

> *On the day that the lot of the slave befalls a man,*
> *The half of his manhood does far-seeing Zeus take away.*

To make matters worse, his purchaser would probably have him branded or tattooed, in the manner of Phoenician slaveowners. Like all body-worshiping Hellenes, although willing to kill, Zopyros was squeamish about branding, circumcision, or other mutilations.

Once during the long afternoon, a camp servant came by with a bucket of water and a dipper. He doled out the water so carelessly that half ran down the prisoners' chins and was wasted. Still the captives waited, as the line inched forward toward the slave block.

At last it was Zopyros' turn. His wrists were unchained; his tunic—his sole remaining garment—was snatched off over his head. A pair of soldiers, watchful lest a prisoner make a break for freedom or try to kill himself, shoved him up on the platform. Other soldiers surrounded the area. Zopyros stared down at the semicircle of dealers and shivered slightly.

"Who you?" asked the auctioneer in pidgin Greek.

Eying the man closely, Zopyros replied in Punic: "I hight Zopyros the Tarentine, sir." He had to watch every word now. He had to impress his purchasers with his value, lest he be sold into a man-killing task like mining. On the other hand, he dared not inflate his worth by too much self-praise, lest his kin could never afford to ransom him.

"What can you do?" said the auctioneer with more interest in his voice. Evidently he was impressed by Zopyros' speech and bearing.

"I am an engineer. I can design and build walls, fortifications, shipyards, docks, waterworks, and engines of war."

"You see!" cried the auctioneer, turning to the dealers. "Behold this fine, big-balled slave lad! A man of wit, learning, and talents, furthermore! What am I bid for this flower of Hellas?"

"One pound of silver," said a dealer.

"Absurd!" cried the auctioneer. "Why, the fact that he speaks the Punic tongue—and with a good Tyrian accent, even—alone should add at least a pound to his value!"

"One pound, thirty shekels," said another dealer.

"You do but jest. He'll retail for ten pounds at least. Look at the intelligent gleam in his eye! Speak some more, fellow, to show these niggards how clever you are."

"Were I as clever as all that, my lord," said Zopyros, "I should not be standing here now."

This fetched a laugh. "One pound forty," said a dealer.

"One fifty."

"Two pounds."

Despite the auctioneer's exhortations, bidding slowed down. The price rose by increments of five shekels only. Zopyros thought he had been knocked down for two and forty-five to a fat man with a sash, when a small, familiar figure pushed through the crowd and called:

"I'll raise that bid to three pounds!"

The dealers glowered at Captain Asto, for they did not like outsiders to buy directly from the army and thus deprive them of their middleman's profit. Nevertheless, the auctioneer sold Zopyros to the little mariner.

With a sudden surge of hope and relief, Zopyros stepped down from the block, donned his shirt, and wordlessly followed Asto out of the guarded slave-dealing area. When they were out of earshot of the soldiers, Asto said softly in Greek:

"I cannot free you here, noble sir, because somebody else would seize you and enslave you again. I shall take you back to Panormos, my present home port. There you shall live with me until the war dies down, after which you shall be free again."

"Thanks to you, dear friend, and to whatever god sent you! Have you perchance seen my wife amongst the captives? She was with her family in Messana when it fell."

"No, I have not; but we might walk about to make sure."

For an hour they strolled the camp, inspecting every catch of prisoners; but no sign of Korinna or Hieron or Xanthos' family did they see. At last Asto said:

"If they were caught, they must have been sold and taken away earlier. Now we must go back to my ship, for I hope to reach a good harbor by nightfall."

"How did you happen along just in time to buy me, Asto?"

"I am carrying supplies for Himilko's army."

"Were you or any of yours caught in the siege of Motya?"

"No, the gods be praised! I prayed, and the Lady Tanith sent me a dream, warning me to move my family to Panormos. It proves what I said on the *Muttumalein* about the gods, does it not? They rule the world absolutely, down to the tiniest grain of sand, and mortals can do nothing without them."

Zopyros said: "I shall save up my price and pay you back every shekel."

"Don't think of it! You saved my life in Syracuse, and I pay my just debts."

During the following months, Zopyros lived as a privileged servant in Asto's house in Panormos. Mindful that his ultimate liberty depended upon the Phoenician's good will, Zopyros tried not to impose upon the good nature of Asto and his family. This was sometimes difficult, for Asto's wife was a sharp-tongued, fanatical housekeeper, while Zopyros' clumsiness led him to break a few small objects—a lamp, a dish, a flowerpot.

When Zopyros' skill as a calculator became known, some of Asto's friends and associates hired him to solve their problems. Zopyros was glad to have a little money: first, to replace the things he had broken and add a few small trinkets to mollify the mistress of the house; second, to save up for traveling expenses when he had regained his freedom.

As time passed, Zopyros heard tales of the war: how Himilko marched around the west side of Aetna on his way south, because an eruption had blocked the coastal road; how the Carthaginian admiral Mago defeated the Syracusan fleet under Leptines; and how the Carthaginians invested the city. He learned of the abortive uprising against Dionysios' rule; of Dionysios' freeing and arming the slaves of Syracuse; of the plague that broke out among the besiegers.

At last, one day in Metageitnion, Asto returned from a voyage with news: "The siege is broken. The Carthaginian forces are all slain, captured, or fled."

"Dear Herakles! How did that come to pass?" said Zopyros.

"When Himilko's army was weakened by the plague, your tyrannos sallied forth and smote the Carthaginians by land and by sea. He led the attacks himself, galloping about like one possessed of daemons.

"When destruction seemed certain for the forces of Carthage, Himilko bribed Dionysios with three hundred talents to let him and his Carthaginians escape by sea, leaving his mercenaries to their fate. The Syracusans routed these bodies of troops and slew or enslaved them, save for the Iberians. These warriors offered so stout a defense that Dionysios enlisted the survivors in his mercenary forces."

Zopyros said: "You seem not so cast down as I should have thought."

Asto shrugged. "Why should I love Carthage? Her hand has always lain heavily upon us Canaanites of Sicily, just as the hand of Dionysios has been heavy upon the Siceliot Greeks. I only hope these masterful men will end their strife and let simple folk like me get back to their proper work. And, in sooth, the African tribes subject to Carthage have revolted, so now war rages in New Canaan. They say Himilko has starved himself to death, to atone for his defeat and his desertion of the mercenaries. ... And now, dear friend, when do you plan to leave us?"

"You mean I'm free to go whenever I wish?"

"You always were, even though for your own protection we kept up the fiction of your servitude."

"You're a great-souled man, Asto."

Asto shrugged and spread his hands. "No worse than most, and better than some. I'll write your document of manumission forthwith."

The following day, Asto brought six friends to his house to witness Zopyros' emancipation. The document, in duplicate, was inscribed on sheets of parchment in Punic and Greek. Asto read the Punic version aloud:

> *Whereas I, Asto ben-Elram, residing in the city of Machanath (called Panormos by the Greeks), have purchased the slave Zopyros ben-Megabyzos the Tarentine for the sum of three pounds Carthaginian, and*
>
> *Whereas the said Zopyros has done for me a service far exceeding the aforesaid price in value, and*
>
> *Whereas it is my wish and desire, in return for this service, to free the said Zopyros from his condition of servitude:*
>
> *Now, therefore, I, Asto ben-Elram, in consideration of the said service, do hereby assign and convey the said Zopyros to the ownership of the supreme god, Baal Hammon (known in the Grecian tongue as Zeus), to serve the said god by righteous conduct as long as he shall live.*
>
> *In witness whereof, I, Asto ben-Elram, have hereunto set my hand and seal this twentieth day of Ab, in the four hundred and eighteenth year after the founding of Carthage, and have caused the said Zopyros and six free Canaanites of Machanath to sign this document as witnesses, and have placed a copy thereof in the temple of Baal Hammon in Machanath, to remain there forever to confirm the fact of this emancipation.*

Everybody signed. There were bows and murmurs of congratulation, and Asto passed a round of drinks of a heavy, sweet wine. After the witnesses had gone, Zopyros packed his scanty gear to leave. Asto asked:

"Have you money enough?"

"Thank you, I have. The money you let me earn by calculating for your friends will take me anywhere in Great Hellas."

"Then whither away? Back to, work for Dionysios, the implacable foe of the Canaanitish people?"

"Nay. Even if he'd have me, I'd liefer toil for a less exacting employer. I think his enmity toward the Canaanites is half genuine only, the rest being but an actor's performance."

"What leads you to say that?"

"I've been thinking of that bribe he took to let Himilko escape. Had his true motive been to extirpate all Phoenician power from Sicily, he'd never have let the Carthaginian general depart. But many of his own people weary of his tyranny; they'd gladly toss him into the Ionian Sea and seize the rule themselves. Therefore he needs the Carthaginians as a bogey wherewith to frighten the men of Syracuse into continued submission."

"You may be right; you may be right. High politics have always been beyond my ken. But, if not to Syracuse, then whither?"

"First, I shall try to find my wife."

"The gods aid you in that quest! Evnos could help you."

"Then, I shall return to Taras, to my father's home, and resume my engineering practice. Farewell, Asto."

"The gods may someday bring us together again; who knows?" said Asto. They shook hands and embraced, and Zopyros walked off toward the waterfront.

Many years passed. Dionysios retained his grip on Syracuse, extended his rule over most of Sicily and southern Italy, built public works, patronized the arts, grew old, and died. In the month of Mounychion, in the first year of the one hundred and third Olympiad, when Nausigenes was Archon of Athens, Archytas, five times President of Taras, sat bent over his desk in his study.

Outside, a late spring rain pattered down on the red roof tiles. The room was cluttered with specimens and models of devices. Oblivious to his surroundings, Archytas scribbled figures and drew lines on a waxed tablet, for he was working out the laws of harmonic progression. Around his feet played four infants, two of them his own grandchildren and the other two the children of his servants. Archytas still retained his fondness for the very young. As these infants grew up, he would have them all educated at his own expense.

A servant came in. "O President! Master Zopyros is here with a friend!"

"Show them in at once! And not a word about our little surprise!" Archytas indicated the toddlers. "Take these little fellows back to their mothers."

Archytas rose heavily and waddled into the courtyard. Skirting the open center of the court, where the rain poured down, he walked around the colonnade toward the entrance vestibule. Halfway around, he encountered his visitors.

"Zopyros!"

"Archytas! You remember Platon of Athens, don't you?"

"Of course! I met him on his first visit to the West—let's see—that must be nearly two decades ago. In those days, people still called Platon by his natal name. Eh, Aristokles, old chap?"

The man addressed took off his dripping traveler's hat and shook the water from its brim. He was about sixty years old, of medium height, stocky, and muscular; stout, but not so gross as Archytas. A thick beard, nearly white, swept his chest. He smiled easily, laughed seldom, and spoke pure Attic in a high, reedy voice, with a delicate charm of manner.

"Good old Archytas!" he said. "Fatter than ever—though who am I to talk?"

"Come on in; get those wet cloaks off. My servants will show you to your rooms. You're just in time for dinner."

"If we're not putting you out ..." said Platon.

"Not a bit, my dear fellow, not a bit. People are always dropping in about this time. But what brings you hither?" As they talked, they moved into the study. Servants brought spiced wine.

"The death of old Dionysios, as a matter of fact."

Archytas laughed. "Poor old Dionysios! All his life he struggled, not merely for empire, but also for literary distinction. Then, no sooner does he finally win the prize for tragedy at Athens than he takes sick and dies. How was that play of his, by the way?"

"*Hector's Ransom*? Not bad; but then, the competition was not very severe this season. They say in Athens that he hastened his end by wild dissipation as he celebrated his victory."

"I don't believe it. He was always abstemious, and it would have taken more than one debauch to kill a man of his physique. No, some disease laid hold of him; and that, together with age, did him in:

For, at the last, black Fates to darkness hurl
And overthrow the lucky, wicked man.

But you were saying, sir?"

"Yes. Old Dionysios' brother-in-law Dion wrote me, begging me to come to Syracuse, to try to make a philosopher out of the young Dionysios."

Archytas said; "Man, you have your work cut out for you! I know that young ne'er-do-well. He's a mere playboy. If he holds his father's empire together for five years, I shall be surprised."

"So Zopyros tells me. But I couldn't very well turn Dion down, when I've been preaching so long about the need for rulers to be philosophers, now could I?"

"I wish you luck, although I fear you've undertaken a Sisyphean task," said Archytas. "I should think your experience with old Dionysios would have disillusioned you."

"The old ruffian was already set in his ways, whereas the young one—I hope—will prove more plastic. As to that, you seem to have done pretty well as a philosophical ruler yourself. Your Taras proves that an honest, enlightened, constitutional republic is possible."

Archytas smiled. "Thanks, O Platon; but it's not really true."

"How do you mean? Are you about to confess some chicanery?"

"No. What I mean is this: I can get up and make a jolly good speech to the Tarentines. I crack jokes. I declaim eloquent passages. Thus I convince them that I'm an honest, wise, able unselfish leader. However, it is just their good luck that I also happen to possess those qualities. Another man—the late Dionysios, say—can make as good a speech and get elected, though he were at heart a self-seeking adventurer. When I'm gone, how do we know whether the Tarentines will choose another Archytas or another Dionysios?"

"As to that, you must limit the franchise to the better sort of people, excluding base mechanics."

"Like me?" said Zopyros tartly.

"Oh, no, no," said Platon. "I count you as a thinker and therefore one of the élite, despite your crassly materialistic interests."

"Thanks."

Archytas said: "When you limit power to the rich—your so-called 'best people'—you still have not solved the problem. For the gentry, as soon as they have power to do so, oppress and exploit the vulgus until the latter revolt. And I needn't tell you how frightful class warfare can be."

291

"As an Athenian," said Platon, "I have of course had firsthand experience with the breakdown of democracy. But it surprises me that you, the world's leading democratic leader, should take so grim a view of democratic government. What government do you, then, deem good?"

"Oh, I am not hopeless about democracy. But it's a new thing in the world. Only the Hellenes, the Phoenicians, and the Romans have experimented with it. It's like one of Zopyros' engines. He may have told you of the struggles he went through to make the first catapult work. The same with a new form of government: it never works as you think it will, and it takes much cutting and trying and sawing and filing to make it work at all."

"How would you saw and file the machinery of democracy to improve it?"

"For one thing, I think the many—your 'base mechanics'—need to be much better educated. People ask me why I bother to educate the children of my slaves. Well, in Taras, we have a liberal policy with manumission and citizenship; many of these infants will someday be voting citizens. It's better for the city if they are well-educated citizens."

Platon gave an aristocratic sniff. "You really think the vulgar head can be made good and wise enough to rule themselves?"

Archytas shrugged. "I don't know, but I'm trying to find out. The trouble with you, my friend, is that you think such questions can be answered by pure reason. If you'd ever been an engineer, you would know that one practical experiment is worth a score of theories." He turned to Zopyros with a curious, secretive smile. "I say, old boy, how's military engineering in Old Hellas?"

"Oh, I made my expenses with something left over," said Zopyros. He was still a tall, lean man, although his hair had thinned on top and his beard had turned iron-gray. "I got as far east as Rhodes and as far north as Pella. My biggest contract was building a pair of heavy stone-throwing catapults for the Athenians. So Megabyzos' Sons will stagger along for a while."

Archytas said to Platon: "When Zopyros says his firm will stagger along, he means he's drowning in drachmai." He sighed. "Sometimes I wish I'd gone into partnership with Zopyros and his brother when they offered me the chance, many years ago. If I had stuck to engineering, instead of this footling politics, I should have been rich."

Platon laughed. "Just a pair of base mechanics at heart, the twain of you!"

"I heard something that will interest you, old friend," said Zopyros to Archytas. "Do you remember that cad Alexis, who built the four-and five-bank ships for old Dionysios?"

"Shall I ever forget him?" said Archytas. "A few other powers of the Inner Sea tried such ships. They were never very successful, considering their cost."

"Ah, but a Phoenician shipbuilder in Cyprus has made a further advance, which renders larger ships practical. He uses but a single bank of oars. These are much larger than normal galley oars, and the shipbuilder sets four or five men to pulling each oar. It works like a charm."

"Plague!" cried Archytas. "Why didn't we think of that, when we were in the business? By the way, what's that clumsy object bound in cloth, which your man carried in with your baggage? Some new device?"

"That's my new portable catapult, which I used for demonstrations on this voyage. Would you like to see how it works?"

"I certainly should!"

Archytas gave a command to a servant, who presently placed the odd-shaped bundle on the mosaic floor before Zopyros and helped him to unwrap it. It contained a catapult about six feet long, designed to be shot while held in the hands. The bundle also contained several foot-long iron-darts for the miniature catapult and a six-foot wooden dart for a catapult of normal size. Zopyros picked up the large dart.

"Behold the arrow of Herakles! I tried to sell the Spartans some catapults, but King Archidamos took one look at this and cried in horror: 'O Herakles, the valor of man is extinguished!'"

"Perhaps it is," said Platon. "You told me on the ship of the Cumaean Sibyl's message, many years ago, about her vision of your shooting Herakles' bow and smashing the world. Old Dionysios started something when he hired men to invent weapons to his order. God alone knows where it will end. Someday one of your engineering colleagues *will* devise an engine to destroy the world."

"The world, luckily, is too large for mere mortals to shatter," said Zopyros. "However, I admit I sometimes brood about it. As far as my own work is concerned, I'm sure the divine Pythagoras would not approve. The trouble is, I'm known everywhere as the leading military engineer of the Inner Sea. Hence the only contracts I receive are military: catapults, rams, fortifications, and the like. I must eat, as Protagoras once reminded your master Sokrates when Sokrates twitted him about charging fees for his lectures."

"Tell him about our screw," said Archytas.

"Yes," continued Zopyros. "Archytas and I worked out a most elegant invention, which we call a screw. You cut a helical groove in a cylindrical rod—anyway, it has many possible applications, all perfectly peaceful. But we can't get anybody to take an interest in it.

"Show me how the hand catapult works," said Archytas.

"I don't want to spoil your plaster—"

"Don't worry. Shoot at that African shield of elephant hide."

Zopyros stood up and put the end of the slide of the catapult against the shield, which hung on the wall. He placed the curved bar on the after end of the trough against his chest, and leaned forward. The slide slid back, telescoping into the trough and bending the bow as it did so. The pawls on the sides of the crosshead rode over the racks with a rapid clicking sound. When Zopyros straightened up, the engine was cocked. He placed an iron dart, a foot long, in the groove.

"Here goes!" he said.

With his left hand supporting the engine, and the curved butt plate resting against his chest, he tweaked the lever on the crosshead. The bowstring twanged. The bolt slammed into the shield.

Archytas whistled; Platon peered behind the shield. "At least," said Platon, "you needn't worry about the shield's falling off the wall. It's solidly nailed in place, now."

Zopyros continued: "I meant the thing only for demonstrations. But on this journey I went all the way to Macedonia. The Macedonians stood around like dumb oxen as I demonstrated—all but their Prince Philip. Although he's still a boy, he took a keen interest in my devices. He swore that someday he'd have a whole company armed with these portable catapults, which he calls crossbows. What have you been working on, Archytas?"

"Oh, mostly mathematics. But here's an amusing device." Archytas indicated a post that stood on a base. A bellows on a low table was connected with the bottom of the post by a tube made of a crane's windpipe. From the top of the post, another tube extended out horizontally for two feet. On the end of this tube was mounted a little wooden model of a bird on the wing.

Archytas stooped, grasped the handles of the bellows, drew them apart, and then closed the bellows with a mighty downward push on the upper handle. There was a hiss of air. The bird moved. Bird and tube whirled round and round like the spoke of a wheel, while the bird's wings fluttered. As the hiss died away, the bird slowed and stopped.

"Zeus on Olympos!" cried Zopyros. "That's clever, Archytas! Let's see—the air travels up the post, and goes along the tube, and is expelled from this hole in the bird. ... We should be able to find some practical application. How would it be to have a galley whose rowers, instead of pulling oars, pump bellows—"

"Good gods, what's that?" cried Platon, starting. A mournful toot sounded from the mass of jars and tubes at one side of the study.

"That means dinnertime," said Archytas. He explained the automatic signal he had developed for the elder Dionysios. Platon said:

"I could use one of those, to signal the start of my classes. You must give me a drawing and a description, so I can have one made to spur the laggard student." As they went in to dinner, Platon continued: "Speaking of students, I wish that young chap from Stageira, that Aristoteles, were here. He's keen to know everything and classify everything, even machinery."

"You mean that skinny young know-it-all?" said Zopyros. "The one who thpeakth with a lithp?"

"That's the one. I left him studying under some of my colleagues. He swears to become a philosopher himself someday, albeit I doubt if he has the needed spiritual insight." Platon swung his feet up on his dining couch and rested his elbow on the cushion. As the servants began filing through with platters, he said: "*Oi!* I see you still do yourself well, Archytas."

"A man must have at least one vice, and gluttony is the least harmful to one's fellow mortals."

Platon dug into the repast piled up on his individual table. When hunger had been somewhat allayed, he said: "May I make a request, Archytas?"

"What, best one? Ask and you shall receive."

"Traveling hither, Zopyros told me some of his early adventures, when you and he worked for old Dionysios. May I ask that he continue? You, Zopyros, had just reached the place where that Phoenician sea captain had freed you from slavery."

Zopyros sighed. "After I left Asto, I spent three years searching for Korinna, stopping betimes to earn a little money by engineering. But I never did find her. Evnos the ransomer also searched vainly on my behalf. By the way, Archytas, have you seen the old fellow lately?"

"Yes; he came through Taras but a few days ago."

"How is he?"

"As usual, he swears that each ransoming journey will be his last. If he ever does retire, he won't know what to do with himself. You and I, O Platon, write noble philosophical treatises on how to improve this cruel and wicked world; but Evnos actually does something about it."

"I should like to hear more of Zopyros' tale, if you please," said Platon.

"Well," said Zopyros, "the boy—my stepson—did turn up."

"Where?" asked Platon.

"In his father's home in Carthage. When he was sold after the fall of Messana, the slave dealer asked him who he was. The child—he's clever, you know—said he was the son of Elazar the building contractor in Carthage. The dealer, knowing a good thing when he saw it, got in touch with Elazar and squeezed a stiff ransom out of him."

"Then what befell the lad?"

"He grew up, married, served in the Carthaginian army, and inherited Elazar's business when the old man died. If he'd been reared in Hellas, he'd have become a famous athlete. He has the body for it. But in the Phoenician lands they consider outdoor games and sports childish."

"Barbarians!" muttered Platon.

"There's something to be said on their side, too. Anyway, I've seen Ahiram—he went back to his Phoenician name—a couple of times when business took me to Carthage. He's gracious to his stepfather but has practically forgotten our adventures with the witch and the slavers. He's almost forgotten his mother, too."

"Then your daring abduction of the boy accomplished nothing, after all?"

"I wouldn't say that. If he'd been living with his father during the Carthaginian civil war that followed the siege of Syracuse, he might well have been passed through the fire to Baal Hammon. As it was, he was safe in the slave dealer's hands at that time and, when next his people offered such sacrifices, he was old enough to escape that fate. Perhaps the gods have a plan for human lives after all."

"How about the rest of your wife's family?" asked Platon.

"Her father Xanthos died of overexertion in belatedly trying to flee Messana, while Glaukos was slain in fighting the Carthaginians. Korinna's mother Eirenê was separated from her daughter in the flight. She found refuge with kinsmen but died soon afterward—of a broken heart, they told me. It was Xanthos' fault for trusting that oracle rather than his common sense. Nearly all the Messanians who had fled the city earlier survived. It was my fault, too, for not having taken Archytas' advice and quit Dionysios' service before that last campaign."

"And Korinna's fault for going back to Messana," said Archytas, "and Dionysios' fault for starting the war, and Himilko's fault for capturing Messana, and so on. It's an endless and useless philosophical exercise to try to pin the blame for any one event on one particular person."

"And have you never married again?" said Platon.

"No. I've never really given up hope of finding her, although I admit it's not logical."

Platon ducked. "You're positively un-Hellenic! The superior man should not allow such a sentimental attachment to interfere with his civic duty of begetting legitimate children—"

"Is that so?" snapped Zopyros in a sudden flare of irritation. "How about your Archeanassa? You preach for years and years on the beauty of a pure, spiritual love between man and man, and then you yourself fall madly in love with a middle-aged hetaira …"

297

Zopyros broke off when he perceived that Platon was becoming angry. Archytas deftly turned the conversation to his mathematical discoveries. As the servants washed and dried the diners' hands, Zopyros gave Archytas a searching look and said:

"Old boy, you're hiding something from me."

"I don't know what you mean!"

"Oh yes, you do! I can tell by the way you try to cover up your smiles. I haven't known you forty-odd years for nothing. Now out with it!"

Archytas sighed. "I never could conceal anything from you! Indeed, I do have a surprise for you." He whispered into a servant's ear.

Soon the door from the women's apartment opened. Korinna entered, followed by Archytas' wife Klea. Although Korinna's hair was gray, she was still shapely and handsome. Archytas and Klea had spared no effort to fit her out. A stole of thin yellow byssus covered her gown of fine purple linen, and a starry silver tiara sat on her hair. Zopyros rose slowly, his mouth open. Archytas, hugging himself with glee, explained:

"Evnos located her at last, plying a loom in a rich man's house in Cyprus. He left her here on his way to Syracuse, to await your coming ..."

He stopped when he saw no one was listening. Man and wife walked slowly toward each other, hands out and tears running down their faces.

"Korinna—"

"Zopyros—"

"It's been a long, long time."

"Nearly thirty years!"

"We still have some time left."

"Yes, darling."

"Let's go home!"

Hand in hand, they walked out. Klea bowed to Platon and returned to the women's quarters. Archytas brushed away a tear and turned to Platon, who stood pensively stroking his beard. "Now, as I was saying about the ratios that underlie the notes of the chromatic scale ..."

Author's Note

The main event of this story—the organization of the world's first military ordnance department by Dionysios the Great in 399 B.C.— is based upon the account in Diodoros of Sicily, Book XIV, sections 41-42. This reads in part:

> ...Dionysios ... gathered skilled workmen, commandeering them from the cities under his control and attracting them by high wages from Italy and Greece as well as Carthaginian territory. For his purpose was to make weapons in great numbers and every kind of missile, and also quadriremes and quinquiremes, no ship of the latter size having yet been built at that time. After collecting many skilled workmen, he divided them into groups in accordance with their skills, and appointed over them the most conspicuous citizens, offering great bounties to any who created a supply of arms. As for the armor, he distributed among them models of each kind, because he had gathered his mercenaries from many nations; for he was eager to have every one of his soldiers armed with the weapons of his people, conceiving that by such weapons his army would, for this very reason, cause great consternation, and that in battle all of his soldiers would fight to best effect in armor to which they were accustomed. And since the Syracusans enthusiastically supported the policy of Dionysios, it came to pass that rivalry rose high in manufacture of arms. For not only was every space, such as the porticoes and back rooms of the temples as well as the gymnasia and colonnades of the market place, crowded with workers, but

the making of great quantities of arms went on, apart from such public places, in the most distinguished homes.

In fact the catapult was invented at this time in Syracuse, since the ablest workmen had been gathered from everywhere into one place. The high wages as well as the numerous prizes offered the workmen who were judged to be the best stimulated their zeal. And over and above these factors, Dionysios circulated daily among the workers, conversed with them in kindly fashion, and rewarded the most zealous with gifts and invited them to his table. Consequently the workmen brought unsurpassable devotion to the devising of many missiles and engines of war that were strange and capable of rendering great service. He also began the construction of quadriremes and quinquiremes, being the first to think of the construction of such ships. ...

The subsequent story of Dionysios' Carthaginian war, including the siege of Motya, occurs further along in the same book. Diodoros is the main source for the life of Dionysios, although additional facts can be gathered from Plutarch (*Dion*) and Justinus. Many anecdotes were told of Dionysios by later writers like Cicero, Polyainos, and Athenaios of Naukratis, although the truth of these is open to question. These anecdotes include the story of the sword of Damokles and the story of "Damon and Pythias" (correctly, Damon and Phintias). True or false, I have used several of them in this novel.

Zopyros of Taras was a real man, although almost nothing is known about him. Iamblichos (*Life of Pythagoras*) lists him along with Archytas as a Tarentine Pythagorean. Biton, the author of a treatise on siege engines in the third or second century B.C., attributes a couple of rather primitive-looking catapult designs to Zopyros the Tarentine, who was more likely than not the same man. From several considerations, Zopyros' period was probably about that of the story; but nothing more is known. (This has advantages for the novelist.) It is a mere surmise that this Zopyros was related to the famous Daduchid family of Persia. This clan had several members named Zopyros, one of whom fled to Athens as told in the story.

Only a little more is known about Zopyros' contemporary Archytas, although Archytas, friend of Plato and seven times President of Taras, was one of the leading statesmen and scientists of his time. There is no positive reason to think that Archytas and Zopyros ever worked as engineers for Dionysios and invented the catapult; but nothing is known to make it impossible, either. It *could* have happened, which is the most that one should ask of a costume romance.

For the technical details of the early evolution of the catapult, see my book *The Ancient Engineers*, pp. 104-8, and my article "Master Gunner Apollonios," in *Technology and Culture*, II, 3 (Summer, 1961), pp. 240-44.

Besides Archytas, Damokles, Dionysios, Plato, and Zopyros, the only historical characters appearing on stage in this story are Leptines and Philistos, although many others are alluded to.

A "penny" is a *hêmitetartêmorion* (literally, a "half-farthing piece") or one eighth of an obolos, which was one sixth of a drachma, which was one hundredth of a pound (*mna*) of silver, which was one sixtieth of a talent.

Opinions differ as to whether *oreichalkos* ("mountain copper"), as the term was used at the time of the story, was real brass—an alloy of copper and zinc—or was instead some other yellow alloy, such as a mixture of copper and arsenic. Later, in Roman imperial times, the word meant "brass" in the modern sense.

Since the less familiar Greek names in the story have no established Anglicized pronunciations, you may say them as you please. Personally I prefer to call Dionysios die-a-NISS-ee-uss, Archytas ar-KITE-uss, Zopyros zo-PIE-russ, and Motya mo-TIE-a.

Most of the tricks employed by the witch Saphanbaal to awe her clients are described by Bishop Hippolytus in his *Refutation of All Heresies*. In the early third century, the bishop constituted himself a one-man Society for Psychical Research. He exposed the deceptions of magicians, such as putting lumps of alum in the fire and gluing fish scales to the ceiling. Of course, this was six hundred years after the time of my story. But, since some of the methods Hippolytus describes have been used by mediums right down to modern times, we may assume for the purposes of fiction that these sleights were already old when he revealed them. As for the burning glass, Aristophanes alluded to it twenty-odd years before the time of the story.

Milton Keynes UK
Ingram Content Group UK Ltd.
UKHW041552290823
427687UK00001B/122